Crossed Pistols

Arthur S. Chancellor

DEDICATION

I'd like to dedicate this story to the Army Military Police Corps and the thousands of my brothers and sisters who have proudly worn the *crossed pistols* on their uniforms and to my closest friend- Harry L. Humbert. Look at us Harry- "We're big now."

ACKNOWLEDGMENTS

No such endeavor is completed without some help. I would like to thank my very good friend Jim Adcock for taking the time to organize, format, and take care of the administrative functions necessary to get this published. Those who know me already know I don't have the patience to do the mundane but necessary tasks to bring this to print. Special thanks also to Jessica Best for editing the text and Marc Dorsett for the cover design. Thanks also to my family for talking the time to read and re-read the various drafts.

I

Oxford Mississippi
March 1973

"Sergeant?"

Sergeant First Class Willard looked up from the crossword puzzle opened on his desk and in rapid succession closed the magazine, sat his ink pen down on the desk, straightened up in the chair, and adjusted his class "A" blouse and tried not to look like he was surprised by the sudden appearance of the young man now standing in front of him.

"What can I do you for today, son?" Willard asked as he brought himself together and began to pass a quick experienced eye over the young man standing in front of his desk. He was in his late teens, wearing a pair of clean Levi blue jeans and a long sleeve shirt. He also noted that the shirt was ironed, buttoned at the cuffs, and he was clean shaven with short well-manicured brown hair. He looked like someone he wished his daughter was dating instead of the unemployed, long haired hippy she had brought home recently. Willard cocked his head to the left to hear from his good ear.

"I'd like to enlist in the Army, Sergeant," the youth answered confidently and with self-assurance.

"You would huh?" Willard felt his interest level rise considerably and started to clear off the papers and magazine on his desk and motioned to the chair next to him. "Well, we're always glad

1

to hear that, come on and sit down over here" Willard motioned to the chair next to his desk.

Walk-ins wanting to enlist were not that common in the days following the end of the draft so even on your death bed a recruiter never ignored a walk in. Besides, based on his first impression, this one actually looked promising and he didn't want to take a chance for a *live* one to get away. Willard took a second even closer look over the young man as he sat into the chair next to him. He was tall, well built, and looked like he was in good physical shape, seemed to carry himself well and was polite. Not at all like some of the other candidates that he was used to talking to; poor blacks or some white trash, trailer park redneck from out in the county looking for the army to rescue them from either poverty or police troubles. Most of his walk-in clientele were looking to exchange a couple of years of service for learning a trade, maybe fix their teeth, or to enlist for just enough time to get the GI bill and then go to college. Since he was in a college town there was also a share of the young immature college punks flunking out of school who couldn't go back home to face mommy and daddy or who were looking for a chance to join the army and avoid some prosecution for a minor offense. They all seemed to stumble into the recruiting office with a sad tale of how unfair life is and desperate for a rescue. But this one seemed different.

Once he was settled in the chair and was paying attention, Willard went into his standard well-recited recruiting spiel, while still trying to judge the seriousness of the young man staring back at him and listening attentively.

Willard began his speech in a controlled non-emotional, almost monotone voice, "The new all-volunteer army or what we call VOLAR offers some good opportunities for a young man like you to get a good jump on life. We offer good careers, good training, and a chance to see the world. Earn the VA college bill and go to college later on or stay in for a career and you can retire in 20 years on half pay with free medical and dental care for you and your family for the rest of your life."

The young man was nodding as if he were taking it all in so Willard continued, "The army can offer you a choice of training, depending on your test scores, and several of our jobs even have a cash bonus. You can also pick where you want to be stationed. Unlike other jobs out there, we provide room and board and a starting pay of $289 dollars a month." Willard paused to see if anything was getting through to the young man.

"Yes sir, I pretty much know that, Sergeant. I've been reading up on the army for a while now," the young man responded politely.

"You have huh? Well, then no sense going into all that if you know it already, is there?" Willard leaned back in his chair and could feel his irritation level starting to rise, now sensing he was dealing with another "know it all" young punk who always talked a big deal but was never able to get the balls to actually sign up. Willard shook off his momentary irritation and began again "Well then, if you're all set, we first need to get some information and then get you tested to see where we can place you." Willard took out a pen and a new form and began to fill out an interview worksheet to document his interview.

"You still in school?" he asked and waited for the response.

"Yes sir, I'm a senior, but I'll graduate this May."

"Good, I'll have to check that out, but good. What's your full name? Last name first."

"York. Sean. Patrick." The young man answered slowly as Willard wrote down each name.

"York, York...." The name seemed to ring a familiar bell and Willard dropped his pen onto the desk and sat up in his chair as if he was trying to recall why that name sounded so familiar. "Where do I know you from?" he finally asked and leaned back in his chair and waited for his response.

"I don't know Sergeant this is the first time I've been in here." The young man looked back somewhat taken aback.

"Yeah? Well you have a familiar name. York ....York....York..... York.....York," Willard repeated a few times trying to recall where he had heard that name before. Then it hit him and he snapped his fingers, "Hey, isn't there a York that plays ball at Ole Miss?"

"Yes sir," Sean answered politely and silently wished they could change the subject, "two of them."

"That's right," Willard snapped his fingers again and sat back smiling, "middle linebackers right? You related to them?"

"Yes sir," Sean nodded and paused for a moment as if he were used to answering the question. "They're my older brothers."

"Well I'll be," Willard responded and shook his head as if he were trying to digest what he just heard. "Boy, I tell you those are two bruisers that's for sure. I saw them play Bama last year. Man, they ate that quarterback up boy." Willard smiled as if recalling a special time in his life.

Sean was momentarily embarrassed and nodded back and sighed to himself remembering that game very well. They had each sacked the quarterback and one intercepted a pass and the other had recovered a fumble. It had been a good game.

"So they're your brothers huh?" Willard nodded approvingly and then came back to Sean sitting next to him. Then slowly his eyebrows lowered and looked straight back at him as if he had recalled some other fact. "Say, wait a minute, don't you play ball too?" Willard asked and leaned back in his chair as if trying to confirm what he already knew.

Sean began to flush, cleared his throat slightly, and then answered in a hushed voice, "Yes sir, I play some high school ball." Sean then began to look down on the floor as if his shoes or the stains on the carpet were suddenly more interesting than their conversation.

"Yeah," Willard snapped his fingers again as if he had suddenly experienced an epiphany. "You're that tailback everyone talks about, ain't you? Yes sir, that's it by God. I read about you in the newspapers, in fact I saw you play this year in the State Championship." Willard was suddenly very animated and pleased with himself having recalled that fact and then continued, "So, your family has that big farm down the road a ways from Batesville, don't they? What's the name of that part of the county, Taco somethin' ain't it?" Willard looked over at Sean quite proud of himself as if had solved some mystery.

"Toccowa," Sean corrected and took a deep breath and exhaled.

"Toccowa, right, OK, that's it," Willard corrected himself and sat up in his chair again as he thought of yet another factoid. "I thought I read in the paper that you're supposed to be gettin' a full ride scholarship to Ole Miss?"

"Ah, well…yes sir, it was offered," Sean looked down on the floor and then continued slowly, "but I'm not taking it." Sean answered and took another deep breath.

"You're not taking the scholarship?" Willard asked somewhat incredulous and looked back again at Sean over his glasses.

Sean looked back at Willard and shook his head no, but wasn't forthcoming with any other explanation.

Willard leaned forward, put his elbows on his desk and put his right hand to his face and began tapping his finger on his lips wondering what was going on. He began again this time a little more cautiously, "So, you're offered a full ride scholarship to the University of Mississippi and you're not going to take it?" Willard looked over at him as if he had finally observed a third eye on Sean's forehead and then he got serious. "You're not in trouble, are you boy? I mean you didn't get your girlfriend pregnant, or steal a car, or rob somebody? You're not trying to skip out on some debt or something are you? 'Cause the army ain't the place to escape that sort of thing, son. This ain't the Foreign Legion, ya know?"

"Oh no sir, nothing like that," Sean was taken aback by the insinuation and straighten himself in the chair.

"So you're not in any other trouble? I mean some sheriff isn't going to come around looking for you are they? 'Cause I'm telling ya son, the army will send your ass right back here to face the music." Willard emphasized his point by tapping his finger on his desk.

Sean shook his head negatively not quite understanding the questions.

Willard continued down his list, "You're not getting kicked out of school or anything? No drugs?" Willard was trying to figure out why a young man, from what everyone says, is from one of the wealthiest families in Northern Mississippi, with a full ride football scholarship to Ole Miss wanted to join the army. "Are you sure you've thought this all the way out son? You know once you're in your momma and daddy won't count for anything with us. Understand? Once you're in, you're in."

"Yes sir, I know exactly what I am doing," Sean responded and looked Willard directly in the eye. "I've wanted to join the army since I was just a kid."

Willard seemed satisfied with his answer and picked his pen back up and looked back over the form in front of him. "Alright, that's every man's decision and it's good enough for me." Willard still didn't quite understand why he wanted to throw all of his advantages away just to join the army but he leaned over his desk again and went back to fill out the form on the desk.

"Let's get started. How old are you, son?" Willard asked pen in hand.

"Seventeen, sir."

"Well, you'll need your parents to sign. Have you talked with them yet?" Willard said as he turned the form over and continued to write.

"Well, I'm eighteen next month, thought I'd actually sign up right after my birthday," Sean countered.

Willard nodded his head. "Alright, sounds like you've thought this through. Well then, let me get some basic information from you." Willard began to complete the remainder of the form asking all of the necessary questions but thinking silently to himself, *"People around here are sure gonna be pissed off at me for bringing this boy into the army."*

No more than two or three others in the whole world knew what he was about to do or how long he had been waiting for this day. Sean had decided he was going to be a soldier when he was six years old and had never entertained another thought the rest of his life. Joining the army isn't necessarily a novel dream or odd fantasy for any young boy; after all, what boy didn't at one time imagine himself to be a soldier engaged in fighting off Indians, defending a tree house against the commie invaders, riding a tank into combat, or flying a fighter against some other mythical enemy? Sean and his many cousins could play alternately Davy Crockett, Stonewall Jackson, or even better, their own personal hero General Nathan Bedford Forest and never tire of the game. Over the years, Sean, his cousins, and school friends, some completely outfitted in homemade confederate butternut gray uniforms, had fought gloriously and died dramatically on the field of battle which was generally somewhere in back of the house or out in the pastures only to be resurrected at supper time to fight and die again the next day. Most boys grow out of their desire for the martial life and move on to other dreams of becoming baseball and football players, astronauts, or some other exciting field of endeavor before they eventually settled down to farming or working in a factory or a hundred other mundane occupations.

As he grew up he had also put away his toy guns and homemade confederate uniforms and moved onto more adult things; but the idea of being a soldier never left him. His teenage pleasure reading was taken up with books like *God Is My Co-Pilot, To Hell and Back, Helmet for My Pillow, Guadalcanal Diary, Patton,* and anything else about the army or the military he could find. He could never get enough. Sean had always known he wanted to be a soldier and had never entertained another possibility. But, it was always assumed and just taken for granted by his parents and relatives that Sean and his two older brothers, like the other men in their extended family for the last 150 years, would grow up and work the land. They would marry, have children, and their children would also grow up and work the land. It was the never-ending cycle of tradition and family. It's simply what "the Yorks" did, and they were just as married to the land as they were their husbands or wives.

His great-great-great-grandfather, Ethan York, was one of the first white men to arrive in what would later become Panola County Mississippi. He was then just a fifteen year old former Tennessee volunteer who had accompanied General Jackson to New Orleans in 1814-15 to defend the city against an expected British attack. He had participated in the battle as one of the marksmen placed into the tall trees to pick off British officers and soldiers as they marched out of the fog with their drums pounding and bagpipes wailing towards the American lines. On their way back to Tennessee, he had contracted dysentery and was forced to drop out of the march along the Naches Trace near what would later be Tupelo, Mississippi, and nearly died. He was left in the care of a few white settlers mixed in with a small group of Creek Indians passing through the Trace towards their home in what would later become Panola County. Ethan recovered and later married one of the maids of the small group of Creek Indians and decided to make his home in Mississippi. It was wild country back then but it proved to be rich farming land.

Just a few years later he had waved goodbye to his in-laws and the rest of his wife's extended Creek Indian family at the small settlement of Toccowa Mississippi, as their branch of Creek Indians departed on the Trail of Tears on their forced relocation to the Indian Territory in what would later become Oklahoma. Some years later Ethan's two older brothers joined him from Tennessee and they got their own claims of land nearby. They worked their farms together and they grew and prospered. What started in the 1820's as a small 20 acre patch of land cleared by hand out of the wilderness grew bit by bit until the 1970's when York Farms was one of the largest single land holdings in the state of Mississippi with over 8,000 acres of rich delta farmland and pasture spread across three counties of Northern Mississippi and a little over 400 acres of pine and hard woods located in the pine belt of Central Mississippi. It was a family run business, with all of the aunts, uncles, and cousins, employed somewhere on the farm or anyone of the related family businesses established in the area. It was just an accepted fact that a York, upon reaching adulthood, would join the family business somewhere. Some went to college first, some just starting working right out of high school where they were needed or where they had an interest. Many times they branched out into related fields such as operating one of their three cotton gins, driving truck or maintaining their fleet of trucks, tractors, combines, and a small logging and lumber operation. A few others branched out to open gas stations or grocery stores each started with a small loan from the family business and then supported by the rest of the family.

When he was six years old Sean had very clearly announced his intentions to break the family tradition one night at a formal family dinner. That night, his Grandparents entertained their congressman and his wife who were making one of their bi-annual pilgrimages back home to Mississippi seeking the York family's continued vote and financial support in the upcoming election. The York family was a large voting block which was actively curried and appreciated by any politician that wanted to win an election and certainly not one to be slighted or ignored. The congressman was an older overweight professional politician who generally wore a dark suit that was too tight with a white shirt that stretched across his chest and belly to the point he almost couldn't button it. He was always outfitted with a big old fashioned wide tie and even in a December ice storm would sweat profusely. He was a Raleigh cigarette chain smoker, and an old style democrat who welcomed the assistance of the extended York family every two years when he ran for reelection and returned the favor when he could through farming legislation. Although his reelection was fairly assured he still believed the only election not to take serious is the one you're running unopposed. His main concern while in Washington seemed to be keeping cotton prices high, and keeping Washington bureaucrats, Communist sympathizers, and every other damned nosey Yankee out of Mississippi and keeping things the way they were and always would be.

"So tell me young man," the Congressman said to Sean as he leaned over next to him at the table, "What do you want to be when you grow up?" It was a simple question asked a million times a day across the country to a million other kids. "You gonna to be a farmer like your daddy and grandpa?"

Sean swallowed the food in his mouth and wiped his lips with his linen napkin as he had been taught and looked back at the Congressman with all the confidence of a six year old and simply stated, "I'm going to be a soldier, sir." Sean satisfied he had answered the question took another bite of his supper and continued being unseen.

His answer generated a polite laugh across the table from the adults and a rolling of the eyes from his two older brothers who were more interested in getting through dinner and out of their good clothes than listening to their little brother drone on about joining the army again.

"A soldier?" he came back in mock surprise. "I should think you were looking forward to working your family farm here with your father, brothers, and uncles. So what kind of soldier do you want to be?" The Congressman decided to expand the conversation.

"Don't know xactly, I just want to be a soldier." Sean announced very positive and succinctly as if he had already made that determination in his mind and then added, "I'm just not cut out to be a farmer." Without so much as a look around the table he continued to eat as if his opinion was all that mattered.

The table broke up in laughter over the honesty and self-assuredness of a six year old.

"Pup has such a good imagination," his silver haired grandmother broke in to change the subject using Sean's nick name. "But don't worry, he'll be out there with his daddy and brothers in the fields one day. It's our family tradition." She looked over at Grandpa York sitting at the end of the table nodding in silent agreement.

Sean started to respond but his mother, sitting next to him, reached out and placed her hand over Sean's on the table. He turned to look at her and she was smiling an understanding smile but clearly was signaling to *"be quiet"*. Apparently his future seemed to be a settled "matter of fact" to everyone else. But, even at six years old, Sean didn't think it wise to further challenge or argue with his grandmother over their "family tradition", whatever that was. So he just smiled and continued eating. But, right then and there his Scotch- Irish stubbornness dug in and he was even more determined. The determination never went away.

As he grew up, Sean never warmed up to the nickname "Pup", but he was stuck with that handle since he was two years old and it never went away. Unlike his father, uncles, or two older brothers Sean was a small baby and toddler. When his father brought him down to the farmer's co-op one day before he was in school, one of the older men decided he just wasn't big enough to be a real York. He was too small and scrawny and was more like a Yorkie, one of those small ankle biter puppies that rich folks up north owned. He became "Pup" ever after.

He was still known as Pup by most everyone in their small hometown even after the 7th grade when he suddenly started growing and filling out. He continued to grow and fill out all through middle school until he was a solidly built 6', 180 lbs and became a welcomed addition to the high school football team. Coach Stanley Fitzhugh was very pleased when he finally arrived in high school. His team was rated as the best high school defense in the state the previous year; but he had lost his solid all-state middle linebacker as Sean's older brother James graduated, and his other brother Robert was a senior and would be gone next year. When Sean arrived, he had gained a speedy tailback and a dynamite offensive running game. It was a tradeoff he welcomed.

Much to Coach Fitzhugh's expectations, Sean had proved to be an offensive tidal wave on the field. He plowed through the defensive line with all the finesse of a bulldozer pushing dirt. His running style was more like a bumper car bouncing off defenders, turning, spinning, but never quite losing his balance and always moving forward. Opposing teams learned painfully if you wanted to stop him, you had to do it in stages. First try to grab ahold of him or his uniform at the line of scrimmage to try and slow him down; then wait for help and gang tackle him. But, if he ever managed to get across the line or got a step on a linebacker, he was into the secondary in a blink of an eye. Then pity any defensive backs left to tackle him in an open field. Sean never had the quick fancy foot moves to misdirect his opponent. Instead he just came straight ahead, lowered his helmet, wrapped his arms around the ball and just ran over them. It was called being *"slobber knocked"* and anyone foolish enough to take him one on one in an open field once he had a head of steam going, seldom wanted to repeat the act again.

Colleges from all over the US had called on Sean and his parents, especially after capping off his high school career with his best season, even managing a 235-yard rushing game in the state's playoff game. Recruiters came to the house and were politely entertained by his parents, allowed to give their recruitment talk, then politely refused. As if it were preordained, Coach Fitzhugh and his parents arranged for University of Mississippi, or more properly Ole Miss, located just a few miles away to come calling with a full ride scholarship. Ole Miss was the family favorite and having two brothers who were already starters and likely All American selections next year didn't hurt. Unfortunately for everyone who was busy planning Sean's life and career, he had never abandoned his dream of being a soldier and had no intention of going to college. He realized that he wasn't ready for school and if he went he would be wasting his time and his parents' money and although he loved to play football, he was done with it. He realized that such thoughts were tantamount to heresy for everyone else, but he had simply reached his limit of interest on the subject and he was ready to move on and do what he wanted to do.

So one month before his eighteenth birthday, he decided it was time to make his own dream come true and instead of coming home after school, he drove over to Oxford to start the enlistment process. Although he didn't like the idea of hiding or sneaking around, he knew it would be easier and less stressful to do this on his own. Besides, he was only a month away from turning 18 and then he could enlist on his own without this parent's permission. It was going to be his first independent adult act and he was looking forward to it.

After their first meeting at the recruiting office, Sean was given an appointment in Memphis to go and take his entrance test and get his initial physical examination to make certain he was physically able to enlist. He continued his silence over the course of the next several weeks and never told a soul of his plans or activity. Instead he cut school on the appointed day, drove to Memphis and spent the day taking one test after another and then got his physical exam. A week later he dropped by the recruiting station to see Sergeant Willard again. When he walked in, Willard had been overjoyed to see him, his entrance tests were high enough for Sean to pick whatever he wanted to do in the army. The decision wasn't that difficult, he had taken several brochures home with him about the different careers in the army. Only one really sparked any interest, the Military Police. Sean looked at how sharp they looked in their uniform and although he had never looked at law enforcement as a possible career, he did like helping people and he didn't like to see people get hurt. He thought it would be a good fit for him. Within two hours they had drawn up the enlistment contract and Sean received another appointment in Memphis, just a few days after his 18th birthday to actually take the oath of enlistment. He had decided to enlist right away in the delayed entry program, but actually not report in until September. That would give him one last summer to help out at the farm and get himself ready to go and say goodbye to everyone, one last summer to spend at home before he flew off into the world on his own, and one last summer to try and change a certain person's mind.

That certain special person was Sharon Fitzhugh the tall, blond, and very attractive, cheerleader that he had known practically all of his life and fully intended to fulfill his other dream and marry her when she graduated college. Sharon was the high school football coach Stanley Fitzhugh's only daughter and Sean had been dating her 'steady' for the last three years of high school. They had known each other since he was in the 4th and Sharon in the 3rd grade, but it wasn't until high school they were finally allowed to "officially date". Sharon had captured his heart when they first really met in Catechism class at Church when they were just kids and even in the 4th grade he had a crush on her. Dating however was somewhat strange; they were already in the same mix of friends all through school, had attended the same small church, and had attended countless family outings together. This made the "talk" by Coach Fitzhugh when Sean first showed up at their house to take Sharon on their first "official date" somewhat anticlimactic after the seven year build up. Coach Fitzhugh wasn't really happy about allowing his daughter to date at 15, but he knew Sean and his family and he made an exception to what was going to be his "not until 16" rule on dating.

But, it was really no surprise to anyone when they started "going steady". Both sets of parents could see what was developing between them and easily came to accept the other child as an expected addition to their family. Sean and Sharon had continued going steady for all but a few weeks in the last three years, breaking up only for a few days when they hit a few teenage rough spots. But, admittedly neither one could face the prospect of not being with the other so they were always able to settle their troubles and get back together. It was always accepted and never disputed by either that they were going to be married after school and live happily ever after. Sharon was still a junior in high school but was already planning to attend Ole Miss to earn a degree in education and then planned to follow her parents into teaching. Sharon was one of the few people he had ever confided in his dream and goal to enlist in the army, but she was not happy with the thought of Sean joining in the army. She was firmly fixed to her family and their small town and had no desire to ever leave the safety of either one, or live anywhere else in the world. She could not for the life of her understand why Sean or anyone else would want to turn down the chance of playing college football, and abandon his family just to go off and be with strangers in the army. Sharon had spent the last year talking, cajoling, sometimes even tearfully trying to change Sean's mind and in one last desperate act, she had finally 'gone all the way' with him after the homecoming dance in his parent's cabin at the lake, thinking she might persuade him from leaving her and their way of life. She truly loved Sean and since she intended to marry him she gave willingly what she was saving for her husband.

When afterwards Sean still continued his plans for the army, Sharon was crushed. But she decided that she still had a chance to change his mind up until he actually enlisted or shipped out. Sean on his part had always believed that Sharon would eventually back down and come with him when he joined the army, thinking she could finish school where ever they happened to get stationed. Sharon had always believed that Sean would eventually change his mind and go to school and settle down in their home town. When the irresistible force meets the immovable object collateral damage is certain to follow. Four days after his 18th birthday, and in keeping with his lifelong plan, he cut school again and drove to Memphis where he filled out even more paperwork, went through a more extensive physical examination, and then along with 50 others he was herded into a large room, raised his right hand, and swore an oath "to protect and defend the Constitution of the United States against all enemies foreign and domestic and to obey the orders of the president of the United States and those officers appointed over [me]". It was a done deal. In just a matter of minutes he was finally in the army. Although there were no fireworks or marching bands, it was his first act as a man and it thrilled him to no end.

Because he was not shipping out directly, he was released to return home to await his orders calling him to active duty. Those who were heading off right away to basic training were gathered up by some sergeant who put them to work right away with brooms and mops to start cleaning up the induction center. Welcome to the army, Sean thought and smiled to himself. He walked outside and leaning up against his car read his first set of orders again; they directed him to report to Ft Ord California in September for basic training. Sean was on cloud nine all the way home. He had never been to California before and he couldn't wait to start this new adventure. He was on a high with his imagination running wild all the way up until he reached the small road leading to his house. Then he suddenly remembered that he still hadn't told his parents or Sharon what he had done and he started getting a sinking feeling in his gut.

The *Big House* was his family home; a grand house of over 4,000 square feet, two story brick with four white antebellum columns up front supporting a wide covered front porch. The house sat on a five acre plot of land carved out of the farm and on top of a small hill that overlooked the circular driveway and lawn, the lower pasture, a two acre fishing pond, and a tree lined gravel road leading to the county road a quarter mile away. The back yard had a large covered and screened patio with a big expanse of lawn, and a well maintained garden filled with his mother's roses and other prize plants. This particular house was originally built by his great grandfather who had placed it upon the foundation of an earlier house that was built by one of his other great grandfathers. It had once been a magnificent plantation known as Toccowa Crossing and prior to the civil war had been the envy of the surrounding farms and other great estates in northern Mississippi. Sean and his brothers had only known it as "The Big House" for their entire life. The Big House had been passed down like some ancient castle and heraldic title to the first born son of the first born son for at least four generations. He first came to the Big House when he was still a child and his grandfather lived there. Later his own family moved into the house once Grandpa retired. It was already preordained and understood that it would eventually be passed down to his oldest brother James once his father finally retired. It was just another one of their many family traditions. Instead of the Big House, Sean and his other siblings and every other York cousin who was interested, would get their own home site up to three acres on a section set aside on the family farm for that purpose and would be allowed to build their own house. Everyone in the county knew that area as Yorktown, because everyone who lived there was related to the Yorks through blood or marriage. Strangers or anyone outside the family had no place there and would never be welcomed.

Finally arriving home, Sean parked his 1969 dark blue Mustang in the front circular driveway and got out and stretched. He looked over the vehicle and was very proud that he was paying for it himself by working on the farm after school and in the summer. Unlike other kids who were given anything they wanted, the Yorks believed in work and responsibility and they were all expected to carry their own weight at the farm and in life. He almost ran up the steps, came into the house, wiped his shoes on the small pad and then walked directly through the living room and parlor and into the kitchen. Opening the door, he was greeted by the most wonderful smell of Miss Hazel putting the finishing touches on her famous chicken and dumplings. It was one of his favorite meals.

Miss Hazel was a heavy set black woman with grey, almost white colored hair that was normally covered in a kerchief. She must have been in her late 70's or even 80's because she had started to work for his grandparents as a cook, house keeper, and nanny for his dad and two uncles and aunt. She had remained with his grandparents and when his father finally moved into the big house after grandpa retired, Hazel was still there and became Sean's nanny too. She was far more a member of the family than an employee. His dad had long ago asked her to retire and out of respect and love said he would take care of her, but she declined and insisted on working and taking care of *her* family. She had lived for 40 years in the small two bedroom house located across the back lawn of the Big House that his grandfather had built for her and husband Dexter. Dexter had also worked as one of the farm hands and later, when he got older, he came to work around the house as a gardener. Dexter took care of his Mom's flower beds and mowed the lawn until the day he died. A few years after Dexter died, Hazel was finally convinced to move into one of the bedrooms downstairs in the Big House so she didn't have that far to walk. Although his parents had hired another woman to do most of the cleaning around the house, Hazel still insisted on cooking for the family as she had done for almost 50 years and three generations of the York family and still took care of Sean and his younger sister Rebecca.

Sean walked over on tippy toes to the stove and the large pot cooking on a low gas flame. He carefully lifted up the lid to take a smell of the wonderful aroma. *My God that was good,* he thought to himself.

"Wow Hazel." Sean stirred the pot with the ladle, "Who are you feeding? There's enough for an army."

"You better get out of that pot boy," Miss Hazel called out without looking around at him. "Go on, you get on out of here or you gonna make a mess in this kitchen and I'll tan your hide if I have to clean up after you. You're too big for that now Sean York."

Sean put the lid back down and was smiling, but Hazel continued talking as she turned to put some biscuits into the oven.

"You're as bad as your brother James. I remember that boy spilt a whole pot of my chicken and dumplings one day all over dis kitchen and Lordy, I busted him a good one dat's for sure. He never messed with my food again." Hazel sort of waddled slowly back to the kitchen sink and started to wash her hands.

Sean knew about that story and smiled. James was in the 4th Grade and he came into the kitchen when Miss Hazel had left for a minute and tried to dip some bread into the pot of chicken and dumplings. He put the bread in too far and it burned his finger and when he pulled back, he hit the pot and knocked it onto the floor, throwing chicken and dumplings and thick gravy all over the kitchen floor. Hazel was walking back into the kitchen at the time and James had a look of death on his face. Hazel never said a word, took his hand and put it under the cold water faucet and then put an ice cube on the finger. She reached over and gave James a big hug. He was certain he was in for a whooping for wasting food which was among their dad's big sins, along with being late to church, showing disrespect to adults and authority, or not putting in a good day's work. Miss Hazel ushered him quietly out of the kitchen and then cleaned up the mess telling his parents that she had knocked the pot over by accident and supper would be late while she made something else.

"Your brothers and their ladies are coming over for supper. It's first Wednesday the men folk have their K of C meeting tonight," Miss Hazel volunteered as she moved across the kitchen.

Sean had forgotten the monthly routine of early supper on first Wednesday so his dad and brothers could get to town and go to the Knights of Columbus meeting at the Church. He was eighteen now and would be able to finally join and attend the monthly meetings too. But that wouldn't happen now he reflected to himself.

"Did you go somewhere today?" Hazel asked softly as she stirred the pot and looked over at him with a look that said she already knew the answer. It was like being ten years old again caught with a bag of cookies inside his room.

"Ma'am?" Sean pretended not to hear, his heart started to race and he put on his most innocent face possible.

"You heard me, I said did you go somewhere today?" she asked while she continued moving about the kitchen.

"Yes ma'am," Sean answered and looked down. He could never look Hazel in the eye and lie.

"Uh huh, and where'd you go?" Hazel asked with the skill of a prosecutor and as if she already knew the answer.

Sean knew it was pointless to try to lie to Miss Hazel. She was part polygraph and part truth serum. She could probably make a crooked politician confess to wrong doings or corruption if she could ever look him directly in the eye; no mortal child ever had a chance to fabricate or conceal any wrong doing with Hazel.

"I went up to Memphis." Sean finally said as if he was confessing to a major crime.

"Did you give your promise to the army?" She continued to stir the pot not looking at him.

Sean looked over with a surprised look on his face; "Well, I......," Sean was caught off guard band started to deny any such action, but then broke down and admitted what Hazel already must have known, "yes ma'am I did." Sean came around to her side. "How did you know?"

"Child, I seen them army papers you tried to hide in your chest of drawers under your shirts and today was circled on your wall calendar." She put her hands on her hips and looked to him over her glasses as if to say "*you're not as slick as you thought*".

"You didn't tell anyone did you?" Hazel looked over at him.

"Didn't think it would be a smart move." Sean looked back as if he were waiting for her reaction. He should have known the one person likely to have found out would be Hazel.

"You probably right on that one," Hazel said as she moved to the sink and washed her hands under the tap.

"You didn't tell anyone did you?" Sean asked hesitatingly.

"Child, that's between you and your folks, that's not my place." Miss Hazel turned back to the stove and adjusted the gas burner under the pot. "But you know there's fixin to be all hell to pay when they find out? Gun be some upset folks 'cause your daddy has his heart set on you goin to college like your bothers. You know that's right." Hazel turned to look at Sean over her glasses as she wiped her hands on a towel.

Sean shrugged, "I know, but I just have other plans. I have other things I want to do."

"I know child." Hazel started to chuckle," You just like your daddy. No one in dis world could tell John York or his brothers anything once they made their mind on a matter. His head is as hard as my cast iron frying pan. And you know, bless his heart, your Grandpa and your uncles Kevin and Henry, they was the same way. Your brothers too, shoot, all you York boys are like that, stubborn and hard headed. I done messed with three generations of you York boys, I know. Lordy, sometimes it was more than one soul could stand." Miss Hazel shook her head and turned back to the pot on the stove. She took a sample taste of the chicken and dumplings and nodded her head approvingly and then turned to him and added, "But you a man now, sad that I am to see it. You got to set your own way in dis world, follow your own heart and head. Your daddy can't live fer you and you can't live fer him." She walked over to the large cookie jar sitting on the counter.

"Come on." She jerked her head for him to come over to her.

As he came over, she opened the large yellow ceramic cookie jar and tilted it down so he could see the contents. Inside were dozens of freshly baked chocolate chip cookies fixed the way he liked them, with just a few chocolate chips per cookie and walnut pieces. Sean grinned and eagerly stuck his hand inside and pulled a few cookies out.

Hazel put the cookie jar down, turned around and grabbed Sean by the shoulders and looked over her glasses at him, "Now listen to me, don't you put off telling your Momma and Daddy what you did. Cause ain't no secrets in this small town and someone gonna tell them one day for sure. They gonna be hurt if it don't come from you. You a man now." Hazel shook him lightly a few times to emphasize her point, "You gots to own up for your decisions whatever you decide to do," Hazel said half scolding half warning and then gave him a big hug which he lovingly returned.

"Yes ma'am I know. I'm just waiting for the right time."

Hazel let him go, Sean stepped back, put a piece of cookie into his mouth and started chewing, not knowing exactly how he was going to tell them.

"Well, don't put it off too much. Now I'm fixin' your daddy his favorite supper tonight so I did all I can do." Hazel looked over at him very conspiratorially as if they were sharing a secret.

"Miss Hazel, you're the best." Sean smiled took another bite of cookie and looked back at Miss Hazel.

"Just a few now, you still have supper coming." Hazel smiled broadly as Sean took the cookie and shoved it in his mouth. Then she turned serious, "Now go on get out my kitchen, I got biscuits coming out and dishes to wash and I don't need no kids all underfoot."

II

Supper was in the formal dining room that was big enough to accommodate a large gathering. And tonight like other first Wednesdays the whole family was assembled. James, Sean's oldest brother, was finishing up his junior year at Ole Miss. He brought Margie Wagner his fiancée from a small town over in Itawamba County just northeast of Tupelo. Robert, the middle brother, now finishing up his sophomore year at Ole Miss brought Beth Fitzhugh, his current serious girlfriend, who was actually one of Sharon's cousins. Both Margie and Beth also attended Ole Miss with his brothers. Margie was tall, fit, and tanned with long brown hair she was wearing in a ponytail. She had a soft but deeply southern accented voice and could jump into the farm chores alongside any other man to pull her own weight, but could dress up and act as the gentle country girl on any special occasion. Margie was sharp as a tack, with a strong personality, hot temper, and a very sharp tongue. As the oldest child of her own family she was used to protecting her siblings and allowed no one to push her or them around. She was seeking an accounting degree and Sean's dad was already eagerly thinking of ways to put her to use in the family farm handling all the paperwork, payroll, and taxes. Over the last year she had been accepted as a defunct member of the family making big marks with his Mom and Dad, by attending Sean's Friday night games, and then Saturday games at Ole Miss sitting next to his parents in the stands. She was exactly what James needed, and everyone agreed James had made a good pick. The fact she began taking instruction to join the Catholic Church and began attending Sunday Mass with the family didn't hurt at all either.

Beth was also a very attractive tall, blonde haired 20 year old, and luckily for her the Fitzhugh bloodline produced very attractive women. Because although she was loyal and obviously dedicated to Robert, otherwise she was, as described by Hazel, "long on looks but short on brains". Sean had once overheard Miss Hazel describe her to his mom as having "more between her legs than between her ears." But Robert was clearly much happier with her than with any of his other girlfriends he had over the years. Beth was shy and not very demanding and seemed to be seeking what everyone in the area knew as a "M.R.S. degree". That is, she was attending college for the sole purpose of finding someone successful enough to marry and be taken care of the rest of her life. Margic had already asserted herself as the oldest future daughter in law, convincing Beth to start attending games with them and since she already was a member of the same church, she was also becoming an accepted part of the family. Sean's parents generally agreed that she was a nice girl, from a good local family, Robert was happy and she was certainly good to Robert, and without a doubt was going to be a "baby factory" which meant lots of grandkids.

Rebecca, his sister and youngest sibling made her appearance as everyone else was coming in and finding their assigned places. Becca, as she was better known, was a sophomore in high school and had enjoyed her status of being one of only two granddaughters of her generation of Yorks among the 14 other cousins. She and her other girl cousin had been spoiled beyond belief by their grandparents especially Grandpa Patrick. But, when she was home she still had to pull her own weight around the house and around the farm. She had also inherited the stubbornness and loyalty to family and out of all the children she had so far given her parents the least cause for concern. But she had no interest in anything that grew in the ground. Her interest and greatest joy were the animals, especially the horses. She had learned to ride at an early age after being presented with "Romeo", a two year old quarter horse from Grandpa, when she turned six years old. In typical York fashion, whatever she was interested in she made it a point to learn everything about it. A broken arm from a fall while barrel racing when she was ten had only kept her from riding for three weeks and made her even more determined to succeed. She spent nearly every free moment down at the stables with Romeo and their other two horses and the two mules her parents owned. Everyone in the family agreed whomever she picked as a mate would have his hands full.

Sean looked around at everyone standing behind their chairs talking and laughing in individual conversations while waiting for his mother to come into the dining room and take her seat so they themselves could sit down. This was home and this was his family and it felt safe and secure to have everyone back home again. James and Robert had moved out of the house years before and were both living on campus at the athlete's dorm. Both were playing football at Ole Miss on football scholarships, and it was expected and part of the general family tradition that they would graduate, get married and come back to work somewhere in the family business. Each would be given the standard 3 acres of land in "Yorktown" a large section of land that was set aside for the York kids to build a house on. That is until James was allowed to move into the big house once his dad and Mom retired and James took over the running of the farm. Once married they would both begin to produce other Yorks who would in turn work somewhere on the family farm and the cycle of York life would continue.

It was just as fully expected and planned for Sean to join the boys next year and play football at Ole Miss. Their cousin Kevin who was Sean's age and was also on the same local high school team as a starting tight end had already signed his scholarship. Robert and James had discussed it amongst themselves for two years as Sean was coming up and looked like he was going to continue the York football tradition.

His dad, John York stood at the head of the table and stood at 6'3", still a reasonably solid 240 pounds, and still with a full head of black hair that was just now turning more and more light grey around the temples. He had also attended Ole Miss back in the 50's where he played defensive end until his college time was cut short when he was drafted into the Marines for the Korean war. Of course he was not supposed to be drafted from college at all, but Sean's grandfather had gotten into a pretty heated discussion with Mr. Everett Hill, one of the local town businessmen that fancied himself as an up and coming county leader and person to be reckoned with, especially backed by the

KKK in the area. It was back in 1948 and trouble started over some remarks made by Mr. Hill who loudly opined the whole cause for World War II and the current problems in American was the result of the number of Catholics and Jews in the government who had driven America into war for their own nefarious reasons. Therefore, they (the Catholics) should all be rounded up and run out of this country along with all the niggers. That would take care of everything.

Sean's grandfather, Patrick York, was a pretty easy going and reasonable man with a pretty thick skin about most things. But with a few shots of store bought whiskey in him and the proper motivation his temper could flare and he was not someone to exchange words with. Grandpa Patrick and his bothers Henry and Kevin had all listened for a while and once Hill sat down after offering his personal unsolicited opinion, Grandpa Patrick stood up himself and politely invited Mr. Hill and anyone else present for the discussion who thought like Mr. Hill, to come and kiss his Catholic ass. The challenge caused Vernon Hicks a local white trash no account, but also a member of the local KKK, to stand up. Being bolstered by alcohol bravery, Hicks voiced a similar opinion and offered to actually to be the one to start forcing Catholics and niggers from the county. Patrick took the challenge and in short but violent order, beat the living crap out of Vernon Hicks, and then walked directly over to Mr. Hill who had retreated to the edge of the group sitting on a hay bale. He had not moved a muscle during the entire scuffle with Hicks and sat with his mouth wide open at Hicks lying on the dirt in the middle of the group trying to get his wits about him. Patrick walked over and solidly punched him once on the nose, sending him sprawling backwards onto his back. Hill made a wise decision not to stand up or say another word. Patrick looked around the group and when he saw that was no one else was going to step forward, he sincerely apologized to the remainder of the men in the small group. Then he and the brothers silently walked away.

The problem seemed to be settled and nothing else ever came of the matter. A complaint was made to the local county sheriff who vowed to do an immediate and thorough investigation; but once Hicks and Hill left his office satisfied they would get the last word on the matter, the Sheriff had promptly thrown his notes into the trash. The Sheriff knew Vernon Hicks was just a no account white trash and had been in trouble on more than once occasion. As far as the Sheriff was concerned Everett Hill and his family were no more than modern day carpet baggers, his family only coming down to Mississippi back in the late 30's to open up a small grocery store after they had gone bankrupt in Indiana somewhere. They had only been in town for about a few years or so, but the Sheriff had grown up with Patrick, Mathew, and Kevin York and knew all of their other kin who had lived in the county for generations. Catholic or not, they were good working people and had never been a problem to anyone. He felt no compunction or desire to act based on any allegation the likes of either Hicks or Hill. The Sheriff also reasoned even if he made an arrest, Patrick York was never going to get convicted in this county for assaulting the likes of Hicks and Hill anyway. It wasn't worth the aggravation or the loss of votes come election time.

The matter seemed to have been forgotten however, the following year Mr. Hill managed to wrangle his way to take over duties as the head of the county's selective service board. Nominally a minor functionary position but when Korea flared up in June 1950, as John York was just getting ready to start his junior year at Ole Miss, Everett Hill promptly arranged for his selection as the county's very first draftee into the service. Mr. Hill then denied every requested waiver or delay and made it abundantly but subtly clear, that John York was going to pay the price for his father's assault and the Sheriff's inaction two years before. Since Mr. Hill couldn't face Patrick York himself he would do the next best thing, he would send his son to the military and probable combat in Korea. It was just icing on the cake to be able to send him off to the Marines instead of the Army or Navy. It was clear to everyone in the county what was going on, but Everett Hill and certain other members of the Full Faith Baptist Church who shared Mr. Hill's views didn't seem to mind at all. By October 1950, John York was in Marine boot camp in Paris Island NC, and by February 1951 he found himself as a replacement rifleman in a marine infantry regiment in Korea seeing combat chasing the North Korean army from Seoul back into North Korea. He was wounded slightly by a hand grenade in a small skirmish, he was taken to an aid station where he was patched up and sent back to the line and they continued the advance north. He had engaged in several tough and bloody skirmishes until September 1951 when he was seriously wounded, this time in the leg by a mortar round. He was finally evacuated from the front back to Japan and then eventually found himself back in the US where he was able to recover. But he was no longer fit for service and finally returned to a hero's welcome in January 1952 as a corporal, medically discharged with two purple hearts, the GI bill, and a slight limp that would last the rest of his life and squash any dreams of returning to football.

Within days of his return home, he married Catherine Sullivan a local girl who he had been dating in college and in keeping with tradition they immediately started producing children. James came late in 1952, Robert in 1953, Sean in 1955, and Rebecca in 1959. Although his injuries caused an end to his football, he was able to finish college and returned to work the family farm.

Grandpa Patrick had never forgotten or forgiven Everett Hill for what happened to his son but he remained quiet waiting for John to come home. His two other sons Kevin and Henry were also drafted in turn immediately as they finished high school and turned eighteen. Neither saw any combat and both came back home, attended Ole Miss and came to work at the family farm, with just a short two year interruption in their lives. But in 1954, Grandpa Patrick and his brothers Mathew and Kevin were coming back from the fields late in the afternoon when they decided to stop in at Sneaky Pete's, a small country jute joint located directly on the county line and about the only place around to get a beer since Panola County was dry at the time. As they walked in they acknowledged the five or six other farmer patrons with a hello or a wave of the hand and sat down. Patrick saw Everett Hill sitting at the bar when they came in, a broad alcohol induced smile came across his face when he saw Patrick come into the bar.

"Well, Pat, how's that boy of yours getting along? I saw him on the square on Saturday. He seems to be doing OK now that he's back home," Hill asked in a loud sarcastic voice almost taunting him. Hill looked around at the other patrons and smiled. It was clear that he had been there a while and was starting to feel his oats.

"Doing fine," Patrick answered sharply as he walked by, sat down with his back toward Hill and ordered a beer, anxious to ignore him. He was no longer in the mood to sit down and relax, but it had been a while since he had the chance to have a cold beer and it had been a tough day. The York men sat down at the end of the bar as far away as they could get and began to enjoy the cold beer.

Henry convinced Patrick to ignore Hill, finish their beers and go home. "Just drink up and forget about this prick."

But, Everett Hill was not willing to just sit down and shut up. "I see he's still got a small limp," he announced to no one in particular while sitting on the bar stool, his back against the bar, looking out towards the other customers sitting at tables. "Damn shame he was never able to play ball anymore," Hill said out loud without prompting. "Yep, damn shame how things happen to some folks. That war is a terrible business."

There are many times when people wish they could take back what they said when liquored up. This would be one of them. Patrick looked at Kevin and Henry who shrugged their shoulders giving their tacit approval for what they knew was about to happen. Patrick tipped his mason jar of beer up and finished it off in a few swallows. Henry and Kevin did the same and then stood up and faced the group in case they were needed. Patrick put the empty Mason jar down on the table, stood up and walked over towards Everett Hill. Everett straightened up on the bar stool not expecting such a response and looked into Patrick's eyes and started to smile.

"You think you're gonna do something in here with all of these witnesses Pat?" Hill asked smugly and waved his arms around the room. "I'll have you arrested so fast you'll be in Parchman in stripes before the end of the month. Or something worse could happen, I have friends remember?"

Patrick paused and looked around the room at the various farmers and laborers that he had pretty much known all of his life.

"Maybe," Patrick whispered as he leaned into Everett and looked directly into his eyes.

Then he turned back and struck Hill under the jaw with his right hand and followed up with a hard left across his right jaw, knocking out two teeth. Hill sank to the floor without so much as a sound and started bleeding out of his mouth. He was dazed, his brain was swimming and he finally was able to spit two teeth out onto the floor. Patrick stood back and looked down at the limp body on the floor and pointed directly at him.

"Everett Hill, the only reason in the world you ain't dead right now is the fact that my boy came home. Everyone in this county knows what you did. You're just a coward and always have been a coward and a piece of shit for as long as I've known you. You need the government or some other trash wearing white sheets to do your fighting. Now if you got a problem with me you bag of shit, we'll settle it man to man."

Patrick looked around the small bar and then back at Hill who was cowering on the floor, "you don't go after a man's children. Now, you best let this go and leave me and my family alone. Because I don't care how many witnesses you think you have." Patrick looked around the room at the others patrons who were all standing looking at the scene. "So, I'm telling you now, in front of God and the whole world, if you or any of your friends dressed up in them white sheets ever sets one foot on York land, you'll die there." He then spoke to the small crowd, "Boys I apologize for causing any trouble or disturbance. We're going home now. Hank," Patrick looked at the bartender and reached into his pants pocket, "do I owe you any damages?"

"None that I see Pat," he answered shaking his head no.

Patrick nodded back and he and his brothers left the bar.

The County Sheriff again decided not to intervene when Hill, this time bearing a black eye and missing two teeth, made a second complaint against Grandpa Patrick. The Sheriff instead expressed a common feeling within the county that since he was still alive after what he had done to John York, he should count himself lucky that Patrick had not killed him outright. But, if he wanted to make a complaint, he would have to take his complaint over to Quitman County, because that's where the alleged assault took place. He wondered out loud how his church was going to react to Deacon Everett Hill drinking at a jute joint and a getting into a drunken fight. Everett Hill was taken aback by the comment about his church that he had not considered. The Sheriff then went on to recommend he avoid any other contact with Patrick York if he wanted to have a long life. Everett Hill didn't take long to decide to pull up stakes, sell his store, and move his family further south to Vicksburg. He was not missed by many. Sean was proud to come from that line of men.

Catherine York, the family matriarch, finally arrived into the dining room and took her place at the table with small apologies for being delayed. Then they all took their own seats. Sean looked around the table as they said grace and then a Hail Mary. Hazel appeared as if on cue, with the silver soup tureen and ladle and began serving portions of the chicken and dumplings on their plates.

"Man, I love Miss Hazel's chicken and dumplings; it's my absolute favorite, I could eat that by the gallons. I think I could have lived on this when I was growing up," his dad said rubbing his hands together in great anticipation.

Hazel beamed in appreciation.

"Sean," his dad started ripping a biscuit apart over his plate, "I'm going to propose your name tonight at the Knights Council to join us. You're eighteen now and there is a 1st Degree ceremony coming up in Tupelo next month. I'd like you to join your brothers and me in the KC."

"Yes sir," Sean answered, deciding not to mention anything about his enlistment until after supper, not wanting to interrupt the family meal. Everyone was served and began eating. Sean was lost in his own thoughts of how to broach the subject, picking at the chicken and dumplings on his plate more than eating, and therefore was not paying attention to the conversation around the table.

"Sean," James finally raised his voice and caught his attention.

He looked up and saw everyone around the table was looking at him. James had obviously been talking to him from across the table and he had not noticed. As he looked up there was laughter as they realized he had been daydreaming.

"Damn Pup, I've been talking to you for five minutes, haven't you heard anything I said?" James asked and everyone chucked again.

"Sorry, I was thinking about something else." Sean flushed and started eating, suddenly very interested in putting something into his mouth.

"I said, I heard you postponed meeting with the coach to sign your scholarship," James repeated and took another bite of a biscuit.

Sean looked up as if he had been caught red handed committing a crime and immediately flushed. He quickly put another bite into his mouth to give himself a few more seconds to think of a reply.

"Well, for crying out loud son, did you postpone the meeting? You never mentioned that to me," his dad now asked looking straight at him. "You know this is a busy time for us, I had to make arrangements so I could be there. I thought we talked about this."

Everyone at the table was looking at him now. The girls were looking down at their plates rather embarrassed for Sean.

"Well sir, I didn't actually postpone it," Sean chewed his food and took another bite as his heart raced. This was not happening the way he wanted it to go.

"You didn't postpone it?" His dad froze with a fork full of food over his plate and tilted his head slightly as if to understand what was being said. "Well then what's this all about?"

"Well I saw the coach this afternoon and he said you called and postponed your signing appointment," James said as if to clarify his question.

"Well, I mean I didn't postpone it; I canceled it." Sean took another quick bite. There. It was out. He was committed to a course of action he could not retreat or delay. Not the perfect time but the only time he was apparently going to be given.

"Canceled it?" His dad sat his fork back down on his plate and leaned back. "What does that mean? When are you going to get together? You shouldn't jerk the coach around son he has a lot to do to get ready for next year. He can't just go here and there on your every whim."

"Yes sir, I know. I'm not trying to jerk the coach around. I....I... I canceled it completely." Sean looked around the table and then like the Charge of the Light Brigade, he knew he was committed and there was no turning back. He took a deep breath and started, "I've decided not to take the scholarship. I'm not going to play ball next year." Sean was now bent over his plate but staring straight ahead his heart beginning to race.

"Not going to play ball?" His dad asked and opened his mouth as if he had been struck by an invisible force.

"What?" asked James and Robert almost at the same time.

"What are you talking about?" James blurted out and the room went suddenly silent.

"Where's this coming from?" Robert joined in.

"Well, I canceled because, well, because I joined the army today." Sean said above the roar of his heartbeat and the chorus of Tennyson, *"Half a league, half a league, half a league onward, all in the valley of death rode the six hundred"* It was finally out. His heart was racing, but he felt strangely better, as if he had been carrying some deep dark secret around for years and was finally released from his vow.

"You joined the army?" his dad asked loudly. "What are you talking about? How can you join the army? No one called us, I have to give you permission." He looked over at his wife almost accusingly, "Did you know about this? Did you give permission?"

"Of course not," Catherine answered and looked over at Sean. "Pup honey what's this all about?"

"Well, I still have to sign and I'm not signing. You haven't thought this out," his dad announced before Sean could respond.

"Sean honey, what gave you an idea about joining the army?" his mother asked again.

"Dad," Sean began addressing his father first trying to remain calm, "I'm eighteen now."

"Eighteen? Four days ago eighteen," his dad interjected.

"Yes sir, but eighteen even so. So, I didn't need your signature." Sean looked over at his mom hoping for some support.

"Son, why are you throwing away all of your dreams and goals and plans? Is there something wrong you're not telling us? Is Sharon pregnant? Is that what this is about?" His dad was visibly upset.

"No sir, she's not pregnant." Sean looked rather hurt at the suggestion.

"Honey, what possessed you to go and do that?" asked his mother.

Sean took a deep breath and started to explain, "Those football and college plans are your plans. I never had dreams to play college ball. If I went now I would just waste your money and my time, besides I've had enough of football." He looked around the table to see the shocked faces of everyone there and tried to continue, "All I've ever wanted to do is join the army. I've tried to tell you all a hundred times but you always laughed at me like I didn't know what I was doing. But I knew what I was doing." He looked up the table at his father, "Dad, you and mom taught me to be my own man and be independent. I've never gotten into trouble, never got into drugs; I got good grades in school. This is my life's choice. This is what I want to do. I'm sorry if you don't understand."

There was silence around the table, broken finally by Rebecca who looked over to Sean.

"Well, I think you'll be a good looking soldier all dressed up in uniform." She then turned to her father, "Daddy, you should be proud of him and the same with you two boys," she looked over at James and Robert and pointed her finger, "We need to leave Pup alone and support him on this."

That caused nervous laughter around the table. Then silence as John York gathered his thoughts.

"Well then," the shock still not registering, John York continued, "apparently this has become an auspicious occasion." His eyes began watering slightly and he reached for his glass of iced tea. "Looks like another York child has grown up. I raise my glass to you son and wish you Godspeed and luck."

The others raised their glasses as well but without much enthusiasm. They repeated the toast "Godspeed and good luck" and all took a drink. The room remained silent as no one could think of anything else to say, each lost in his or her own thoughts. The mood was broken after a few seconds by John.

"Now, if ya'll please excuse me from the table," John got up and wiped his mouth and the napkin and sat it down on his plate. "I need to get ready for the Knights." He rose up and walked into the kitchen where he saw through tear filled eyes Hazel busily cleaning up. He wiped the tears away and cleared his throat.

Hazel walked over and put her arms around him, like she had done a thousand times before in his life.

"Did you hear, Miss Hazel?" John asked.

"I heard you both and I'm proud of both of you."

"But he never asked. We never talked. He's just a boy and doesn't know what he's getting into."

" Dat boy wanting to join the army is the worst kept secret in this world son." Hazel reached out and reassuringly put her hand on the back of Johns head. "He's been saying it all his life. You just never paid attention." Hazel smiled and John nodded against her shoulders as if he really deep down knew. "Johnny, you raised these boys to be men. He's trying to be a man and this is what he wants to do." Hazel patted him on the backside, "This child is more like you and your Daddy than the other two boys."

"I know," John recovered, stood up and wiped the water from his eye, "but I guess I just realized it tonight." John reached out and hugged Miss Hazel again. "Thanks Miss Hazel."

"That's alright son, boys always grow up and seek their own way."

III

Telling his parents was difficult but had gone far better than he could have imagined. After supper when his brothers and dates went back to their dorms, his father invited him down in his small office to talk. His dad had not been able to come to full terms with his decision but there was nothing to be done about it. He ushered him into his office/den and broke out a bottle of Jack Daniels. He poured them each a two finger drink and then, for the first time in his life, he started talking about his own military service. In his entire 18 years, his dad had never talked much about being in the Marines or fighting in Korea, his medals, or any of his marine buddies. It was as if that time of his life had not really existed. Sitting in the two easy chairs in front of the desk, they talked really for the first time over such manly things.

He smiled as his dad began talking so animatedly with such great enthusiasm and humor over his experiences. It was as if he had been holding the memories back for all of these years. For the first time in his life Sean heard his dad say the word "fuck" and nearly choked on his drink, he had no idea his father even knew the word. His dad saw his expression and they both laughed out loud, a big belly laugh that almost brought tears to his eyes. His dad then momentarily panicked and got up quickly to look down the hallway to make sure his mom had not overheard anything. When it was all clear they laughed again. As the third son, Sean had never felt ignored, left out, or shoved to the side, and he knew his parents loved him. But that night he felt for the first time that his dad was really proud of him, not because of some football award or other childhood accomplishments, but perhaps because for the first time in his life, Sean felt like he was becoming a man, at least in his father's eyes and that was so important to him. The memory of them sitting together, in the office, his dad telling his Marine stories, each drinking whisky in a crystal glass, straight up with a little ice, would remain with him as one of his best moments in his life.

Sharon was another matter. She was gone for a few days at a spring softball tournament in Memphis and was not due home until Friday afternoon. He was going over to talk with her about enlisting and break the news to her and try one more time to get her to listen to reason or to accept this decision. But, he had forgotten Beth was Sharon's cousin and in true southern small town fashion, Beth had immediately called her uncle and got the number for the hotel in Memphis where Sharon and the other girls were staying. In a long dramatic phone call she told Sharon about what happened at supper that night. When Sean arrived at the Fitzhugh's house in the early afternoon it was apparent that Sharon already knew. As she opened the door Sean could see she had been crying as her eyes were red and puffy and she was blowing her nose. She opened the door without saying a word and then turned and walked inside leaving the door open for him to follow. He meekly followed as if expecting an ambush. She went into the kitchen where Mrs. Fitzhugh was sitting at the table drinking a cup of coffee; Sharon sat down in one of the chairs where a small cardboard box was sitting on the table. The box was loaded with several picture frames containing pictures of Sean or of them together, along with several knickknacks he had given her over the years, and on top was his high school letterman's jacket.

"This is all I could find for right now," Sharon said hesitatingly as she sniffed her running nose. "I'm sure there is more; I'll collect it and send it over to your momma and dad." She was looking down not wanting to look Sean in the eyes.

"Babe, I..." Sean started to explain.

Sharon held up her hand as if to make him stop. "Beth called me last night. I shouldn't be surprised; I knew you had to join that damned Army, you've always said so and I guess I always knew you would. I just, I guess, ... I thought maybe........" Her lips were trembling and the tears began to flow again, "so I know now I can't stop you," she said haltingly, "but I'm not going to go with you either. You just go on and find yourself. I'll be here for a while. I'm not leaving." She held out her hand and when he reached over to it she opened it up to show his high school class ring that she had kept for two years. She turned her hand and the ring fell into his.

"Sharon I…"

He was cut off again by Sharon that held up her hand as if signaling him to stop. "It's going to be hard enough for a while, so you need to go please."

Sean hesitated and was frozen in place not sure of what to do. He wanted to take her in his arms, he wanted to shake some sense into her, and wanted to hold her so bad it hurt.

Mrs. Fitzhugh stood up from the kitchen table and spoke up, "Pup, you need to go ahead and get your things and go on now hon. Let her get herself together. I'll take care of her." She stood up and walked over to Sean and opened up her arms and gave him a big hug and patted him on the back whispering into his ear, "I'm proud of you, now you take care of yourself now and don't be afraid to write. We'll all be here whenever you can come back home."

"Yes ma'am," Sean whispered meekly back to her.

She pulled back and looked him in the eye and nodded her head. Sean knew it was time to go. There was no need for dramatics. He gathered up his things and stated walking towards the front door not even looking back. This had not gone exactly as he had hoped. But the die was cast and things set into motion that could not be reset.

Mrs. Fitzhugh walked slowly behind him and spoke as he opened the door, "Now be careful and we'll see you all at church Sunday."

"Yes ma'am," Sean said over his shoulder as the door closed behind him.

There were just a few weeks left until high school graduation and they were a blur of getting ready, and the endless rounds of explanations to other family and friends. His cousin Kevin was one of the few who understood and was one of the few people in the world that was aware of what Sean intended to do. Although admittedly, he had always believed in his heart Sean would eventually change his mind and they would be playing football together in college. Kevin and Sean were the same age and had gone through school together and they were closer together than any of their other siblings or cousins and Kevin was the one person that Sean sought out after the break up with Sharon.

Sitting down at their favorite fishing spot on a small creek in the middle of Yorktown, they brought a cooler of beer and two lawn chairs and talked, just the two of them. Kevin also brought out two marihuana joints and lit one of them up. He offered it to Sean, but like all of the other times Kevin had offered, he declined. Kevin shrugged his shoulders and the two drank their beer, laughed, and talked about their lives growing up, and what lay ahead for them both. High school graduation came and was gone without a lot of drama. As a graduation present he received the title to his Blue 1969 Mustang that his dad had bought but Sean had been making payments on by working on the farm and at the cotton gin. His parents decided since he was going out on his own, he didn't need a car payment and every man needed a car. His dad considered the car debt paid in full with his high school diploma.

After graduation, Sean was back on the farm working on a daily basis as he had done his entire life. Only now as he drove one of the tractors he was thinking about the Army, about leaving town and getting out on his own, and about Sharon. There was a large empty space now that no matter what he did he couldn't seem to fill. He would see her around town, and at Sunday Mass and although she was always nice and polite, and seemed like she wanted to talk with him, she would always find some excuse to depart early and took to sitting on another pew sometimes on the other side of church. Over the course of summer she finally started to talk with him on the phone, but would never allow the subject of Sean's entering the Army or of her leaving town to come up. She would either change the subject or would make a quick excuse to hang up.

There were a few get-togethers with friends out at the lake where they drank beer and howled at the moon at being out of school and at the same time, most of his friends were still trying to figure out what they were all going to do. Almost all had settled down working for their own parents, or were still actively engaged in looking for work. The break up with Sharon and his entry into the Army eventually became common knowledge around town and lead to a lot of speculation and rumors for folks that were very disappointed that he would not be playing college ball.

Not too many people seemed to understand his desire to leave or join the Army; some even took it very hard. Wilber Tanksly, or "the Tank", was one of the guys on the football team. As the name implies

Tank was a 5'11", 250-pounder and like most country boys was built solid. He played offensive tackle on Sean's high school football team and many a yard Sean gained was a result of the Tank's effort to knock a hole in the defensive line for him to run through. Tank took his going into the Army very hard, because he was also trying to get a space on the Ole Miss Football team. However, he wasn't certain he was ever going to get a chance to play again because of his academic grades.

Whereas Sean had enough of football, Tank knew the only thing he had to look forward to in his young life was a chance to continue playing football, because afterwards there was only an eventual return to spend his life in his father's junkyard. Fueled by frustration over his prospects and a 12 pack of beer, Tank took Sean aside one night at a get-together at the lake with other teens and basically promised if he wasn't able to play any more football, that he was going to 'kick Sean's ass" for giving up the chance to play ball. Tank promised once Sean left town, if he ever saw Sean again he was going to do it. He then laughed and Sean laughed and they shook hands still friends and had another beer. But deep down he knew Tank meant what he said. During that last summer Sean also had a chance to make peace with his brothers. Robert was supportive and thought it was good to get out and see the world and could understand. James was not as appreciative on his decision thinking he was selfishly leaving the family. But in the end they had accepted Sean's decision and they adjusted their lives. They were filled with stories once summer football camp started, James for his last year and Robert for his junior year. It was a tough camp and the coaches all let it be known to them that were not very happy with Sean's decision. After losing Archie Manning two years before, the offense was sputtering and they had all expected Sean to fill out a hole in the backfield.

Sean did go out on a few dates with local girls, but they really never amounted to much. Most of the local girls knew he was leaving and he really wasn't interested in establishing any new relationships. The summer came and left, with Sean becoming more anxious as the day to leave approached. He was already starting to mark off the days on the calendar. Many times he regretted his decision to wait, thinking without Sharon it might have been easier to just ship out and get away instead of dragging the process out. On the weekend before he left he had what could be described as a going away party at nearby Sardis Lake at a place out of the way where the local teenagers used to go to drink beer, neck, and generally get away from parents and responsibility. His brothers came along with Beth and Margie and they sat around talking and laughing and teasing. After a while, Sean walked over to one of the large boulders that surrounded the area and sat down and looked around at his brothers and friends. James and Margie had finally settled on a wedding date following graduation next year, but they were already behaving like a married couple. Robert and Beth had become informally "engaged" shortly after football camp started and Sean laughed to himself thinking of his father's own observation of Robert and Beth that they were behaving like "two rabbits in heat."

Rebecca came out as well after a special invite and when she saw Sean walk away by himself, she walked over and sat down next to him.

"Last weekend Pup," she said and looked over at him, "are you ready to go?"

"Yeah, I suppose. I sort of wish I had gone earlier." He smiled and took a sip of his beer.

"I think I got you all figured out," Becca announced as if she had come across a family secret.

"Figured what out?" Sean answered with a quizzical look.

"You and this Army thing," Becca answered and took a sip of her soda. "I was looking through some of my books from last year this morning and I saw my notebook about Greek mythology."

"Yeah?" Sean wasn't catching the connection.

"Well, I remembered the myth about the Sirens, you remember? They were like these female creatures that played enchanting music and could sing songs that lured sailors as they sailed by their little island. Well the sound was so sweet the men couldn't resist so they sailed toward the voices to find them, but instead of finding the women, their ships ran into hidden rocks and they all were killed of course." Becca was impressed with herself for figuring out what happened to her brother and smiled as her comment sunk in.

"So what does that mean? What in the world are you talking about?"

"Well, I think you've been listening to some Siren who's been secretly singing in your ears all of these years."

"A Siren huh? Singing in my ear?" Sean smiled to himself and took another sip of beer.

"Well she's gotten you to leave home and your girlfriend, so it must be a sweet song." Becca took a sip of her soda and smiled at her ability to figure it all out.

"I don't know, I didn't think it was that big of a deal. I just want to be a soldier." Sean looked back not sure of what to say.

"Well, no matter," Becca said back, "besides, I think you're making a good decision and I'm glad you're getting out of here."

"Yeah?"

"Yeah, cause I'm getting out of here too," she announced.

"You? Where are you going?" Sean was surprised. "You hear a Siren too?"

"No, I'm not leaving altogether, I mean not permanently, but I've decided to go to Vet School."

"Gee that's no surprise," Sean smiled.

"Yeah, not a big leap was it?" Rebecca looked at him and smiled. "But, now that you're breaking away it's going to be easier for me."

"What d'ya mean?"

"Cause, I'm going to Vanderbilt." She said with self-assurance.

"What?"

"Yep, Vandy for me. Now that you broke the mold it's going to be hard not to let me go where I want to go."

"Oh my God I want to be a fly on the wall when you tell them that."

"No problem, you did your thing, so can I. Besides I'm daddy's little girl," she said and looked over at him with an angelic smile and batted her eyes and they both started to laugh.

"Hey Sean, hey Becca," came a female voice out of the darkness.

Sean looked up to see Loren Payne, a tall slender auburn headed 18 year fellow graduated classmate, standing in front of them.

"Hey Loren," Sean answered back.

"Hey" Rebecca chimed in and took another sip of her soda watching as she came up to them.

"I just came over to say hello. Am I interrupting a big family something?"

"Nah, not really. We were just sitting here talking," Sean looked over at Rebecca and then back at Loren.

"In fact, I'm going to go get another soda," Rebecca said suddenly feeling like the third wheel. She stood up and lightly punched Sean in the shoulder and walked towards the fire.

"Mind if I sit for a while?" Loren asked as she moved next to Sean.

Sean patted the rock next to him and she sat down. Sean had once wanted to date her when he had broken up with Sharon for a few weeks at the start of his senior year. Loren was very attractive, very personable, a lot of fun to be with, and very experienced in the world of love. She had always seemed very interested in Sean all through high school, but sadly it was not to be. There were still some people that viewed Catholics as being unacceptable and despite everything else that was going for him, her daddy was not going to allow that to happen.

"So you're leaving in a few days?" Lauren said and reached out to take the beer from his hand to take a drink.

"Yeah, I fly out Tuesday."

"Wow, just three days left." She took another sip and handed the beer back. "You know you sure fooled everyone in town. No one expected you to run off and join the Army." She picked up a stick and was making designs in the dirt in front of her. After a short pause as if she were collecting her thoughts she spoke again. "You know, I always wanted to get out of this place too. I used to dream at night someone would knock on my door and sneak me out of the house and just take me out of here, somewhere far, far away from this little town."

"Who did you dream about coming to get you?" Sean asked and took another sip of his beer.

"You. It was always you, Sean. I wanted you to come and get me and take me out of this place and away from this town. But you never knocked on the door did you?" She sighed and smiled and looked back down at the designs she was making in the dirt.

"With your father standing right behind you with his shotgun or following us down the road? Not a nice thing to think about," Sean patted her on the knee. "Your daddy is a pretty big man. Makes you think first."

"And he's a good shot, too." She smiled and reached for his hand taking it in her own and whispered lightly, "but, daddy ain't here now." She took his hand to her face and kissed his fingers and rubbed them across her face. Sean turned towards her as she leaned forward to kiss him, showing more cleavage than he had ever noticed before.

"Sean, take me away from this place," Loren whispered into his ear, "I'll be good to you and take care of you." She then kissed him softly on the lips.

Sean was taken by surprise and was immediately aroused by the smell of her perfume and soft kiss. She placed his hand over her shirt and pressed his hand over her left breast and leaned against him, the kiss becoming more passionate. Her breath became heavier and Sean was experiencing discomfort as he became aroused.

"Pup," came a whispered voice from in front of them. "Pup."

Sean broke his kiss and turned to see Robert walking up to them.

"Hey, Sharon's here." Robert whispered and then turned around and headed back to the main group.

Sean broke up his embrace with Loren who sat up and smiled back at him, wiping her lips with the back of her hand. She reached out and took his beer.

"I thought you guys were over," Lauren said and learned back on the rock her arms going behind her.

"Yeah, she broke up with me," Sean explained as he stood up and adjusted himself and wiped his mouth off as well.

"I guess I don't have really have a chance do I?" Loren asked.

Sean looked back at her and didn't know what to say.

"You better go; it'll be worse if she sees you with me." Loren stood up and walked away in to the darkness by herself.

Sean turned around and walked back to the group and saw that Sharon was saying her hellos to everyone. Sean walked up but stopped a few feet back to catch his breath and to think of what he should say. Sharon saw him hesitate and walked up to him and handed him a fresh beer.

"I guess this is it?" Sharon said as she opened her own beer and took a sip while waiting for a response.

Sean looked back at her but she had already turned her head as if she were watching everyone else.

"Yeah, I guess this is it. I fly out Tuesday morning at 8 a.m. to California."

"Well I see you have a big turnout." Sharon looked around at the group and then back at him and then back down to the ground.

Sean didn't know exactly what to say and Sharon was equally lost in her thoughts.

"I have something for you," Sharon finally said and handed her beer for Sean to hold. She then opened her purse that was strapped to her shoulder. "It's just a little something I know you need and have wanted to give to you for a while."

"You didn't have to do anything like that," Sean responded feeling somewhat uncomfortable.

"Here," Sharon had a small jewelry box in her hand and exchanged it with Sean for her beer.

Sean opened the box and tilted it towards the fire to see it was a gold St. Christopher medal on a gold necklace.

"I know you lost your other one," Sharon's eyes were watering and she was fighting back the tears.

"Babe," Sean started to talk and quickly embraced her in his arms and gave her a hug, but Sharon stepped back and turned to the left slightly to avoid the hug.

"It'll help you find your way home," she began. "I wanted you to remember that I'll be here for a while but don't be gone so long."

"Sharon I," Sean started again but Sharon shook her head as if to say she couldn't or didn't want to hear what he wanted to say. She wiped her tears and turned and walked away, followed by her friend she arrived with.

"Sharon," Sean called out as he started to walk towards her, but instead of stopping, she began to walk faster towards the cars parked in the area, leaving Sean looking back at her as she went away. Sean put the small box back into his pocket and returned to the group who had grown silent watching Sharon leave. He took another long drink of his beer but was no longer feeling the celebration.

When Tuesday morning finally arrived, he was grateful that the wait was finally over. He was ready to go. The last couple of nights he had packed away his personal things and went through his closet giving a lot of his shirts and sweaters to Rebecca, who had eagerly accepted. It was as if he was dividing his life from "before the Army" to "in the Army". There were a lot of pictures and newspaper clippings, trophies and other memorabilia a teenager might collect. Most were boxed up with the promise to his parents he would come back for them one day.

His dad volunteered to drive him to the airport and his mom wanted to go, but his dad insisted that he wanted some time alone with Sean to say things a father tells his son. Although she was not very happy, his mother had reluctantly agreed. It was hard watching his mom cry as all moms cry when one of their children leaves the nest. It wasn't as bad for her when James and Robert left since they really only moved 30 or so miles away to attend school and they were certainly coming back. Rebecca would also probably go to college and then come back, with a husband in tow, who would work somewhere on the family farm. But, Sean was really heading out of the nest and she was not certain if he was going to come back. He didn't have the look of someone who was tentatively checking the water. He looked more like someone ready to dive in and start swimming.

SFC Willard was waiting for him and 10 others at the Memphis airport when they arrived at a little after 6 am that morning. He shook hands with Sean and his dad, visibly relieved he had showed up as instructed. It was a nightmare sometimes to get these enlistees to basic training. Recruiters didn't receive credit for the enlistment until the enlistee actually showed up at basic training so it was a constant nightmare come travel days as to who would show up and who he would have to track down. He handed Sean a sealed yellow paper envelope with his name and social security number written on the outside. Inside the sealed envelope and far from Sean's sight was his enlistment contract and travel orders. Sean received the envelope and moved away from the others that had also showed up and were obviously waiting to ship out. Sean was taking only a small bag with a change of underwear, a shirt and a few toilet articles. SFC Willard was pretty explicit when he explained that he would not be allowed to have any civilian clothing and anything he brought with him was going to be sent back anyway so he limited what he brought. It should make the traveling easier. The individual groups of enlistees and their families milled around the area, each ready to send someone they loved into the unknown world. It made Sean feel somewhat uncomfortable standing next to his dad, each wanting to say something but neither knowing what they could say. It was almost a welcomed moment when Sean heard a familiar voice call out.

"ALRIGHT gentlemen," Sergeant Willard spoke up in a loud voice that carried across the airport, "it's 0730, say your goodbyes, we're heading down to the terminal and getting on board the flight." SFC Willard looked around to make sure everyone heard him and then added, "family members, this is as far as I want you to go please. So, say your goodbyes now and we'll be leaving in a few minutes to get them on the aircraft."

Sean turned back to his dad and each pushed an invisible rock across the floor with their feet trying to find the right words. Finally his father broke the uncomfortable silence.

"Well, I'll let you go," he began, but hesitated for a few seconds to keep his voice from breaking. "You know your Grandfather took me to the train station when I shipped out to boot camp. He shook my hand and said, boy I'm sending you into the world. You bring everything back you leave with. I think what he meant to say was...,"

"Take care of yourself?" Sean smiled as he could imagine Grandpa talking to his dad in just that manner.

"Yeah I think that's what he meant. You'd make your momma cry if anything ever happens to you."

"Yes sir, I know. I can't do that."

"No, it would be bad for all of us." John tried to smile at the joke.

His dad stuck out his hand and Sean took it and shook it, he then reached out and they hugged.

As they embraced John gave his final advice, "I'm proud of you boy. I probably should have said that a long time ago." He released Sean and began to rub his nose, "now, remember always do the right thing, do what you're told, and don't forget the way home."

"Yes sir." Sean gripped his small travel bag and stated walking down the terminal towards the gate, the others enlistees straggled behind in ones and twos. His father watched until he turned the corner and then turned around himself and walked towards the parking lot. John now understood why his father, so strong and gruff as he was growing up, had tears in his eyes as he boarded the train to take him away.

Sean walked with the group down the terminal. He was lost in his thoughts and fairly oblivious to his surroundings. He walked right past the small coffee shop found in most airports; he was lost in thoughts and apprehensions and did not see Sharon sitting at the table.

As the group moved by towards the gate, Sharon stood up and walked into the terminal hallway and followed slowly and tentatively behind the group. By the time she had made it to the gate, she could just see the back of Sean's head as he walked through the terminal door and into the gangway to board the plane. She walked over to the large windows and remained there until the plane backed away from the gate and started moving towards the runway, tears flowing down her cheeks. Minutes later she was still watching as the plane took off. She placed her hand on the window as if to catch one more touch of Sean and then turned and walked away.

IV

Northern California
October, 1975

"Sergeant York," a loud voice called out from the orderly room across the street. The voice was directed towards the group of soldiers noisily offloading from the 24 passenger army bus, forming a single line and moving into the arms room located in the basement of the old building to turn in their weapons.

"Hey, is Sergeant York over there?" the voice called out again, louder this time.

"He's still on the bus," a soldier finally called out in answer more as an effort to stop the yelling than to provide an answer.

"Tell him to come to the orderly room when he gets the chance, I got something for him," the voice called out again.

"Yeah I got something for you too, you piece of shit," one of the soldiers called out causing the group of soldiers standing around to break into smiles, chuckles and laughter.

"Eat shit, you suck ass, Vincent," another voice called back causing another round of chuckles and jeers. The soldier gave up and retreated back into the relative safety of the company headquarters. The remaining soldiers continued to pile out of the bus slowly one at a time, each loaded down by their individual load of equipment, steel pot, M-16, web gear, 5 magazines of live 5.56 ammunition, .45 pistol with 3 magazines, flack vest, and finally a gas mask. A couple soldiers carried an M-60 machine gun and a few others carried the ammunition can with its belted ammunition. They were all tired from their guard shift but bolstered by their major accomplishment of the day, marking one more day off their enlistment. Each stepped off the bus and then got into another line to the arms room to turn in their weapons.

"Sean," one of the soldiers called out to him as he stepped down from the bus, "they want you in the orderly room."

"Who does?" Sean asked as he arched his back and tried to stretch from being jammed into the small bus seat during the fifteen minute bus ride back to the company area.

"I don't know that suck ass Vincent was calling for you," another soldier volunteered as he stepped down into the arms room to turn in his weapon.

Sean looked with disgust towards the orderly room and company headquarters. Specialist Vincent was one of the clerks in the company HQ, and because he could type, he had landed a soft administrative job in the company headquarters on a permanent five day workweek, with no additional duties, no chance of going out to the high security area, with all weekends and holidays off. He was pretty much hated by the remainder of the company who enjoyed no such privileges.

Sean looked down and shook his head as if thinking, *"what now?"* He slowly dropped his own flack vest, steal pot, and gas mask on top of the clearing barrel outside the arms room. He put his baseball cap on his head and slung the M-16 rifle over one shoulder and his pistol belt and web gear slung over the other and walked across the street. He climbed up the steps and into the orderly room where, as expected, everyone appeared to be hard at work doing nothing.

"Sergeant York," Vincent raised his right hand in the air and called out from his desk in the corner as Sean entered the company orderly room. "Been waiting for you." Vincent waved him over to the chair placed next to his desk.

Sean acknowledged the voice with an uninterested wave of the hand and walked across the room. He still hadn't gotten used to being addressed as Sergeant. Because his unit was critically short of junior Non Commissioned Officers, he was selected as one of the few troops to be elevated to the unenviable position of "acting sergeant" or more informally as an *"acting jack."* Meaning he wore the three sergeant stripes on his collar as his rank and was now officially supervising troops, but he only received pay of an E-4. This really amounted to having all of the responsibility of a sergeant but none of the pay and other prerogatives of a real NCO.

"What's up?" Sean asked as he walked up to Vincent's desk and collapsed in the chair.

"Got something for you to sign," Vincent reached back and took a clipboard mounted on a nail on the wall behind him and retrieved a yellow envelope from a stack of other yellow envelopes on his desk.

"My discharge?" Sean asked flippantly and listened to the chuckles across the room.

"No such luck, but might be just as good. Here's your levy notice." Vincent continued to flip through the papers on the clipboard until he found the right one.

"My what?" Sean asked, not sure he understood what he was being told. His heart started to beat faster.

"Your levy notice, looks like you're finally getting out of here. You're heading across the pond." Vincent handed him the sealed yellow envelope and pointed on the clipboard where Sean was to sign acknowledging receipt of his notification.

Sean's heart started beating faster in anticipation. A levy meant overseas assignment. It meant he was finally getting out of this dump. He was being paroled, reprieved, and rescued.

"Levy? Where to?" Sean asked with a sudden great interest as he signed the form on the clipboard.

"Does it matter?" Vincent quipped and looked up at Sean who was obviously not in a joking mood. Vincent decided not to press the point and looked down on his paperwork. "Korea," Vincent finally announced in a matter of fact take it or leave it manner as he withdrew the clipboard.

Sean began to eagerly open the sealed envelope and withdrew the official orders inside and read. "*York, Sean P. Specialist,*" Sean skipped a few lines, and continued reading to himself, "*is alerted for overseas assignment.*" his heart started to race and he continued to skim the document, "*gaining unit Headquarters and Headquarters company 728th Military Police Battalion, reporting date to be established for March 1976.*" The "seven deuce eight," Sean recognized the unit immediately. It was a line duty unit which meant white hat or regular MP duties; he had been told over and over again this was the best duty in Korea. His thoughts were interrupted by Vincent who was trying to pass along some other information.

"Ok, your levy briefing is 1300 next Wednesday over at personnel; they'll get you squared away with port call, transportation, and everything else you need. They'll do your orders after you work all of that out with them." Vincent looked up to make sure he understood.

"God damn," was Sean's only response and he sighed as if a great weight was being lifted from his shoulders. He went back to reading the levy notice. "Man, it's about frigging time," Sean said out loud to no one in particular and sat down in the chair by Vincent's desk momentarily. How many times had he requested a transfer or overseas assignment? Four or five at least, and finally here it was. A million thoughts raced through his head as he continued to scan the document. "...*individual must re-enlist or extend to meet service obligation for overseas assignment.*"

"So I have to extend or re-up to go huh?" Sean asked and continued reading.

"Yeah, you got to have at least 13 months remaining on enlistment before you go across the pond. Don't worry, personnel will work that out with ya next week."

"OK, so I have a reporting month of March," Sean paused and then asked the most important question of his notification. "So, when can I get out of this shithole?"

Vincent turned back around to face Sean again but looked like he had become bored or uninterested in the conversation. "I don't know man, it's not my bag, and personnel will work that out with ya. But, probably early February maybe late January depends on how much leave you take."

Sean did some quick figuring in this head, "early January could put me right around 90 days left then, right?"

Vincent only shrugged his shoulders as if to say *"it's not my problem,"* and started typing again.

Sean stood up and looked around the room and at other soldiers sitting behind desks and typing and called out, "well, I guess I'll be seeing you, you bunch of sorry sons a bitches." He raised the levy notice over his head as if he was suddenly and unexpectedly paroled or was being freed from indentured service. He was, for a moment, lost in his own thoughts and his own little world as he looked around at everyone who had already lost interest and were already busy trying to look busy. It didn't matter, it was as if someone from above had finally listened to him and was now reaching down to personally rescue him from this god awful place. Apparently purgatory does have a time limit.

After turning in his weapons and a short platoon NCO meeting he was released for the day. Sean had talked to a few of the older NCOs who gave him a rousing congratulatory and envious shake of the hand and pats on the back. A few of the older sergeants were able to talk about great and fond memories of their time with his future unit and made him even more excited about the new assignment. It was with great relief Sean finally managed to get back to his barracks room, a small one man room located on the second floor of a dilapidated WWII wooden, two story barracks. Only these barracks had been modified fifteen or so years before from the large open bay area and made into separate rooms where two, sometimes three soldiers crammed into a room together with a common latrine and showers down the hallway. One of the few advantages of being a sergeant, or even an acting sergeant, was getting his own room without a roommate. At least he had a little privacy. He got out of his uniform and boots and left them in a pile on the floor and walked over to the small refrigerator for a cold beer. He needed one tonight to celebrate.

Sitting down in his chair at his desk, dressed in only his white tee shirt and white boxer shorts, he read and then reread the orders over and over again. Every once in a while he took a sip from his beer but never really took his eyes off the paperwork. Looking up, he picked up his calendar off the wall that he was using to mark off his days and did some quick figuring, counting backwards from various days in March silently working out several possible scenarios and options. His main thoughts and fantasy seemed to be fixated on getting out of that place as soon as humanly possible. After working out all of the different possibilities, he realized it provided no real answers and only created more questions. He sighed in frustration and tilted the beer up draining it completely and throwing the empty into the trash. He sighed, because he knew it did no good to make any plans until he could get his levy briefing and get his port call. Anything else at this stage was just wishful hoping and he had already spent a lot of time in the last 19 months hoping to get out of that place and go anywhere else.

Sitting back down on his desk chair he reached for the 8 X 10 gold picture frame containing Sharon's high school graduation photo sitting in a prominent position on his small metal desk. He put the frame against his chest and rubbed it on his t-shirt, trying to remove the small layer of dust that had accumulated since the last time he had gazed at it. He held it out in front of him and took a drink of his second beer. Sharon was pictured in her long sleeve black sweater and her mother's pearl necklace, her hair was so blond in contrast to the dark sweater and background he could not believe it. She was smiling in her large naturally straight toothy smile that brought out her dimples in both cheeks that she hated and he loved.

He had gone home the previous two summers, once for James and Margret's wedding after their graduation from college and Sharon's High school graduation. Then this last summer, he had returned home again for a week to attend Robert and Beth's wedding after they had both graduated from college. Sharon had just completed her freshman year at college and was living in some sorority house on campus. She was especially invited to both weddings by written invitation and then a few personal phone calls made by Margret, Rebecca, and his mom to ensure her attendance. In both events she had been "seated" at the same table with the rest of his family and right next to him. Whatever conspiracy the York women had plotted, Sean was very happy at the results. For those few days he had gone home it had been literally like old times. They had spent nearly every waking hour together and there was no talk of the army or even an acknowledgement that they were even separated from each other. Instead it was as if he had been gone for a weekend trip and then came back. They laughed, and teased each other like old times, and during quieter moments when they managed to get away and be alone, they had embraced and kissed passionately and Sean felt himself falling in love with her all over again. Robert's wedding was even more special, thanks to Margret, who managed to borrow the keys to his parent's cabin at the lake and slipped them to Sean. They were actually able to sneak away and spent their first night ever alone and slept together in the same bed, making love, talking, and holding each other. Waking up realizing they didn't have to rush right off to take her home or worry about not making her curfew was a thrill of their newly realized adulthood. Instead they had spent the morning waking up slowly, entwined in each other's arms and talking about their first experience at the cabin and their lives.

Sean put the picture down and reached up and took the gold St. Christopher's medal and necklace she had given him before he left for the army. He held it between his thumb and finger as he did many times when he was thinking of Sharon. He smiled to himself thinking back to them lying in bed talking last summer. Sharon was so pleased that he was wearing the necklace and he assured her he never took it off. He was lying on his back in bed when she rolled over and reached out and momentarily held it in her hand.

"I gave you this not just to protect you," she slyly started to confess, "I wanted you to think of me every time you wore it and imagine that I am right there next to you no matter where you go. That way you would be reminded of me every day." Sharon had smiled and leaned over to kiss him again.

Unfortunately each visit home had passed quickly and before he was really ready to go he was leaving again. Although it was never officially discussed, at the end of his last leave both considered themselves to be back together. Each long separation was highlighted by letters and sporadic phone calls, but the long distance romance was taking its toll on both of them. Sean sat, looked over at the alarm clock on the desk and realized he had to get dressed; evening chow opened in a few minutes. That was a major milestone in his daily existence over the last year or so, because after chow he could come back to his room and officially mark another day off of his calendar. He pulled on a pair of jeans and a polo shirt and slipped barefoot into a pair of tennis shoes and sat down behind the desk again. Taking another sip of his beer he reached out for his calendar and noted that this month was two years since he had gotten on the plane in Memphis, leaving Mississippi, his family, and Sharon to join the army. He had long ago come to the conclusion that enlisting in the army had been both the best thing he had ever done and the fulfillment of all of his boyhood dreams and yet for a substantial period of time, it had seemed like one of the worst mistakes he had ever made. He said a mental prayer that his upcoming transfer would finally bring him to the army he had expected and wanted to be a part of and not what he was living now.

Basic training and MP School or Advanced Individual training (AIT) were everything that he thought the army was going to be and from the very first day of basic training he knew he was right where he belonged. He liked the feeling of belonging, of doing something different, being a part of something, and yet being independent and out on his own. But the 'army way' was a shock to some of the other young soldiers. He could remember lying in his bunk during the first days of basic training totally exhausted and trying to get some sleep and listening to whimpering or sniffling of others who were having a tough time adjusting to the army way of life. He was confused at the difficulties of some of the others had following simple directions or conforming to the army way. Most of those having problems were city kids that were unused to discipline, any kind of manual labor, or that had been spoiled as they grew up and had probably never been responsible for anything in their lives. Some had no idea how to even wash their own clothes or make their own beds. It was clear to him even in the first few days that the army had a particular way for everything and demanded simple and unhesitating compliance and uniformity in everything it did.

To be successful you simply had to learn what the army wanted or expected and then do it. Failure to follow instructions, fighting the army, or acting independently inevitably lead to unpleasant attention by their Drill Sergeants and some "extra training" such as your entire wall or foot locker pushed over or turned upside down spilling its contents all over the floor, with instructions to try it again. There were a lot of things he did have to get used to with the army life, being raised in a nice house with his own bedroom, bathroom, and a house keeper. In the army, he found himself living in an open bay with 30 others with his individual living area defined by a double bunk bed and two wall lockers and two footlockers. The bunk beds were pushed against the wall lockers of the soldiers adjacent to them and the wall lockers of the other area were pushed against their bunk beds. A bathroom in the army was called a latrine; in basic training consisted of a large open area with one wall lined with fifteen sinks, the other wall lined with urinals and seven toilets in the corner, four along one wall and three against the other. There were no stalls or anything else to give anyone any semblance of privacy. You did your business along with everyone else. At the end of the duty day there were always six or seven of them at one time relieving themselves together, talking and smoking and joking to each other as each did his business, with a line of several more soldiers waiting their turn. The showers were in a smaller room where there were eight shower heads and like in gym, everyone came and went and no one wanted to drop the soap.

They graduated basic training on a Friday in early November and the next day he arrived at the MP school at Ft Gordon GA. A few days later, that unit filled up with others who were coming in from other basic training forts across the country. A week later, he started training to be a military police man and the adventure continued. The MP School was designed much like he envisioned a civilian police academy would be and he excelled in learning everything he could about the law, police procedures, and traffic enforcement. Unlike basic training, AIT was about going to school and training, so there was a lot more free time. Basically once released for the day, they could pretty much do what they wanted until they had to get up the next day and go to school. Weekends they could come and go as they wanted as long as they came back for training Monday morning. Thanksgiving came and went and then ten days of Christmas exodus where all trainees were encouraged to go home on leave while the schools closed down and the drill sergeants and school instructors were given some much needed time off. Sean went home and tried to go by and see Sharon, but she was still upset at his leaving. Although he came over for a visit a few times, it was at first very strained. Towards the end of his leave, Sharon seemed to warm up some and although she was still upset, she had at least agreed to write him while he was away. It was a small victory but Sean was at least happy to have opened up communication again as he returned to complete his training

The remaining weeks flew by and a week before graduation from MP School, everyone received their new assignment instructions. Sean had not picked an assignment when he enlisted so there was no telling where he would end up. When his name was called out he reached out to receive a copy of his orders and scanned looking for where he was going. He read the orders several times but had to ask the cadre about his assignment; no one had ever heard of Yuma Proving Grounds or even knew where it was located. It certainly did not have the same allure as a Ft Hood, Ft Campbell or Ft Benning, or any of the other large forts. Even Germany or Panama where so many of his classmates were headed most of the senior soldiers knew where they were located and what could be expected, but Sean had no idea what to expect. On graduation day in January 1974 still dressed in his winter greens, he boarded a plane at the Augusta, GA airport where the January weather was a cool and crisp 40 degrees and that night he landed in Yuma Arizona a little after 8 pm to 80 degree weather. Sean had almost melted as he stepped out of the small plane and into the dry warm heat of Arizona, instantly realizing his wool winter greens were likely not going to be worn around this place much.

Yuma Proving Grounds turned out to be some 900,000 acres of empty Arizona desert located 30 miles from the city of Yuma, Arizona. Although one of the largest bases by land area, it was one of the smallest by troop size with only about 500 soldiers assigned to a few units engaged in various testing of aircraft, machines, and artillery in desert conditions. Sean was assigned to the 64th MP Platoon, a small 35 man MP Detachment responsible for police and security duties. Sean was a welcomed addition to the unit and had the distinction of being the first and only lower enlisted member assigned to the unit who was not a draftee. All other enlisted members below the rank of sergeant were draftees and most were on their last few months of service. All were ready to go home and were already counting down their final days in the army.

Sean had a hard time adjusting to his new environment. He was used to the heat and humidity of the delta and the *greenness* of Mississippi, but Arizona was dry, sandy, and hot. In early summer the temperature went to 115 in the shade and while standing around on the roadway checking security badges of workers coming to a secured area to work, Sean looked down and actually saw his polish on the tips of his black leather start to melt and run down the toes of his boots. Another MP described it best as, *"Yuma wasn't quite hell, but it's in the same area code."* Yuma was a small backwater installation much like the small town he came from and not quite the "army" he had expected and yearned for after training. But at least the time went by fast. Sean found himself locked into what came to be known in the MP world as the 9 and 3 rotating schedule. Meaning he worked three midnight shifts- going to work at 2200 in the evening, working until 0600 the following day. Then a 24 hour break and came in at 0600, and worked until 1400 for three day shifts, then a short break coming in at 1400 in the afternoon and getting off at 2200 and then three days off before you started the routine all over again. It was the worst type of shift work and his body never seemed to recover and get into any type of established routine. Work itself was a combination of a little MP police work and a lot of physical security work, mostly shaking doors or working in secluded guard posts all over the desert. Off duty there was almost nothing to do but play cards and drink beer. Their barracks were located across the street from the bowling alley and after work they could walk across the street and have a few beers. Sean learned to play a mean game of Spades and after a few weeks, actually became a sought after partner. He spent many a three day break playing cards, walking over to the mess hall, eating, walking a few streets over to the liquor store, buying beer and then coming back and playing cards again until everyone went to sleep exhausted.

V

He got quite an education from the draftees and through osmosis picked up a little of their attitudes. They were not very happy about being in the army. Several had been in college on their way to other things when the draft caught them and took them away from their regular lives. Apparently it was vital to the national defense to have them break up their lives to guard rocks in the Arizona desert. Draftees wanted no trouble and no responsibility; they just wanted a discharge and a trip home. Sean didn't care for Yuma very much although he did pick up another stripe and a raise in pay. But the duty was nothing like he expected and his surroundings were even worse. He tried to keep a good attitude and volunteered for overseas assignment twice but was turned down both times because *"he had not been on station long enough."* Sean took each 'no' with a grain of salt and resolved to try again as soon as he could. But, as he would find out, even though he hadn't been on station long enough to go overseas, when it came to *'the needs of the army'* they could move heaven and earth or do anything they wanted. He had only been at Yuma for six months and was just getting acclimated and established when he received notification he was being transferred. Once he received his orders he again went to the senior NCOs in the unit and asked them about his new unit and installation, Sierra Army Depot. But like a now familiar song, no one had ever heard of it.

In September 1974, to mark his first year in the army, Sean found himself standing outside the orderly room at Sierra Army Depot, with orders in hand and signing into his new unit. As he left Yuma, he had consoled himself with the thought that at least when he eventually transferred he would go to a better place since this was certainly the worst place in the army. Instead he discovered the truthfulness of an old army adage, *it may not ever get better; but it can always get worse.* The soldiers at Sierra Army Depot had concluded if God were ever to give the world an enema he would most certainly put it into Sierra Army Depot, because this was truly *the asshole* of the world. He had thought Yuma was bad, but after a few months at Sierra Army Depot he longed to be back in the Arizona desert again. Sierra Army Depot was located some 50 miles north of Reno and at least another

30 miles away from any real town. Looking at a map one might suppose this was an ideal spot as it was also located bordering the shores of Honey Lake. Unfortunately, Honey Lake was an alkali lake, not more than 2-3 feet deep and surrounding the lake was a high desert.

At Yuma there were at least some law enforcement duties, but at Sierra Army Depot it was physical security only. Each day the MP's went to work, armed with M-16, .45 pistols, M-60 machine guns, steel pot, flack vest, and gas mask. They went out to guard ammunition bunkers and fight boredom in a small fenced in high security area. Like Yuma, there was really nothing to do for the MPs assigned there except to work and drink. After looking forward to being in the army for so long, Yuma and then Sierra Army Depot were indeed a crushing letdown. He was assigned to a unit with a collection of malcontents who were not interested in anything excepting getting out of the army and away from that horrible place. It's not that they weren't good guys, some could have been excellent soldiers in other conditions, but the duty and lack of off duty diversion, poor living conditions in the barracks, poor morale, and poor leadership sucked the life out of even the best of soldiers, leaving them empty and bitter. Sean himself was falling into despair. With literally nothing else to do, he started drinking far too much for a young man of 20. He started caring less and less about his military appearance, his duty performance also dropped, and he gained over 30 lbs in a short period of time mostly from lack of exercise and too much beer. His once trimmed athletic body was now pudgy and he became winded from just walking up the steps to his 2nd floor barracks room.

Even worse, after reestablishing some contact with Sharon and beginning to exchange sometimes twice weekly letters and a few phone calls, the disappointment and frustration of his current duty sank in. His letters home started to slow down and the calls home became more infrequent. He was slipping into a depression and there was simply not a lot to talk about anymore. He had waited his entire life to join the army and suddenly he went from one bad place to another that was even worse and he felt like he had been tricked. After a few months it was all he could do anymore to motivate himself just to get up and go to work.

When he received his written invitation to Robert's wedding he was of course happy for his brother but actually was ambivalent to returning home again. The entire thought process of arranging a flight, asking for leave, and finding something that could fit him as he was now seriously out of shape and overweight was almost more than he could bear. Actually any excuse to get out of that place would have been welcomed, but he hesitated to go home looking the way he did. It was easier to send a card, express his well wishes to his big brother, and have a drink or two for him at the club that night. Had it not been for Margaret and Rebecca, that's likely what would have happened. But within a few days of receiving the invitation, he received a call on the payphone in the barrack's hallway from Margaret who was evidently well engaged in helping out her future sister in law get the family together. Margaret had also noticed the change in Sean over the last couple of months from talking with his mother and thought he might be considering not showing up. This would have crushed the rest of his family and she took it upon herself as 'his new big sister' to call and make sure he was coming home. Sean had been polite and pleasant but noncommittal on his attendance. He had been very impressed with Margaret for at least reaching out on a personal level; she was clearly a good pick by James and would undoubtedly be able to ride roughshod over the wild bunch when his mother gave up the reins.

Whereas Margaret was still polite while acting as the oldest sister in law, Rebecca was more like his mom. Being a York herself she knew how to be direct and brutal when it was needed. As the youngest sister she didn't feel like she had to pull any punches to any of her older brothers and whereas she could never match them on a physical level, she could hold her own with her sharp tongue and stubbornness. It only took a few minutes and a vague but serious threat to "personally" fly out to California and drag him back home, for him to finally acquiesce and commit to coming home.

The trip home was uneventful but he actually had started to feel better as he was driving to the Reno airport to fly home. Maybe it was just putting distance between himself and his unit that actually started to make him feel better. The flight was long but once airborne and on his way he started to feel better about coming home again. He was met in Memphis by his dad who was somewhat surprised at his appearance but was obviously happy to have him home again. This time it truly felt good to be back home and away from California, the army, and his miserable existence. June was hot and humid and the countryside was green and had familiar sights and smells and Sean started to relax almost immediately. The whole week home had been hectic with very little time to just sit around and relax. He had spent as much time with Sharon as he could but still had a chance to visit with James and Margaret who had already set up a nice house in Yorktown. They decided to buy a house from one of the cousins instead of building one of their own since they were eventually going to move into the big house once his parents retired. Margaret was an outstanding homemaker and had furnished and decorated the house very warmly. Cousin Kevin showed up at the wedding and reception looking very fit. He would be starting tight end in his second year at Ole Miss and managed to corral Sean at the reception to go out back where they had a beer together. He filled him with the wild stories of college and what all Sean was missing. But of course the main event was seeing Sharon again. He had been taken totally by surprise when she had been placed next to him at the reception at the large family table. He was sitting directly across table from his mother who was smiling approvingly when Sharon sat down next to him. She had also been surprised at his appearance, but was aware more so than anyone else how unhappy he was. She was secretly happy that he seemed so miserable and took it as a sign that he might want to get out of the army and come home. She did everything she could do to make him feel homesick and remember how nice it could be if he would only come home.

The whole week just flew by and he was genuinely down when he realized he had to leave the following day and go back. The night before he was packing his clothes in his room when his dad called him down to the study to sit and have a talk. His dad in typical fashion, didn't talk round an issue, instead confronted it head on.

"Son, what's the matter with you?" He started almost immediately when Sean sat down in the easy chair as he handed him a brandy snifter.

"Sir?" Sean answered and took a sip of his drink not knowing exactly what his dad was trying to say.

"I said what's the matter with you?" His dad raised his hand and swept it towards Sean, "Look at you; you're out of shape, I can tell you're drinking way too much; your letters have dropped off to nearly nothing and you're starting to worry your mother. Now what's going on? Are you on drugs?"

Sean nearly sent his drink through his nose. "Dad, no way, where's that coming from?" Sean wiped his mouth off with the palm of his hand.

"OK, well then what's going on?"

Sean sat back momentarily and took another small sip and then started to unloaded all of his disappointment with the army and his current duty. He continued on for several minutes outlining all the complaints felt by all of the soldiers in his unit and the general stupidity of the army. His dad listened very patiently and nodded his head as if he understood. Sean actually felt better as if he were getting all of the built up frustrations off his chest for the first time.

"So, the army ain't quite what you figured huh?" His dad leaned back in his chair and took a sip from his own drink.

"Nah not really," Sean looked down into his drink not quite certain how to respond.

"Well son, you never came to me before you enlisted so we could sit down and talk about it. You acted on your own," his dad responded back.

"Yes sir I know," Sean answered back and sighed.

"But, let me ask you something. You wanted to be an MP, so are you an MP?"

"Yeah, I'm a physical security MP." Sean nodded but not satisfied with his answer.

"OK, but an MP right?" He looked over at Sean who nodded his head. "Now, are you getting paid?"

"Yes sir of course I get paid."

"Well, then what's the problem? The army did what it said it would do. For whatever reason the army says you're needed there in California. So they trained you and sent you there and are paying you to be there. Seems to me you got everything you asked for."

"Well I guess so, but dad that place sucks."

"Shit son, hasn't anyone told you yet there're only two good places in the service? The place you're going to and the place you're comin' from; the place you're at always sucks." His dad took another sip from his drink shook his head back and forth twice and then continued and grew serious. "But now listen to me, you enlisted and volunteered on your own. No one came looking for you; you signed your name, you gave your word, and you took an oath. A man is no man who goes against his word, son. It's your bond and your mark as a man. Your Grandpa once told me there are two things a man is born with and no one can ever take away, if they lose it, they must voluntarily gave it up themselves. The first is your immortal soul." He took another drink and looked to see if Sean was following and then began again, "Son even the devil can't steal your soul, did you know that? You have to willingly give it to him. The second thing is your honor. Every man is born with honor and a good name, no matter how poor. You have to willingly give that up yourself too. Now your word and honor is basically the same thing, you give a man your word on something and you're bound by it. Right now it's riding on your oath to the army. Are you ready to give up your honor because things aren't exactly the way you want them to be? Well, boo hoo son, things aren't always the way we like them to be. Are you just going to give up?"

Sean looked into his drink and took a deep breath. "No sir, I ain't ready to give up."

"Well then reach down into your gut son and man up."

"Yes sir."

"Now, you have, what, a little over a year left? If that ain't your cup of tea then do your time and get out. But leave with your head held high that you did the best you could. You give an honest day's work for an honest day's pay. Then you can always come home and get back to school and get on with your life."

Sean looked over at his dad and felt his eyes water. "Yes sir I can do that."

"I know it son," his dad nodded his head and looked over at him, "I was proud of you for standing up for what you thought was important and taking off and becoming a man. Now don't disappoint me and don't dishonor your family by being a little wussy."

"Yes sir," Sean said back almost in a whisper and looked up at his dad who looked back and raised his glass in a silent salute. Sean returned the gesture and took another sip.

Sean returned to California and his unit somewhat renewed and recharged. He was determined to get his attitude adjusted and get back into the 'game.' The first day back Sean got up early in the morning dressed in shorts and tennis shoes and started to run again. His first day, he was winded in less than a ½ mile, but he kept with it and little by little he increased his run. Within just a few weeks he was running 3-5 miles at a time. He quickly realized how good it felt to be working out; the first few days his body had ached terribly and he really realized how out of shape he had become. But he kept with it and as he ran he actually felt like he was alive again. He spent the first few days cleaning the rest of his barracks room and straightening the place up. He then took out his uniforms that were stuffed into his wall locker and broke out his iron and started to iron them before work. At the same time, he started applying more polish to his boots that were eager to get more than a slight brushing to remove the dust. They would take some work to get a shine back onto them but at least he was starting.

Over the course of the next several weeks after his return, Sean started to get back into life again. He slowed down his visits to the NCO Club and instead focused on running and hitting the gym and was doing his best to get back into shape. His overall military appearance improved and so did his general attitude and duty performance. His hard work did not go unnoticed by the platoon sergeant who noticed a distinct improvement. Suddenly Sean became a super trooper and volunteered to take on additional responsibility for training of the new people as they were assigned to the platoon. By the end of the summer, he was selected to appear before the sergeant's promotion board and shortly thereafter was appointed as 'acting Sergeant'.

Sean reflected that once his attitude changed and he quit feeling sorry for himself, everything seemed to change for him. Although he still hated where he was at and the duty, he had reconciled with his life and decided if he couldn't get out of there he would just do his time and go home. His letters and calls to Sharon became more frequent and they actually began to talk about a future together again. Although Sean was quick not to promise, it was evident to Sharon that he was looking forward to coming back home again and she also began to imagine their life together back in their small hometown. She had also noticed a change as they talked on the phone and in her letters.

Then came his levy notice and his world seemed to change overnight.

VI

Sean had decided not to say anything about the transfer to anyone at home. He had originally planned to take some leave and come home for Christmas. Instead, Sean worked out a deal with the platoon sergeant for him to work over the holidays and allow a few of the platoon mates to go home and the platoon sergeant would support his leave request for 45 days prior to going overseas. Normally only 30 days was allowed, but for special reasons it could be extended. This would now put him able to sign out in mid-January and start the out processing right after the New Year. Sean had calculated that he was less than 60 days away from finally getting out of that place. His attitude improved even more as he was able to start counting down the remaining days.

Sharon and his family were both disappointed when he was unable to come home for Christmas but seemed to take it in stride. It was difficult for him not to say anything to anyone about his expected tour in Korea. Sean decided that if he were to ever hope to have a relationship with Sharon he would have to look at her face to face and tell her about his overseas tour and about his plans to stay in the army. He did not want to take a chance in breaking the news over the phone; things were starting to look up again, he would have to do this face to face.

Sean's remaining time seemed to fly by. Thanksgiving came and went, Christmas was just another duty day and shortly after New Year's he had received his orders and clearing papers and happily started processing out of the installation. As a soldier processed out of his current duty station, he was taken off all duty rosters and he had a lot of free time to get his affairs in order. Movers came to pack up his personal property; some were being sent forward to Korea where he would get them back and some were packed up to be sent home to wait for his return. The 15th of January was his last day; his Mustang was packed up and he waited quietly around the post office to collect his mid-month pay check. But he was so ready to go that when the mail was delayed, Sean decided he had enough money to get home and he left without his check, knowing he would eventually get his pay straightened out. He put the car into drive, put Sweet Home Alabama into the 8 track and turned it up to the pain level, and punched the accelerator throwing up dust and gravel all around the car. Happiness was truly Sierra Army Depot in the rear view mirror.

He drove home almost straight through stopping only for gas or something to eat and once or twice to sleep in the car for a few hours at a truck stop. Then he was up again and back on the road. Eventually he stopped at a truck stop, called home and spoke to his parents and let them know he was coming home on leave. Two days later he arrived home in the early evening and was greeted with open arms and welcomed back into the house. Hazel fixed him a huge sandwich and he hit the shower and then collapsed back into his bed.

Sharon had been ecstatic to have Sean home again. He had surprised her by just showing up at her sorority the next day after class. Sharon had cried to see him again and for several minutes she just held him in her arms not saying anything. Sean could feel her tears on his neck and his cheeks as he held her back. It would be one of his most cherished memories of their time together, just holding each other standing on the sidewalk in front of her on-campus sorority house. Sean had made reservations at one of the smaller more expensive and trendy restaurants on the town square in Oxford. Sharon had happily accepted the invitation to what seemed like a romantic dinner. As she was getting dressed she vividly imagined Sean asking her to marry him. She was convinced his sudden appearance, the romantic dinner, and the rekindled relationship added up to a marriage proposal and his leaving the army and coming home. Sharon confided in her roommate her suspicions and hopes and they had giggled with excitement like school children. Sharon had always known deep down in her heart that a proposal was coming and although it had certainly taken its time getting there, she was going to enjoy it nevertheless.

Dinner however, had been an unmitigated disaster and had ended with Sharon in tears, walking out alone before the main course was even set before them. Sharon could hardly believe her ears as Sean began talking again about the army again in positive terms and suddenly from nowhere, he's leaving the country for a year. But worst of all, Sean had actually extended his enlistment in the army in order to be able to complete this assignment. If he had not extended, he could have been out of the army in nine months. But he had added time to his enlistment and now he had a fourteen more months. Far worse than anything else, she realized that he was not coming home and was not getting out of the army. Her dreams of a romantic proposal, of her planning her wedding, and their life together were smashed in a matter of minutes.

"This is why you brought me here?" Sharon had asked trying to hold back her tears, "To tell me you're leaving?"

"Well," Sean started to explain but was broken off by Sharon.

"To tell me you're going back to the army?" Sharon felt her own words stab her in the heart.

"Sharon," Sean began to plead, "I had to get out of that place."

"I thought you were getting out, and now you tell me you extended your enlistment?" Sharon leaned forward to emphasize her point.

"Sharon it's a year tour, but a chance to get out of what I was doing. I've been miserable for two years now."

"Maybe you've been miserable because you've been in that....that" Sharon stumbled as she tried to find the right word, "that fucking army? Did you ever think of that Sean? It's the damn army that was making you miserable?" The tears were streaming down her face at this point. "Did you ever think about that?"

Sean was taken aback not knowing what to say. Sharon picked up the linen napkin from her lap and wiped her eyes. Her makeup had started to run and small dark lines were now running down her cheeks.

"Sharon I was," Sean started to speak but was interrupted again.

"I,...I,....I,..... Always I, I, I. You have to do this, you have to do that. What about us Sean? As in you and me? It's never going to be about us is it?" Sharon looked over and took his lack of response as an answer. She quickly stood up and lightly threw her napkin onto the table. "That's what I thought."

Sean stood up as Sharon turned and walked towards the door. Unfortunately for Sean the best intentions along with logical arguments did not always change things for the better. Sean reached into his pocket and put a fifty dollar bill on the table and then ran outside after her. She was walking very fast and it took several seconds to finally catch up with her. He finally caught up with her and reached out to grab her by the arm to make her stop and talk.

"Sharon, will you please wait a minute?" Sean called out to her.

"Don't touch me, Sean York, just don't touch me ever again." Sharon snapped back, jerking her arm away and continued walking without so much as breaking her stride.

"Sharon, can't we at least talk for a minute?' Sean continued walking behind her pleading.

Sharon stopped on a dime and turned swiftly around, facing Sean. She stopped so quick that Sean almost knocked her over.

"I'm sorry," Sean reached out to her after accidentally jostling her.

"Sean, there is nothing to talk about. I haven't changed my mind and apparently you haven't changed yours."

"Sharon, I love you. We can work this out." Sean tried to explain.

"Sean, stop saying that," Sharon said through gritted teeth and then out of emotional frustration she struck him on the chest with her fist.

"Hey, goddamn it." Sean rubbed his chest, "Settle down, will ya?"

"No I won't. You hurt me Sean York." Sharon pointed her right index finger straight at Sean, "and you're going off again to that damned army as if I don't mean anything to you."

"You mean everything to me," Sean opened his arms and walked forward to take her into his arms.

"Everything, Sean? I mean everything to you. Really? Then why are you leaving me again? Is this what you mean by everything?" Sharon reached up and dried her eyes on the backs of her hand and then put both hands stubbornly on her hips.

"Sharon, this was my way to finally get out of California and finally do what I've been trained to do. You know how miserable I was out there."

"Exactly!" Sharon almost shouted in frustration. "That's what I've been trying to tell you," Sharon started to tear up again. "Sean, you're such an ass." Sharon started at him momentarily and then turned and started walking down the street again.

It took a little cajoling and convincing but finally Sharon accepted a ride back to her sorority house by Sean who had run back to retrieve his car and had started driving slowly down the street. She got reluctantly into the car only because it was cold outside. Although Sean did his best to talk to her, Sharon ignored him and only stared out the window until they arrived at her sorority. She quickly got out, slamming the door hard behind her and walked quickly to the front door. Sean waited until she got inside and then drove slowly off, not seeing that she had turned and looked back at him through the small glass pane in the front door. After he drove away and she could no longer see his tail lights, Sharon walked to her room and fell upon her bed and began to sob. This is not what she had expected or wanted and her heart ached like never before.

Sean slowly began to realize that they were headed along two different paths and wasn't certain if they were ever going to come together again. Other than a few times going out with Kevin and his brothers, Sean spent most of his time working out at the small workout room his father had built for them when they were all playing football. On days without the winter cold and ice, he was out running. His running distances increased as he found himself trying to get his life in some semblance of order and as he worked out the pain he felt in his own heart.

Sean hoped Korea might bring something better.

VII

The long leave was now just as painful as the long separation had been and Sean began to count the days remaining on leave as eagerly as he counted his days remaining in California. But they passed by slowly even painfully. Instead of enjoying the time at home he grew impatient and began to take long walks in the middle of the day just to get out of the house and have something to do. Finally the last day came and they all had a nice family dinner sat around and talked for a while and then mercifully everyone went home early. After the last family member left, Sean bid his goodnight to his parents and Hazel feeling nearly worn out for the wait and anticipation of his new adventure. He slept fitfully spending more time tossing and turning than sleeping and was more than ready to go when the alarm finally went off at 3 am. He was already packed and after shaving, brushing his teeth he shoved his shaving kit onto one of his smaller bags and in just a few minutes he was dressed in his class "A" uniform and ready to go. Looking in the mirror to check out his appearance he actually felt good being back in uniform, although he was slightly upset at having to take off the sergeant chevrons from his uniform and replace them with the specialist rank. When he left his last unit he lost his acting sergeant stripes and had to revert back to his actual rank od Specialist. It was really his only disappointment from leaving California.

He had said his goodbyes the previous night and did not expect his mother or Ms Hazel to be up, but when he made it downstairs they were both sitting there at the smaller table in the kitchen drinking coffee. Ms Hazel had gotten up early and fixed a thermos of coffee for their ride to Memphis. His dad finally showed up in the kitchen himself and looked as if he too had a difficult night. Thankfully his dad was ready to go and after only a moment or two of uncomfortable small talk it was time to go. Sean gave both women a large hug and kissed them on their cheeks and then he was off.

The ride to the airport with his dad was reminiscent of his first departure, but not so traumatic. Sean was already two years older, had been out on his own now and had matured greatly. Sean was now more excited and looking forward to a new adventure than apprehensive and uncertain when he left for the army. His dad filled the ride with more of his tails from the Marines and his time in Korea some twenty years before and the time passed quickly. Probably before either one was ready, his dad pulled the truck up to the curb of the departing flights and momentarily parked. He walked around as Sean was unloading his duffel bag and two smaller leather suit cases onto the side walk and adjusting his garrison cap on his head.

"Well son, I have some stuff to do today so I'm just going to have to drop you off and skedaddle back home."

"I know dad it's OK, I can handle it from here."

His dad came over to stand in front of him and looked him over standing in his class "A" greens. "You've really grown up in the army son, it seems to fit you."

"Yes sir, I think I got my head straight now." Sean lookup at his dad who was smiling nervously.

"Alright well, I want to tell you how proud you mother and I are of you." John paused and kicked around an invisible stone with his foot then continued," Now get over there and do the right thing. Remember what we talked about before."

"I know dad I'm OK now, my head's in the game." Sean smiled back understanding the meaning of the caution.

"Right. Well, remember what your grandfather told me when I shipped out?"

"Yes sir, he said for you to come back with everything you went over with." Sean smiled remembering the phrase.

"There you go," His dad smiled and then stuck out his hand, "Well, I guess I got to go, take care son. Come home safe."

"Yes sir," Sean answered as he took his father's hand. They shook three times and then dropped their hands. His dad reached up and patted him twice on the left shoulder and looking into his eyes they nodded at each other. His dad then turned and walked around the truck and got inside. The truck fired up right away, he looked around to find an empty spot in the slow flowing traffic. He looked over one last time and waved and then entered the flow of traffic taking him out of the terminal. Sean watched the truck for as long as he could then turned to his luggage on the ground, reached down and grabbed the duffle bag and put the carrying strap over his shoulders, then picked up the two small leather bags in one hand and a small briefcase with his orders and files in the other and walked inside. With a million thoughts running through his head he was ready to go.

Hours later he was standing in line in the Seattle airport snack bar, a sandwich and soda in hand, Sean was tapped on the shoulder by another soldier also dressed in class "A" uniform.

"Hey, MP right?" the soldier asked and pointed to Sean's cross pistol brass on his uniform collar identifying him being in the MP Corps, "Reggie Phillips," Reggie stated matter of factly and stuck out his hand at Sean.

"Sean York," Sean adjusted the sandwich and cola in his hands and reached out and shook the open hand.

"Great. You headed to the Land of the Morning Calm?" Reggie asked and got into line behind him.

Sean looked back at him with a blank look not really understanding.

"Korea, are you headed for Korea?" Reggie deciphered his comment and reached out and picked up a candy bar from the counter onto his tray.

"Oh yeah, "Sean remembered reading in some army pamphlet he was given that Korea was known as the Land of the Morning Calm. Sean put his sandwich and soda down on the counter and paid the attendant.

"Yeah me too," Reggie replied as his sandwich and soda were rung up. "Hey let's go cop a squat," Reggie motioned to go sit at a table.

"Cop a squat?" Sean repeated not sure what he was talking about.

"Yeah, you know go sit down. You never heard that before?" Reggie didn't quite understand why he had to translate that bit of slang.

"Yeah OK," Sean was somewhat confused but followed Reggie over to a small table.

Reggie was as tall as Sean but a thinner, with thick blond hair and wore gold framed glasses and never seemed to lack for something to say. They seemed to hit it off real well and Sean was enjoying talking to someone his own age with his own interests. He had been home living around civilians for the last month or so and was dying to talk to another soldier who at least understood what he was thinking. They started with the typical army basics, where you from, where you been, do you know such and such, when was basic, when did you go to MP School, what had done in the army so far.

As they were talking a few other soldiers, each wearing the cross pistol brass on their uniform wandered by introduced themselves and joined into the small group conversation.

Reggie explained was from a small town outside of Pittsburg Pennsylvania and after high school decided that he would rather be in the army than be in school and had already finished his first three year enlistment. He had spent a little over a year at Ft Hood with the 1st Calvary Division's MP Company, and then came up on orders for Korea. He ended up in Pyeongtaek with Company B, 728th MP Battalion at Camp Humphreys. He explained that he liked it so much that when he tour was about up, he extended to take another tour and transferred up to the 142nd MP Company in Yongsan, which was located in Seoul and is one of the largest of compounds in Korea. He loved Yongsan even better and had met and was living with his Korean girlfriend, but when he tried to extent for a 3rd tour he was denied and had to return to the US.

"It pisses me off," Reggie explained," I didn't want to leave- I wanted to extend and stay in country but I had a piece of shit first sergeant who thought it was bad for someone to spend so much time in Korea so he refused to let me stay. So I said fuck you" Reggie shrugged his shoulders and continued," I ETS'd and got out of the army, went home for a few weeks' vacation and promptly re-enlisted and I'm heading right back." Reggie smiled as if he were happy to have gone around the system that stood in his way.

"I'm gonna try to get back to Yongsan, you know right in Seoul, my girlfriend works there and still has our apartment, but who knows it's like throwing dice. Once you show up you're at the whim of the 8th Army and where ever they need you at the time is where you go."

"I have pin point orders for the 142nd," Collins, another one of the MPs who had joined the group as they were talking and seemed very proud of what he considered to be a cherry assignment.

"Yeah," Reggie replied and knowingly shook his head," hate to tell you this, but most MP's, have orders for the 142nd. I think that's the way they get guys to go over without putting up a fight because they think they all think they're going to Yongsan. Trust me man, those orders aren't worth shit once you hit the Replacement Company."

Collins looked incredulous," But I got pinpoint orders I'm not going anywhere but the 142nd .

"Hey," Reggie shrugged, "You'll see, you're about to come into contact with the 8th Imperial Army man. They don't listen to big army back in DC. They do pretty much whatever they want. No matter what your orders say; if the man with the Indian Head patch comes calling you're heading up north for certain. "

"Indianhead patch?" Collins asked.

"Yeah, the 2nd ID man, you know the 2nd Infantry Division." Reggie looked around to make sure everyone was picking up on what he was saying," That's Camp Casey if you're lucky. Maybe Camp Stanley, but you also have a chance to get Gary Owen, or Howze." The unfamiliar names rolled up Reggie's lips as if everyone knew where he was talking about and he continued non-stop, "You'll see guys start crying when they find out they're heading to the 2nd ID. But, the 2nd Division gets first pick of everyone. Once they're full, then the other units can get filled. I guess it all works out, but things are certainly dicked up man. But you know there are plenty of other good places too. I was with the seven duce eight, the 728th you know? It was good down in Humphreys, then there was Camp Walker, Camp Henry, man there was a lot of good stick time, and lots of stuff to do. It's all pretty much white hat line duty, except for a couple of shit hole places."

Sean nodded his head that's what he wanted to hear. White hat duty was known as the traditional law enforcement duty in the military police. It came from the fact that a lot of unit's the MP's at the larger posts wore the class "A" Green or Khaki Uniform while on duty and wore a white hat with a patent leather bill. White hat duty meant law enforcement to an MP.

Reggie managed to change his seat assignments with the soldier scheduled to sit next to Sean and they talked all the way to Alaska, where they had another short layover and changed flights again. Reggie continued talking almost the entire way across the Pacific Ocean to Tokyo Japan. Sean dosed on and off for a while as they flew, daydreaming of the chances of finally going to a place where he could do what he was trained to do but had little chance over the previous two years.

Traveling to Korea was really a two day adventure, because of the midnight to 4 A.M. national curfew; no one could be out on the street or driving around; even commercial airliners couldn't land in Seoul after a certain time at night. So all replacement soldiers coming into Korea via commercial air were forced to stop and overnight at some hotel in Tokyo then proceed the following day to their final destination. Arrival in Tokyo was a welcomed break, after some seventeen hours of riding cramped in a plane Sean was ready to get off and finally stretch his legs a little bit. They arrived late in the afternoon, losing a day by crossing the international dateline and as they filed off the plane they were herded all together by a transportation NCO at the terminal who brought them to their luggage carousel, where they reclaimed their bags and then all loaded onto a couple of buses that took them all to some hotel in Tokyo. Sean's eyes were heavy and he could smell himself from having been in the same uniform for what amounted to two days already. As they all grabbed their gear Sean could think of nothing of little else than to get a shower and lay down. But once on board the bus he found himself wide awake looking around at the strange sights and sounds of the orient. He had never seen so many people before in such a small place. It was as if he were suddenly part of an Ant society with everyone scurrying around in and out of the ant hill. It was ever stranger to discover the Japanese drove on the left side of the street.

Reggie and Sean shared a room at the hotel and they talked well into the night about Korea and what it was like. Their bodies were still on American time so when the morning finally arrived it was tough to get back up, get dressed again and then go downstairs and back onto a bus back to the airport and to a new flight to Seoul. They somehow all managed to get downstairs wolfed down some pastries for breakfast and back on the bus to the airport. Then placed into another commercial aircraft and finally settled down for the two-hour flight to Korea. They arrived at Kimpo, airport just outside of Seoul by mid-morning. As they were landing Reggie pointed out the window to Sean showing him the air defense batteries that surrounded the airport that was both a Civilian commercial and military air field.

"Takes some getting used to," Reggie explained to Sean who looked somewhat confused," this whole country is waiting for the next invasion from the north." When you drive down on the highways every ten or so miles there's suddenly a huge wide space that is like four or five lanes on each side of the highway and it is a perfectly flat terrain."

Sean nodded as he was listening.

"Well those are emergency air fields, so if the north ever comes down again, the South Koreans have like a hundred or so places they can land aircraft. So no matter if they destroy the regular air fields they can still find a place to land and service their aircraft. Pretty smart people if you ask me."

Sean nodded in agreement as he looked out the window and all the activity at the airport. They were finally off loaded into the terminal and met by another transportation NCO who gathered them all together and then went to claim their bags and then escorted them to five or six large army buses that were parked in a row in the small parking lot waiting to take them to the replacement center. They all got on board and much quicker then Sean thought possible. Obviously the transportation people have the routine down pat. In an hour they were loaded up and on the move.

The bus wound itself through the traffic in Seoul, and Sean thought how similar to Tokyo with all of the people walking, riding bicycles, motor scooters, and cars all competing for a small space in the roadway. Roughly three hours after their arrival at Kimpo, they were at the Replacement center at Camp Coiner in Seoul. One by one they filed into a small room where they were assigned a bunk in a pre-1960's Quonset hut barracks, received some bedding, and turned in all of their various personnel records and orders. They were then released to go and try and get some sleep and get adjusted to the new time zone. Sean was ready for a quick nap and a chance to finally stretch out. But only a few hours later and in the middle of a good dream Reggie shook him awake.

"Sean," Reggie half whispered and shook his shoulder.

"What?" Sean was wide awake now and somewhat upset when he realized where he was and how much he wanted to return to his dream.

"Hey, I'm getting ready to go see my girlfriend; you guys still want to go downtown for a while?"

Sean thought quickly to himself," Yeah, I need to get up anyway."

"Well get up I'll go get the others and see if they still want to go." Reggie walked away and left Sean on his back staring up at the ceiling gathering his thoughts and waking up. Finally Sean decided it was time to go and he sat up and put his feet onto the cold floor.

Reggie had explained on the flight over that his girlfriend lived in a small apartment in Seoul not too far away and he was bound and determined to go and see her. It had already been almost two months since he had left and now that he was back in country he wasn't going to let something like a "new comers" restriction to base stop him. He had asked if Sean and the others wanted to go downtown and check things out and without a moment's hesitation they all had agreed. Sean silently got dressed and walked outside were he discovered he was the last of the small group of MP's that came over with them.

"Alright, I think that's everyone, "Reggie the Korean tour guide or the Army's version of the Pied Piper announced and they all stood up like lemmings and followed him as he walked down the road. As they walked Reggie continued his indoctrination of the proper interaction with the Korean people, how to talk to the Taxi drivers, and where they wanted to go and then how to get back to Camp Coiner.

"Alright let's try it. Itaewon Dong. " Reggie tried to enunciate clearly as the group of soldiers walked down the road toward the back gate of Camp Coiner.

Sean and three others repeated as a chorus, "Itaewon Dong." Sean looked around as they walked wondering if they were going to be able to find their way back that night. He was already completely lost, but Reggie assured them he knew the way very well.

"OK, that's close enough. They'll understand their used to stupid and drunk GIs." Reggie seemed to be proud of his efforts in the indoctrination of this group of Turtles.

As they had found out unceremoniously upon their arrival, all replacements or new guys arriving in Korea were known universally as "Turtles" and Camp Coiner a small section of the Yongsan military reservation in Seoul, was known as the "Turtle Farm," where all the "turtles" are taken upon their arrival into Korea and then processed and then sent out to their respective units throughout the country. New guys were called Turtles because each one of them was going to be a replacement for someone else who was already in Korea. The soldier they were replacing had been waiting for them and their ticket home, for over a year. So why did it take so long for them to get there? "Because those damn those turtles walk too slow. "

"OK, we can get there alright. But how do we get back?" Someone asked.

"Tell the taxi driver, Camp Coiner." Reggie announced self-assuredly.

"OK, Itaewon Dong." Sean repeated out loud one more time. "Camp Coiner."

"There you go. Look they're going to understand what you're talking about if you're even close. Believe me they pick up a hundred GI's a day they know where you want to go." Reggie said in great confidence as they continued walking towards the gate.

Sean continued looking around at the various light bluish green painted cinderblock buildings that lined each side of the street and thought back over the exhausting whirlwind last few days had become. He had just about given up on Sharon and shut that particular door to his heart, realizing they each wanted two different things and he didn't know how to reconcile their differences. Perhaps a short trip down town or to the 'ville' as Reggie informed him as the correct vernacular was in Korea would be just what he needed.

Sean was jerked back from his daydream by the other soldiers talking to Reggie.

"So ok, after we get to Itaewon-Dong, then what?" asked one of the four new guys as they started to approach the gate.

"Well you're on your own then; I can't be there to babysit. You can see a street headed up a small hill. Just start walking up the street you'll see all of the clubs lined up on both sides, just pick one, they're all basically the same, some have different types of music you'll find one that you like believe me. It's better if you use won to buy drinks but they'll take dollars. The official rate right now is about 480 won to the dollar- but in the bars think about 500 to the dollar for easy conversion cause that's what you're going to get in the bars. But, whatever you do don't try to use any Japanese Yen if you still have any from Japan. You're liable to get your ass kicked, they still have hard feelings for the Japanese and they take great offense to you trying to pawn Yen off on them." Reggie looked around and saw that everyone was nodding.

Reggie continued, "OK, you guys need to be back before 2200 tonight because Mr. Chou is off at 2200."

"Who's Mr. Chou?"

"He's the back gate guard I worked with him when I was assigned here. He's going to let us out without a pass and let you back in- But his shift changes at 2200. I've no idea who's coming on so you want to avoid a problem, get back here before 2200 alright? Trust me try to get back on without a pass can be a bitch unless you have it worked out with someone beforehand."

Reggie finished up his briefing," One last thing; if you decide to stay overnight or get too fired up remember there's a national curfew from midnight till 0400 - so you have to be off the street. The police will pick your ass up in a heartbeat and you're in for a world of shit if someone has to come and get you, you guys got it?" Everyone nodded their head in understanding.

They finally got down to the back gate and Reggie walked over to the South Korean Security Guard, a civilian employed by the US Army to help guard the installation. He was dressed in a summer Khaki uniform, black leather boots, and had a black cloth Brassard pinned to his left shoulder sleeve with the letters SP topped with a Shiny black Helmet liner.

"Mr. Chou," Reggie called out and expended his hand to the guard. "An-nyong ha say yo"

"Ah Flipi," Mr. Chou said and laughed out loud and warmly shook his hand and bowed slightly. Koreans along with other Orientals always had a hard time pronouncing the letter "P" and generally was said as if it were a "F." Where you go?"

"I go Stateside for short time remember?" Reggie reminded him.

"Stateside? OK. Adaso." Mr. Chou nodded understandingly, "Now come back?"

"Yeah, now come back." Reggie nodded and patted him on the shoulder. "Mr. Chou we go ville. " Reggie continued on, "These are my Chingo's, "he then pointed to all four of them, " One, four, two, Humbyum," indicating in broken Korean, pidgin English, and sign language the group were all friends of his and were newly assigned MP's to 142nd MP Company, and he was vouching for them.

Mr. Chou understood right away they wanted to go downtown without a pass or authorization, but he also knew Phillips was a good American, respectful and generous to him and the other Korean Security Guards, always good for a pack of cigarettes or a bottle of Whiskey every now and again.

Mr. Chou knowingly smiled and tapped his index finger on his watch face, "ten clock I go home." His meaning was clear, if they wanted back in the gate they had better be back by then. He waved to them as they walked through the small gate and allowed them all to pass.

Reggie gave him the thumbs up sign, "Mr. Chou you numba one." The five of them continued walking out the personnel gate. Seconds later they were outside on the street in Seoul Korea a change from night to day. Inside the gate they could have been at any installation in America. Passing through the gate was like going through the looking glass into another world. Without hesitation Reggie flagged a taxi down. He opened the back door and paused.

"OK, dudes- I'm going to go see my girlfriend are you guys all set?" Reggie asked and looked at each one to see if there were any last minute questions. The others looked at each other and shrugged. Obviously it was sink or swim now.

"OK I'll see you guys tomorrow- remember get your asses back here by 2200 and there's no problem. Come late and you're on your own, *me na hum ne da*." Reggie smiled and got into the backseat of the cab.

"Me na hum what?" Collins asked.

"Me na hum ni da, is like tough luck, sorry about that shit you know?" Reggie translated and smiled back at the group he was leaving behind. He closed the taxi door waved through the back window and it disappeared down the street and into the heavy traffic. In a matter of seconds it was lost from view with the hundreds of other vehicles vying for space in the busy road. The four remaining soldiers found themselves on the street in a foreign land looking at each other not knowing exactly what to do. Moments later a blue taxi cab pulled up in a fog of blue exhaust and without hesitation they all climbed in.

"Itaewon-Dong." They repeated in unison and then started laughing. The driver nodded his head as if he understood the terrible pronunciation of his language and flipped the meter on the dashboard down and started off. As they drove down the street Sean sitting in the front seat looked at the dash board and saw there was an actual split down the dashboard where it had separated. Looking closer he could see that the split was actually held into place by bailing wire that was wound through smaller drilled holes each side of the split.

"Oh my God, look at this" Sean pointed to the visible crack in the dashboard where the metal had actually separated but was bound together by wire wound around the crack- "That's bailing wire."

"Hey, look at the steering wheel," someone from the back called out.

The steering wheel had at one time been cut or had broken at the two o'clock position. It was secured back together using gray duct tape and one could actually see the two ends were no longer a single unit and fixed together but had again separated- but the duct tape was keeping them from separating any further. The driver was wearing slightly soiled white cotton gloves and seemed to have a death grip on the steering wheel as if he were speed racer.

"Geez, this is a death trap."

"Talk about red neck engineering. Here's proof that duct tape and bailing wire can fix anything"

"Man, now I know why they call 'em "Kimchi cabs".

"Man I need some air."

"Yeah, well I need a drink."

"I gotta fart."

"Better open a window, I've been through one of his farts, he can kill us all"

They all laughed out loud, the driver in turn laughed as well and was patted on the back approvingly by those in the back seat. Not really understanding the joke, the driver wanted to be polite to the American's and perhaps earn a small tip. It only took a few minutes to wind through traffic to have the cab suddenly pull over at a street intersection and stop. They all piled out and Sean looked and saw the meter for 400 Won. From quick figuring this was a little less than a dollar. Sean pulled out a 500 won bill he had exchanged for dollars earlier that day, and gave it to the driver and then waved his hand as if to signal no change. The driver pulled out a leather wallet and change purse and smiling broadly he put the money inside and then looked towards Sean and bowed slightly in recognition of the tip.

"Kam sa ham ni da." He said smiling broadly, at the Americans who all seemed to be so rich and generous. That is until they got drunk and turned mean.

"OK, "Sean closed the door and looked up the street. On each side of the narrow street were clubs, and shops. As they walked up it was thrilling to take in the sights the smells. As they walked up they peered into the various shop windows with the bounty of the orient on display, as well as copies of anything you could imagine.

"Check this out," Collins called out to the others as he looked into a shop filled with framed paintings. "It's the friggin the Mona Lisa."

The others gathered around and looked into the window and saw an unmistakable copy of the Mona Lisa in a fancy wooden frame mounted on the wall inside the shop with a small light directed on it. They spent several more minutes looking through the shop windows discovering several other copies of famous paintings.

"I bet these people can copy anything man," Collins stated the obvious to everyone.

"Hey," one of the group whispered to the others, "Check what's coming up the road."

The group turned in unison back towards the roadway and saw two black soldiers walking up the road. The first was dressed in a patchwork of tan, brown and black leather pants, vest and jacket, with a white shirt with very large collar laying outside of the jacket. He was wearing matching shoes that clicked as he walked as if he wore taps on the bottoms.

The second soldier was wearing a pair of white polyester pants, a shiny black shirt, with large collar and unbuttoned midway down his chest. A gold chain necklace with large links, could be seen underneath. He was wearing a flowing white crushed velvet coat that ended just above his ankles, but it was open and flowed as if it were a cape, he was topped off by a matching crushed velvet wide brimmed hat and large white Ostrich feather on the right side tucked into the hat band. He was wearing 4" platform shoes in a white and black checkerboard pattern.

Both were wearing dark gold rimmed sunglasses and were walking slowly up the small incline with a matching cool swagger.

"Jesus Christ," one of the group said to no one in particular, "What the hell is that?"

"They can't be serious," commented another.

"I don't know, almost looks like that Superfly deal."

"Superfly?" Sean asked

"Yeah the movie Superfly, didn't you see it?"

"Man I ain't ever seen anything like that," Sean answered back and continued to stare as the soldiers walked past them.

"Toto, we ain't in Kansas anymore," Collins observed out loud and the rest of the group laughed and turned in mass and started walking all abreast up the slightly inclined street looking at the various bars and shops, that lined the road until they found themselves in front of one of the clubs.

How about this place?" Collins asked pointing to a glass doorway to a club.

"Six of one half a dozen of the other."

"Ah, who gives a shit I'm thirsty."

They looked at each other and after ambivalently shrugging their shoulders decided to go inside. One place was as good as another and their thirst and curiosity was over powering. The club was warm, dark, loud, and smoky but a welcomed change from the cooler evening air. Their eyes adjusted after just a few seconds and they found their way to an empty table, took off their jackets and coats, and placed them over the seatbacks and sat down. Seconds later Peter Frampton's "Show me the way" started blasting through the stereo speakers. As their eyes adjusted they looked around the room, the other tables were all occupied by other soldiers, some in deep conversation, some with their arms wrapped around some young Korean in a short skirt who was returning the hug. Without a doubt there were some very attractive, short skirted, Korean women who doubled as hostesses, waitresses, and prostitutes. Reggie had already explained 'the trade' or the legalized prostitution that took place inside the various 'tourist clubs' and what they could expected when dealing with the females.

The legal prostitutes were those working inside the various tourist bars and were registered by the government and required to go to weekly medical examinations to be checked and screened for venereal disease. They were also required to show their "VD cards" to any customer to verify they had been checked out and were required to have a card if they were ever seen in the company of a soldier. Street prostitution was illegal and not regulated by the government. In order to protect the Western Soldiers who were frequenting the tourist bars and the prostitutes, the Korean government placed several laws wherein almost any single Korean woman found in the company of a westerner without VD card in her possession they would be treated as if they were unregistered street prostitutes. It could earn the female a trip to the police station and a very heavy fine.

The women referred to their profession and each other as "business women" and their business was selling sex. Most of the women in the clubs Reggie explained, were bonded to the bar through a debt to the "mamma san" who owned the bar and also operated a brothel located somewhere close to the bar where the girls might actually live or where they took their customers. While waiting for customers they would work in the bar and entertain the men and encouraged the customers to spend as much of their money as possible. In one of their many conversations, Reggie explained the rate for services was pretty standard and really only varied when a large troop surge took place such as when an air craft carrier group came into port. A short time or what someone would call *a quickie* was on average $10.00 and a "long time" meant overnight was on average $20.00. For a long time, you could have two or three sessions and spend the night in bed with the girl, generally having to get up at 0400 in the morning after curfew to try and get back for duty. This was important to know because if the soldier was not so educated it was not unusual for the price to go way up and he paid for his inexperience. According to Reggie, the women could ferret out a new guy in a matter of minutes and had the best intelligence network imaginable.

They looked at each other and with a shrug of the shoulders they decided to go inside. The club was warm, dark, loud, and smoky. After a few seconds to adjust their eyes to the darkness they found their way to an empty table and sat down to a loud refrain of Peter Frampton's "Show me the way" blasting through the stereo speakers. As their eyes adjusted they looked around the room, most of the other tables were all occupied by other soldiers, some in deep conversation with each other, some with their arms wrapped around very attractive, short skirted, young Korean females who worked as waitresses and legal prostitutes. But, even knowing they were prostitutes the women were nothing like he had ever seen before. They were beautiful. He at last began to understood Reggie's comment to him while they were having a beer in Japan, Korea was America's best kept secret and even the ugliest most homely man in America could get laid in Korea. Drink orders were by one of the waitresses and shortly four beers were served.

But, even knowing they were prostitutes the women were nothing like he had ever seen before. They were truly beautiful, especially in the dark and probably more so after a few drinks or when you were especially lonesome. Drink orders were taken and shortly four beers were served to them. They picked up the bottles and raised a toast to each other. Sean took a drink and immediately was greeted by the taste of one of the worst beers he had ever had.

"Oh my God." Sean held the bottle in front of him. "What the hell does OB mean? Old beer?"

"This is piss water man."

"I think piss would taste better."

"I heard they put formaldehyde in the beer."

"I heard it was in the liquor."

"Man if this is the local beer this is going to be a very long tour."

"I don't know if I can do another one of these. But we better try don't ya think?" They all laughed and looked around at the bar and forced themselves to take another sip. The clear deep base riff of Black Sabbath's "Iron Man'" came across the speakers at what best be described as the pain level. Sean leaned back and enjoyed the music and tried to take it all in Then one by one a Korean bar girl came by and sat down next to one of them and began plying their trade. By the end of the song there were four women sitting around their table.

"Hello GI, my name Sunshine," said the very attractive young Korean female who came up to Sean.

Sunshine, as she called herself sat on Sean's left leg and crossed her legs which caused her short black mini skirt to rise up even higher on her thigh and looked directly into Sean's eyes and smiled. She was slender and petite, with short black hair and huge almond eyes and red lips, Sean estimated her to be in her early 20's. She was wearing a black mini skirt and black fish net stockings and a low cut white blouse. She was very attractive and certainly friendly. But she had a very boney butt and was cutting into the top of his thigh. He moved her over slightly and she put her arms around Sean and hugged him several times, bringing his face against her breasts.

"You Turtle boy?" Sunshine asked as she leaned back to get a better look at him, her arms still around his neck.

"Yeah. We just got here." Sean answered and tried to adjust himself.

"Ah ha, I love GI Turtle boys. You buy me one tea?" Sunshine asked apparently very familiar with the script.

Tea was generally exactly that, tea. Probably more colored water then tea, and especially made for the hostess to drink. It was obviously very good tea at 3 bucks a glass. But it kept the girls around for a while as it slowly took money out of your pocket.

"Sure I'll buy you one tea." Sean smiled playing along with the game.

"You buy Tea? Sunshine asked again and when Sean nodded and took a drink she called out for a drink from another waitress. "You good man." Sunshine smiled broadly revealing almost perfect teeth.

"You have cigarette?" Sunshine continued with the script to decide what all she could get from this soldier.

"I don't smoke." Sean responded.

"No smoke? Good." She abruptly changed the subject" Smoke numba ten," Sunshine wrinkled her nose and made a disapproving face and then asked "How long you stay Korea?"

"We stay one year."

"You stay Korea one year?" Sunshine looked over at him and tilted her head as if thinking, "I no think so."

"No, we just got here. One day in Korea now."

" One day? No, I don't believe you. You stay Korea long time, yes?" Sunshine looked around for support.

"No just one day."

Sunshine decided to change the subject "So, handsome GI, you have girlfriend? You have Yobo?"

A Yobo Sean had learned from Reggie on the flight over, literally meant wife or spouse, but it also referred to a live in girlfriend. It was not unusual for a soldier to find a bar girl or sometimes lucky enough to find another Korean woman and "Yobo" or move in with them. The Yobo bargirls are generally paid an agreed upon monthly stipend, for which the soldier received all of the benefits of married life, but none of the long term commitments. They stayed together as long as they wanted and when the soldier rotated he simply left and she went back to the bar.

Many times however, the soldier fell in love with the Yobo and they were married and she went back to the states with him. Being a Yobo was especially sought after by the women because it meant they no longer had to work in the bar and date and have sex with different men. Instead they would have a soldier to take care of them and they could have a more normal life. They were always looking for a Yobo, although many suffered through mental and physical abuse from soldiers it was still better than the endless nightly tricks, and possibility of disease while working the bars.

The girls also wanted to be certain they were not cheating another business woman out of her money. Much like a marriage, a single man was fair game, one with a Yobo or girlfriend was considered to be out of bounds and any soldier cheating on his Yobo was considered to be very bad in deed.

"No Yobo." Sean answered back and smiled looking Sunshine over.

Sunshine leaned down and hugged Sean, and whispered in his ear, "You take me Yobo. I take good care of you. I'm good Korean woman. We make good love. Long time, many time, I promise you."

Sean became somewhat excited by the hug and soft touch and from the sweet smell of perfume. Sean leaned back to look in her face, "I believe you, but I will be leaving Monday."

"You leab soon? Go stateside?"

"No not yet," Sean smiled politely.

"Where you go?" Sunshine leaned back to look into his eyes to see if he were lying to her.

"I don't know," Sean answered.

"Adaso." Sunshine seemed to understand and went onto another tack," OK, you take me now for short time. You handsome man, I take good care of you good long time love." Sunshine whispered softly into his ear and then hugged him around his neck.

Sean was forced to adjust himself again, but he eventually turned down her offer, although she was very attractive. The women stayed at the table for a while. But when they realized the soldiers were there to drink and would not be going back to their rooms, and they were not buying any more tea, they left for other customers to try and 'catch' a soldier for the night to pay their bills.

The group stayed for a only a short time more, laughing at each other as they adjusted to the new environment and each had a few more OB beers which were all just as bad as the first one. Sean looked around and saw Sunshine sitting on another soldiers lap across the small bar. She was leaning forward and whispering something in his ear, but then turned to look back at Sean smiling at him the whole time.

It had been interesting but they decided that sleep was more important and more interesting than anything else that was happening at the bar so they got up and walked back down to the main street and hailed a cab. Remembering Camp Coiner to the driver who knew exactly where they wanted to go. Several minutes later then found themselves walking up to the personnel gate where Mr. Chou was waiting for them. They greeted him warmly and he smiled in return.

VIII

Korea
March 1976

Sean woke up with a raging case of the Turtle Trots or the Kimchi two step described as the local diarrhea that hit most new guys coming to Korea while they processed through Camp Coiner. Collins had fallen asleep Sunday afternoon underneath the open window, with a brand new portable radio/cassette player on the window ledge plugged in and playing on the Armed Forces Radio Channel in Yongsan. When he woke up it sounded as if the radio was fading out. He stood up and discovered his nice new and expensive radio was missing, in its place was a 6 transistor Japanese radio also playing on Armed forces radio.

"Slicky boys," commented Reggie when he heard. "Korean thieves are about the best in the world. They can steal the air in your lungs and not wake you up."

"Shit I guess so. First time someone stole my radio and left the music playing."

Reggie broke into a war story, "Hey, once I was working the back gate and this ten ton dump truck that was used to haul the garbage was on the way out. It hit a big pot hole just up from the gate and suddenly we looked up and a radio antenna was sticking up and waving in the air. We stopped it and looked inside. They had stolen a jeep with a radio and everything, loaded it into the bed and then covered it in garbage and were on their way out the gate. I'm telling you man, no one is better than the Korean slicky boy."

Processing started early the next day with all of the new arrivals from the preceding day and those remaining from the day before, stood in line outside the in-processing building. Inside was the typical army routine of hurry up and wait. A group of soldiers file into a room and waited to be called. One station they turned in their Finance records. Go sit down and wait. Fill out and turn in travel vouchers. Go sit down and wait. Next station was the review of medical records, make sure you've had all your shots, then go sit down and wait. Next station review of personnel records. Go sit down and wait. Go here then there and then wait some more. Most of the day was spent in a waiting room talking, smoking, reading, or taking a nap while the fifty or so new soldiers were waiting to be processed. The day's never ending wait being broken up only by the walk over to the mess hall and lunch. Then the walk back to sit around and wait again.

As they continued through their processing they could look over and see the next group of soldiers had arrived and were being issued their bedding, while the group arriving before they got there were turning their bedding in and getting ready to ship out. Collins offered that at least they weren't the newest guys in Korea anymore. The day passed and although it was not strenuous the endless waiting had been exhausting mentally. Reggie made an appearance two or three times that day but never seemed to stick around as everyone else was being processed. They went to lunch and Reggie filled them that they should be receiving orders on Tuesday and shipping out Tuesday afternoon or Weds morning. Monday night Reggie skipped supper and instead went back to his area, changed out of his uniform and into civilian clothes and waved goodbye as he headed down to the personnel gate and back to his girlfriend's apartment.

Tuesday morning Reggie showed back up at Breakfast looking especially chipper and in a good mood. Knowing the moment of truth when everyone received their orders was coming dampened the mood of breakfast. Everyone still held to their belief that they were going to get a good assignment.

Reggie decided not to remind them of the stark truth that some of them were going to get screwed. One by one everyone left the table leaving only Sean and Reggie sipping a cup of coffee and talking.

"I got a surprise for you," Reggie offered and smiled at Sean

"Yeah what's that?"

"Nah, can't tell ya, then it wouldn't be a surprise would it?" Reggie smiled and tossed Sean a copy of the Stars and Stripes the

American Forces newspaper and stood up with his tray. "I'll see you this afternoon."

"Thanks," Sean called out as he picked up the newspaper and waved at Reggie. At least he would have something to read for a while as he waited. Sean looked up at Reggie who was turning in his tray and silverware to be cleaned and smiled. Reggie was a good ole boy and had already become a good friend in the short time they've known each other. It would be cool to be stationed together.

Tuesday morning it was really more of the same as they continued to file through the in processing routine, picking up where they left off the preceding day. But, as promised, that afternoon orders and assignments were finally being received. There was noticeable tension in the air as a an older grey haired, chain smoking, senior NCO wearing the 2nd ID Indianhead patch on his left shoulder walked into the room with copies of orders.

"Alright at ease everyone," came the general call to pay attention delivered by someone used to giving such orders." Hey, listen up." The sergeant shouted louder to get everyone's attention. He began again after everyone calmed down, " The following individuals have been assigned to the 2nd Infantry Division and I have your orders. Now, I know not everyone will be happy, so let me help you out right now. Life sucks. The 2nd Division needs you whoever you are and whatever your job. I don't care what orders you had prior to arriving were, you're going with the needs of the army. If you have a problem with your assignments, go to 8th Army replacement and make your case. I personally don't care so don't bother me about it. The buses for Camp Casey are leaving tomorrow morning at 0800, outside this building." He pointed in the general direction." Clear your billet space and turn in your bedding at 0600 tomorrow. You'll need your cleared hand receipt from replacement company supply to get on the bus. Everyone got that?" He looked around and saw the general nods of agreement.

The room was silent as he called out names and handed out sets of orders. There was lots of grumbling including Collins who was convinced he was going to stay in Yongsan. He wasn't. His was the first name called out.

"Fucking army." Collins said under his breath." I only came over here because of those orders." He walked up and received his orders and then came and sat down. "2ⁿᵈ MP Company, Camp Casey. Fuck me man."

Two dozen other names were called out one at a time, before a collective sigh of relief went out when the Sergeant announced "that's all folks." There were general smiles and pats on the back as if everyone else in the room had avoided something bad.

About a half hour later, a female Staff Sergeant came into the room with a stack of orders for the remaining 30 or so soldiers still remaining in the room.

"Listen up, when I call your name I have your orders right here. Come up and get them, if you have any problems don't bring them to me I can't help you. If you think there is a problem with your assignment go back to G-1 in the back and talk to them. You got it? Your assignment is not my problem." The Sergeant looked around as if to make sure everyone understood her comment. Then one at a time she reached into the stack of orders and started calling out names of the remaining soldiers.

Each soldier answered when his name was called and as if walking to a firing squad walked slowly up to get their orders and find out where they were going. Reggie came into the room from parts unknown and sat down next to Sean. He had been noticeably absent during most of the day while everyone else was in processing.

"You're about to get your surprise and you owe me a beer." Reggie leaned over and whispered into Sean's ear.

"Oh yeah, how so?"

"You'll see. I took care of you man, you're gonna thank me."

"What the fuck are you talking about?"

Reggie just put up his hand as if to quiet Sean down.

"York, Sean P." The female sergeant finally bellowed out his name.

"Here Sergeant," Sean answered and stood up his moment of truth finally at hand. He walked up and took the set of orders and started reading as he walked away his heart beating faster. *Permanent Change of Station, York, Sean P, Specialist, ...will proceed on a permanent change of station......* he scanned down further to find what he was looking for.....*assigned to 3rd Military Police Detachment, APO SF 96358.* It still didn't register with him.

"Where's this?" Sean held up his orders to Reggie.

"Dude, it's a cherry assignment, believe me. "Without even looking at the orders Reggie leaned over to him, "You're going to I Corps at CRC- Camp Red Cloud. It's totally white hat duty man, no field time."

"Yeah?" Scan seemed pleased but curious as to how he knew." Well where are you going?"

"Hey, I told you it was a Cherry assignment." He reached into a manila folder and pulled out a set of orders. "I already got my orders, I'm going with you! " He started laughing

Sean looked at him not totally understanding.

Reggie motioned for Sean to come closer and Reggie whispered in his ear, "Hey, see the female Sergeant?" Reggie pointed out the female NCO who was finishing passing out the orders. "That's my cousin, "she took care of us." Reggie explained very conspiratorial," There was nothing open here, so we got the next best place available. We could have gotten the 728th down in Pyongtek but I Corps is a better assignment. Besides it's just down the road from my girl."

Sean had no idea in the world what he was talking about, but decided to roll with the flow for the time being. They gathered up their paperwork and field jackets and started to file out of the door. Meanwhile they could see Collins and several others in a group surrounding the female sergeant who were upset at their orders change.

"Like I said," Reggie motioned towards the group," This is the 8th Imperial army over here man, big army don't matter. You go where 8th Army says you're going Man," Reggie smiled and patted Sean on the back," you'll be buying me beer for a while over this. "

Sean looked back once more and saw a uniformed MP walk into the room and walk towards the crowd.

"They always have a MP at the replacement building just in case." Reggie explained as they finally made it outside." Sometimes folks can get pretty upset. Come on let's get out of here and get some chow and pack up your shit. We can beat the crowd at the mess hall. Besides, I need to go check on my yobo. She misses me terribly when I am away too long"

The next day's bus ride to Camp Red Cloud was long and for Sean tedious with the stop and go intercity traffic until they got out of

Seoul. He had never been through such a large city before with so many buildings built so high and stacked so tightly together. Even worse, was the traffic. He imagined they were all in some type of Ant Farm with all the other ants scurrying from one side and then to the other. Everyone with a certain specific thing to do; but always on the opposite side of the ant farm then where they started. How could anyone drive in a place like this? Along certain stretches of road there were some type of traffic police directing traffic spaced out no further than 50 feet from each other for several city blocks. Each dressed in their blue uniforms, with blue hats, white cotton gloves, and every two seconds blowing on their police whistles for some reason or another. Sean sighed and momentarily longed for the open and flat Mississippi delta again.

Reggie had sat next to him as the bus weaved through the traffic, filling him in on more of the major do's and don't s of Korea. As a third tour vet he was officially becoming what is known in the army as "Asiatic". He really had no desire to ever go back home he loved it over in Korea and if the army would only leave him alone he would stay here forever with his girl who he claimed to be madly in love with. Reggie explained how he had met her in Seoul when she was enrolled in an English language school and he was trying to hustle some extra money by working there as an "instructor." It had been a good deal. He didn't have to worry about any real English lessons or even know anything about English grammar. He was mainly there just to speak English so the students could hear a native speaker. All he had to do was go and read from a book of simple English phrases and allow each student to practice their English on him. It was an easy $10.00 a night for a couple hours of work.

After a few lessons, they had started seeing each other after class for more practice. He would teach her English and she would teach him a few words in Korean. She was a good girl from a good family, Reggie was quick to point out, she wasn't working in the bars she was working for her father in a department store but wanted to learn English. Then they started dating, and then they started living together. Reggie had been uncertain about meeting her father when they started dating, Koreans don't typically like outsiders, but he was actually very supportive and very warm towards Reggie and Americans in general. Her father and his family had been rescued by some US Marines during the Korean war and brought from North Korea to

South Korea, so he loved Americans and was OK with having his daughter date an American.

The entire ride had been a learning experience for Sean. The bus finally arrived and dropped them off at the bus stop on Camp Red Cloud near the main gate. They stumbled off the bus with their duffel bags and looked around. With no one there to ask directions they walked the short distance over to the main gate to where they could see another MP working the personnel gate, checking passes and Identification from everyone coming in or going out and in the middle of the street on a small concrete platform was a ROK MP or Republic of Korea Military Police who was directing vehicle traffic into the post.

"Hey sarge, where's the Detachment Headquarters were just signing in." Reggie asked the MP who was standing with his back turned and looking out the gate.

Sean was very impressed as the MP turned around. The MP was from top to bottom what they called STRAC; his uniform was heavily starched and properly creased down his trouser leg and down the arms of the uniform blouse. He looked like he filled it out very well. Jump boots were shined like mirrors, the green pistol pistol belt was secured in the front with a large highly shined brass buckle, his pistol was secured in a customized and unauthorized high ride holster, a snow-white lanyard attached to the butt of the .45 pistol with the loop around his right shoulder. A customized night stick holder, also unauthorized and wooden night stick on his left hip, with a series of belt keepers placed around the web belt and through his trouser belt that kept it steady on his waist. He had added unauthorized epaulets to his uniform blouse and he was topped off with a mirrored shiny black helmet liner with the letters "MP" Stenciled on the front and the number 3 on the right side.

"You assigned to 3rd MP?" He spoke with a gravelly voice.

"Yeah, just getting in." Reggie responded.

"I'm the Ghost. Sgt Kasper." He reached out to shake both of their hands and Sean could see the name tag clearly. "Stand by." Sgt Kasper said as two soldiers walked up to the pedestrian gate with their ID Cards and passes in their hands as they approached.

"Button your pocket," Sgt Kasper directed as they came up to the gate and pointed to his own left blouse pocket.

Both soldiers looked down and the offender buttoned his pocket. Sgt Kasper looked over their passes and then waved them through.

"You're in luck" Sgt Kasper retuned his attention to Sean and Reggie. He pointed towards another building across the street," The PMO, MP Station, and the detachment are right over there."

"Thanks Sarge." They turned and started across the street.

"Hey, Turtles," Kasper called out to them. "Forty-five."

They both stopped and turned around.

"What?"

"Forty-five. I have forty five more days, and then back to the world." Sgt Kasper smiled at them and turned back to the gate.

As they walked across the parking lot towards the building, they noted the sign out near the street, the background was painted MP Green, with white letters that Proclaimed: I Corps/ROK (US) Group, Military Police Station. I Corps was a joint command consisting of both American and ROK army units. It was commanded by a three start US General with a two start Korean General as the deputy commander. Camp Red Cloud was the Headquarters of I Corps.

As they walked into the parking lot towards the main entrance a jeep pulled up alongside them. "Military Police" was painted in black under the windshield with a large single rotating blue light mounted on the top windshield frame. The side doors were removed and both occupants were wearing their MP helmet liners. The driver was a very dark complexed black Specialist.

"Hey, are you two our new Turtles?" he spoke to them in a very deep Alabama country drawl.

"Yeah, just signing in." Sean answered back and sat his duffle bag down.

"Hot damn, where you been boy? I've been waiting for you for a year now." He smiled and started laughing.

The vehicle passenger another younger black male looked over and said," "T" you better carry those bags inside for them, if they trip and break their necks or get a hernia, you'll be here till the next one comes in. You know Turtles don't grow on trees man."

"Shit, I'm too short for any manual labor." Then he looked over at Reggie and Sean and proudly announced," Twenty two days

Turtles," The driver and passenger both started laughing "Hey man, go inside check with the Desk Sergeant. He'll send you back to the detachment."

Sean and Reggie nodded their heads and the jeep drove off the occupants laughing at their own personal jokes.

"How long are we going to have to put up with this shit?' Sean asked as his picked his bag back up.

"Ah, another GI Custom, man." Reggie picked his duffle bag up and started walking." It's the unofficial welcome to the new guys. You know to them we're just a couple of FNG's- you know Fucking New Guys to everyone here."

They trudged their way into the front door that opened into the MP Station. To the immediate right was the MP Desk, a large elevated platform, surrounded and enclosed by Plexiglas, where the MP Desk Sergeant conducted business. The ROK military police were situation to the right and the American Military Police were to the left of the long Plexiglas enclosed platform. There was a very large and shiny brass rail that ran the entire length of the platform two foot in front of the desk. Attached to the front was another green sign that proclaimed in yellow lettering"

Military Police Motto
"Of the troops and for the troops"

Then directly underneath and on the same sign:

3rd MP Motto

"Do unto us as you would have us do unto you."

They both walked up to the American side, where a bald, light skinned black Staff Sergeant ,was sitting typing on a manual typewriter with a sideways pencil in his mouth. They walked up to the opening in the Plexiglas to address the sergeant.

"What do you two need and don't touch my brass rail," barked the Sergeant who continued to type without even looking up at them.

"Looking for the detachment HQ Sarge, we need to sign in." Sean said and stepped back from the rail not wanting to take a chance he would touch and therefore smudge the brass rail.

"New guys huh? Where you coming from?" The sergeant finally stopped typing and asked in a definite New York City accent.

"142nd in Yongsan" Reggie piped up.

"Sierra Army Depot." Sean chimed in.

"Yeah, well welcome aboard, we've been waiting for youse guys. I'm staff sergeant Wallace- I got the 2nd squad. Drop your shit right there and take your papers back to the orderly room down the hall first door on left. I'll have a patrol take you up to the barracks when you're ready."

"Thanks sarge."

The sign in process was about the same as any other unit. Sign the SIDPERS document; showing your official arrival at the unit; provide three copies of your orders, give up your 201 personnel file, then your medical, dental, finance, and training records. Receive in return a form to get your new military driver's license, your weapons cards, your pass to get off the installation, ration control plate so you could get into the PX, special MP Identification card, and various company supply forms.

As they were being processed Sean began to look around the building and walked down the hallway into the next office identified as the pass and ID section, walking by he looked inside and a Korean man in civilian clothes was on the phone speaking Korean to someone, on another desk typing was a young early 20's very attractive, Korean female with very long straight black hair that fell below her shoulders. She was wearing a light blue sweater over a white blouse that was buttoned to the top with a multi colored silk scarf around her neck. Sean was mesmerized momentarily as she typed away.

"Hello" Sean surprised himself by calling out to her.

The typing stopped as she looked up towards the door. She smiled at him and his heart increased a beat.

"Hello, may I help you." She answered in a soft voice.

Sean' heart was racing and was suddenly tongue tied." I wanted to say hello I'm a new man just got here."

"I see, you are coming to three MP?" She spoke nearly perfect educated English with just a slight oriental accent, not like the Pidgin English he had heard from so many before. He felt stupid for assuming all Koreans would speak so uneducated.

He flushed red and tried to recover, "Yes, I just arrived and was looking around."

"Welcome to you, my name Miss Park."

"Miss Park?" he repeated asking more than responding, flushing even more at his boldness which was not like him at all.

She slightly blushed as well, "Yes, Miss Park." She smiled back warmly at him.

Sean was searching for something to say when his train of thought was interrupted by male voice originating somewhere up the hallway.

"York" someone bellowed from up the hallway where he was obviously being missed.

"I'm sorry- My name is Sean. Sean York," he began and walked into the office to shake her hand.

"YORK!" came the bellow again, this time very impatient.

She took his hand and it was incredibly petit and soft, he noticed she was wearing red fingernail polish, and caught a slight whiff of a most pleasing perfume.

"God dam it YORK, "the voice was much more insistent and growing irritated.

"I think they look for you now," she smiled again.

"Yeah, well, I guess have to go, nice to meet you." Sean walked backwards waving. He looked over at the other office occupant who was not off the phone and he stepped forward to quickly shake his hand "Sean York, nice to meet you." He then turned and walked out. Wow.

As he walked down the hallway to the detachment HQ an older Senior NCO stepped into the hallway and looked back and forth.

"Are you York?" the sergeant demanded.

"Yes sergeant," I was down the hallway."

"Get your ass in here, the Commander is waiting for you. I'm Sergeant First Class Grubner, the Detachment sergeant." He stuck out his hand and Sean shook it. Grubner looked back down the hallway to see where he had come from and then ushered him into the commander's office.

Sean entered the office and came to the position of attention and saluted, "Sir, Specialist York reporting as directed."

The Captain returned his salute and pointed to the empty chair next to Reggie who was already sitting. Sean took his seat and the captain began.

"I'm Captain Cruz, the detachment commander." The captain leaned back in his chair and folded his hands across his stomach.

Sean looked at the commander and sized him up. He was older, early 30 maybe, slender and athletic, obviously Latino, both from appearance and from accent, probably from Texas. He had a bushy mustache, and gold rimmed glasses.

"We've been waiting for some replacements to get here we're short right now and got lots of people getting ready to rotate." Captain Cruz hesitated a moment and then started again," The 3rd MP Detachment is sort of unique in the whole country. We belong to I Corps, which is a joint command we work with the ROK military police, we have no KATUSAs in this unit we work strictly with the ROKs."

A KATUSA was a Korean soldier who was because of family position and influence or luck of the draw was doing his national service assigned to and part of an American army unit. They were serving Korean soldiers, but were trained, equipped, fed, and paid for by the Americans. A KATUSA'S life was considerably better than the average ROK army soldier and tended to go to the sons of the rich and connected.

"You probably noticed our MP Station is also a ROK Military Police station. They also do military police functions. We leave them alone and they do whatever they have to do. We share the facility with them. Our detachment is on the left side of the building; their detachment is on the right. "Cruz looked over at Reggie and then back at Sean trying to seize them up as he spoke, "Our mission here is to provide general law enforcement throughout our area of responsibility. In time of war, our sole mission is to protect the Commanding General of I Corps. So day to day we do normal MP line duties, if the balloon ever goes up, we're the General's body guards and we go wherever he goes. It's pretty simple. I run a pretty tight ship. If you do your work correctly there is no problem. I expect you show up when you're supposed to, be sober and ready for work. Any questions?"

"No sir," they both stood up and answered in unison.

"Detachment sergeant, "Captain Cruz bellowed," finish getting them squared away and onto the duty roster" He looked up at them." Alright welcome aboard and dismissed."

They both saluted and did an about face and walked out of the office and were met by Grubner.

"There's a patrol coming for you outside to take your shit up to the barracks. Phillips, you're assigned to 2nd Squad Staff Sergeant Wallace. York, you're assigned to Staff Sergeant Whitehouse, 3rd Squad. Go get yourselves squared away at supply, draw all your field equipment, bedding and get your barracks assignment. Take the rest of the day off to get your shit squared away and be back down here tomorrow morning 0730 I have a small detail I need finished up. "He looked over and saw them both nod they understood and then he abruptly walked down the hall to his own office.

They gathered up their gear and walked out into the front parking lot waiting for a patrol vehicle to arrive.

"Hey, did you see the little honey in the back?" Sean asked

"Nah missed it, was she nice?" Reggie asked.

"Man, she was something else." Sean shook his head and smiled.

"That's what they all say."

It had taken the rest of the afternoon to get situated and get their barracks assignment. At company supply they received another full duffel bag of field equipment and extra winter uniforms and another smaller bag containing their MP equipment including their web belt with a large brass belt buckle, night stick, and black MP Helmet liner. They struggled across the street to their individual room in the small detachment billets area.

The MP Detachment occupied a small corner of the camp and consisted of eight Quonset huts placed in two rows of four and separated by a small lawn and two drainage ditches. A Quonset hut was a metal, prefabricated, un-insulated, building that dated from around the Korean War. Each was built over a poured concrete slab, without any indoor plumbing. Showers and the latrine were in another cinderblock building located in the middle of their small area. Sean was placed into 3rd Squad area and took over a small portion at the end of the building defined by four wall lockers set adjacent to each other, spaced out from the wall creating a small private area where his bed was located.

There was a small desk, lamp, and a small 3x5 piece of green carpet on the floor and that was it. He was fortunate to have three windows in his area and being on the corner of the building allowed him some cross breeze for the coming summer. As part of his indoctrination, he was introduced to his house boy, Kwan, thin but wiry, late 30 year old Korean male that was employed to do most of the menial labor around the detachment such a mowing the lawn and general cleaning of the area, as well as taking care of Sean's personal area. For a the use of the house boy, there was a monthly charge to a general fund managed by the supply sergeant, if he wanted Kwan to do his laundry and shine his boots and otherwise take care of him, then he would work out a separate arrangements with him. Using a houseboy to do his laundry was voluntary, but Sean laughed and shook his head when he learned there was no washer or dryers he could do his own laundry on the entire compound.

Sean and Kwan came to quick terms; for an additional $30.00 a month, Kwan agreed to do his laundry and shine his boots and clean his personal area in the billets. Kwan also needed a box of detergent, box of starch, and a can of shoe polish every month. Sean only needed to put his dirty clothes into his laundry bag and it would be washed and then put away in his dresser when it was done. His uniforms would be heavily starched and pressed using one of the old non electric irons, heated from a small stove they also used to cook their Raman soup every day. Immediately following a hand shake after coming to terms, he took Kwan over to his area. Kwan looked around and pointed to a wall locker. "TA 50?"Kwan asked, pointing to one of the empty wall lockers where Sean's field equipment would be set up on display.

"Yeah sure sounds good," Sean shrugged his shoulders not really knowing what to say. Kwan nodded and looked over at his duffle bags and suit cases as if he were trying to figure out where everything was going to do. Sean moved to his duffel bag and set it on the chair and started to unpack and put his things away. But Kwan interrupted him by literally stepping in front of him actually blocking him from his

"OK, ok, you go now, I fix," Kwan said and waved him off as if to shoo him out of the area.

"OK, I just want to make up bed," Sean pointed to the bed and the bedding lying on the mattress.

"I do I do, " Kwan made a motion for Sean to get out of the way. Sean shrugged his shoulders not sure what to do and walked out of the Quonset hut door, almost running into three other house boys who were trying to get inside. They momentarily bumped into each other at the threshold and the house boys ran into each other like a keystone cop movie and all started laughing at each other. They stepped back and bowed slightly and waved their hand in a greeting. They allowed Sean to step out and then they went inside.

Sean looked through the window and saw four of the Korean houseboys standing just outside of his area inside the hut. Kwan was talking to them and pointing and then suddenly as if by magic they were suddenly dumping out his duffle bag of clothes and uniforms and another dumped out his other duffle bag full of his field equipment onto the floor. They all started to work together to get his area squared away.

He shook his head in amazement as Reggie walked up to him. He had already changed into civilian clothes and was smiling broadly.

"Amazing aren't they?" Reggie asked and looked through the window at the houseboys

"Yeah, no kidding," Sean answered in amazement

"I'm telling you I'd have married by first houseboy if he were a little better looking," Reggie patted Sean on the shoulder. "Han was good to me, but man he was an ugly old guy. And talk about shit breath, man that guy could stop rust."

"Stop rust?" Sean chuckled and shook his head not quite certain exactly what Reggie was talking about but decided it was meant to be funny and played along.

"Yep, it was that bad. Come on let's check this place out, I got to hit the PX anyway."

"Hey Reg," Sean asked as they started walking, "You never said why you wanted to come back here anyway."

"Shit man that's easy. Man, I got the fever." Reggie offered with a smile and zipped up his windbreaker.

"The fever?" Sean asked not understanding the comment.

"Yeah, you know the Yellow fever; I love the little yellow people."

"Koreans?"

"No shit Sherlock, who did you think I was talking about." Reggie started to laugh "You came back because you love Koreans?" Sean looked over at him and tilted his head in mock nonbelief.

"Well, one particular Korean actually." Reggie smiled to himself and then offered an explanation "Look I admit it, I have a bad case of the fever and I tell you if you ever catch it you'll never get rid of it.

"For me, I got a good ole lady man, she's a looker, smart, and she takes good care of my ugly ass. Most important she screws brains out," Reggie paused and then raised his index finger up to make a point," and she does so with great enthusiasm I might add. So as far as I'm concerned you can keep all those round eyes to yourself."

"So that's the Yellow Fever huh?" Sean smiled and shook his head in mock disbelief.

"You laugh, but I'm serious man. The Yellow Fever is very contagious and if you ever catch it there's like no cure you know?" I know you're full of shit," Sean answered back as they walked.

"Well maybe," Reggie laughed back. "but, you can trust me, I'm from your government and I'm here to help."

It took them almost 45 minutes for them to walk from the detachment area down to the Post Exchange and snack bar and check out all of the sights in between. Along the way Reggie happily recounted his reunion with his girlfriend and their plans to get an apartment off the compound where they would live together again. His girlfriend was going to give up her job and move to be with him and look for some work in the local area. Things were looking up as far as Reggie was concerned, he was back in Korea where he wanted to stay in the first place, and he was getting back with his girlfriend who seemed to genuinely make him happy.

Sean deflected any real questions about his own personal situation deciding he didn't want to talk about his own love life or lack thereof. Sean envied Reggie as he talked away and thought briefly about his own situation with Sharon and if things were ever going to come around and they would be able to work their problems out. He was almost to the point of closing the door in his heart on the whole situation. He was coming to the realization that things were simply not going to work out like he had planned or like he wanted and perhaps he needed to get on with his life. They grabbed a couple of beers at the snack bar, had a cheese burger and fries and then walked back. The beers loosened Reggie even more and he was in animated conversation the whole way back about his earlier tours in Korea, his girlfriend, and other adventures. Sean enjoyed the walk and managed to throw in a story or two of his own whenever Reggie took a breath. Sean wasn't in a mood to really talk but he was enjoying listening to Reggie rattle on about nothing.

Once they got back Reggie offered to go round up a few more beers, but Sean declined the offer deciding to go to bed early and try and catch up on some sleep. He bid Reggie a good night and returned to his own area.

Sean entered his area and was pleasantly surprised to see the entire area was squared away. His suitcases were stacked on top of his wall locker, his bed was made, clothes put away. Opening up his wall locker he saw all of his clothes hung up with his uniforms placed in proper order as required, his other clothes were in his dresser folded or rolled up neatly. His second wall locker was filled with his field gear and was also all set up as if it were ready for an inspection. Sean smiled as he kicked off his shoes and took off his pants he liked Kwan already. He pulled out the chair from under his desk and sat down. He looked over to the desk and saw the gold picture of Sharon's graduation. It was a nice touch of Kwan to set that up and he smiled. Reaching over he picked up the photo and held it in his hand. Rubbing the glass over Sharon's face with his thumb softly as if he could somehow reach out and touch her, he wondered to himself if he was ever going to be able to do that in person again.

He opened the desk drawer and found his writing tablet and envelopes and took out a pen and wrote two quick two page letters one to his mom and dad and the other to Sharon. He wasn't sure how the letter was going to be received but he still held out hope that she would answer now that she had a chance to calm down a little. Both letters were rather brief and perfunctory letting them know he had arrived and provided his own address. He was too drained to really sit down and write any more. After addressing both letters he sat them down on the desk and became lost in thoughts. He was at the start of a completely new adventure and he was happy. So far it seemed as if he was finally joining the army like he had always imagined, but at what sacrifice? He was even further from home and Sharon and now in a foreign country. His thoughts were interrupted by the crackle from a large metal speaker mounted on the telephone pole two Quonset huts down.

He looked at his watch and saw it was fifteen before ten and second later a bugle began to play over the loudspeaker. Within a few notes he recognized the bugle call as "Tattoo," the old Calvary call that was supposed to tell the troops to return to their barracks and get ready for Taps and lights out. Sean knew the bugle call well hearing it almost nightly for the last couple of years and it was soothing and reassuring to him. It was one of the traditions and customs of the army that he had grown to love. Sean listened to the final notes of the long and sad song and the speaker went dead as it was turned off. He sat motionless for a few seconds and then finally reached out and turned the picture of Sharon slightly towards him and smiled.

IX

He had gone to sleep to the sound of Taps and was awoken the next morning by the loud and excited bugle call of Reveille blaring from the metal loudspeaker. Seconds after the first bugle notes over the loudspeakers, Sean's clock radio alarm went off with a click and then a loud verbal blast.

"Goooooooood morning 2nd Division," The radio announcer shouted loudly out, "It's a fine PT morning here at Radio Indianhead, Tong du son Korea home of the 2nd Infantry Division." The radio continued with its own rendition of Reveille, the bugle breaking the morning quiet throughout the barracks.

"Jesus Christ," Sean said to himself as he quickly rose up and reached over to the small night stand to turn the radio off. He fell back onto his back, "Radio Indianhead?" he thought to himself. These guys are brainwashed up here. After a few more eye blinks to fully wake up, he threw the blanket off and rolled out of bed, stood up and put on a set of shorts and tee shirt and walked next door to the latrine to shave and brush his teeth and get ready to go. It was still a little cool in the March morning so he walked fast to the latrine and the warmth inside. Opening the latrine door he was greeted by a blast of warm and humid air from the accumulated steam and hot water from the morning showers and other activity of the oncoming MP Shift. There were small puddles of standing water on the floor much like a gymnasium locker room, but there was no movement. He was joined in a few minutes as he brushed his teeth by Reggie who was also coming in to get ready for the day's activity.

Sean looked up and started laughing out loud. Reggie had obviously slept on something with a raised pattern because his face was dotted with a pattern of slightly red indentations, his hair was messed up with a large cowlick in the back and his eyes were bloodshot.

"Damn," Sean called out and spit into the sink, "What the hell happened to you?"

"What?" Reggie responded sleepily and then turned to look in the mirror.

"Man, you look like you were rode hard and put away wet." Sean laughed and continued to brush his teeth.

"Yeah," Reggie looked into the mirror mounted above the sink and rubbed his face. "Yeah I feel like I was hit by a friggen truck; and then he backed up to see if he really hit me."

"I think he hit you both times man." Sean offered as he gathered up his razor and toothbrush and put them into his shaving kit.

"Yeah, I think you're right." Reggie leaned forward towards the mirror with both hands on the side of the sink, turning his face from side to side to check out the indentations.

"What happened to you?" Sean asked as he picked up his things.

"Soju and Fanta," Reggie announced as he bent over and threw water on his face.

"So what?"

"Soju and Fanta," Reggie stood up, his face dripping water. He looked around and realized he didn't bring a towel with him and looking quite helpless and confused Sean threw his towel to him hitting him in the head. "Thanks man." Reggie patted his face dry which seemed to revive him somewhat.

"Couple of the guys were playing Spades last night in the NCO hooch so they invited me over. All they had was some Soju and Orange Fanta." Reggie shrugged his shoulders as if to say, 'what's a man to do?'

"What's Soju?" Sean repeated tentatively.

"It's Korean liquor, very deadly. I advise you to stay away from it." Reggie threw the towel back to Sean, "Thanks man. I think I'm gonna make it, but I need some coffee. And aspirins."

"Go get dressed shithead and let's go." Sean shouted over his shoulder as he started for the door.

"OK, but don't shout." Reggie answered.

Sean left Reggie leaning over the sink again and returned to his area and noticed for the first time that his uniform was hanging on a hanger in front of his wall locker. It was neatly pressed and he noted that Kwan had already added epaulets onto the shoulders, strictly unauthorized anywhere else in the world. They were added to uniforms in Korea so the MP's could wear a lanyard for their weapon and be able to wear their MP brassard. He had a difficult time unbuttoning the shirt because of the heavy starch and had just as much a hard time trying to put his arm through the sleeve, it actually took some effort to 'break starch'.

The blouse was so starched that the crease stayed in place the length of the arm even after he had managed to get it on. The trousers were another matter. He had to balance himself against the wall locker as he tried to put his legs through the pant legs. He had never experienced such heavy starch, but he loved it. He finally had to do a couple of deep knee bends to break the starch before he could manage to even walk in them.

His boots were next; he had given Kwan a set of jump boots that he had shined before and thought were looking good. He looked down at his boots now and could not believe the mirrored image in the toes and heels. He was impressed. It was a pleasure to tie his boots and then stand in front of the mirror in the middle of the barracks and look at himself. Man he looked sharp, like never before. He walked outside to the cool morning air and felt great. Moments later Reggie walked up to him and looked much better.

"Ah you look good GI. Numba one!" Reggie offered as a good morning. The indentations on his face were nearly gone and he looked much better.

"I see you've recovered." Sean answered as they began to walk towards the roadway.

"Yeah, miracles do happen."

"Man I can hardly walk in these things." Sean looked down at his uniform.

"It's the Rice Starch they use," Reggie offered as an explanation. "It will really get worse as it builds up but it feels good doesn't it?" Reggie looked at the sharp creased uniform, "Come on," Reggie motioned towards the two jeeps coming from down the road towards them, "I bet day shift is dropping off nights and we can probably catch a ride over to the mess hall. I need to get something in my stomach."

They walked across the small street towards the detachment day room. In a matter of seconds, the two jeeps who were screaming up the roadway towards them suddenly came to a screeching halt in front of the dayroom. They stopped so suddenly it made all of the occupants in the back seat come forward smashing into each other or into the gun mount in one of the jeeps.

"Ow, you dumbass motherfucker," came a loud voice from the rear seat along with laughter from the others who had not hit the gun mount.

"You said step on it," one of the drivers answered in return. Laughter and good natured teasing to each other as the six MP's from the off going shift all disembarked from the two jeeps, stretched and started walking back to their individual spaces. Time for a little shut eye before it got too loud to sleep.

"You the new guys?" One of the drivers asked Sean and Reggie who were walking over to the jeeps.

"Yeah, Sean York." Sean offered and leaned over to shake the driver's hand.

"Reggie Phillips," Reggie followed suit leaning over as Sean stepped aside.

"Good to meet ya, Don Hughes." The driver answered back.

"How about a ride to the mess hall?" Sean answered.

"Climb in, that's where we're headed," the driver answered back and put the jeep into gear.

Reggie climbed into the back as Sean sat in the front passenger seat of the leading jeep. They made small talk as the jeep made its way over to the mess hall several streets away. Both jeeps parked along the street and the drivers were starting to secure the steering wheels with a chain that was bolted to the floor boards, wrapped around the steering wheel and secured by a pad lock. Since the jeeps were a tactical vehicle there was no traditional ignition key. If they weren't locked up, they could be gone once they came out.

The PRC/46 tactical radio mounted in the rear compartment crackled to life signaling radio traffic from the MP Station, "One Zero, Noble."

The driver in Sean's jeep reached forward for the microphone, "Noble, this is one zero and one-one, we're both ten-one-two at the

Mess hall CRC." The driver answered the call for both units with their currently location.

"Negative one zero and one-one, I need you both to ten-one-seven right now I have some distro and a duty call." Sean recognized the New York accent of SSG Wallace directing the return to station for both patrols.

"Roger that, in route." The driver spoke into the microphone, paused to hear the reaction from the radio and then looked up at Sean, "Shit, looks like it's starting already, gonna be a long day."

"Noble clear, zero six one five," the radio crackled one last time and then went silent.

Both Sean and Reggie decided to forgo the mess hall and instead were dropped off at the PX snack bar a short walking distance from the PMO and MP station. After a short breakfast and a Styrofoam cup of coffee to go, they were ready to walk to the PMO for whatever special duty was waiting for them. They arrived just as the Grubner was walking out of his office.

"Ah, York and Phillips, right on time, hang here a minute, I have a special detail for you two." Grubner walked back into his office and then returned seconds later carrying some keys. "You two follow me," Grubner announced and then started walking down the small hallway to the end of the building and out the door and continued over to the next building. Opening a side door secured by a hasp and padlock they found cardboard boxes stacked nearly to the ceiling completely filling up the room.

"All right, see these boxes?" Grubner waved towards the room. "These are old MP reports, blotters, journals, pass and ID paperwork and other unit records. It's built up over the last five or six years and you two are going to get rid of it. Miss Park from pass and ID will be in this morning and is going to help out. She'll go through them and decide which we keep, which need to go to Yongsan for record retention, and those we can just get rid of. Now, don't give Miss Park any trouble; she knows how this is supposed to be filed so just do what she says."

Grubner looked to make sure he made his point to the two and then finished, "This should take you guys a couple of days and then you join your squads. Understood?"

"All right Sarge, can do," Reggie answered.

"Good! Now don't screw around, I want this thing done in a couple of days." With that, Grubner walked out of the building and returned to the PMO.

They watched as Grubner walked away back into the PMO and then both of them looked back at the boxes inside the room.

"Oh my aching back," Reggie sighed and stood before the door looking at the towering stack of cardboard boxes.

"I don't know, I think this might be a good gig," Sean answered back.

"Are you ......," Reggie started as he turned around to face Sean but then caught sight of Miss Park walking out of the side door of the PMO and walking towards them, "...crazy?" Reggie's voice tapered off and he looked over at Sean who was staring intently at Miss Park as she approached.

He stepped up and nudged Sean. "Wow," Sean responded and he watched her every move.

"Wow? Is that all you're going to say?"

"Holy shit," Sean whispered as his jaw dropped. He was otherwise speechless.

"Oh yeah, that's a better conversation opener." Reggie chuckled.

"Bite me," he whispered back in response.

She was obviously casually dressed for the expected work in the store room, but still she was attractive and outfitted in a brand new pair of light fitting Khaki pants, a brown long sleeve sweater over a white blouse, tennis shoes and her long black hair pulled back in a pony tail, tied in the back with a white ribbon, with just the hint of makeup. Sean immediately concluded that she was one of the most attractive and alluring women he had ever seen and felt his heart begin to race, his stomach start to knot up, and he almost forgot to breathe.

Reggie turned around to face the room and leaned back towards Sean and whispered, "You hear that?"

"Hear what?" Sean answered not taking is eyes of her.

"That little buzzing sound," Reggie whispered back at him, "it's that damn Korean mosquito and it carries Yellow Fever."

"Get away from me you dipshit," Sean mumbled through clenched teeth and quickly checked out his uniform to make sure he was a squared away.

"Ah, Specialist York," she began in her soft and accented voice, "nice to see you again." She smiled as she walked up to him.

"Hey," Sean began, although he wanted to say more but found himself tongue tied. He finally managed to blurt out, "I hear we're under you today."

"Under me?" Miss Park was momentarily taken aback not understanding and made a face of incomprehension. "I don't understand."

"Oh, I... I... I mean, we're working with you today," Sean quickly came back, his face suddenly flushing.

"Ahhhhh, adaso, Ok." She smiled and blushed slightly herself, "Yes, we work together today."

Pok Suk Park, better known at the PMO as Miss Park, would have been secretly pleased to know the reaction she was causing in Sean because she had been very interested in him when he came into her office the previous day. There was just something about him that sparked a deep interest she had never experienced with any other American solider she had worked with. Pok had worked for the Americans for nearly two years now, obtaining her job at the PMO right after graduating from the University in Seoul with a degree in English and Administration. She was only 23 and the daughter of a very wealthy industrialist involved in the manufacturing of electronic devices. Her father was also a retired general officer from the ROK Army and apparently had played a minor role in the military coup that brought the current Korean president Park Chun Hee, also a former general officer, to power.

She was the only female in her entire extended family that had attended college and then obtained employment outside of the household. The remainder of her female cousins was all married off in their late teens or early twenties by their respective families in basically arranged marriages. Pok had politely but stubbornly refused such a fate and with the final acquiescence and slight disappointment of her father, she had gone to college and then applied and was hired with the US Army. She almost caused a scandal within her family when she declined to work in her father's company and instead moved out of her parent's house in Seoul. She found a large brick, three bedroom house, with a modern bathroom, kitchen, wooden walls and floors, on a corner lot with a cement fence surrounding a small yard with a small flower garden away in the city of Uijombu located outside of Camp

Red Cloud. There was even a small store across the street where she could get most of her basic needs.

She could never had afforded the house under normal circumstances, but the home owner was suffering from bad times with several sick relatives, a faltering business, and needed the rent money more than he needed a nice place for his family to live. The owner had initially hesitated but unbeknownst to her, Pok's father made a personal visit and had worked out a mutually agreeable arrangement. Pok's father had also provided a substantial advance rental payment and the owner agreed to ensure there were no security or safety issues. After being assured that his investment was going to be protected he readily agreed to Pok's lease for what she thought was a very reasonable rent.

She had been very proud of herself for finding such a bargain on such a nice house and she was pleased to show her parents that she was doing so well for being right out of college. She had a house that was even better than her older brother who was now a Major in the Army, stationed further south and much like what her younger brother would have once he finished medical school.

It had taken her awhile to get used to the informal nature of the Americans who were not what she had expected or what she had been told all of her life. Americans were not rich and lazy; they actually worked very hard every day and took their duty very seriously, but were still quick to laugh at themselves, tease and play tricks on each other. They were very welcoming to everyone and generous in everything they did. They had never failed to include her in such things as picnics, Thanksgiving, Christmas, and her favorite of all, their 4th of July celebrations. After talking to several other Korean female workers at the Korean Snack bar where she went once or twice a week for lunch, she realized she was very lucky because she was not treated in the same manner as they described. Apparently many of the American soldiers equated all Korean females with the prostitutes they came into contact within the bars, someone that was more than willing to have sex with them if they came up with the right price. There had been several soldiers in the last two years who had approached her with offers of dates or a chance to live with them for money. It was embarrassing, but she had politely refused. She was not that kind of woman and if there was one thing she wished she could change about those GI's, it would be their impressions of the Korean people. They were not all prostitutes, houseboys, or slicky boy criminals.

She was feeling more comfortable in her second year, the work was challenging and still interesting and she was continuing to develop her English ability. But, the working conditions were becoming somewhat problematic once the new detachment Sergeant Grubner was assigned. He was older then her by fifteen years but even in her short time working with Americans she could tell he thought he was some kind of ladies' man. He frequently came into her office and leaned over her from behind, to show her something on her desk, and then 'inadvertently' brushed up against her from behind or he'd make a point to put his hands on the top of her shoulders.

She was born or cursed with larger and fuller breasts than most petite Korean women and one warm fall day she made a mistake of wearing a lower cut dress. Grubner had spent the day coming next to her and seemed to be doing everything possible to be in a position to be able to look down her dress. After that day she only wore dresses or blouses that could be buttoned up to her neck. He had made it clear through innuendo and hints that he wanted to have a relationship with her, but the thought had revolted her. She was not like that at all and was not happy with his attentions towards her. She knew it was only going to be for a year and no more; she could be patient and he would leave and she could relax and enjoy her work again.

She had been pleasantly surprised at seeing Sean come into her office the previous day. He was young, handsome, well built, and had the softest of southern accents. She had smiled when she realized that he had embarrassed himself trying to talk to her. She had never had that seemingly genuine effect on anyone before and it made her equally interested in this new soldier.

After he walked out of her office, Pok had gotten up and walked towards the front door, stopping just inside the doorway to see him walk to the MP jeep, get inside, and drive away. She was quite thrilled when she found out Sean was going to be assigned to help her get rid of the files that accumulated over the last five or six years. She had brought this up when she first started working at the PMO but no one had bothered to take care of it. No one seemed very concerned at all until there was no more room in storage and something finally had to be done.

They both smiled at each other and Sean looked deeply into her eyes. Pok responded for a few seconds and then jerked her head away smiling. They began to engage in the timeless Kabuki dance of young people mutually attracted to each other, with neither knowing exactly how to proceed further. Each was guarded in what to say and how to say it with each phrase and word being dissected and deciphered for any possible hidden meaning. The day progressed in alternating work and conversation, with each asking questions about the other intermixed with deciding which old files were to be stored and which were to be destroyed. Reggie had popped in several times, but it was clear Sean and Pok were in a personal conversation that he did not need to participate in. They had each ordered a Ramen noodle soup delivered from the Korean Snack bar and then ate in her office in the PMO still talking with each other.

Sean was familiar with Ramen noodle soup, but not the Korean style, which was considerably spicier then anything he had ever had. He went through two soft drinks but could not finish all of the broth because it was too hot. They continued working until 1600 when it was time to straighten up and for her to get ready to go. They both left the building at the same time, Pok walking to the left to go out the main gate and home, Sean walking to the right to go to the mess hall and back to the barracks. They stopped momentarily before they parted and said their polite goodbyes, each wishing the other would say something more, but each hesitating to be the one to say it.

They finally laughed and started their way home, each turned around in time to see the other turn around for a last look. They waved and laughed and walked to their respective destinations. All of this comedy was not lost on Grubner who was looking at their parting through his office window that opened into the front parking lot. He was not appreciative of this new guy honing in on what he considered by virtue of rank, *his piece of ass*. It did not sit well with him at all. If nothing else he knew as a Sergeant First Class, and detachment sergeant, he could make a young Specialist's life very miserable if he chose to do so. He would have to see if it became necessary.

The next morning Sean and Reggie walked across the small parking lot and into the PMO lost in their conversation. Entering the main door to the PMO, Sean almost ran over Grubner who was standing in the doorway. He stopped suddenly and Reggie who was not paying attention ran into his backside.

"Sorry Sergeant," Sean sputtered, "I didn't see you there. Are you OK?"

"York," Grubner recovered, "we don't need you here anymore."

"But Sarge, there's still a bunch of boxes to go through," Sean protested.

"Don't worry about it, Phillips will finish up.

"Hey Sarge, I don't mind, I'll be glad to finish up," Sean protested slightly.

Grubner shut off any other conversation by holding up his hand. "I want you to head over to the detachment and find Staff Sergeant Whitehouse and get settled in. He's doing his duty roster. You're on duty first thing tomorrow morning with the rest of your squad. Phillips, you finish up with that mess back there."

"All right Sarge," Sean was chest fallen and a little confused but resigned himself to obeying the order. He stood aside thinking Grubner was walking out of the building; he at least wanted to tell Pok what was going on so she didn't think he had simply disappeared.

"What's the matter, you got lead in your feet?" Grubner looked down on Sean.

"No Sarge, just waiting til you passed so I can go talk to Miss Park for a second," Sean answered sheepishly.

"You don't work for Miss Park, don't worry about it. I'm sure she'll survive without your presence. Now, hit the road up to the detachment and do what I told you to do. Phillips, go get that shit wrapped up." Grubner jerked his head towards the door to Reggie. "I want that finished today."

"Right Sarge," Reggie spoke and looked over at Sean and waved.

Sean stood back confused as if he didn't understand what was being said then about faced and walked back to the detachment. What was that all about?

X

He walked back up to the detachment area and found SSG Whitehouse sitting in a cloud of tobacco smoke in the NCO Lounge located in one of the Quonset huts set aside for the NCOs of the detachment. The lounge consisted of the typical army issued dayroom furniture - a metal framed couch with removable cushions, couple of chairs, a card table, a refrigerator, with snack and coke vending machines. There were two counters across the width of the hut which resembled a bar - in fact the whole place looked like it might have been a bar at one time. The walls were loaded with pictures of former unit members in glass frames and it was generally off limits to the lower enlisted unless you were invited.

The meeting was rather brief as SSG Whitehouse was not known for having long conversations with anyone. Whitehouse seemed to be a good guy. He was older, late 30's, chain smoker, short and thin, balding, and when he did speak, had a distinct Midwestern accent. He was one of the detachment squad leaders and was already on his second tour with the unit, having just married his much younger Korean wife, he was looking to stay even longer. He actually lived off post in what they referred to as *the ville* in a small apartment but had to come back to the detachment to do his weekly walk through the barracks and post the duty roster for the next week. They were scheduled to start their six day stint of duty the following day.

Whitehouse shook his hand and waved Sean to an empty chair around the card table. Sean waved the cloud of standing smoke away and sat down. Lighting up his third cigarette in ten minutes, Whitehouse began his traditional new guy briefing. He explained they were working 12 hour shifts from 0600 to 1800 for three days, then a short 12 hour break, then three nights, and finally three days off, then start back to days again. Sean had worked 12 shifts before, it certainly made the time go by faster.

"You're on the E5 promotion list right?" Whitehouse asked and took another long draw of the cigarette.

"Yeah, couple more months, I should make it, I was an acting jack my last unit."

"Alright, well I'm going to put you with my assistant Sgt Martinez. He's going to rotate in about a month or so; as it stands you're the next ranking enlisted so you'll take his spot when he leaves." Whitehouse knew Martinez was aggressive and tended to need a partner who was not afraid of a fight. He looked at Sean and decided that he could probably take care of himself. Whitehouse spelled out his philosophy to Sean simply and uncomplicated.

"This is a pretty good outfit. But this is the Wild, Wild, West up here. Plenty of stick time for sure. If you want to be accepted up here, you have to be ready to back your partner up. If you don't back a partner up no one is going to back you up. We've got no use for someone who isn't ready to fight when needed. I have some simple demands. When you're told to do something, do it. When you're told to be somewhere, be there. Got it? It's real simple."

Sean nodded understanding clearly what he meant, "No problem Sarge, you can count on me."

"All right, we'll see." Whitehouse seemed satisfied and didn't feel it necessary to go into any details or any war stories about the bar room fights or the obstinacy of a young soldier, liquored up, and away from home for the first time, and thoroughly impressed with his assignment to the 2nd Infantry Division. Whitehouse welcomed him to the unit and basically told him to go find something to do for the rest of the day and be ready to go to work the following day shift. Sean was more than ready to go and at least try to get some fresh air.

Although the 12 hour shifts were brutal he was finally in a place he knew he wanted to be, the army became what he always envisioned it would be. Whitehouse ran a good squad and everyone was highly motivated. Sean looked forward to going to work. He especially liked the heavily starched uniform and spit shined boots. The other guys in his squad had taken him down to the local shoemaker and he had purchased his high ride style leather holster and leather belt keepers, both highly unauthorized back in the states, but certainly in fashion in Korea.

He also ordered his own grey insulated nylon flight jacket. The grey nylon flight jacket was a coveted prerogative that the MP's in Korea guarded well. According to 8th Army and I Corps regulations, only General Officers, flight crews, and Military Police were authorized to wear them as a part of their military uniform. It looked sharp, but it also served another purpose; it added more padding to the shoulders, arms, and chest. This was useful not just for the winter, but also when required to use physical force to apprehend a soldier, it put that much more between them and the bad guy who decided to use a broken bottle, a knife, or razor blade. On average an MP went through two or three jackets over the course of their tour, the cost of which was borne by the individual MP himself. But the cost was worth it. If the jacket was ripped or torn by some GI in a fight, there was going to be an ass whipping. This special privilege was especially guarded by the MP and anyone other than a general officer, flight crew member or MP was taking it off. Period. No exceptions.

The work was everything SSG Whitehouse said it was going to be. Dayshift was pretty much go here and go there, playing taxi for everyone at the PMO, occasionally they would take reports of thefts or other offenses down at one of the units and determine if an investigator was needed and then secure the scene until they arrived. Nightshift however, was completely different. Nightshift was almost always some action somewhere. Very few nights were spent on endless patrolling with nothing going on. Most of the nights were spent on walking town patrol, going through the various clubs, basically as a moving and constant reminder that if a soldier acted stupid or did something stupid, there was someone around to take care of them.

Sean was somewhat pleased when Martinez took him downtown on foot patrol for the first time. They called out of service and parked their jeep outside the Korean Police Box or police station and locked up the steering wheel with the chain and padlock.

"Look," Martinez started off and turned to the right to look directly at Sean sitting in the passenger seat. "We're down here alone, ok? By ourselves, get it? Once we get out of this jeep we have no contact with anyone. No radio, no phone, so no way to call for help. We can't afford to be taking any shit from anyone. We don't do any pushing and shoving or throwing punches with these shit heads.

Because when you fuck around with these assholes a crowd starts to form. A crowd of drunk GI's forms, we'll get outnumbered real quick and then we got some trouble. If we get trouble inside a bar it's really bad because there are too many weapons they can use. Bottles, chairs, you name it. It'll be 10 to 20 minutes before we get any help. Get it??"

Sean nodded as he understood what Martinez was trying to emphasize.

"All right, so, if we ever have to take anyone in, don't fuck around. Take him down, use your night stick or flashlight and get him to the ground. That generally gets their attention. Once they're on the ground, cuff them. No matter what, we don't exchange any punches with these assholes. Let them punch; we get them to the floor and cuff them. You understand?" Martinez looked over to make sure the message was being received.

"All right, got it." Sean nodded.

"OK, because I want to get my brown ass back across the pond OK? I got no interest in going to the hospital." Martinez looked into Sean's eyes to make sure he was receiving his message.

Sean nodded in agreement and they got out, straightened their uniforms, adjusted their pistol belts, put their night sticks in their carriers and then started walking down the street taking in all of the sights, sounds, and smells.

As they walked Martinez continued with his training, "After we cuff them, we don't fuck around, we get them away from their friends and back to the jeep. Main thing, never give these guys a chance to fight back." Martinez stopped to make sure Sean was paying attention and to look over at a small group of soldiers who were standing outside a club smoking a cigarette.

Once he was certain that the soldiers were behaving themselves, he continued with his training, "These shitheads all think because they're with the 2 ID, and they take Tae Kwon Do for part of their training that somehow they're such bad asses. Because they think they're such bad asses, they think they get to do anything they want or they don't have to listen to anyone. Take that attitude and throw in some firewater, and you have a potentially bad mix. Believe me, if you give them a chance, someone will kick your ass one night. I don't want to be sending any letter to your parents telling them how stupid their son was for trying to fight it out with these assholes. Comprende?"

"Yeah, I don't think my mom would like that either," Sean answered and smiled back.

Sean was impressed when they walked into the first club. As they opened the door, they could make out the blasting music from the stereo, walking downstairs into the cellar bar they could smell the thick heavy tobacco smoke. It took a few second for his eyes to adjust to the dimly lit bar, which was just an open space with 20 or more tables spread out and a small dance floor with ten or more soldiers and Korean women dancing. Martinez walked over to the DJ who was sitting in a booth up front, and he tapped on the glass enclosure with his nightstick. The DJ looked up and saw the MP helmet liner and immediately turned the music slightly down and then adjusted the lights to turn them back up. Martinez then motioned for Sean to follow him; as he approached each table Martinez directed, "pass and ID on the table, pass and ID on the table." Martinez repeated this as he walked through the club. Each soldier in turn opened his wallet and provided a pass and their Military Identification card. Martinez walked around each table, took a cursory look at each one, then handed it back and said "Thank you."

Around the bar they went, Martinez made a motion to Sean and he began to check out the documents as well. Most of the soldiers provided the documents without question and without hesitation, an irritant they just had to deal with as the price of a ticket to get off camp even for a couple of hours. Other soldiers did so, but were not so resigned to the requirement; add some alcohol and too much testosterone and it could be a bad combination.

"Pass and ID," Martinez called out to a table of 7 soldiers who were cooperating but doing so slowly in an effort of passive resistance. Martinez was looking around the club waiting for the soldiers to provide their documents when one of the soldiers called out to their friends sitting at the table.

"Hey, you smell that?" one of them volunteered to his friends.

"Yeah, like it just came into the bar." The other answered back looking innocently at Martinez.

"Smells like pig shit doesn't it?" The first solider spoke back to his friends but looked straight up at Martinez with his pass and ID in his hand.

"Yeah, you're right, getting stronger man," a third soldier spoke up joining in with his friends.

"Yeah, someone better flush or this whole place is going to stink." The soldier looked up at Martinez as if challenging him. Martinez looked back and took a deep breath. Looking up he caught Sean's eye and motioned for him to come over to the table. Sean returned the documents to a soldier he was checking and walked over to the table. The first soldier was leaning back in his chair and Martinez saw that he was wearing a white tee shirt that announced in red letters "FUCK IT" across the chest.

Martinez looked at the soldier and smiled. "That shirt is in violation of I Corps Regulation, you have to cover it up," Martinez directed.

"What?" The soldier leaned forward to hear Martinez.

"I said you have to cover your shirt up or you have to leave. You can't wear that shirt here."

"Says who?"

"Says me and I Corps Regulation, It says no profanity written on any outer clothing. It's considered disrespectful. So cover that shirt up or you have to leave and go back to camp, or you're going to go with us back to the MP Station."

Sean looked at the other soldiers sitting at the table and moved his left hand over to the handle of his night stick. Sean could tell that no one there wanted any trouble and they began to call to their friend.

"Paul, shut up and put your jacket on. Can he put his jacket on?" one of the soldiers asked.

"Sure, put your jacket on or cover up the shirt."

"I'll just take it off," the soldier leaned forward and started to take it off. Martinez noted that there wasn't another shirt underneath.

"Can't take it off, you'll expose your naked chest. That's against I Corps Regulations. I'd have to take you in."

"Paul, put your jacket on and shut up," one of his friends spoke up.

"There you go, cover it up and no problem. But when I come back, if that shit is visible again, I'm taking you in. Got it?" Martinez leaned forward to look the soldier in the eye.

The soldier reached back and put his jacket on and stared straight ahead.

"You have to zip it up so no one can see those words." Martinez spoke again.

The soldier looked back as if he wanted to say something.

"Dude, zip your jacket up and shut the fuck up," another soldier called out.

"Man it's hot as fuck in here," the soldier protested but zipped up his jacket and then leaned back in anger folding his arms across his chest.

"There you go. Now you're in compliance." Martinez handed the soldier's pass and ID back. Then he walked around to the offending soldier and leaned down and whispered in the soldier's ear, "By the way, that wasn't pig shit, that was chicken shit you smelled."

Martinez looked around to see if anyone else at the table wanted to say anything else. The other soldiers looked straight ahead and remained silent. Once the point was made Martinez signaled Sean it was time to go and they walked outside. As they walked out, the club the lights were turned down and the music was turned back up.

"Look it's not the shirt, I mean who really gives a shit, I'd have never said anything," Martinez explained to Sean as they returned outside and were walking down the street to the next bar. "It was the smart assed comment, it was a direct challenge. Can't let them challenge you, because if these fuckers lose their respect or even worse they lose their fear of you, we got chaos man. Did you hear his friends? No one wanted to start any shit. You know why? Cause we woulda kicked their asses and dragged them in and they'd get restriction to compound for a couple of weeks. You can't let that go by; because next time we come back they get braver and braver."

A few days later, they were on a walking patrol and as they walked by the Korean police station they saw one of their other patrols inside. A soldier was sitting on a bench, handcuffed to a small ring mounted on the wall. A Korean prostitute was standing in the middle of the room loudly speaking in excited Korean and pointing at the soldier. Mr. Kang, the MP interpreter, was doing his best to calm the prostitute down and translate the complaint to the other MP patrol. Martinez went inside to see what was going on; Mr. Kang looked very relieved to see him there.

"Hello," Mr. Kang said as he bowed slightly to Martinez and smiled, "Happy to see you. Sarge Martinez, we got fuck up situation here."

Sean always laughed when he heard a Korean trying to cuss in English. Looking around at the Korean police, it seemed as if they were waiting for the American MP to decide what to do next.

"What's up?" Martinez asked as he approached.

"This businesswoman," Mr. Kang pointed at the Korean female (using the euphemism "businesswoman" for prostitute), "says this soldier raped her. But, I think this is case of he just not pay."

"He use any force?" Martinez asked.

Mr. Kang translated and then waited for her reply. The woman listened and then came back in very rapid Korean. She put her two hands to her throat to demonstrate that she was choked, then pointed to her knees both had abrasions and were bleeding slightly, then to her hands to show her broken fingernails.

"Yes, much force, try to choke her, push her down, hurt knees." Mr. Kang translated.

Martinez looked at the prostitute. He put his arm around Mr. Kang, walked a few steps away and whispered "Mr. Kang what do you think?"

"I think this a failure pay just debt. This is no rape, I don't think so." Mr. Kang shook his head.

Martinez then walked over to the soldier sitting on the bench. "Hey," he kicked the soles of the soldier's shoes. "What happened?"

The soldier woke up and tried to straighten up and mumbled a greeting.

"Hey Sarge."

"What happened?" Martinez repeated.

"Sarge, I don't know. I paid her for all night. We come back and get it on, I fell asleep. I wake up a while later and I'm ready to go again, we do it again and everything is great. I get up and want to go to the club again and she wants more money. I said what the fuck I paid for all night I'm not giving you any more money." The soldier looked around to see if his explanation was getting through. "Then the bitch starts scratching me and throwing shit at me, man, look at this," he leaned forward showing a small cut on the top of his head, "she hit me with her fucking alarm clock, man."

Martinez looked at the woman and Mr. Kang was standing by listening. The soldier continued, "Look, I grabbed her to make her stop beating the shit out of me and then I tried to get out of there. I mean I don't want no trouble. I get to the street and she starts yelling bloody murder. She grabs me by the leg and won't let go. I'm trying to get out of there, but she won't let go and I guess I dragged her for a while down the street until the police showed up and they threw me down and cuffed me."

"How much did you pay her?"

"Ten bucks all night, standard price," the soldier responded rubbing his head.

"Where are you from?" Martinez asked.

"B battery at Camp Maxwell," the soldier explained.

Camp Maxwell was one of the smaller Hawk Missile Battery located some distance from Uijambu, and Martinez understood right away the problem.

"Well, the standard prince for all night here in the big city is $20 minimum," Martinez explained.

"It is? Shit, I thought she was trying to screw me over you know, charging more because I was new to town."

"You don't have any trouble paying more?"

"Nah, if I knew that's the price. Hell I was going to ask her to spend the weekend with her man she has some talent Sarge. You know, she knows what she's doing."

Martinez walked back to the Police Captain and through Mr. Kang discussed the problem.

"The Captain asked, what does the American MP suggest?" Mr. Kang translated.

"The American MP suggests we allow the soldier to pay the proper amount, plus some extra for injuries."

Mr. Kang translated and the Korean Police Captain nodded in general agreement.

"And no arrest by Korean police and we take soldier," Martinez added and Mr. Kang translated.

The police captain waited for the Korean female's response; it was presented to her that the soldier would pay $20.00 plus $10.00 for her cut knees. At first she was uncertain but then she somewhat reluctantly agreed.

The soldier was presented the same option, pay the $30.00 and leave without any charges and return to Camp Maxwell or stay there and get prosecuted by the Koreans for rape. It had taken about 15 minutes to finish up some paperwork. Mr. Kang prepared a form for the Korean female to acknowledge that she had received $30.00 in payment from the soldier and did not want to press any charges against him. The soldier then turned over the money which was witnessed by the police captain.

The two were then released and they walked out of the police station. Martinez and Mr. Kang talked with the police captain while Sean walked towards the door and looked out at the prostitute and soldier walking down the street together apparently talking to each other. After a few feet they stopped and Sean saw the soldier reach into his wallet and pull out some more money and give it to the woman. They then walked down the street to the corner arm in arm, flagging down a taxi they both got inside and drove away. Sean could only shake his head. Unbelievable. What a country.

XI

Over the next few weeks, Sean got into the routine easily enough and still managed to find the time to see Pok especially working day shift or his days off. Whenever possible he would go with her to the Korean Snack bar for lunch or they would talk over a cup of coffee when he was taking a break at the PMO. He tried repeatedly to ask her out, but she had always smiled and in the oriental way, never said yes, and never said no, leaving Sean hanging in the wind like never before, not knowing where he stood with her. Perhaps this was her plan because he was becoming more and more infatuated with her, seeking every excuse in the world to be with her or talk with her throughout the day.

She had been especially interested during the previous weeks of his constant flow of pictures he was receiving from his family back home in his once or twice a week letters. His mother was a prolific letter writer and often included newspaper articles of what was happening around town. Rebecca wrote once a week like clockwork talking about her trials and tribulations. She had applied to Vanderbilt and with her grades, had already been accepted, but had not yet told their parents. Pok had seemed more interested in his family than he thought possible and seemed to genuinely want to hear all about what was going on back home. He tried to ask the same questions about her family but she always tried to deflect the questions. Sean felt like there may be tensions between her and her family and decided not to press her.

It had taken several weeks of coffee and lunch and casual conversations before she finally agreed to meet him off duty. It was several more weeks of long walks on weekends where they talked endlessly. Pok even allowed Sean to hold her hand for short periods of time as they walked, but would break his hold if they were ever approached by another Korean as if she were uncertain of the reaction of her holding hands with a soldier. Sean was encouraged when on occasion Pok would allow herself to be kissed, never more than a peck, but it was a kiss nevertheless, as they said their goodbyes or hellos.

Sean was probably more confused on where he stood with Pok than he had ever been before. He found himself thinking and day dreaming of her constantly, yet he was careful not to force intimacy on her. Perhaps this was the Korean custom and Sean decided to be patient. But he was beginning to lose heart that Pok was really interested in any type of relationship and perhaps she was just being polite and would never consider him more than just a friend. Reggie convinced him to hang in, that this was the Korean way. It was not surprising that Pok hesitated in going out with him; it was not socially accepted for proper Korean females to be seen with occidentals. Koreans were very particular about interracial relationships and they were not very accepting. Pok was obviously weighing what she would probably experience with the rest of her family and Korean society with what she could gain from a relationship with Sean.

Sean had never considered that possibility and became concerned that he might not have a chance because of some cultural prejudice. When she finally agreed to go out in public with Sean to a restaurant he was overjoyed and took it as a sign she was interested or perhaps he had finally been able to show her he was a good guy and worth taking a chance on. Although she agreed to go out with him, she would not let him pick her up, instead she insisted on meeting him downtown. The appointed time did not seem to pass quick enough and when the day finally arrived he found himself standing on a street at the agreed upon meeting spot, impatiently pacing slowly back and forth glancing at his wrist watch every ten seconds. Sean looked up as a taxi stopped just ahead and was caught off guard when she exited out of the back, paid the fare and then started walking towards him. She was in a long but tight fitting strapless yellow dress with a white sweater draped over her shoulders. Her long shiny hair was wrapped into a small bun in the back held together with a gold pin. She was wearing yellow leather high heels that made her a few inches taller and was wearing just a hint of eyeliner makeup. As she walked towards him his heart melted as she broke into a wide toothy grin.

Sean of course said a silent prayer of thanks for at least wearing a pair of slacks and a button up shirt. He still had not spent a lot of money on civilian clothes and was even wearing his army issued low quarter dress shoes. He hoped that he would at least pass the initial test. As she came up to him she reached out with both hands to take his hands and then walked up and gave him a quick kiss on his left cheek and then stepped back to look into his eyes. Sean looked back into the large brown deer eyes and felt his knees grow weak and noted a mild reaction in his trousers. He could make out just a hint of what he thought were roses from her perfume or shampoo as she took his hand and walked him towards a doorway nearby. The restaurant entrance used the same entranceway of one of the tourist clubs frequented by soldiers but instead of walking further up the stairs, Pok lead him to the left and downstairs to a small dimly lit Korean restaurant. He had recognized the main entranceway to the club, but had no idea of the presence of the restaurant below.

They were met at the door by an older Korean waiter dressed in a white long sleeve shirt and bow tie, shiny red vest, and black pants. He bowed in a polite and traditional welcome and ushered them into the small dimly lit restaurant which consisted of ten or twelve western style small tables, each with a white linen table cloth, and a candle on each one. Pok was assisted to her seat by the waiter and Sean also sat down. The waiter began to speak Korean and handed both of them menus. Sean dutifully opened the leather bound menu and was confronted with the chicken scratch of the Korean writing. Sean looked over the menu briefly and then looked across the table at Pok who was smiling and looking over at Sean seemingly enjoying his confusion.

"May I order for us please?" Pok asked politely.

"Ah, yeah that might be better. No telling what might happen if I do it."

"Would you like beer or drink?" Pok asked.

Sean thought back to what he remembered of OB beer and decided to go neutral. "Ah, no beer. How about tea?" he responded tentatively.

Pok smiled and then spoke in rapid Korean and received a bow in return. Pok then smiled and turned to look at the waiter and started speaking Korean. She paused and the waiter looked over at Sean and also smiled and bowed slightly in his direction. The conversation was all lost on Sean as they spoke together. Sean looked up as they came to a halt. The waiter reached out for their menus and Sean gave his back and received another slight bow in return.

"He was very impressed you are trying Korean food," Pok explained as the waiter withdrew.

"Oh yeah?"

"Yes, many Americans come to our country and never get out of nightclub, never meet real Korean peoples." Pok seemed genuinely pleased that Sean was making such an effort. "He say you are first American to eat here in many years."

"Well, I wanted to be with you," Sean said.

"Oh yeah?" Pok answered and smiled in the coy way she did when she didn't know how to answer back.

They made small talk and very shortly the waiter returned with hot tea and then shortly after returned with small metal containers of white rice, a rather large platter of seasoned beef, and smaller bowls of rice, fresh vegetables, and Kimchi. They were all laid out on the table and a plate put before each of them. Sean looked around as the food came and noted there was no silverware on the table. Instead was a set of wooden chopsticks. Pok looked over and saw his hesitancy.

"Would you like fork and spoon?" Pok asked seeing his lack of confidence in chop sticks.

"Nah, I'm gonna try these out. I've been practicing," Sean answered back and managed an uncomfortable smile.

Pok smiled and they began to eat. Sean was somewhat slow at the beginning, but was able to manage to get most of the food into his mouth and luckily none onto his trousers. His feeble attempt led to many chuckles and laughs between them as they ate and talked. As they ate and talked, Sean felt his heart melting away. Pok also seemed to warm up some and she finally talked a little about her family. He learned about her father being a former officer in the Army and her brother was a Major stationed near Pusan, and her other brother was in medical school, soon to be a doctor. Sean talked more about his life in Mississippi, working the fields, his family, and the army. The dinner went by far too quickly. After dinner they walked outside onto the street and stood for a few moments while they contemplated their next move. Sean noted the number of soldiers walking through the area along with other Korean civilians who all seemed to be coming and going somewhere. Not wanting the evening to end, he asked Pok to go to one of the clubs or go somewhere else to dance or perhaps sit and talk more. She politely declined but offered to walk a ways with him. They walked together along the street talking and looking into the various shop windows and Sean smiled a broad smile when he 'accidentally' brushed against her hand and she took his in hers. She smiled as well but looked down towards the street not knowing exactly what to do either. Koreans were not known for public displays of affection or holding hands and he could tell she was trying to come to terms with the decidedly western cultural expression. They walked a length of the shopping area but most of the stores were closing up and they reversed their direction.

"Sean, I'm sorry but my foot hurting," she looked up at him and smiled, "I think maybe I go home."

"OK, let's get a taxi OK?" Poks nodded and they quietly walked over to a number of cabs that were parked waiting for passengers. As they came to the first cab the driver started the engine and Sean opened the door for Pok to step inside.

"You know its American custom for a man to escort his date home to make sure she arrives safely," Sean offered as Pok sat into the back seat.

"American custom?" Pok smiled back.

"Yeah, very important, I could lose face." Sean looked down at her and smiled.

"Ah ha, so you want protect me?"

"Of course."

"OK, better come with me, I will feel safe."

Sean ran around to the other side of the taxi and entered, certain that if he didn't move quickly she would change her mind. Sean adjusted himself in the back seat and reached his left hand out; Pok took it in her right hand and smiled. As the taxi drove away into the night, Pok moved closer to him and slowly leaned up against his left shoulder and placed her left hand on his left arm. Pok eventually placed her head on his strong shoulders and for the first time felt secure, warm, and safe. She sighed deeply in satisfaction. They rode the rest of the drive in silence, each enjoying the quiet and closeness. The taxi ride was far too short for Sean who got out asked the driver to wait for him thinking he would need a ride back to camp.

"Would you like to come in?" Pok asked coyly as she looked into her purse for her keys.

"Well it's almost curfew," Sean answered back, his heart starting to race.

"Yes, but no curfew inside." Pok responded as she found her keys and started for the metal door leading into her small yard.

"No there's not." Sean closed the door to the cab and walked over as Pok opened the door and they both went inside.

XII

Sean woke up the next morning with sunlight coming through the window across his face. He looked over at the small alarm clock on the dresser and saw that it was 7 am. It took a few seconds for him to realize where he was at and what all had happened the previous night. He looked over to the other side of the bed and saw that it was empty. He could hear clattering in another room and then water running and could smell what he thought was coffee brewing. He rose up on the side of the bed and pushed the covers off and saw that he was naked. He reached down onto the pile of clothing on his side of the bed to find and put on his boxer shorts and pants. Although he had nothing to drink the previous night he woke up feeling almost as if he were hung over, primarily because they had spent most of the making love to each other and he was still tired but felt wonderfully fulfilled.

He walked out of the bedroom, stretched, and then followed the sound into the kitchen where Pok was standing in front of the sink washing some dishes. He could see the coffee pot on the small counter top with two small cups and saucers already in place. Pok must have heard him walking into the kitchen because she turned around. She was wearing a white cotton terrycloth bathrobe that went just above her knee, and her hair was put into a ponytail behind her back and tied with a rubber band. Sean thought she was one of the sexiest women he had ever seen standing there in front of him. He walked quickly over to her and reached out and took her in both of his arms and lifted her off the floor. She smelled fresh and her hair was still damp from a morning shower.

"Ahhhh," She laughed and groaned as she was picked up off the floor, returning his hug. Sean finally lower her back onto the floor but continued to hug her.

"Good morning," she said lightly into his ear. She leaned back to break the embrace and looked into his eyes. "Go take shower, I buy toothbrush from the store, it's on the sink. I bring coffee then have breakfast," she said pushing him towards the door. "Go shower, breakfast ready soon." She shooed him out of the kitchen to the bathroom and returned to the sink.

Seconds later, Pok knocked on the bathroom door, opened it slowly and came in with a steaming hot cup of coffee. She handed it to Sean, who accepted it gratefully, then stepped back to let him shower. Sean took a sip of the coffee, it was terribly weak, about the color of strong tea, but it was a considerate thought and he wasn't about to say a word. He set the cup and saucer down and looked into the mirror mounted on the wall over the sink. His hair was messed up and he still looked like he had just gotten up. But he smiled and made the sign of the cross as if praying and thinking to himself, *if this was a dream I don't want to wake up yet.* Sean quickly brushed his teeth, then stepped into the shower and let the water wake him fully up. It was steaming hot and it felt good. He was trying to remember the entire evening; it had been so totally unexpected and more than a little erotic. Pok was more than he had ever expected or had ever wanted in a woman, both giving and then demanding at the same time. He could have stayed in the shower for much longer and enjoyed the moment with the instant replays from last night running through his head, but the water started to turn cold and he knew he had to find out if he were still dreaming.

Showered, teeth brushed, hair combed, and relaxed, he was feeling fantastic when he walked back to the kitchen, where he could still hear Pok rattling around. He could smell something good being prepared, but his mouth literally fell open when he came into the kitchen and saw the table Pok set out for breakfast. On the table were sausages on a small plate along with a few strips of bacon, fried potatoes were in another dish, a couple of fried eggs were sitting on his plate, along with several pieces of buttered toast, and what looked like white gravy in a small bowl. He sat down and was almost overwhelmed. Pok brought over a new cup of coffee and a small glass of orange juice that only added to the overfull table.

"Is this OK?" Pok asked uncertainly.

"Oh my God, who else is coming over?" Sean looked at all the food; it was like a Thanksgiving Breakfast.

"I know American love big breakfast," Pok announced proudly.

Sean laughed, "Yeah when I was working on the farm. But damn!" Sean looked over at everything.

Pok seemed somewhat disappointed, completely misunderstanding his comment. Sean saw her reaction and reached out and put his arm around her waist.

"Oh no, I'm very happy, I'm just surprised. You did this all for me? How long have you been working on this?"

"Yes this is all for you, I wanted today be special day." She smiled broadly and hugged him back. She quickly sat down across from him. "I wake up early and go to market," she said very proudly.

"Pok, it's beyond fantastic." Sean was of course surprised; he was not much of a breakfast person unless he was about to do a hard day's work. But he took a big plateful careful not to hurt her feelings. She smiled and sighed in relief that her first attempt at American cooking seemed to be so successful.

After a long and enjoyable breakfast, where they talked and laughed and teased each other, Sean helped clean the table and wash dishes. Pok had initially insisted that she would do it all herself, but Sean was just as insistent and they started to laugh over arguing about cleaning up. Once the kitchen had been cleaned and their breakfast had settled, Sean took Pok by the hand and returned to the bedroom and they made love, yet again. This time, it wasn't the lustful, excited, and intense love making from the previous night, but the slower more deliberate and emotional enjoyment that two people share. Afterwards Sean rolled over onto his back and Pok put her head on his chest and her leg across his legs, and she listened to his heart race and then slow down as they both fell asleep.

Since it was a nice warm Saturday afternoon by the time they got up, they decided to venture downtown to walk around the various shops together. The sights, the smells, the multitude of people walking around was a new experience for Sean, as he had never been downtown in the daytime, only at night when the area was crowded with off duty soldiers bar hopping. As a small town boy, he had never been to such a large city. For him, shopping was rather limited to the local town square or maybe driving over to Oxford's. Every once in a while they would really go crazy and jump in the car driving over an hour up to Memphis and hitting one of the malls. But during the summer and fall there was almost no time between chores to skip out for a full day of 'shopping'.

Pok took Sean from one small open stall to another, picking and choosing various food items for later. They spent a great deal of time looking into the shop windows and every once in a while venturing inside to look around at the wide variety of electronic goods, counterfeit cassette tapes, and records. He had seen many of the shops through the windows, on foot patrol, but had never really stopped inside to take a look. At Pok's gentle insistence, they went into what he discovered was a tailor shop in the middle of the market place.

"This is good tailor; you should get a nice clothes made here." Pok grabbed his arm and lead him into the shop.

"But, I'm not a dress up guy," Sean protested.

"I know, but you are a handsome man, and one day you take me out to very nice restaurant. So you need a good clothes," she continued in her near perfect English and smiled. Sean's argument and protest ended with those magic words spoken by every female who was bound and determined to get her way or win any argument. "It make me so very happy."

"All right, if it would make you happy." Sean sighed, resigned himself to the new purchase and his first rule in becoming an eventual successful husband: *If it makes her happy, you'll be happy.*

"Yes, please." Pok smiled broadly in her female victory and then covered her mouth with her hands in the oriental way not to show her teeth.

"Ok Ok," Sean resigned and took a deep breath and walked inside. They were immediately greeted by an elderly man with large, thick lens, black framed glasses, with a cloth measuring tape placed around his neck like priest vestments. Pok and the man exchanged slight bows and pleasantries in Korean while Sean was left to walk around the small shop. On a small table were several GQ and other men's and women's fashion magazines. Sean was leafing through the magazines as Pok came over to him.

"We find picture in magazine first, then pick material," Pok explained. "They make for you here. Whatever in the magazine, they can make for sure. Today pay half and when ready, pay other half." Pok looked to see if Sean understood.

"They have all of these patterns in this little shop?" Sean pointed at pictures from the magazine.

"No, they make suit from picture," Pok said as they began to look through the magazine. "Don't worry this Korean tailor, they make anything. You see." Pok looked up and nodded as if to validate her statement.

"OK, if I have to get some nice clothes, then you have to get a nice dress," Sean announced.

"Oh no, I no need dress. I have many nice dress." Pok was taken aback uncertain how to respond.

"Maybe, but they won't match my new clothes. If I have to buy some fancy new clothes, then you have to buy a new dress too. Don't worry I have money." Sean smiled back at her and she, with just a slight perfunctory polite protest, finally agreed. Secretly however, she was very pleased and gave him an unsolicited peck on the cheek and a smile. He would have bought her the world at that moment.

They sat down next to each other and leafed through the various magazines; Sean through GQ and Pok through several of the female magazines. It took several minutes, but they both finally decided on patterns and then materials. Pok then showed the magazine pictures to the elderly man and pointed to the materials for each outfit. The man nodded in understanding and began to scribble notes on a pad. He then quickly took the necessary measurements from each one of them and once satisfied, went back to his counter to add up the costs. After the price was tabulated, Sean looked over at the estimated bill and started to reach for his wallet. Pok took her hand and placed on Sean's as a signal *"not so fast"*. Pok then began speaking in polite Korean. There was a several minute back and forth conversation between the two of them. In the end, he obviously surrendered to Pok and began to refigure the expected bill. Pok looked at the calculations again, then nodded and smiled in agreement. Sean looked at the bill again and noted that it was substantially lower.

"OK, total price 150 dollar US. Can you pay 75 dollar now?" Pok asked.

Sean reached into his wallet and pulled out four twenty dollar bills. "I only have $80. No change."

Pok spoke to the tailor who nodded eagerly in agreement.

"Ok, give to him please." Pok smiled and Sean handed him the money. In return, Sean received the receipt and another piece of paper.

Sean looked at the paper where he had written something incomprehensible in the chicken scratch Korean alphabet. Pok and the elderly man spoke politely back and forth and then said their goodbyes. The elderly man shook his hand and bowed slightly as they departed. Apparently to Sean, everyone was happy with the deal, although he was slightly bewildered by the whole exchange.

Once outside, Pok explained there were two prices in the smaller shops, one for Americans and other westerners and one for Koreans. Mostly because everyone knew the Americans had more money and therefore would be willing to pay a higher price, and because they knew Koreans would never pay so much. Pok explained, with the exception of food items, it was always necessary for Sean to haggle over the stated price of almost everything within the smaller shops. The shop keeper expected the haggle and enjoyed the give and take. They took a mild offense at Americans who simply paid whatever price was offered to them.

Sean thought to himself, *well maybe here, but we don't do that in America* and wondered how that concept would go over at Mr. Haskel's hardware store on the town square back home. He imagined the conversation something like: "Gee Mr. Haskel, you have this priced too high I just can't buy it at this price."

With the answer something like: "Yeah, well then, come back when you've saved enough money, now go put it back on the shelf where you got it from." Mr. Haskel would then spit tobacco juice into the coke bottle sitting on the counter, and likely go back to reading the paper. Sean doubted there would be a lot of negotiating with Mr. Haskel, whatever the price.

Pok continued, stating the other list was for thread the tailor suggested they buy at the American PX. Pok explained that the material was generally OK, but the Korean thread was inferior to American thread. The tailor was offering the option of using American thread if Sean would buy it at the PX and he would only use the American thread. Sean smiled and shrugged his shoulders in confused acceptance but Pok smiled as if it were normal course of business.

As they continued walking though some of the back alleyways, Sean discovered a whole new world once they reached the farmers market area. This area was quite different than the night clubs, small food stands, or the other small shops located outside the main gate, which catered strictly to the military. There you found the tailor and cobbler shops where you could get uniforms tailored, patches sewed on or a nice set of jump boots at a reasonable price. Now he suddenly took in the sights, the hustling of the people, the odd and unusual smells, of people and food. For the first time in a long time, Sean was feeling alive as if he was actually seeing Korea for the first time and he liked it.

Walking slowly through, Sean almost gagged when Pok asked to stop at a small stand that was selling dried fish. He decided right then and there it was the ugliest fish he had ever seen and it was impaled on what looked like a sharpened dowel and dried to a beef jerky consistency. Looking to the back of the same stall and hanging from a series of strings running the length of the stall, were rows of dried squid. Pok purchased one of the dried squid with its long tentacles dangling out of the small piece of paper in which it was packaged. Pok snapped off a small piece of the tentacle and tried to hand it over to Sean. It only took one look to decide he was not interested; he made a face and shook his head.

Pok giggled and put the piece in her mouth, "it's good, you try?"

"Maybe later," Sean declined, deciding almost immediately he wasn't nearly as adventurous as he thought.

Pok laughed and put another tentacle in her mouth. She pulled on it until it snapped off and began eagerly chewing it like a piece of licorice. Sean shook his head and decided he could avoid that part of Korean life with no problem. They continued walking and exploring through the market place and then quite unexpectedly, Pok reached out to him and lightly brushed the side of his hand. Sean naturally took her soft delicate hand in his and looked over to her, surprised at the unexpected display of public affection. She looked up and smiled as he looked into her eyes, pulled her hand to his lips and softly kissed it. Hand in hand they slowly made their way through the market and Pok, like a professional tour guide explained to Sean the many different sights and customs.

It was early afternoon when Sean decided he had seen enough Korean culture for one day and they mutually agreed it was time to be alone. They returned in the early afternoon to her house quite exhausted from the walk but again made love to each other. When they were spent, Sean lay on his back and was almost drifting off to sleep when he felt Pok sitting on the edge of the bed next to him, nudging him awake and forcing him out of bed. Wordlessly taking him by the hand, Pok brought him to the bathroom, where she had drawn him a hot bath and instructed him to climb in. It was almost scalding hot; Sean now knew what a crawdad must feel when it hit the pot and felt instant sympathy. He took several minutes to slowly lower himself into the hot tub and finally lean back. It felt remarkably good and relaxing to soak as Pok kneeled down beside the tub and began to apply soap to a bath sponge.

"What are you doing?" Sean asked looking over at Pok.

"This is Korean custom. It shows much affection and attention by woman for the man," Pok explained as she put the sponge onto his chest and began to wash him.

"I like this Korean custom." Sean tilted his head back and closed his eyes grinning ear to ear.

Pok took the sponge and washed him all over and later used her fingers to massage him, pampering him like a king in an oriental palace. He asked her repeatedly to join him in the tub but she playfully declined. He finally managed to talk her into joining him, because as he explained, "this is GI custom." She playfully giggled and then dropping her terrycloth robe and slowly lowering herself into the tub, she nestled herself between his legs, finally comfortably leaning back against his chest. They soaked, talked, and laughed with each other and he returned the favor of slowly washing and massaging her back and shoulders, kissing her neck softly and exploring her other areas.

They remained in the tub until their skin began to wrinkle and the water became uncomfortably cool and neither could take it any longer. Pok reluctantly stood up, stepped out of the tub and put her terry cloth robe back on. As Sean stood up, she opened up a towel for him as he stepped out to the cold tile floor. She hugged him from behind wrapping the towel tightly around his waist. They both looked up, saw themselves in the fogged up mirror over the sink and grinned, both silently reading each other's mind.

Sean slowly awoke in the morning, stretched out on his left side, Pok snuggled up against his back, right arm wrapped around his waist, so close he could feel her breath. As he gained his awareness he went back over the last two days and then it came to him; it was already Sunday morning and suddenly came the realization the weekend was about to be over. Sean would have to go back to Camp that night to be ready for work the following morning. The thought of not being with her for even a short time was already causing him distress and he sighed deeply. The motion of his chest rising caused Pok to momentarily wake up.

"You wake?" she quietly spoke.

"Almost," Sean answered and caressed her forearm tenderly.

"You want coffee?" Pok gamely offered.

"No, go back to sleep." Sean patted her on the arm. "But I have to pee," Sean announced and then slowly rose up and placed his legs over the edge of the bed. Looking back, Pok had changed into a fetal position and adjusted her head on the pillow and fell back to sleep.

XIII

Sean got up and tended to his morning business and then went to the kitchen and put a pot of coffee on and sat at the table. He was not certain exactly what had happen that weekend, but he sensed he had finally arrived at a place he was supposed to be. He realized he had not thought of home or Sharon, or the Army, or anything else in the last two days. He was still lost in his thoughts when Pok walked into the kitchen dressed in her white terry cloth robe.

"How did you sleep?" Sean asked and sipped from his coffee cup

"I sleep good and you?" Pok asked as she walked over to sit down on his lap and poured a cup of coffee.

"I slept real good; you wore me out woman." Sean smiled back as he hugged her.

"I wear out?" Pok asked playfully bristling and looking back at Sean.

"No you wear me out. You were too much." Sean tried to explain the compliment.

"Oh OK, then maybe not so much love next time OK?" Pok offered innocently and smiled.

"No, no, no, it's OK, believe me. I like being worn out by you."

They talked through the morning and enjoyed a relaxing uneventful afternoon but each realized their time was coming to an end. They both knew Sean had to return to Camp so he could work the next day.

Although they knew they would see each other in a matter of hours, if someone had been watching their goodbye, one would think they were expecting to be gone from each other for months. Sean finally kissed her one last kiss and walked out the door towards Camp

Red Cloud and the Army. Making his way along the dark pothole packed gravel road the cool night air helped him think. He could not recall a time when he had been so happy. It all seemed so strange how his life seemed to change so radically in a matter of a few weeks. Over the space of one weekend he found himself going in a new direction with his life. Suddenly things seemed so clear to him.

He was still locked in deep thoughts as he came through the main gate at just past 1900 hours. Reggie and another MP were both talking and leaning against a MP jeep parked at the personnel entranceway.

"Hey, where are you coming from?" Reggie called out. "I've been looking for you all weekend."

"Down in the ville," Sean answered, somewhat evasive. "How about a ride to the detachment?"

"Sure, hop in," Reggie said and moved into the driver seat and started the jeep. "I'll be right back," Reggie called out to the other MP who waved back in acknowledgement.

Sean climbed in and Reggie took off speaking into the radio microphone.

"Noble, this is one two. I'm giving a courtesy ten-ten to Mike Pappa York to the detachment."

"Roger, Noble clear nineteen oh five."

"So, where've you been?" Reggie asked as they drove away.

"Downtown," Sean answered nonspecifically, taking a deep breath and sighing.

"I know you were downtown dickhead, where downtown?" Reggie persisted.

"What difference does it make, I was downtown, and what are you writing a book?" Sean was looking out the door into space feeling a little annoyed.

"Yeah I'm writing a book, what about it?"

""Well leave out a chapter and make it a mystery."

"Eat shit and die," Reggie laughed and then turned serious, "Now tell me did you take her out?"

"Take who out?" Sean asked unconvincingly.

"Hey, I'm silly not stupid, don't confuse the two," Reggie grinning a knowing grin.

"Yeah I took her out."

"And?"

"And?"

"Well, come on, don't leave me hanging, give me some details."

"Ain't no details. She's a good woman."

"No shit, I know that," Reggie sat back in the seat and started smiling and enthusiastically slammed his hand against the steering wheel. "You've been bit. Damn! It got you too, I can tell."

"Oh yeah? Well why don't you bite me?" Sean replied and started to smile looking out the side of the jeep as they drove.

"Nah, you've been bit man, you're catching the Yellow Fever, I can tell. Ole Doctor Phillips always knows. Don't worry it's not a bad thing." Reggie suddenly turned back into the great Korean expert, "Look, Koreans are great people and the women, man they know how to take care of their man that's for sure. It's like it's in their genes you know?" Reggie looked over all knowing towards Sean as if he were passing along a great secret.

"So you say." Sean was noncommittal.

"So I know. Why do you think this is my third tour here?" Reggie looked over as if expecting an answer. "Hey, in all seriousness, listen to me." Reggie became more serious as he maneuvered through the large trucks parked on the side of the street, "Korean women are great, none better. But, the Korean Fathers not always so. They aren't always cool with daughters marrying a Mi Guk you know, an American? To most of them we are still all barbarians."

"Whoa on the father-in-law shit man, it ain't like that yet."

"Hey, listen to me she's not like a business woman or some casual Yobo. You can tell, she's a classy girl and she's educated too. That means she's from a good family and not just out for a quick time shack job or some sugar GI to take care of her for a year. What's her father do?"

"Runs a factory or something somewhere in Seoul."

"See, that means they have some money and probably some political power too," Reggie let it sink in.

Sean decided to let the comment go and stared straight ahead until they pulled up to the detachment. Sean started to get out as the radio came to life from the back.

"One two, this is Noble," blasted the recognizable New York accented voice of SSG Williams over the radio speaker.

Reggie reached for the microphone that was wrapped around the front hand hold on the dashboard.

"This is one two, detachment area CRC," Reggie answered with his call sign and location.

"Roger one- two, ten one five Hamilton Club, reference fight in progress. Your partner is heading down with unit one-one."

"Roger, in route." Reggie put the microphone down.

"Noble clear at 1915." And the radio went silent.

Reggie looked over at Sean, "It's Sunday night for crying out loud, can you believe it? Fucking GI's." Reggie put the jeep into gear again and shouted, "Hey," as he was backing up, "I picked up your mail yesterday and put it on your desk. Who's that babe in the picture?"

Sean paused for a second to think about his answer. "Just someone I used to know, no biggie," Sean finally answered back and exited the jeep. "Thanks Reg."

"Hey no problem, but word of advice?" Reggie turned his head towards Sean, "Korean women are mighty jealous. Might want to ditch that photo if you know what I mean." Reggie didn't wait for a response; he waved and hit the gas to head downtown to the reported fight.

Sean waved back and started walking into his living area; he could hear the jeep rapidly accelerating down the street. A siren went off in the distance, probably the other MP unit leaving the MP Station headed towards the Hamilton Club and another fight. Sean returned to his bunk and saw several letters and a small package waiting for him. He looked at the small package wrapped in brown paper and recognized Hazel's writing immediately. He knew what was inside, another batch of his favorite chocolate chip cookies, but made with just a few chocolate chips and walnut pieces. He opened it quickly, took a few out of the box, sat down, and began reading her short hand written note:

"My soldier boy, these are for you, so you don't forget us. I love you, Hazel."

Sean knew Hazel's arthritis made even this short note a major effort on her part. The cookies had brought back some wonderful memories of home. He looked over the other letters; he recognized the first two letters right off. They were both in light pink colored envelopes, addressed to him, written in Sharon's dainty hand writing, and he could smell a slight hint of her familiar perfume. He looked at the letter for a long while and then at the picture on the desk. Finally, as if making a decision, he opened the top desk drawer, put the unopened letter and the picture inside and then closed it.

Looking over to the other letters, he saw one was from his Mom and another from Rebecca. He read them both and they were filled with the local happenings and a few pictures. Both included mention of Sharon as if they intended to keep him from forgetting her. He reopened the desk drawer and tossed the other letters onto the pile.

He undressed and took a shower; as the hot water sprayed down onto his head he tried to imagine what his family's reaction would be if he were to bring Pok home. He knew they would have no problem within the army community; there were thousands of Korean wives married to soldiers, it was so common the very idea raised no concern or interest. But he knew it would raise some eyebrows in their small home town, the mixing of any race was not really accepted, although his mom and dad had never openly subscribed to many of the racial sentiments and prejudices of the day back in Mississippi. When integration came to the local schools in the late 60's, the York kids all remained in public school. A lot of the white families decided it would be better to send their kids to a new private school in the area, rather than let them attend school with the blacks. He had no problems attending school or playing ball with any of the blacks, and Ms. Hazel was every bit a part of his family as any of his brothers or sister and he knew his dad loved her as he loved his own mother.

But bringing home a foreigner, he wasn't so sure. He briefly remembered when Aunt Sarah, his dad's sister, brought home Uncle Frank from Illinois. Sarah was in her early 30's at the time, single, never married, and still living at home in the big house with his grandpa. Sarah and Frank had apparently met in Memphis at some club on Beale Street when Sarah went to the city to do some shopping. In the course of knowing each other for only two days they up and got married by a justice of the peace somewhere in Tennessee. It was a scandal for months around their small little town; such things were simply not done, especially marriage in the spur of the moment, presided over by some justice of the peace instead of in the Church.

But the real problem was not because they had met in a bar and eloped to get married without telling anyone. That was bad enough and had created fireworks to match any Fourth of July celebration, but the ultimate atomic bomb was Aunt Sarah had married a *damned*

Yankee. Sean's family was visiting Grandpa's house at the time when Sarah first brought Uncle Frank home and introduced him as her husband. The words from his Grandfather when he shook Frank's hand were very memorable. They were in the 'old old house,' built in the 1850's before it was torn down and the current "big house" was built in the mid 1960's.

"You know the last time someone from Illinois was in this house they tried to burn it down?" Grandpa shook Frank's hand and looked directly into his eyes.

"Well sir," Frank said looking around the living room, "it sure doesn't look like they knew what they were doing."

Grandpa was referring of course to the small Union Calvary detachment that was sent out during the last year of the civil war to destroy the plantations and farms in an effort to ruin the local economy and hopefully the South's ability to continue waging war. In reality North Mississippi was already on its knees and was not contributing very much to the war effort any longer. After bloody defeats at Shiloh, Tupelo, New Albany, Jackson, and Vicksburg the fight was just about out of Mississippi. Some units of Union Calvary were not about interrupting the war effort, they were about punishing and pillaging the local area. They would suddenly appear at a plantation and demand money or simply hold the owners hostage while they ransacked the house. Grandpa's Grandpa and several of the farm hands and slaves demonstrated the mistake of sending out too few troops to do a dirty job when fifteen Union troopers were all killed in a quick and violent confrontation outside the house. They were all then buried unceremoniously in one mass grave in the corner of the family cemetery. A week later a second small detachment showed up to both check up on the other group that seemed to have disappeared and to complete the destruction of the farm and buildings. That second detachment met a similar fate and like their compatriots were all buried in another large mass grave next to the first. The horses, guns, and other equipment from both detachments were provided to the local Confederate Army who was still trying to harass the Yankees. No other Union soldier ever returned to the farm even to find out what happened to either detachment and the York property was one of the few that escaped damage or destruction during the war.

Some things down south were not forgotten so easily, but Uncle Frank managed to hang on and turned out to be quite popular when they eventually moved back home. Sarah received her three acres of York land to which she was entitled, and they built their house. It also helped when they discovered Frank's family was actually involved in the textile business up north. Soon York Cotton was sold at a very good price to Hampton Textile Mills outside of Chicago and eventually they agreed to buy almost their whole crop. Frank was given a position at one of their cotton gins and seemed to have a real knack for running the dirty business. Once he converted to Catholicism, the two were remarried in the church and Sarah's rapid production of four new grandkids helped cement Uncle Frank's merger into the family.

Sean was not so certain what Pok could possibly bring to the family other than she loved Sean and he loved her. He sighed and shook his head wondering why he was even worried about all of that now, any such question was a long way off. Although he was mentally and physically exhausted, he did not sleep well. His mind continued to toss and turn over the preceding weekend with Pok. The morning came far too quickly, announced by the radio alarm. He got up slowly and could hear everyone else in the barracks slowly getting up themselves. It was going to be a long day for sure.

Before he went to bed, he walked over to the desk and picked up Sharon's portrait in the gold frame. He looked over it very quickly and then opened up the bottom desk drawer and set it down. Then picked up a few letters he had received from her and dropped them on top of the picture and frame inside and closed it. He hesitated for just a moment and realized he had turned another page in his life and he was moving forward.

XIV

Almost immediately after guard mount and before he had a chance to even get a cup of coffee or get any breakfast, he received a summons from SSG Whitehouse who was sitting on the desk sergeant platform. Sean walked up to the side of the MP Desk and paused momentarily to look at the soldier sitting in the detention cell, on the long metal bench with his head hung down and arms folded across his chest.. His hair was messed up and there was some blood on the front of his shirt. He looked up as Sean walked by and Sean noticed his puffy, swollen, face, black eye and several stitches over his left eye, looking like he came out the worst of an ass whipping.

SSG Whitehouse pointed back to the D Cell, "Take this soldier up to the 51st Signal Battalion. You know where that's at?" SSG Whitehouse asked, taking another drag from his cigarette.

Sean nodded and looked back at the prisoner who had returned to his head down position.

"Take a jeep and run him up to battalion HQ," he pointed to the D Cell, "and release him back to the rear detachment on a DD 629." SSG Whitehouse handed him three copies of the form all stapled together with sheets of carbon paper in between and continued, "his unit is in the field and couldn't come over to get his ass last night and I want him out of here. I'm not running a damned hotel." SSG Whitehouse tossed him a set of keys for a jeep outside. "Take one-one and then comeback and help the gate until the PX opens, you got ID Check today."

"Sure Sarge," Sean caught the keys and took the form from Whitehouse. The DD FM 629 was a receipt for a detained prisoner used to document the apprehension of a soldier and release back to the unit. Sean read the form and noted the soldier had been apprehended for Drunk and Disorderly conduct, engaging in an affray,

Assault and Battery, and resisting apprehension. Sean put the form in his clipboard and turned for the D cell just as Reggie came out of the small room used for guard mount and writing reports.

"Hey man, good to see you, you look rough," Reggie offered as a greeting.

"Yeah, tough night," Sean smiled.

Reggie motioned to the D Cell and began to explain, "This is the guy from the Hamilton club last night."

"Yeah, what happened?"

"Typical bullshit, couple of engineers started some shit, and ole Broadbench here nearly kicked four of their asses. Then he got sucker punched from someone else and went down. They worked him over pretty good until we got there and broke it up. He punched one ole boy right in the nose man, probably broke it."

"No shit?"

"Yep, turns out he's one of your southern boys from the big city of Bucksnort, Tennessee wherever that is." Reggie smiled.

"Bucksnort?" Sean laughed. "I know where that's at; it's in Tennessee between Nashville and Jackson. Hell, we're almost neighbors."

"Yeah? So check this out, we pick two of them up, this one and the guy with the busted nose, and we haul them both up to the dispensary. The other idiot is bleeding like a stuck pig from the nose, but starts talking some shit on the way inside about catching Broadbench here downtown and how's he and his buddies are gonna fuck him up. Well, ole Broadbench here doesn't say a word but suddenly just takes off running and head butts the boy in the friggin head, knocked him flat out man. I mean he went down like a sack of shit; we had to carry him inside. Ole boy here gets a cut on the head then walks inside, doesn't say a word to anyone." Reggie laughed. "This is one tough motherfucker man."

"No kidding?" Sean smiled listening to the story.

"Yeah, but he's OK, never gave us a hard time," Reggie explained.

"Broadbench," Sean called out to the soldier as he walked up to the D Cell and put the key into the door lock. "Come on, get up, time to go home." Sean turned the key to open the cell door. Broadbench stood up somewhat warily as if trying to regain a sense of balance.

"Do I need to cuff you or are you going to behave?"

"I got no problem with y'all," Broadbench said with a heavy southern accent as he walked outside.

"Well, then y'all take care then. Hurry back now ya hear?" Reggie walked away smiling.

Broadbench and Sean looked at each other and Sean shrugged his shoulders. "OK, come on let's get you out of here. You hungry?"

"I could eat. Coffee would be good."

Sean nodded and they walked outside and drove over to the PX snack bar. Sean got a cup of coffee and a Sausage and biscuit. Broadbench got a coffee and some biscuits and gravy. They both sat down at a table and began to eat.

"You're OK man," Broadbench commented in between bites, "I appreciate it."

"Hey, treat me like a human and I treat you like a human, you know?" Sean answered him back.

"Yeah, makes sense," Broadbench put his finger inside his mouth as if he were checking on one of his teeth. "Man, got a lose tooth."

"Yeah, sucks man," Sean volunteered. "So you took on four guys?"

"Nah, they started some shit with me, I was just sittin' there drinking and chasing some tail."

"Yeah?" Sean took a bite and listened.

"Yeah, some little guy with an attitude. You know, those engineers, they're always talking shit like they are bad asses or something. I stood up, downed my drink, and started to walk out and go to another club.

Then someone threw a bottle at me and hit me on the back." He took another bite and continues talking while chewing. "Well, I turn around and I see the little guy strutting his stuff around like he was some tough guy, you know? So I walked up and just punched his ass. He went down hard and really didn't get back up, so I thought that was it. I started to walk out again."

He interrupted his story to take a drink of coffee, "Well, then the other three guys jumped up like musketeers or something and came at me so, well, I started whooping up on them. I mean, there wasn't any need for any conversation at that point."

"So you kicked all of their asses?" Sean asked incredulously.

"Well, shoot, those were all city boys. I wasn't having all that much trouble. But, I didn't see the fifth one though; he sorta sucker punched me in the right ear with something hard and I went down." He took another bite and slowly chewed and then started again, "When your boys showed up they was working me over pretty bad. No telling what could have happened if they would have had any more time."

They talked for a few more minutes, finished the quick breakfast and then headed out the door back to the MP jeep. Sean almost felt like he was back home riding with one of his neighbors. He was use to country boys guys like Broadbench, who were never really looking to fight, but if someone made the mistake of challenging their manhood, impugn their honor, insult their family, or throw the first punch then you were likely in for the fight of your life.

"Well, sounds like you have a good chance not to get into much trouble," Sean offered as they drove away.

"Well this thing was pretty much self-defense. But," Broadbench looked over at Sean, "But, when I catch the other fella that sucker punched me, that's different. That'll be premeditated." He looked straight ahead and Sean recognized the redneck attitude about settling old scores.

Sean pulled into the parking lot of the battalion, turned off the engine and turned to Broadbench. "I don't guess it would do any good to say just let it go, would it?"

"Nah, not really." Broadbench shook his head and looked away.

"I didn't think so," Sean looked over and smiled. He knew a fair fight was one thing, but the sucker punch required a response, at least a 'one on one' ass whooping. In other more extreme examples, it could mean death. It was just it was for a southern man.

"Well," Sean took a breath, "I can certainly understand what you're thinking and really I can't say I don't agree with you. I don't know, maybe if something like that happened to me, I'd feel the same. Hell I know I would feel the same way. But you know, if you go get that guy, you realize I'll have to come out and apprehend you again."

"Yeah I know," Broadbench seemed resigned to that fate.

"You realize that I'll have to write another MP report and your commander is going to have to do something to you right?"

"Probably," Broadbench shrugged his shoulders.

"But the guy who hit you is probably going to get away with getting his ass kicked while you lose a couple of stripes. Hell, they might even kick you out of the Army. You know we can't have folks going off on their own settling their problems."

"Yeah I guess," Broadbench was agreeing out of politeness not agreement.

"So tell me, you have some good job waiting for you back in Bucksnort, Tennessee that you can afford to get your ass kicked out of the army?"

"Hell, ain't no work back home, you know that."

"Yeah I know. Army's about the best thing we ever had isn't it?" Sean sympathized with him. "Hell, was probably your first store bought shoes, weren't they?"

Broadbench looked over and they both laughed out loud.

"Well, it's the first pair I ever had to shine up," Broadbench sat back and looked as if he went into a deep thought. "Well let me think on it."

"Might be better for you," Sean said. "Look, you have a good case for self-defense for the bar room fight. The part at the dispensary might be touchy, but you have a pretty good chance to walk away with just a slap on the hand. But, it ain't gonna happen if you go after the other guys. Look, why don't you point this guy out to me and let me take care of him? You know who he is?"

"I know who he is." Broadbench nodded to himself as he sat back in the seat and folded arms across his chest.

"Well think on it." Sean pulled out the chain and wrapped it around the steering wheel and locked it.

He met Broadbench around the front of the jeep.

"Ready?"

"Hey," Broadbench called out to Sean and stuck his hand out, "My name's Jamie. Jamie Broadbench."

"Sean York," Sean held his hand out and accepted his and shook it twice.

"I do appreciate you taking the time and you're probably right and all, but it doesn't set too well with me. But I'll think on it."

"Good. Let me know that guy's name and I promise I can take care of him."

Sean released him to the staff duty office and then returned to the MP Station and walked over to the main gate for something to do and to see Pok again. Just a few minutes later he saw Pok walk up; she was dressed in one of Sean's favorite outfits, a very tight fitting and short black leather skirt, with a white blouse, buttoned at the top. Her hair was put into a pony tail. He almost lost his breath when she walked up and smiled at him. He could feel his heart melt.

"Good morning Yobo, you look beautiful today," Sean smiled as he took her pass.

"Yobo?" Pok smiled and mimicked. "You think I'm Yobo?" She looked around to see if anyone else was watching, reaching for Sean's hand holding her pass she placed her hand over his and squeezed slightly. Looking around again, she smiled and whispered, "Maybe so," and then giggled slightly. " I make special dinner tonight, for handsome soldier boy."

"Oh, how nice. Do you want me to find one for you?" Sean teased back and smiled.

"No, I find already. Thank you so much," Pok smiled back and started to walk towards her office.

"You're welcome so much. Maybe I should come by to meet him," Sean called out to her as she walked away.

Pok kept walking but turned around and started walking backwards, "Maybe. But he is big strong soldier boy so be careful."

"That's me, always careful," Sean called out.

"OK, 6:30 please." Pok turned back around and increased her pace.

"OK, 6:30. I'll be there."

"Don't be late," she called over her shoulder one last time and smiled.

Sean watched her walk away and sighed to himself. He ended up spending the remainder of the day working at the main gate. His assignment was changed when one of his squad mates was put on light duty for a sprained ankle and could not be used on patrol or the main gate. Instead he was placed at the Post Exchange. Sean was just as happy to be at the gate where he could at least walk around, get some fresh air, or sit down and take a break. It was going to be a beautiful day and he spent most of his time pacing around just outside the gate shack, thinking about the special dinner waiting for him. The remainder of the day had been uneventful and he was anxiously awaiting a chance to turn in his weapon, change out of his uniform and then catch a ride to Pok's. He planned to stop and buy some flowers at one of the small shops outside the main gate, thinking that it would be a nice surprise. He learned that from his Dad and remembered how pleased his mom always was when she was presented flowers for no reason.

The weather had warmed up and many times the cool breeze that came across the rice patties surrounding the camp brought with it the pungent odor of the human waste that was pumped into the fields by the 'honey wagons' and used to fertilize the rice crops. The thought of fertilizer had him thinking about back home for the first time in a long while. He knew it was a busy time with plowing, planting, and fertilizing their own fields; the weather was also growing warmer back home and the days longer. It made for a pleasant daydream and passed the time.

Six o'clock finally came and Sean was ready to go. Once his relief finally started walking across the street, Sean was already halfway to the MP station. He turned in his weapon and ran out to Reggie who was waiting for him in a jeep in the parking lot. Reggie had offered to wait for him and take him out to Pok's. Reggie drove him up to the detachment area; he ran inside his Quonset hut and quickly changed out of his uniform. Kwan was waiting for his return so he could polish his boots, shine the helmet liner, and deliver his uniform for the next day.

XV

Once changed into blue jeans, tennis shoes, and a pullover shirt, he ran back outside towards the waiting jeep when he noted someone walking out between the Quonset huts towards him in civilian clothes. Sean did not immediately recognize him being part of the MP detachment so he slowed down to a slow walk to see who it was. It was unheard of for anyone else to be walking around the detachment area. Sean was almost upon him before he recognized Broadbench from earlier that morning.

"Hey," Sean began somewhat confused, "What are you doing up here?"

"Looking for you," Broadbench said as he came towards him.

"Yeah, why?" Sean asked as he looked quickly at his watch.

"Wanted to thank you for this morning, you're right. I'm going to let that thing go. No sense to it. My Captain talked to me this afternoon and I told him what all happened. He said exactly what you said. I'm a good soldier, and was just defending myself. So he already told me I'm just going to get a small fine and restriction to Camp for two weeks. If I wouldn't have hit the guy outside the dispensary I probably wouldn't have even gotten a fine."

"Good, glad it all worked out. No sense creating any problems." Sean started walking towards the jeep as if he were ready to break off the conversation and get going.

"I want to thank you," Broadbench called out to him.

"OK, consider me thanked." Sean turned around and reached out his hand to shake hands, "But right now I got to get going."

"Well OK, but I got something to tell you," Broadbench reached out and grabbed a hold of Sean asking him to stop and talk, "and well I'm headed to the field for at least two weeks tomorrow so I gotta tell you now."

"Tell me what?"

"I got some information on criminal activity that you could use."

"Like what?"

"Well I know of a senior NCO who's pimping some female soldiers, selling dope, and loan sharking."

"What?"

"There is a senior NCO, a Sergeant First Class, who is pimping some soldiers. They're selling pussy in the barracks and the NCO is protecting them and taking care of the money."

"Soldiers are prostituting in Korea, the land of prostitutes?"

"Yeah, but this is round eye stuff . You know?"

"All right."

"Well you know some GI's just aren't into the slant eyes and would rather have American; they're willing to pay for it too man. They're making a lot of money."

"OK, but I'm just a uniformed MP, what am I supposed to do about it?"

"Yeah, I know but you know who to talk to and you can get credit. It's my way of saying thanks for talking me out of being stupid."

"Well, I appreciate it, but you need to go to CID man, that shit is beyond me. There's nothing I could do with that."

"I'll be gone for at least two weeks in the field, who knows what might happen? What if some GI gets hurt or something."

"Jamie, man I appreciate it, but…"

"But……I thought you were going to be able to help me. You said give you a name and you'd take care of the guy who hit me. I'm offering you another criminal but you don't have the time for me?"

"Come on man, that's not it. But look, I have to be somewhere and I don't even know what I could do with any information."

"Hey, you can go to CID and tell them, it'll make you look good. I can give you everything, names, dates, places. You cops can go right over and bust them, man."

"Shit Jamie, I don't know if I could do anything, best you go to CID."

"Look, I don't want to get involved with them, I'm not their snitch. I just thought," Jamie let his thought die out and turned to walk away, "I guess I'll go and mind my own business then." Broadbench walked a few steps and then turned around, "I only came to you because you said you were "the man" and I could count on you. You talk big shit dude, but I don't think you can deliver. Guess I am going to have to beat the shit out of that guy after all. Take my chances of getting caught."

Sean looked at his watch then over at Reggie who was sitting in the jeep reading a Stars and Stripes. "All right, look I can at least listen I guess, but I have to make a call first and then we talk and then I'm out of here."

Jamie turned and walked back, "All right, this is going to get you promoted."

"Shit, this is going to get my assed kicked," Sean held the front seat so Broadbench could get into the back bench seat. Reggie drove him back to the MP Station where Sean used the off post Korean telephone to call Pok. He looked at his watch; it was already six twenty-five when he called.

The phone rang twice and Pok answered, "Yoboseyo."

"Hello Yobo," Sean began, not certain exactly what to say looking around at everyone at the desk looking at him.

"Sean? Where are you? Dinner all ready," she responded somewhat sharply.

"I'm sorry, I'm going to be a few minutes late."

There was a slight pause and then a disappointed Pok answered, "OK, how late?"

"Just a few minutes I have to talk to someone, it's very important."

"But I make special dinner for you." The irritation was starting to come through her voice.

"I know and I'll be there soon, just a few minutes late, OK?" There was a longer pause and Sean asked again, "OK?"

"OK, thank you for call." Pok then curtly hung up the phone.

"Korean women don't like to be stood up, this better be good," volunteered Reggie who was leaning up against the elevated platform of the MP Desk.

"Yeah no shit." Sean hung up and walked outside where Jamie was sitting on the jeep hood.

"OK this better be good Jamie, because I just pissed someone off to talk with you," Sean looked over and gave him a stern look.

"Well, all right," Broadbench spoke up and slid to the ground, and took some pieces of paper out of his pocket. Sean pulled out his green memorandum notebook and leaned back against the jeep and started to listen. It was almost an hour later when Jamie finally ran out of gas. It took another 30 minutes to answer questions and get every last detail that Sean could think to ask. As he was listening to Broadbench he realized how far out of his league he was playing. He understood the basic problems and allegations but had no idea how to proceed. He knew he was going to have to coordinate with CID to pass on this information, he had no idea how reliable Broadbench was or how he even got this information in the first place.

They finally parted ways, Jamie walking back to his barracks to get ready to go to the field, and Sean walking quickly back to the MP Station to call Pok and try to get a ride out to her house. He looked at his watch, it was almost eight fifteen.

"Yoboseyo?" Pok answered the phone in two rings.

"Hey, Yobo," Sean started, "I'm sorry I just finished, can I still come over."

"It's late now, I clean up already," Pok explained in an obvious tired and disappointed voice.

"Ah, Ok, I'm sorry I had to do something it was important. But I can still come over?"

"No, not tonight. I tired now go sleep."

Sean wanted to plead his case, but there were too many people around the MP desk.

"OK, I'm sorry I'll see you tomorrow, OK?" Sean asked almost begging.

"OK, maybe see tomorrow," Pok answered abruptly. She quickly hung the phone up, turned and fell face first onto the bed. Had she made such a bad mistake? Was this just a wild weekend of sex for this man? Pok had sought to make a traditional dinner and pamper him and had planned this evening from the time Sean left her arms on Sunday. Monday had been spent on cloud nine, feeling as if a great weight had been removed from her shoulders and the stone wall she had built around her heart had finally been knocked down. Now she was racked again with doubts and fears and didn't know what to do.

Sean stood there looking at the telephone receiver and although he wanted to slam it down onto the cradle out of frustration, instead he carefully up and walked outside into the cool night air. He realized he was hungry and decided to walk off camp to get something to eat. As he walked through the personnel gate, he waved at the MP who was sitting inside reading the Stars and Stripes and to the Korean Security guard that was standing outside in the fresh air. Out the gate, down the main street, and then over the railroad tracks, Sean's thoughts alternated between his personal feelings with Pok and his professional dealings with Broadbench.

Sean understood why Pok was upset; she had probably gone to a lot of trouble. No, not probably, he *knew* the trouble she went through to make him a special dinner and she had every right to be upset. But what was he supposed to do? Could he really ignore what Broadbench was trying to tell him? It was like he was being torn in two by conflicting equally important responsibilities. Of course he wanted to go to Pok's and wanted to be with her. He was even thinking long term and they had just started dating. She was becoming one of the most important things in his life. But there was also the pull towards his duty that had to be answered. This is what he was paid to do, what people expected him to do, to protect them, and to sacrifice himself. After hearing Broadbench's allegations, he was even more convinced that he had done the right thing.

He walked towards the small shop a few hundred yards from the main gate where a Korean family had a small take out stand where you could buy chicken and handmade onion rings, fried in a large wok, heated over a block of coal. The shop stayed open late to catch the drunken GI crowd heading back to camp after a night of drinking and debauchery in the 'ville'. Sean ordered three pieces of chicken and an order of onion rings and then stood outside the small shop leaning against the wall while the food was cooked. If he didn't have to work the next day, he would have had a beer or two just to relax and put his mind at ease. Instead he leaned back and focused on meeting with the CID the next day and passing along the information. He had seen one or two of the agents since he had been at Camp Red Cloud but had never really talked to anyone. He looked over his notebook and suddenly started doubting himself. Here he was a street MP, with no real experience. He thought the information was important, but what if CID wasn't interested? Would they think he was just trying to be a junior "G" man with this stuff?

So, what was he going to do? He poured over his notes again and realized if Broadbench was telling the truth, and he thought he was, then this was going to be some big stuff. CID would be interested all right. He knew he was doing the right thing to pass it along and let CID develop it. The bottom line was clear; he could not be aware of these serious allegations and not report it. Regardless of how it impacted his own relationship with Pok, he had to do the right thing, come what may. His food came. Sean paid for the order and accepted the chicken and onion rings wrapped in several pieces of paper that were already starting to soak in the cooking oil from the food. He looked down at the paper and noticed the paper actually looked like some type of printed material. Walking under a street lamp he examined the printing in the dim light. It was in English and took only a moment to realize that his chicken was wrapped in some soldier's change of station orders, and his onion rings were wrapped in a few pages of a technical repair manual for a hawk missile system. Damn, Sean thought, the Koreans don't waste anything. Both pieces of paper were probably pulled from the trash and recycled to carry his food. He shook his head in wonderment and walked back to Camp lost in thoughts of "what ifs".

On his way back, Sean decided to pick up a six pack of beer, and then get a ride back to the detachment and turn in early. Walking through the main gate he glanced at his watch and noted it was almost closing time for the class VI store located about a hundred yards away. He picked up the pace and as he came up to the store first noticed the taxi cab parked in front of the door, with the engine running. A figure was leaning against the trunk of the taxi smoking a cigarette. As he got closer he recognized the figure as the female clerk from the MP Detachment.

"Bea," Sean called out cheerfully, "What are you doing here?"

Beatrice Finch was a mid 40's petite, red head, and in her earlier life was probably very attractive. But, after five years in the army and three failed marriages, the years were beginning to show. She tried to recapture some of her earlier life and tended to keep her hair dyed to eliminate the gray. She wore too much make up to try and cover up the crow's feet and other wrinkles. Bea was very popular with the other troops in the unit and she went out of her way to take care of 'her soldiers' who affectionately referred to her as 'Mom'.

"Hey," Bea answered back in a slightly raspy voice caused from too much smoking over the years. "What are you doing?"

"Just headed back to the detachment, wanted to get a couple of beers. What are you doing?"

"Oh, just waiting for a ride home," Bea said in a noncommittal voice.

"All right, well I guess I'll see you tomorrow." Sean waved and walked into the small store and over towards the beer coolers. He picked up a six pack of beer and walked to the counter. There was one customer there at the counter whose purchase was being put into a cardboard box. Sean placed the beer onto the counter and then looked over at the other customer. Only then did he recognize him as Sergeant Grubner.

"Evenin' Sarge," Sean greeted Grubner respectfully.

Grubner turned around with what could only be described as a deer in the headlight look and paused for a second before answering, "What are you doing here?"

"Ah just picking up some suds," Sean motioned towards the beer on the counter. "You?"

"Me too. Just picking up a few things," Grubner answered and then looked over at the box in front of the counter. Hw quickly reached out to close the flaps on top, picked it up, and balanced it on his left hip as he got change back from the cashier.

Sean had already glanced over at the seven bottles of various types of liquor inside the box and the three cartons of cigarettes. Normal ration was 4 bottles of liquor a month and four cartons of smokes.

"Looks like you're having a party," Sean offered as Grubner collected his change.

"Nah, just stocking up," Grubner answered him and then started for the door.

"Goodnight Sarge," Sean offered as he opened the door.

"Yeah, goodnight York," Grubner said dismissively over his shoulder as he opened the door and walked outside.

Sean walked the few steps over and looked out of the glass front door. He saw Bea get into the back seat as Grubner and the driver were putting the cardboard box into the trunk. Then they quickly got into the taxi and as if they had just finished a pit stop at a stock car race and were suddenly heading towards the main gate. *That was weird*, Sean thought to himself. It seemed to confirm what had been rumored in the detachment, that Grubner and Bea had a thing going on and were probably shacking up. It sure looked like he was into the black market. That much booze said it all. They would probably be sold to some bar owner downtown for double the price he had paid and then sold back to soldiers by the shot, but no Korean tax paid. Sean shrugged his shoulders as it was of no concern to him what either one of them did on their off duty time. He made his purchase and walked outside, popping a top from the Budweiser, and took a long drink of the beer. It seemed to hit the spot, and after a well-deserved burp, he started the short walk over to the MP Station to look for a ride back to the barracks.

XVI

Oxford MS

"Look ya'll," Rebecca pointed down the side walk at a couple exiting from one of the small shops on the old town Square in Oxford.

"Isn't that Sharon?" Elizabeth asked and leaned slightly forward, squinting as if it would somehow help her see better.

"I think so. Who's she with?" Margaret asked as she squinted to make out her companion.

"I don't know," Rebecca answered as they walked and switched their packages from one hand to the other, "I can't make him out yet."

All four York women Margaret, Catherine, Elizabeth, and Rebecca had decided to get out of the house and get away from their men and the farm for a few hours, and spend a nice spring Saturday morning out with the girls that included shopping and lunch. With Rebecca heading off to Vanderbilt at the end of the summer, these days of getting everyone together were going to be fewer and fewer and they had looked forward to it all week long. Four abreast, they walked slowly up the sidewalk towards Sharon who was talking to a young man while standing on the corner waiting for traffic before crossing the street.

Sharon and the slender young man were talking and laughing oblivious to anyone else around them. Sharon was wearing a pair of blue jean shorts, a pair of tennis shoes and ankle socks. But most notable to the four women coming from behind, was the white football jersey bearing the number 25 with the name YORK spelled across her shoulders in black letters.

"Momma, she's wearing Sean's jersey," Rebecca pointed out to everyone.

"I see that, but who is she with?" Catherine asked.

"Oh my God that's Miles Dorn," Rebecca whispered towards her mother as they continued to walk towards the corner.

"Miles Dorn?" Catherine responded uncertainly. "Is that Richard Dorn's son?"

"Yeah," Rebecca whispered.

"Richard Dorn, the lawyer?" Margaret asked.

"Yeah, he's going to Ole Miss too and then to law school," Rebecca said not very impressed.

"How wonderful, another Dorn lawyer," Catherine whispered to them all sarcastically. "Just what this world needs."

The comment made them all start to laugh and giggle.

"Oh momma, he is so pompous," Rebecca leaned over as if she were telling them all a secret.

"He's been chasing Sharon ever since Sean left for the army," Elizabeth offered.

"Really?" Margaret asked somewhat irritated.

"Oh yeah, he's been like a puppy dog in heat," Elizabeth explained.

They were within a few feet of the corner when Sharon turned around and saw the four women walking up behind her. She was somewhat surprised but immediately broke out into a smile and called out "Hey you guys!" She turned full around and opened her arms and gave each one a hug and pat on the back in turn in true southern style. "Hey Miss Catherine."

"Hi Honey," Catherine responded and kissed her on the cheek. Sharon turned to the next in line.

"Hey Becca," Sharon said and reached out to give another hug.

"Hey yourself," Rebecca gave a warm hug back.

Followed by Margaret and a special hug to Elizabeth

"Hey cuz," Elizabeth smiled and patted her on the back.

"What are you guys doing here?" Sharon asked as she stepped back to take them all in.

"Well we decided to leave our men folk out in the field and go spend all their money in the big city," Catherine responded and smiled, looking first at Sharon and then towards Miles who had walked back a few steps but remained in the background.

"Hey Ms Catherine," Miles finally decided to break a momentary silence.

"Miles, isn't it?" Catherine reached out her hand which was taken by Miles.

"Yes ma'am," He took her hand shook it twice and then looked over at Rebecca and Elizabeth and raised his hand in a greeting, "Hey Becca, Hey Beth."

"Hey Miles," Rebecca and Beth answered together but unenthusiastically, in the southern forced politeness.

"Miles, I'm Margaret, James's wife." Margaret stepped forward and thrust out her hand and looked him in the eye and smiled. But it wasn't really a friendly smile as much as it was a warning smile, about like a rattlesnake that was warning of a potential strike.

"Nice to meet you," Miles shook her hand and began to flush and retreated a few steps back uncertain what to do next.

Not wanting anyone to think that she was actually out on a date with Miles, Sharon volunteered, "Miles and I were just hanging around killing time until I have to go to work in an hour."

"Well it's a nice day for it," Catherine smiled back to keep a conversation going.

"Yes ma'am, going to get hot though," Miles volunteered the obvious and then looked around at the other four women, who all looked back at him in silence with polite smiles.

"What a putz," Rebecca leaned over to whisper to Margaret, who tried not to smile and nudged her with her elbow.

Miles looked over and saw the whisper and nudge between the two and decided his best tactic was to retreat and make himself small, so he put his hands into his back pockets and stepped back, feeling very much as if he had interrupted something.

It was all Rebecca could do to remain calm, when she really wanted to put Miles into a head lock and throw him to the ground like a steer at branding time. It was a shared telepathic thought between Margaret although she thought he only needed to be punched in the face. Elizabeth was still trying to figure out the attraction Sharon might have to Miles Dorn. Although Sean and Sharon were not officially together anymore, none of the York women had ever really accepted the idea that they would never be together.

"Have you heard from Sean?" Rebecca finally asked and looked past Sharon towards Miles who looked down to the street and then suddenly became interested in the passing traffic.

"Well, not recently, I got a couple of letters from him after he first got over but there nothing recently. I guess he seems to like it over there. I don't know why. He did send a couple of pictures when he first got there." Sharon answered. She set her shopping bag onto the ground and then opened her purse and pulled out an envelope with several pictures inside. She handed them over to Catherine, "Take a look."

"Well thank you honey, we've only gotten one or two ourselves when he first got there." Catherine looked over the few pictures taking a quick look and then handing them over to the other girls. "Sean's not so good at letter writing, if we ever get one or two pages we consider that a major accomplishment."

"Wow, Momma he's lost all that weight, he looks good," Rebecca noted and passed the pictures one at a time over to Margaret and Elizabeth who then handed them back.

"Well," Catherine spoke as she finished the last of the photos, "we were on our way over to some lunch would you care to join us?" Catherine asked Sharon.

"Sharon, please come I haven't see you in such a long time," Rebecca insisted

"I'd love to ya'll, but I have to go to work in a little while, I just snuck out to get a few things for my apartment."

"Apartment?" Elizabeth asked.

"Yeah I'm sharing an apartment with a couple of other girls from the sorority. I can't seem to get any studying done at the Sorority house," Sharon explained.

"Well, I guess we're going to run then." Catherine decided it was time to go, "You kids be careful."

"Yes ma'am," Miles responded, grateful at their departure.

Sharon walked up and gave Catherine another long hug and spoke quietly into her ear, "Miss Catherine, if you hear from Sean, can you ask him to write? I miss hearing from him."

"I will honey," Catherine responded to the big hug and answered quietly, "I'm sure he misses you too."

XVII

SSG Whitehouse was sitting up on the MP Desk Platform, the omnipresent cigarette burning next to him in the ashtray already piled high and overflowing with previously extinguished butts. He was leaning over the manual typewriter, an eraser pencil clenched in his teeth, deeply engaged in the quick but inaccurate tap, tap, tapping with two fingers on the typewriter. Sean came and stood by until he stopped for a second to wait for Whitehouse to make a correction. Sean knew it wouldn't be that long of a wait. As if on cue, Whitehouse let out with an exasperated "Shit," and grabbed the pencil out of his mouth and started to erase the original followed by the six other carbon copies of the report.

"Hey Sarge, I need a few minutes this morning, I have to drop by CID," Sean quickly inserted himself into Whitehouse's thought process.

"Yeah? What for?" Whitehouse asked leaning forward and blowing the eraser debris off the page. He took a drag from the cigarette and blew the smoke into the stagnant cloud hovering above his workspace.

Sean continued, "I picked up some information last night and I need to pass it on." Sean waved his hands back and forth in front of his face to break up some of the smoke.

"God damn it," SSG Whitehouse spat out to no one in particular as he misspelled another word. Reaching up, he took the staple puller and removed the staple holding the original and six carbon pages together and repeated the erasing exercise. He looked over briefly at Sean and asked, "Are you sure you don't know how to type?"

"Not me Sarge," Sean denied emphatically. He threw both hands up as in self-defense and started to back up towards the door.

"You know what? I think you're bullshitting me," Whitehouse shouted at him as he tried to make an escape, "You're getting ready to make sergeant, you need some training on this friggin typewriter and I need a break." Whitehouse continued to swear to himself as he tried to realign the pages together and continue to type. "So you just might find your happy ass up here pretty soon. Now leave me alone, I got to get this shit done by this afternoon."

Sean retreated from the desk and heard SSG Whitehouse swear again as he made yet another mistake. Looking up at the clock on the wall he noted that Pok should be coming through the gate soon. He decided to try and catch her and talk with her before she made it to the office and so many other people were around. He only had to wait a few minutes before Pok walked through the personnel gate.

"Good morning," he asked tentatively as she walked through the gate.

"Good morning, how are you?" she replied in a dispassionate manner and then looked down as if she were embarrassed.

"I'm sorry about last night," Sean tried to offer his apology.

"OK, I forgive." Pok looked up at him and then quickly back down as she tried to walk away.

"Can I take you to lunch today?" Sean asked.

"I have a lot of work today. I bring lunch," Pok said holding up a small paper sack as she continued to walk.

"Look, I'm sorry; I know you made a nice dinner for me, but this isn't the end of the world. Can I please can I take you to lunch?" Sean implored and reached out his hand to get her to stop walking.

Pok paused a moment in the middle of the street and tried a thin smile of surrender. "OK, I would like that,"

"OK, I'll come by and pick you up around noon, OK?" Sean asked in the form of a question not certain of her response.

"OK, I see you later." she answered somewhat non-committal, but her ambivalent remark hid her excitement and relief over seeing Sean again and hearing his voice.

Sean took a deep breath as she walked away. He could tell that she was still upset; obviously the dinner the previous evening had been something special and he knew he would have to eat some humble pie, but it would be worth it.

Sean paced around the main gate helping check passes and ID cards of the various Korean employees as they came to work and of soldiers returning back from their night in the 'ville', or downtown. He was passing time until he could go to the CID office and unload the information still spinning around in his brain. Finally, at 0800, Sean walked back to the MP Station, opened the side door and called, "Sergeant Whitehouse, I'm going to CID."

"Don't be gone all day." Whitehouse yelled back and started cussing again.

Sean jumped into the patrol jeep and in a minute was parking in front of the small cinderblock building with a white metal sign identifying its occupants as the Camp Red Cloud Branch Office, 7th Region, USACIDC. He straightened up his uniform and walked inside the front door. He was greeted by a Korean female secretary and another black SGT both typing away on manual typewriters.

"May I help you?" The female asked looking up from her work.

"Yes ma'am. I'd like to talk to an agent please," Sean didn't know what else to say.

"Do you know which one?" she asked perfunctorily.

"No ma'am. I don't think it matters, just a CID Agent."

"OK, one moment please." She stood up and walked to the back of the building down a short hall and into another smaller office. She returned moments later and waved to Sean to come back to her. As Sean approached, she pointed to the office for him to enter.

Sean entered the smaller office which consisted of two straight back metal chairs and a metal double pedestal desk with several piles of manila folders stacked on top. Behind the desk was an older man, heavy set to the point of being overweight, dressed in a tight fitting white long sleeve shirt and red tie, wearing black framed glasses with very large and thick lenses.

"Morning. I'm Mr. Bateman. What can I do for you Specialist?" Bateman asked and leaned back in his chair giving Sean a critical once over.

Sean walked partway into the office and could smell the stale smell of cigarette smoke. "Good Morning, Sir, I'm Specialist York from the MP's," Sean felt awkward reporting on the obvious, "eh, last night I picked up some information that I think might be of interest to CID."

"You did, huh?" Bateman made a motion to come into the office and sit down in the straight back chair located to the left of the desk. At the same time he reached for the open pack of cigarettes on the desk, placed a cigarette into his mouth and struck his Zippo lighter to the end. The desk was suddenly covered in blue cigarette smoke forcing Sean to lean back slightly as the smoke wafted towards him.

"Let's hear what you got," Bateman directed and took a deep drag from the cigarette, the end glowing red.

"Well sir, it's about a senior NCO and an Officer involved in criminal activity," Sean looked over to judge the interest level.

"Go on," Bateman seemed a little uninterested.

"Well, I had a soldier tell me last night that this NCO," Sean looked down at his notebook, "a Sergeant First Class and," Sean leafed quickly through his other note pages, "a First Lieutenant are involved in some criminal activity and wanted to report it." Sean looked over at Bateman.

"OK, you said that already. So what type of criminal activity?" Bateman leaned back and took another drag on his cigarette.

"Well the Sergeant is involved in some loan sharking and running some prostitutes," Sean stated but was interrupted.

"Hold on a second," Bateman continued to puff on his cigarette, "You don't have any personal knowledge of this alleged criminal activity?"

"No sir, I had another soldier tell me about it last night."

"I see," Bateman responded rather nonplused, "let me get this straight, you're a uniformed MP and an informant tells you about some nefarious criminal activity last night?"

"Yes sir," Sean answered and shrugged his shoulders. "Well, no. I mean, I don't know about an informant, he was just a guy I know." Sean really didn't know if it was nefarious or even what nefarious actually meant.

"Well what is your Informant's name? Who gave you this information?" Bateman flipped his ashes in the general direction of his ashtray on his desk but they fell short and hit the desk.

"Well, he only told me the information after I promised not to tell you his name," Sean answered.

Bateman straightened up and leaned forward, "Well, we'll need to talk to your source ourselves."

"Well he didn't want to talk to you himself; not you personally," Sean tried to point out, "just CID in general. It's kind of complicated you know?"

"No, I don't know. You say this other soldier has information on some criminal activity, OK fine, then I need to talk to this other soldier. No sense wasting my time with you."

"Well, can't I just give you the information and you can do whatever you need to do to check it out?" Sean asked.

"No, it doesn't work that way." Bateman began to raise his voice as if he were trying to intimidate Sean. "Specialist, how it works is, I ask you questions and you give me answers. Now you say you have information on a criminal act, well I want to hear about it. But I'm not playing any guessing games here, not with some uniform MP who is trying to be some kind of a super cop." Bateman leaned back again and let his words sink in. "You know what we call that? It's called Obstruction of Justice or Misprision of a Felony. In other words, you have information about a crime and fail to tell us about it. That's a criminal act in itself."

Bateman leaned back in his chair and took another deep drag of his cigarette, exhaling the smoke directly at Sean and filling the small office with another cloud of smoke. Sean looked over at him and started to smile. He could feel his blood start to boil and he took a deep breath to try and calm down. His brain was swimming from being ambushed by Bateman's attitude. Here he was trying to give information to CID and he was being treated as if he somehow had committed a crime. His eyes were diverted to a photograph frame sitting on the end of his desk. Sean looked over and could tell it was Bateman and a Korean female; it was a standard wedding type photograph but it made Sean briefly think of the saying, even Godzilla can get laid in Korea for twenty bucks.

"Well?" Bateman said impatiently as the long ash from his cigarette fell off onto his tie, causing him to quickly rise up and start to brush off the hot ash with his hand.

Sean was about to stand up and walk out of the door when his thoughts were interrupted by a voice from outside the office.

"Bateman," a voice from down the small hallway called out.

"Yeah," Bateman answered and leaned forward to crush out his cigarette. He looked at his tie to see if it was burnt.

"Chief wants to see you. And bring your PX file," the unknown voice called out.

"I got an interview going on here," Bateman called back and looked over at Sean.

"Send him over here, I'll finish up, but go see the Chief right now," the voice replied.

"All right," Bateman stood up and reached for one of the manila file folders on his desk. "Come with me," he said to Sean.

Sean stood up and hesitated for a few moments not certain if he wanted to stay or if it would be better to just walk out the door and go back on routine patrol. He put his pride in his pocket and decided to try again. He followed behind Bateman who seemed to waddle more than walk as they went down the small hallway to the next office. At the doorway, Bateman turned around and extended his arm into the office inviting Sean inside. Once inside, Bateman leaned against the doorframe and folded his arms across his chest. Sean was wondering to himself if he had made a good decision to even come by the CID. The reception was not quite what he had expected.

The younger and taller man sitting down behind his desk was wearing a long sleeve blue shirt and red tie and a suit jacket draped across the back of his chair. The desk top was clear except for a single manila file folder opened before the man. Towards the right side of the desk sat another man in a straight back chair.

Bateman then turned to York, "This is Agent O'Toole and this is agent O'Brien." Then to the other agents he introduced Sean, "This is Specialist York from the local MP's. He says he has some information for us but won't give it up. I was about to throw his ass out of here and call his commander."

Sean turned around to face Bateman and wanted desperately to say something in response. But the other man sitting in the straight back chair also dressed in a suit and tie caught his eye and he shook his head. He held up his hand as if asking Sean to hold his tongue and motioned for him to sit down in the empty chair in front of the desk. Sean nodded, sat in the chair and faced the man introduced as O'Toole behind the desk. He put the chair's arm rest into a death grip. There was an awkward moment of silence before the man behind the desk looked up at Bateman who was still leaning against the door frame.

"Chief's waiting for that file," O'Toole finally spoke to break the silence.

"Yeah, let me know if you have any trouble with this guy," Bateman came off the door frame but still had his arms folded on his chest, "I know the Detachment Sergeant down there real well."

"OK, I will," O'Toole smiled back. "Hey, why don't you shut the door on your way out?"

Bateman nodded in agreement and walked into the hallway and shut the office door. O'Toole waited a few seconds until he could hear him walk down the hallway.

"You got to be shitting man," O'Brien finally spoke from behind Sean.

"See what I mean?" O'Toole said looking over at O'Brien who was shaking his head in almost disbelief.

"York," O'Toole stood up and reached out his hand across the desk to greet Sean, "I'm Tom O'Toole and this is Pat O'Brien; we're what is known as the Irish Mafia in CID."

Sean looked back and smiled.

"York, ..."O'Toole contemplated for a second, "You Irish?"

"Scotch-Irish." Sean smiled back.

"Hell, aren't we all?" O'Brien laughed.

O'Toole leaned forward on his desk with his forearms on the desk top "Look, Bateman is....well a little high strung. He means well but he is lacking a little in the fine arts of human conversation," O'Toole tried to explain. "So he's a little rough."

"He's a penis with ears," O'Brien offered as another opinion. They all laughed and Sean suddenly felt a lot more comfortable.

"I understand you have some information," O'Toole brought out a tablet and pen and motioned for Sean to begin. "Whatcha got?"

"All right," Sean looked at both agents and began again, "as I was telling the other agent, I got this from a soldier last night. I just met the guy so he's not like an informant or anything; just a guy I helped out and he gave me this information. He said, well, he said it would make me look good, you know?"

"Make you look good?" O'Brien asked.

"No, well, I mean this is what he said when he gave me the info that it was so good it will make me look good, you know? As if I was somehow going to make an arrest myself or something. But, look, this is beyond me, I just want to give you guys the information and then you do what you got to do. I don't even know if it's true or not. I don't even know how to check it out. I'm just trying to do the right thing here."

O'Brien and O'Toole looked at each other and then back to Sean.

"OK, I can live with that, let's hear it," O'Brien spoke.

Sean then opened up his memorandum book and started to relate the facts as Broadbench gave him.

"All right, this is about a Sergeant First Class Bishop, he's a black male, platoon Sergeant over in the Supply and Transportation Battalion at Camp Sears. He lives in," Sean looked through his notes, "Building 501, room 10." Sean looked up and saw O'Toole writing notes on the tablet and then continued, "According to this soldier, he's running four female soldiers who are all assigned to his platoon, as prostitutes."

Sean paused a moment while O'Brien scooted his chair closer to him.

"Go on man, I'm sorry I just wanted to hear this," O'Brien said as he sat down and glanced over at O'Toole who was busy making notes.

Sean continued, "Well he runs them out of room," Sean looked at his book again, "out of the Headquarters Company Barracks, rooms 210, 212, 214, and 218. It supposedly costs $50 dollars for a shot of pussy or $25 for just a blow job. I guess there are other things you can get up to $100." Sean flipped the page over and looked up, not sure if he needed to continue.

"Tommy," O'Brien broke into Sean's story and stood up. "I'm going to go get the raw data file from last month."

O'Toole nodded as O'Brien stood up and walked towards the office door.

"All right," O'Toole began, "go ahead man, I'm listening. ut first, what's your first name?"

"Sean"

O'Toole scribbled onto the tablet. "OK, Sean, me boy, continue. I am all ears." O'Toole spoke in a terribly fake Irish accent with his pen poised over the tablet.

"Well," Sean looked back down at his memorandum book, "It works like this. On paydays, Bishop and another soldier named LaShaun Belk, they call him L.A, he's with the 1st of the 15th Field

Artillery at Camp Stanley, I don't know which battery..." Sean looked up to see O'Toole writing his own notes, "Ok, so on paydays, they throw the regular soldiers out of their rooms in the barracks and, well the girls move into their rooms. They sell pussy from like 2000 hours until just before midnight. Bishop collects the money and Belk keeps the peace so to speak or settles any disputes. There's at least one other soldier, maybe two others, also over at Camp Stanley that are involved," Sean paused and leafed through his notebook, "Shit, I guess I forgot to ask who they were. Sorry about that."

"Don't worry about it." O'Toole broke in. "What do you mean they force the soldiers out of their own rooms?"

The door opened up and O'Brien came inside. He had a file opened and marked.

"Excuse me one second." He gave the file over to O'Toole who found the marked spot and began to read. When he was finished he looked up and then over at Sean.

"Sorry, what about throwing the soldiers out of their own rooms?"

"Well, the guy says, on paydays they physically make those soldiers leave their rooms for four or so hours, you know when they are prostituting there. The soldiers have to go somewhere else during that time. The guy said, when it first started, the occupants each got a reduced rate and got to go first with the girls. But now, because they all owe Bishop so much money they are just told to get the fuck out and come back at curfew when the business is closed out."

"So this operates only on paydays?"

"I don't know. I guess it operates in the barracks during the whole payday weekend. According to my friend, you can make an appointment with Bishop and he makes an arrangement somehow if you want something through the week. The guy only knew you could make an appointment to buy some pussy but didn't know how that worked."

"So how is it that Bishop can keep something like this going and no one reports it?"

"Well, I asked him that because you know I thought someone would eventually make a complaint. My guy said that Bishop was pretty intimidating, and could make your life easy or hard as the platoon sergeant. But that this guy Belk, and the others from Stanley would just beat the shit out of you if you couldn't pay or if you got out of line, or if they thought you were going to rat them out."

O'Toole nodded in understanding and made more notes, "You said they were loan sharking?"

"Yeah," Sean turned the pages back towards the front and started to read from the notes again, "you know GI's they can never keep any money, so they're always doing short term loans between each other. OK? So, Bishop set himself up like a credit union you know. The GI gets a loan of twenty bucks, and when payday comes you pay back thirty. You take fifty bucks you pay back seventy-five. They're supposed to be paid back every payday, but if the soldier is short, Bishop accepts an interest only payment of like ten dollars or whatever the interest is supposed to be, but then carries the loan over to the next payday."

"So the next payday the soldier is still expected to repay the original thirty dollars?" O'Brien said out loud.

"Yeah, but in the meantime, these soldiers sometimes end up taking another loan, because, you know, they can't manage their money anyway. So they're now looking at sixty dollars or more to repay. But most are only able to make the interest payment of like twenty dollars now, for the two original loans of forty dollars," Sean explained while looking at his notebook.

"So literally we have guys that are never paying off their loans to Bishop." O'Toole leaned back and started thinking. "They're just getting further and further in debt, without ever paying off the actual loan."

"Yeah. That's the problem. If they decide to say anything then someone comes around and beats them up. But, my friend said there is a way for the soldiers to clear their accounts."

"How so?" O'Toole asked.

"Well, that he didn't say exactly. He said he just he knew they were able to do something and then the debt was repaid, but no details."

"All right, what about the girls?" O'Brien asked.

Sean looked through his notebook again and sighed in frustration, "I would assume they're assigned to one of the units on Camp Sears but that's just a guess. I don't think I asked that either, sorry." Sean looked around the room. "This all sort of took me by surprise."

"No problem, we can sort it out." O'Toole was scribbling notes rapidly and continued to write as he tried to confirm, "but they're soldiers, right?"

Sean shrugged his shoulders again, "I'm pretty sure that's what he said, but I don't have it written down."

"All right, what about the drugs? You said they were doing drugs, too?"

"Oh yeah," Sean picked his memorandum book up again and flipped through the pages until he found the right entry. O'Brien and O'Toole looked at each other and nodded affirmatively.

"Well, they're supposedly selling marihuana in dime and quarter bags, nothing bigger. But that's mostly this guy Belk and some other GI from Camp Stanley. But, it's Bishop that's supposed to have the contact with some Korean who either works on Camp Sears or from downtown somewhere and so he gets a piece of the action."

As Sean was flipping through his memorandum book and going over his information with O'Toole and O'Brien, SFC Grubner happened to drive by the CID Office in the Detachment Commander's jeep. He observed the MP patrol jeep parked in front of the CID office and turned his head towards the office as he drove slowly by. He couldn't see inside but hadn't heard any units call out of service or be dispatched to the CID office. It made him wonder. He returned to the PMO and upon entering walked directly up to Whitehouse who was still trying to type out his report.

"Whitehouse, whose vehicle is that over at CID right now?" Grubner asked.

"Probably York's," Whitehouse answered back without looking up and continued to type.

"What's he doing there?"

"I don't know, he said he had something to pass onto them." Whitehouse looked up with the eraser still in his mouth.

"What does he have to pass onto CID?"

"I don't know I didn't ask." Whitehouse looked back down to the typewriter and continued to type.

"You didn't ask?" Grubner asked in a rather condescending tone.

Whitehouse removed the eraser from his mouth and he leaned forward in his chair, "Hey Top is there a problem? One of my guys says he has something for CID, so I sent him to CID. I mean what the fuck over? Who gives a shit?"

Grubner didn't reply but looked back at Whitehouse who had already dismissed Grubner in his mind and resumed his position over his typewriter. Grubner flushed a bright red with the passive snub, did an about face and walked rapidly back into his office and closed the door. He threw himself into his chair behind his desk and thought how much he hated CID and these MP's who were always such "holier than thou" types.

When he was in his first assignment in Germany, CID had tried to work a case on him for black-marketing. He was a medic back then working in a small troop clinic and they had come right out and accused him of selling American cigarettes and whiskey to one of the local bars outside the Kasern in Schweinfurt . They had tried to put him through the ringer, but they could never prove anything. He was black-marketing of course, but not to really make any money. He was trying to date the owner's daughter and well, he bent a few rules. It wasn't as if he were stealing, so as far as he was concerned, it was no harm, no foul. But the experience had left a bitter taste in his mouth towards anything CID and their little brothers the MPs. It was irony that some ten years later he found himself in military law enforcement. It certainly was not by choice, it was mostly the lesser of two evils. He was on orders back to Viet Nam assigned to a Divisional medical unit, which meant a return to the field and fighting and a chance to get killed. Instead, he took an option to change MOS and go to another school and thus get out of his orders. The only thing really available that didn't send him back to a combat unit was the MP's. So he re-enlisted and took a new MOS and set up some long term plans to eventually return to the medical field. Rank came faster than he anticipated and he found himself promoted out of a chance to return to his original MOS.

So Grubner was stuck where he didn't want to really be. The mere fact that he was engaged in black-marketing again while he was in Korea didn't cause him to lose any sleep at night. Again it wasn't for profit, it was just to help pay for an apartment that he shared with Bea downtown. But he was worried about some young snot-nosed, straight laced MP who had it out for the detachment sergeant and would keep book on him waiting for a chance to drop a dime on his activity as a way to get back at him. He considered Sean to be one of those young punks. Grubner lit another cigarette, flipped his rolodex around until he found the number he was looking for and dialed it. Seconds later he could hear the phone ring.

A voice answered after a few rings, "CID Bateman."

"Robert," Grubner responded, "this is Grubner at the PMO. What are you up to?"

"Hey, just doing some paperwork, you know the drill," Bateman chuckled into the phone.

"Yeah I sure do. Hey, tell me, you have one of my soldiers down there, is he in any trouble?"

"One of your soldiers? Oh, yeah, York is down here, said he had some information he wanted to pass along about some Sergeant First Class and some Officer involved in something together."

"A Sergeant First Class and an Officer, did he say who or what about?" Grubner asked and took another drag from his cigarette.

"Nah, not that I know, sounded like BS to me anyway. I passed onto one of the new guys. You know I got too much shit on my own plate."

"All right. Hey, let me know what he was talking about, OK?"

"Yeah sure, will do. What's the problem?" Bateman responded.

"Well York is a problem child down here, so you have to take anything he has to say with a grain of salt. Just be careful with anything he might tell you."

"All right, I'll pass it along. It sounded like it was going to be bullshit to me anyway."

"All right,, well thanks for the info. Anything comes up let me know please," Grubner took on last deep drag from his cigarette and then crushed it out.

"Sure, will do," Bateman responded and then they both hung up.

Motherfucker, Grubner thought to himself as he put down the phone onto its cradle. He tried to recall if he had ever come into contact with York before the previous night when he was with Bea or when he was at the Post Exchange. Whenever he was going to do any black-marketing, he always took a jeep over to Camp Stanley or one of the other smaller camps scattered throughout their area or hit the CRC Post exchange at closing time when most of the patrols were downtown. He recalled running into him once over at Camp Stanley with Bea in the jeep, but they were on an authorized dispatch and they had never actually talked to him that day. He decided until he found out what York was chattering about, he and Bea would have to redouble their effort to be more careful. No way was he going to let some snot-nosed MP get him into trouble, he was looking at E-8 next year and with two more years until he could pull the pin and retire. Grubner stood up and paced back and forth in his office thinking of his options. He decided to make the first strike and walked over to the Commander's Office and knocked.

"Come in." Captain Cruz called out from inside.

Grubner opened the door and walked inside and closed it behind him.

"Hey Top what's up?" Captain Cruz dropped his ink pen down on the desk and put his hands behind his head and leaned back in his chair.

"I think we got a problem." Grubner started to pace in front of the Captain's desk.

"Yeah, how so?" The commander straightened up and was all ears.

"I think we got a snitch in this detachment," Grubner came to a stop and turned to face Cruz.

"A snitch?" Cruz repeated, not certain he understood.

"Yeah, a little shithead that drops a dime on his chain of command if he doesn't get his way."

"Top, what are you talking about?"

"I'm talking about York, that fucking pain in the ass York."

"York?" The Commander looked at him incredulously. "What would York have to complain about?"

"Doesn't have to be anything, to get CID involved you only have to make allegations, innuendo, or just fucking lie about it." Grubner was turning red but was trying to remain in control, his heart starting to race.

"Top, I'm still not following you. Would you calm down and explain yourself?"

"Look, York is over at CID right now, I just talked to one of those guys I know who works there. He's making a complaint against a Sergeant First Class," Grubner pointed index finger at his chest, "and against an Officer," Grubner pointed his index finger at the Commander.

"But about what? What has he got to complain about?"

"Well he's upset at me because I ordered him to leave Miss Park alone. He was sniffing around there like she was in heat or something and she couldn't get any work done, and I don't think she was as interested as he thought she was. She mentioned something about being uncomfortable around him."

"So, you think he's upset because you told him to leave Miss Park alone?" the commander asked.

"Could be. I know he was upset, you know I got eyes and ears in this detachment. I know what everyone is doing, that's how I knew he was up there at CID running his mouth and destroying our careers."

"Well I just don't see what he would really have to complain about."

"Well, how about you and your little girl from the Million Dollar Club?"

"What?" the commander asked and started to turn red.

"Think he doesn't know about her?"

"What do you mean?" Cruz was suddenly paying attention as his face was now beet red.

"Look sir, didn't you mention running into him while he was on town patrol a couple of weeks ago right?" Grubner let the thought sink in. "Hey sir, even in Korea there is a thing called Adultery, and for you there's Conduct Unbecoming an Officer; which if you look in the UCMJ it includes associating with known prostitutes." Grubner leaned over the desk and stared straight at the Captain.

"So what do we do?" Cruz asked still not totally convinced but was running possible consequences through his mind. He wasn't really worried about the Army, but what would his wife say?

"Sir, you just leave it to me. Just be careful out there, don't give him any more ammunition and I'll take care of you like always."

"OK Top, you handle it." Cruz nodded in agreement uncertain exactly what Grubner had in mind.

"Yes sir," Grubner stood up, walked out of the office and returned to his where he closed the door, lit a cigarette and pondered his next move.

After a short break the CID agents continued talking with Sean now very eager to listen to what he had to say.

O'Toole began, "Now what about the Lieutenant? You said that some Lieutenant was involved. How so?"

Sean adjusted in his seat, "Well I got the impression that he was maybe like protecting Bishop by not making him do his job or whenever someone made a complaint he told the soldiers to shut up and then told Bishop. Bishop then would talk to the soldier himself."

"OK, got a name?" O'Brien asked without looking up from his notes.

Sean looked down at his notes, Prichard. Lieutenant Prichard. I think he works down at the motor pool." Sean continued answering question after question for over an hour before finally reaching the point where he had nothing further to offer and neither O'Brien nor O'Toole could think of anything else to ask him.

"All right, you did good, but we're eventually gonna have to talk to this guy who gave all this to you." O'Brien finally said.

It was the moment that Sean knew was coming, "Well I sort of gave my word I wouldn't tell anyone who he was." Sean put the memo book back in his pocket and looked between O'Brien and O'Toole.

"Well, I appreciate that, but we need to talk with him and see where he's getting his information," O'Brien persisted.

"Well, I gave my word," Sean looked down on the floor not sure of his position and certainly didn't want to create a problem. O'Brien stood up next to Sean and looked over at O'Toole who was listening with his elbows on his desk and hands folded together, chin resting on them both. O'Toole shook his head briefly and O'Brien stepped back.

"All right, we'll see what we can do. We have enough for right now; if it becomes important, we'll be in touch. Fair enough?" O'Toole looked at Sean who nodded readily in agreement.

"All right, well we got a lot of work to do to check this all out. Obviously you don't need to be talking with anyone about any of this."

"Sure I can keep my mouth shut. All right, well thanks guys I hope this all works out." Sean was relieved to have it all off of his chest so he could go about his life.

"All right, but if you talk to your friend again, ask him to come in and talk himself, OK?"

"Yes Sir, will do," Sean stood up and shook both of their hands and walked out of the office towards the front door.

O'Toole held up his notes to Sean, "No matter what happens or how it turns out you did good. You picked up some good information then passed it right on. That's the way we're supposed to be working together. I'll have to remember you." O'Toole patted him on the shoulder.

"Good job, York," O'Brien reached out and shook his hand. Sean walked out of the office and back into his jeep. He felt both relieved to have passed the information onto CID and then exhilarated that they had genuinely thought he had done a good job. He felt on top of the world. Looking at his watch, he realized he had spent almost the entire morning at their office. He had to get to the PMO and take Pok to lunch.

After Sean drove away, O'Brien and O'Toole closed the door and looked at each other almost in disbelief. Then without uttering a word, they walked directly back to the Special Agent in Charge's or the SAC's, office.

"Chief," O'Toole began as he walked into the open doorway. "You're not going to believe this." He made a motion for O'Brien who was following him in. O'Brien turned around the shut the door.

CW3 Robert Stack was affectionately known as Elliot Ness to the CID Community, based on the old TV show, The Untouchables. Stack was the Special Agent in Charge of the CID office at Camp Red Cloud and had been in CID since the mid 70's. He had seen it all, from working Check Point Charlie as an MP in Berlin in 1961 when the Berlin Wall was actually built, to cutting his teeth as one of the agents assigned to work on the famous Kaki Mafia case, involving the theft of money from the Club system by senior NCOs throughout Viet Nam. He worked against one of the most senior NCO who would actually become the Sergeant Major of the US Army, the top enlisted man in the entire army, before he was arrested and court martialed. He had a smaller role in the Mi Lai mass murder investigation when he interviewed a lot of the soldiers who had already returned to the US.

Stack ran a pretty tight ship and was immensely popular among his troops, but was terribly demanding. There was not a lot of sitting around drinking coffee all day in the office and looking good in civilian clothes. Stack believed a detective's place was out on the street doing some walking and talking. That's where he expected his agents to be, out on the street and solving cases.

"The dynamic duo," Stack looked up as O'Brien and O'Toole came into the office and shut the door behind them. Stack leaned back in his chair and reached for his cup of coffee. "Why do I always have a bad feeling when I see you two together?"

"Hey chief, you gotta hear this, this is some good shit," O'Brien offered as he sat down, looking at O'Toole who was still standing in front of the desk.

"Yeah, well I ain't got all day," Stack took a sip from his coffee and then sat back to listen.

O'Toole started to repeat Sean's information, laying out the entire scheme as reported by Sean's soldier friend, O'Brien chirping in on occasion to emphasize a point. Over the course of the last month both had received similar partial information from other sources that seemed to confirm a lot of what Sean had just reported. At the time they received their info it was just somewhat fragmentary with no real specifics, now suddenly it all made sense. It was as if Sean had provided the Rosetta Stone and brought everything together.

"Chief, listen to this," O'Toole picked up a file and turned to the marked typewritten page, "We picked this up last month. This came from some guy Pat, catches on a possession of marihuana beef, says the following: there are some American women prostituting themselves over in the Camp Stanley area. The source identified them as three civilians and one soldier. They get fifty dollars apiece, and they are being managed by some black soldier in the 15th Field Artillery at Camp Stanley. The source says that's all he's hearing so far. Now Pat tells the guy to check it out further. But so far hasn't come back with anything. Well, last week, I catch a guy on a bad check and forgery case out of the CRC and Stanley Post Exchange. You know the Ransom Case, the guy who was spreading bad paper all over the place?"

O'Toole stops momentarily to make sure that Stack is listening. "Yeah, I remember, the case. Said he needed it to pay off debts or something but would not say what debts he had. Sounded like bullshit you said," Stack started to rub his chin a sure sign he was listening and putting the facts all together.

"Yep, same guy." O'Toole continued, "Well, he's from Camp Sears, right?

He's assigned as a mechanic and driver. He lives in the Headquarters barracks, room 212. Chief," O'Toole let his word sink in, "this is the same room York's source says they are using to sell pussy."

"So this Ransom never mentioned that small point?" Stack asked incredulously.

"Nope, he never wanted to talk about why he had any debts, only that he needed to pay someone and was cashing bad checks to do it."

"Tell him the rest of the story," O'Brien chirped in, smiling.

"Well, York then says his source gave him the name of two soldiers who know everything about what's going on and could fill us in to anything else we wanted to know. Guess who?"

"Let's see. Wild guess...Ransom?" Stack volunteered just to get the game over with.

"Yep, give the man a cigar! Ransom, and his roommate Slavin," O'Toole was smiling like the Cheshire cat.

"Slovinkay," O'Brien interjected.

"What?"

The roommate's name is Slovinkay." O'Brien corrected.

"Hey what-fucking-ever man." O'Toole was smiling, "Another fucking Polack for all I care."

Stack leaned back in his chair and contemplated for a few seconds in silence. "All right, who wants it?"

"Come on Chief, it's the Irish Mafia, we do things together." O'Toole protested and looked over at O'Brien who looked equally offended.

"You shitheads scare me sometimes," Stack smiled and rose up in his chair and picked up his now empty coffee cup. "All right open it up on a preliminary investigation and see what you two can turn up. Tom you're the primary agent on this one. Make sure your brother Paddie here keeps his reports up. If there's anything to it I'll call the Field Office and give them a heads up we might need some help. I want an investigative plan and your conversation with York in a detailed report and on my desk ASAP. What's this York want for all this?" Stack walked around his desk heading for the door.

"Nothing Chief, I think he just wanted to do the right thing."

Stack stopped at this door and turned around, "all right, what about his source of information?"

"York says the guy wanted nothing to do with CID, he told York everything and York passed it to us."

"All right, check this York out. Make sure he is on the up; sure seems like an awful lot of information for someone to get from someone else. But who knows, just check it out to make sure." He looked over at O'Brien and O'Toole who nodded back, "Right now we got like ten days before payday so we're on a tight schedule. Let's check this shit out and let's bust them."

"Got it Chief," O'Brien replied and walked out the door behind Stack with O'Toole right behind him.

After leaving the CID office Sean was literally floating on air. It was the first time he had spent any time with a CID agent actually talking about an investigation. As far as he was concerned the CID were those guys running around in civilian clothes driving civilian cars. He knew they were responsible for conducting investigations, but really he had no idea what all they did or how they operated. As he left, he realized he was very impressed, not with everyone, but certainly with O'Brien and O'Toole. As they talked, he had tried hard to remain passive and just answer questions as they were asked and not volunteer his own thoughts.

After all he was just a MP with very little actual Law Enforcement experience, and certainly had no experience in conducting any investigations. But as they talked back and forth about the information, he found his mind working overtime, swirling around with hundreds of things he thought they could do to check things out. The whole experience turned out to be a great personal epiphany; as if his eyes and mind were suddenly opened to conducting investigations and he understood almost immediately what was involved, maybe not the complete ins and outs of the process, but he firmly grasped the concepts. He was thrilled beyond belief. He liked working regular uniform MP duty and liked the action of the street because there was always a lot going on there was always something to do. But for the first time he was able to see the "other side", criminal investigations, where you actually could use your brain not just your brawn, pitting your own intelligence, determination, and training against a bad guy's. Like this Sergeant Bishop, here he was running a criminal enterprise under everyone's nose making a lot of money thinking he is so smart. But here they were, sitting down planning how they were going to destroy that enterprise, and send him to jail, without Bishop knowing what was about to happen.

He drove away from CID with his imagination and fantasy alive and kicking. He felt both satisfied and vindicated that he had made the right decision, as painful as it was in his personal life. He hadn't wanted to miss the dinner and he wanted to be with Pok more than anything, but if he hadn't made such a sacrifice, there is no telling how long Bishop would continue to victimize his soldiers. He would have to make amends, but someone had to do it. He drove to the PMO and saw Pok was standing out in the front patiently waiting for him. As he drove into the parking lot she looked up and gave him a broad smile of welcome. He stopped the jeep and she climbed carefully into the front passenger seat trying not to snag her nylons. As they drove away, Captain Cruz happened to be looking out his front window and caught Pok's broad smile as Sean drove up and stopped in front of her. He recalled Grubner's assertion that York was bothering Miss Park and was told to leave her alone, he rubbed his chin and thought to himself, it sure didn't look as if York was bothering Miss Park. In fact, it sure looked as if Miss Park was enjoying any attention York was giving her. He would have to store that fact away for the time being until he could see how everything played out. He also thought it was time to scale back any future trips to the Million Dollar Club downtown just in case.

Sean drove to the small Korean Snack bar, which was becoming their favorite place to meet because they could sit down and talk and be left alone for a few minutes. It was just down the street from the MP station so it only took a minute to get there. It was still early so they were among the first ones to show up for lunch. They ordered ramen soup and a soft drink and then sat down at 'their table' in the back near the window where they could catch an afternoon breeze as they ate.

"Hey," Sean began. "I want to say, I'm sorry about missing dinner, but I can explain," Sean began as they sat down and he could look into her eyes.

"It's OK," Pok reached out and put her hand on Sean's hand which was resting on the table in front of him. She looked into his eyes and smiled, "I should not make a big problem, it's only a dinner."

"No, it was right to make a problem." He tried to find the words to express his thoughts but they did not seem to come. "I...."

"Sean," Pok leaned slightly forward and spoke lightly, "I was afraid I make big mistake." She lowered her head in a slight embarrassment, "I think I have sex with you too soon, and maybe you think bad thoughts of me and have no respect." Pok hesitated as her eyes filled with tears and she blinked several times to clear them before she spoke again, "I not like business woman." Pok shook her head from side to side and looked deep into his eyes. "It was very special to me, understand?"

"I know," Sean started to speak but was cut off by Pok's raised hand.

"Shhhhhh, let me speak please," Pok interrupted and Sean nodded his head. "I have been with only two men like that in my life. The first was Korean man. He was student and boyfriend in college. But, things happen and we not get married like I thought. You were the second. I don't know how to explain how it happened but I was so happy. When you did not come to dinner, I think I make another big mistake. Maybe you think I was like whore. Whore that is bad woman, yes?" Pok asked.

"Yes, bad woman, something like that," Sean nodded and placed his left hand over hers.

I not like that." Pok shook her head from side to side again to emphasize her point.

"I know honey, I have been driving myself crazy to talk with you to explain."

Pok smiled and then continued, "Reggie talk to me this morning, he told me about the soldier last night. He said you tried to go but this soldier must talk to you. Now I understand. You are soldier, you must obey orders, you have duty, and you must always do duty first."

"Pok, I don't think you understand my feelings for you."

"Sean," Pok looked into his eyes, with her own eyes tearing, "you are my only one now, I promise."

"Pok, if you will forgive me, then you will be my only one, and I promise you."

Pok smiled for the first time as a tear rolled down her face. Sean reached out and wiped the tear with his hand. Pok smiled and reached for his hand and brought it to her lips and kissed it and then smiled broadly.

"OK, no more sad talk," Pok announced, "you come home tonight for dinner?"

"Yes, six thirty?"

"Yes please." Pok smiled again.

Looking up, one of the Korean cooks arrived at their table and served their ramen soup in individual brass sauce pans. They both adjusted the pot and started eating. They laughed and held hands throughout lunch and afterward Sean dropped her off in front of the PMO so she could go back to work. He wanted so desperately to kiss her goodbye but knew that was not a good idea. He settled for a wave goodbye and drove off

Sean spent the remainder of the day on cloud nine. As soon as they were relieved, he drove straight back, changed clothes and then caught a ride back to her house. He knew short of nuclear war he was not going to be late. He arrived at Pok's house that night at six fifteen, and discovered the table set with candles. She had made a feast of Korean Barbeque beef, known as Bulgogi, white rice, fresh cucumber Kimchi and even managed to make a small pitcher of iced tea. They talked about their day and for the first time Sean talked about maybe going to CID and about passing along the information and how excited he was with the process. He could not tell her exactly what it as about, but she understood that he had a great personal victory that day and now she had become a part of it. She was thrilled to see him so excited and to have him back at the house with her. They cleaned up the dishes after dinner and then and lay down on the bed, opening the large window and feeling the cool night breeze blow across them. They were in their own special world and slowly each faded into a deep sleep still holding each other.

XVIII

Following their meeting with Stack, O'Toole and O'Brien started earnestly to track down their informant at Camp Stanley. It had taken a few phone calls to track him down but finally they managed to reach him. It's easy for a soldier to avoid a phone call if he really wanted to, it is impossible to avoid a summons by his commander who held his life and free time in his hands. After trying to locate him through normal channels, O'Toole finally picked up the phone and called the battery commander. It was not an unexpected surprise that the source was on the phone to them within thirty minutes and seemed very cooperative. It had been nearly two weeks since the source had been apprehended and brought to the CID Office and was interviewed. During the course of his arrest and processing, he had agreed to provide information about criminal activity in his unit or over in the Camp Stanley area; such information was to be exchanged for CID talking to his commander about what punishment he should receive. It was a common tactic to exchange information on other crimes for potential leniency or a good word to their commanders. Both O'Toole and O'Brien stood behind their word and if the soldier really truly helped them out and gave them good solid information, they did in fact go to the commander and brief him on all of the assistance that he rendered.

Most commanders were also experienced enough to know if CID or someone from the MPs were not willing to speak up for their soldier it was likely because for some reason they declined to help out CID or were unwilling to turn in another criminal. Commanders also took that into consideration when they had to decide their punishment. The source was just a small time doper, unlucky enough to have been caught within 30 minutes after making his purchase of a small bag of marihuana. Although such a small amount of marihuana was not really a CID case, he had been identified by yet another CID informant as having made the purchase and being in possession so they kept the case themselves instead of giving it to the MPs. Although he admitted to possessing the marihuana he had declined to talk about where he had gotten it from; instead he was willing to offer up some other information that he was aware was going on. Being a source or snitch was not really something any soldier wanted to do and it could become quite difficult to have a normal life if anyone found out. In some cases it could be a real safety concern.

It was not totally out of the question to have a CID source who was unlucky enough to be found out by other members of his unit and beaten up for cooperating with the police. It was obviously a dangerous undertaking, but that was the price you paid for smoking dope, stealing, or getting involved in criminal activity and then getting caught. In the army there was always a price to pay for criminal conduct. Sometimes it took the form of demotions in rank, sometimes fines and restrictions, and other times it came with a price tag of playing Judas with your other criminal friends. But when it came right down to it, there was really no loyalty among thieves or other criminals; and it was very infrequent when a soldier did not want to cooperate in some manner. Self-preservation was a very strong motive.

O'Toole and O'Brien had arranged to meet the source outside a small, little, out-of-the-way bar in the 'ville' outside of Camp Stanley. Like some spy movie, the source was told to stand on the corner, and if he had a sweatshirt with a hood, that he should wear it and put the hood up. They would drive up to him in their unmarked civilian CID vehicle and he was to get in the back seat and lay down. They had a small blanket and he was to cover himself up. They would then take him elsewhere and talk with him. This was to avoid anyone seeing him in the company of police or in the backseat of a police vehicle. It went fairly smoothly without a hitch and they drove all the way back to Camp Red Cloud and their office, making polite small talk the entire way. They ushered the source through the front door and into their own office in the back. They all relaxed as O'Brien went to the refrigerator located in the reception area and brought out three cans of soft drinks. They had already talked about the source's lack of communication with them over the last two weeks. The source attempted to explain why he had not called them back as he was initially instructed to do. O'Toole described his explanation as "a sad tale of woe" and was thoroughly unimpressed.

Both O'Brien and O'Toole had already decided that they were going to hit the source directly with the new information and see whatever he might know and not play around with him. Sometimes you had to shock a source into understanding how tightly you had his balls in your hand. The question was just how hard they have to squeeze.

"All right, let's get down to business," O'Toole started out.

"OK, sure," said the source as he sunk down while sitting in his chair.

"Tell me about Belk." O'Toole looked at the source to see his response.

The question seemed to take the air out of his lungs. "Who?" The source looked down to the floor and then straightened up as if he was suddenly more interested in paying attention. It was clear they had struck a nerve. It was not lost on either of them.

"Who? Who? What are you, some kind of fucking owl?" O'Toole answered. "You know who I'm talking about, so don't dick with me. LaShawn Belk. Do ya know that name?"

"Well he's in the battery that's all I know."

"He's in your battery?"

"Yeah, Bravo Battery."

"What's he do?" O'Toole leaned forward.

"He's a gun bunny like me."

"What else does he do?"

"What do you mean?"

"Jesus Christ, what do I mean?" O'Toole raised his voice, "what do you think I fucking mean? This is getting really boring."

"I don't know," answered the soldier pretending to sound surprised by the question. He looked over at O'Brien for support that was not forthcoming.

"Hold it," O'Brien interjected and held his hand up. "Let's make this a little easier." O'Brien caught the sources attention. "I think I see the problem here. So, tell me, did you ride the short bus to school?"

"What?" The source looked up, not understanding.

"Did you ride the short bus to school? You know, the one for all the retards?" O'Brien leaned over and looked the source directly in the face.

The source looked back and forth from O'Brien to O'Toole not understanding at all, "No, I walked to school."

"Ah ha, so you're not such a dumb ass after all. Is that what you mean?"

"No," The source shook his head and took a sip of soda.

OK, then let's try this again just, a little more direct." O'Toole started out again, "Tell me about Belk and him selling dope. I mean, he is selling dope, right?"

The source looked at his fingernails as if he were suddenly interested in his personal grooming, "Yeah I guess so," he finally answered and took another sip from his soda.

"You guess or you know?" O'Toole asked.

"I know." The source finally answered and looked down to the floor.

"You know because you bought dope from him before?" O'Toole bored down on the source.

He hesitated for a few seconds and answered, "Yeah,"

"OK, the dope you got caught with at the main gate at Camp Stanley, was that the same dope you bought from Belk?"

"Well sort of,"

"What does "sort of" mean?" O'Toole looked across at O'Brien and raised his arms as if to say what's up. "Jesus, this is like asking my kid who broke the fucking living room lamp. One more time, did you buy the dope from him or someone else?" O'Toole asked directly to the source and leaned down to look in his eyes. "Am I speaking English here?"

"No, this is like being at the fucking dentist." O'Brien said exasperated. "Are you sure you didn't ride the short bus to school?"

The source began hesitantly, "I meant that he was there, but so was Jefferson."

"Jefferson? Jefferson who? Jefferson Davis? Did you buy your dope from the Confederate president himself?"

The soldier smiled meekly at the joke, "No Lionel Jefferson. Sergeant Jefferson. He's in my battery, too."

"Well thank you very much." O'Toole rose up and started pacing around his small office," Look we knew all that way back when I first talked with you. Did you know that? But I waited for you to man up and grow a pair." He raised his hand and started pointing directly at the source and continued, "I was depending on you to come forward on your own. Remember when I said I can find out anything I want to find out? I have so many friends over at Camp Stanley, I could find out anything I want? Remember that? I was giving you a chance to help yourself out. Now I realize how fucked up you are. You don't care about helping yourself out. "O'Toole looked over and continued, "If I wanted to know the last time you took a shit, I could find out if I wanted to." O'Toole then leaned down and looked straight into his face to emphasize his point.

"Yeah I remember." The source answered and looked back down to the floor.

"But you didn't believe me, did you?"

"No, not really."

"OK, so tell me, does Jefferson work with Bishop too?"

"Bishop? Who the fuck is Bishop?" The source looked up with a blank stare but his face flushed a bright red giving away how much the question bothered him.

"Now suddenly we have amnesia again huh?" O'Brien barked back in from behind.

O'Toole fired back, "Let's see if I can stimulate your memory again. I'm talking about Sergeant Bishop. You know, the guy who is running the whores over there and at Camp Sears. Does that sound familiar? Does that strike a bell? Do you remember telling me about the whores when you were here before? You tell me the whores were tricking, but forgot to tell me you know all about the guy who's running the whole fucking scam, didn't you?"

O'Toole started pacing back and forth behind his desk then suddenly spun around and looked the source directly in the eyes, "So you see, I reached out to my other friends and I checked it out myself. Easy as can be." O'Toole snapped his fingers to emphasize his point.

The sudden movement caused the young soldier to jump and gasp in surprise and stare blankly back.

O'Toole, not giving him a chance to recover from his shock, opened the file on the desk top and began reading, "So listen up, Marvin Ervin Bishop, E-7, born Detroit Michigan, home of record

Detroit Michigan, MOS 63 Bravo 40 wheel vehicle mechanic."
O'Toole continued reading from the file and spouting off personal
details including date of birth, social security number, and next of kin
and their address. O'Toole finally stopped talking, pulled out a small
photograph, and shut the manila folder. Holding up the photo of
Bishop, he demanded, "Now do you know who that is?"

"Yeah, I know him."

"How do you know him?"

"You probably know already don't you?"

"Of course we do, but I want to hear it from you." O'Toole
looked over at O'Brien who nodded in approval and began taking
notes.

"Well I..." his voice dropping off as if he didn't quite know
where to start.

O'Brien decided to try a ploy, "You're in his book, aren't you?"

They had both figured with so much going on Bishop must
have some way to keep track of how much money he had out and who
owed him. It was likely in some kind of notebook that he was able to
keep with him all of the time in case someone tried to repay a loan or
wanted more money. Likely everyone that dealt with Bishop would
know about the notebook.

"Yes, Sir." He finally answered meekly.

"Is that why you didn't say anything before?"

"Yes, Sir."

"How much do you owe?"

"Two hundred."

"You owe him two hundred dollars?" O'Toole asked for
clarification.

"No, 200 a month" he answered and then looked up briefly
and then back down at his fingernails.

O'Brien and O'Toole looked at each other and shook their
heads in amazement.

"OK, so you owe him two hundred dollars a month. Is that
just the interest then?" O'Brien asked and looked while the source
nodded his head affirmatively.

"So how are you thinking you're going to pay that
motherfucker off?" O'Brien asked.

"I don't know, Sir; I'm in so deep, I'll never get out." Tears began to well up in his eyes, his shoulders sagged, and his face took on the look of absolute defeat.

O'Toole, sat down in his chair taking a deep cleansing breath and began in a calmer voice, "You've always had a way out; don't you know what it is?"

"No, Sir," the soldier looked up confused.

"It's me," O'Toole whispered.

The soldier, wiping the tears from his cheek, looked up at O'Toole.

"I'm your way out of this mess. I can fix just about everything."

The soldier looked up and slowly nodded as if he finally understood.

"All right, even though you didn't do what I asked you to do before; I'm willing to give you one more chance. But that's it," O'Toole spoke in a calm and controlled tone. "Because if you will do as I tell you to do, then I can make Bishop and Belk and Jefferson and the others all go away."

The source nodded in agreement and for the first time acted as if he were genuinely interested in what O'Toole was selling. He brushed away his tears and wiped his nose with the sleeve of his shirt.

"OK, well we're going to sit down and talk tonight and you're not going to bullshit us anymore are you?"

"No, Sir," the soldier said with total agreement.

"All right, fine. And you're going to tell us everything we want to know and no more holding anything back, right?"

"Yes, Sir."

"All right, then we'll get you out from under Bishop and those other assholes. Agreed?"

The source nodded his head and took another sip from his soda. He looked as if he wanted to cry again.

"OK, then let's get started." O'Toole leaned back in his chair and the source started to talk.

It took several hours to finally extract all of the information and details. By the time they were finished their brains were swimming. They had suspected that the operation was more involved than even what York had provided but they had no idea how extensive it was. They had finished up, taken the source back to his Camp and then returned to the CID Barracks for the night; they spent almost an hour debriefing Mr. Stack over their latest meeting with the source.

Sean awoke the next morning with a start at the loud pounding on the metal door down by the street in front of the house. He was first confused and uncertain where it was coming from, and then he looked over at the clock adjacent to the bed; *Shit* he thought to himself, it was almost five thirty, guard mount was in 30 minutes. He was immediately wide awake and rapidly thinking. He could still hear the pounding on the outer gate metal door and Reggie calling his name. He went to the opened window over the bed and could hear Reggie calling from outside.

"Sean, Sean, you shit head get up," Reggie then hit the metal gate bam bam bam, "Sean get up."

"Coming Reg, two minutes," Sean called out and closed the window. Thank goodness the pounding stopped before it woke up the other neighbors.

Pok also woke up with a start once Sean yelled out the window and immediately reached out to hold him as she was trying to bring him back to bed.

"Honey, I'm sorry but I have to go, I'm late." Sean jumped out of bed still naked from the night before and jumped into his pants, grabbed his shoes, but did not even try to put them on. He ran out the door barefooted and bare-chested down to the front gate. Opening the gate, he jumped into the passenger side of the jeep that was parked literally on the sidewalk already running.

"Come on you dumbass," Reggie laughed as he put the jeep into gear. He popped the clutch and jerked the jeep forward.

"Thanks man." Sean finally exhaled as the jeep flew off the curb and turned to the right, screaming up the road as Reggie ran through the gears.

Reggie leaned over and shouted over the roar of the engine, "I got flag call, so drop me off and you take the jeep to the barracks and get changed. I'll catch a ride with the other patrol, OK?"

"OK," Sean was trying to wake up and not fall out of the jeep as they raced through the deserted city street.

"Well, did things get worked out?" Reggie asked in a shout over the roar of the engine and road noise.

"Yeah, everything is OK." Sean braced as the jeep came up to a small rise in the road that supported the railroad tracks. The jeep flew up almost clearing the ground landing solidly on the other side but throwing Sean forward.

He quickly recovered and yelled to Reggie, "Hey man, I didn't have a chance to say thanks for talking with Pok yesterday."

"That's what friends are for amigo," Reggie shouted and the jeep raced around a Korean bus that was out making the first run of the morning. "Hold on boy." Reggie shouted and started laughing as the jeep went into something similar to hyper drive, veering into the left lane screaming past the bus and then almost immediately recovering back to the right lane. They roared through the gate and Reggie kept the jeep floored all the way up to the post HQ. Reggie braked hard in front of the small concrete pad where the three flag poles and the 70 mm pack howitzer used to fire the salute to the flag were placed.

As they pulled up, both the MP and the ROK MP's were already starting to form up to march to the three flag poles: one for the Korean National Flag, for which the ROK MP were responsible, the US Flag for which they were responsible and the UN Flag in the middle for which responsibility was traded back and forth between the MP and ROK. Whoever had the UN flag, the other fired the cannon salute. Reggie jumped out, leaving the jeep running but in neutral with the emergency brake on. Sean hobbled into the driver side still barefooted and put it into gear and took off up to the detachment, checking his watch every two seconds. Sean may have broken an unofficial land speed record tearing through the Camp to the detachment area, changing into uniform, and then racing back down to the MP Station, but he was still almost ten minutes late when he arrived. He stumbled into the MP Desk, with his boots on but still not laced up. He still had not tucked his uniform pants into his boots; his uniform blouse was not tucked into his pants, his pistol belt was over his right shoulder and his overnight bag with his shaving gear and toothbrush was in his other hand.

"Well the prodigal son returns, eh?" SSG Whitehouse asked as he came through the door. "I thought you flew the coop or something."

"Sorry Sarge, I woke up late, no excuse. It won't happen again." Sean was almost breathless.

"All right this one's on me, next time, it's on you. Go get yourself squared away." Whitehouse sat back down behind his typewriter, lit another cigarette and began typing some report.

The telephone at the MP desk rang and Whitehouse answered after two rings, "I Corps MP Station, Sergeant Whitehouse speaking Sir," Whitehouse said almost automatically.

"Whitehouse, who just came racing through post in an MP jeep?"

Whitehouse recognized Grubner's voice right away. "Well I don't know, I'll have to check. What's the problem?" Whitehouse answered, but was really unconcerned.

"The problem Sergeant," Grubner responded to Whitehouse's attitude, "Mario Andretti is driving one of my MP jeeps screaming through this installation like they were on fire."

"I see, well I guess that was probably York, he was running a little late this morning, I'll talk with him." Whitehouse acknowledge and continued typing.

"How late was he?"

"About ten or fifteen minutes or so," Whitehouse answered off the cuff.

"I want a counseling statement."

"A counseling statement? About what?"

"York was late for duty, that's a failure to repair and I want a written counseling statement to that effect." *That motherfucker*, Grubner thought to himself. *I got him already. This was almost too easy.*

"Well I already talked to him, that's good enough."

"Sergeant, is there any problem with your hearing?" Grubner snapped back.

"No, my hearing is good."

"Then I want a counseling statement in writing and I want it when I get in there, is that clear?"

"Clear to me top," Whitehouse leaned back and took another drag from his cigarette and hpaused.

A counseling statement was a more formalized and official version of "you did something wrong and don't do it again." To get hurt by a counseling statement alone, you would have to roll it up tight and stick it in someone's eye, but string them together they could be powerful evidence of misconduct or of a need for more formalized counseling or perhaps even non-judicial punishment. It was seldom used when verbal counseling seemed sufficient or when the soldier in question responded. This whole deal struck Whitehouse as odd, especially since he had never had any problems with Sean whatsoever. In fact, his verbal comment to not let it happen again was all he thought necessary. A counseling statement was used to get someone's attention who was not listening to you, and it seemed redundant to Whitehouse. But it was clear from Grubner's tone that Sean must have pissed in his Wheaties recently.

"Anything else?" Whitehouse answered in a dismissive tone. He was answered by a loud click as the phone was slammed on the cradle. "God damn it," White house said out loud to no one in particular, throwing his eraser pencil across the desk. Now he was going to have to type up another piece of paper.

Whitehouse looked up from his typing as Grubner walked into the PMO and he took another long drag of his cigarette. Grubner made a beeline straight for Whitehouse.

"Give me that counseling statement on York," Grubner demanded.

Whitehouse paused and took another drag from his cigarette in an effort of passive contempt and then leaned forward and reached for the paper sitting on the desk top. "Here it is." Whitehouse somewhat contemptuously spat out, "you know this is bullshit, right?"

"I don't really care what you think, Sergeant. I care that you do what you're told to do. But you should know, your super soldier there that you think is all that and a bag of chips, well he's a *bookkeeper.*" Grubner stated as he read. "You know what that is?"

XIX

A bookkeeper was understood to mean a tattletale, someone writing down anything and everything that happened that may go wrong or any mistakes made by the chain of command, to be used at some time when it is most advantageous to the bookkeeper. They were a hateful lot because it meant everyone always had to be on their guard as to what they said, what they did, and everything had to be done according to regulations. If not they might find themselves explaining their actions to the Inspector General or a higher headquarters.

"Says who?" Whitehouse asked.

"Says me. You know he was at CID the other day?"

"Yeah, so?"

"Did he tell you what about?"

"I didn't ask him," Whitehouse looked around for an ashtray to flick the ash from his cigarette.

"Exactly. So you gave him time to go to CID to open up his little book to those suits." Grubner looked down at the counseling statement. "We both have a lot to lose; you're coming up on eighteen aren't you?"

"Yea, another year to go," Whitehouse answered back. Whitehouse knew what he meant. Eighteen was the magic year for soldiers, after you hit eighteen years you were "locked in" or assured to make your twenty and be able to retire. It was the eighteen year mark that soldiers really looked forward to and not twenty.

"Well you know how a bookkeeper can twist things around to suit whatever they want to say. Would be bad not to make it to go all of this way and not make your twenty, wouldn't it?"

Whitehouse stared back for a moment, "Yeah, well there isn't anything to keep book on, so who gives a fuck." Whitehouse looked back contemptuously and tried to end the conversation. "Is there anything else, top?"

"This will do it." Grubner turned and walked away towards his office.

Whitehouse leaned back in his chair steaming mad. He knew Grubner was a backstabbing idiot and he was not convinced York was involved in keeping book. But it was clear Grubner had set his sights on York for some reason. It would only be a matter of time before he could have York up on something even if it was made up. He had seen Grubner's type before and many a good troop's career destroyed for no apparent reason. Hard to say what was behind these intentions but it was clear he had a bull's eye on Sean's back. Only thing is, York was his soldier. He knew he wasn't going to allow that to happen. He'd been down that road before.

"Hey, Lewis," Whitehouse yelled back to the others in the break room.

"Yeah, Sarge," came the reply followed by silence to hear what he was saying.

"Go relieve York at the gate and tell him to beat feet over here ASAP," Whitehouse called out and started to lean back in his chair. A few short minutes later York walked into the PMO and up to the MP Desk.

"Hey Sarge, you want me?"

"Come on let's go get some coffee." Whitehouse stood up and step down from the desk, "Beasley come over here and answer the phone. I'll be back in a while, going to get some coffee."

The soldier nodded and stepped up to sit in the chair on the desk. Whitehouse waved at York to follow him outside. Whitehouse climbed into the driver's seat, started up one of the patrol vehicles and drove over in silence to the PX snack bar. York started to ask him what was up but Whitehouse held up his hand to be quiet. He was trying to formulate some questions and a plan of action. Once inside, they each bought a cup of coffee and then sat down at one of the tables.

"All right look, I'm not a very complicated guy. I don't bullshit or beat around the bush. When I want to know something, I just ask. So I'm just asking you straight up and I want a straight answer." Whitehouse looked straight into Sean's eyes.

Sean was taken aback at the directness and was confused. "Sure Sarge."

"You keeping book on me?" Whitehouse asked and took a sip of his coffee.

"What?" Sean responded, not quite understanding the question.

"Are you keeping book on me or anyone else in the detachment?"

Sean smiled, still thinking it may be a joke, "No Sarge, I don't know what you're talking about."

"The First Shirt says you're keeping book on folks in the detachment that's why you went to CID."

"Sarge, are you serious? I had someone tell me some information about dope. I just went to CID because it's like their thing. Why would I want to do that Sarge? Wait a minute, let me show you something."

Sean unbuttoned his blouse pocket and reached for his memo book and turned to his notes obtained from Broadbench. He passed the book over to Whitehouse who started reading the notes. "Sarge, this is what I briefed CID about, right here."

Whitehouse looked him in the eye and was satisfied. "All right, I thought it was a bunch of shit." Whitehouse was more than satisfied. "Look, you need to watch your step because Grubner has it out for you. Did you piss in his Corn Flakes or something?"

"Hey Sarge, I try to stay out of his way."

"Well there must be something," Whitehouse lit up another cigarette and took a deep drag.

"Sarge, I think I know where this is coming from." Sean took a sip of coffee and sat back. "I'm dating Miss Park, and he had been trying to score with her since he got here."

"What?" Whitehouse almost shot coffee through his nose.

"I'm telling you Sarge, that's gotta be why."

"You're dating Miss Park? That little cutie in the back of the PMO?" Whitehouse leaned back and smiled.

"Yeah, I think I'm going to be moving in with her, we sort of talked about it last night."

"Holy shit, I'm proud of you. That's a nice one." Whitehouse looked at Sean with a little more respect.

"Yeah I think so, too."

"All right, that answers that one. It makes sense to me, he's banging Bea and thinks he's God's gift to women." Whitehouse turned serious, "Look, you watch your ass; he has a hard on for you and that counseling statement this morning was like the first step. I know guys like Grubner, he's a sneaky shit and he'll lie to screw you over. Just stay the fuck out of his way will ya?"

"Will do, Sarge." Sean held his coffee cup up as if he were giving a toast to Whitehouse.

Later that day, Sean was working the main gate, checking passes and identification of everyone wanting to come into or leave the camp. It could be a boring tour or it could be OK if you got outside and enjoyed the warm weather and exchanged some polite conversation and greetings with the soldiers as they passed through.

Sean looked up the road and saw a familiar face walking towards him.

"Jamie, how you doing?" Sean asked as Broadbench walked up and came to a stop a few feet from Sean.

"Hey, I'm doing OK. You know, trying to get through the day," He answered back.

"So, what are you up to?"

"Well just checking to see if you were able to use that info I gave you?"

They were interrupted by three soldiers walking through the small gate. Sean checked each out and waved them into Camp.

"Well, like I said, there was nothing I could do about it, but I did pass it along to CID and they said they are going to look at it hard," Sean explained.

"Well OK, just as long as someone is going to check it out,"

"But they sure want to talk to you, Jamie. I mean, you're the one with the actual information, I'm just parroting what you're saying." Sean tried to explain.

"Nah, I don't want anything to do with those guys. I trust you and that's all. You promised not to tell anyone who you got that from. You know that could get my assed kicked right?"

"I know, but they sure want to talk with you. It's sort of putting me in a hard place."

"Well I trust you. I have your word on it,"

"Yeah, you do," Sean acknowledged but wished it wasn't so.

"So you get everything squared away with your girl?"

"Yeah we're all set; she was mad, but got over it,"

"Well good," Broadbench commented and then asked, "So if you don't go downtown in the bars, where do you take your girl to go out?"

"Well, you know, we find somewhere to go. This Saturday we're going downtown to pick up a dress we ordered for her,"

"Yeah, right here in the ville?" Broadbench motioned out the gate with his hand.

"Yeah there's a tailor shop downtown in the market place," Sean explained.

"Oh yeah, maybe I'll have to check it out. I could use some dress up clothes."

"Yeah, might do you some good," Sean joked and the two laughed.

"Well, guess I'll head down the road, good to see ya man. I'm counting on you to keep your word now," Broadbench said over his back as he walked away.

"Yeah, I know," Sean acknowledged yet again his mistake and then turned to check out the identification of another soldier coming through the gate.

Over the next several days O'Toole and O'Brien tracked down some additional leads and finally got ahold of the soldier named Ransom. They had worked a case on him for spreading bad checks all over the area. The unit agreed to send him back to the CID office allegedly for an interview about some additional bad checks that they just discovered. The unit was already well versed as to the problem of PFC Ransom's bad checks and this was but another request by CID to re-interview him. Once he arrived at the CID Office however, he immediately realized they were no longer interested in any bad checks. Instead, he found himself talking about what else was going on over at Camp Sears.

Both O'Toole and O'Brien thought they had a good understanding of the extent of Bishop's involvement of criminal activity, but they were in for a real shock when they finally debriefed Ransom. Ransom could only be described as a small town naive and immature teenager, complete with a box shaped head, black rimmed glasses, and the body shape and physique of a mild mannered Casper Milk toast. He had been thrown by luck or fate into the pack of wolves of Bishop and his crew and he and other sheep in his unit were being fleeced. But for all his timidity and mistakes, Ransom was very intelligent; and like many intelligent men, knew he could make it in any world because he was smarter than any of those who could physically tower over him. O'Toole and O'Brien learned fairly quickly he was very cleaver indeed. Once he was convinced they were aware of Bishop's activity and were interested in shutting down his organization, he opened up. It was like a dam bursting open and he continued late into the evening. Ransom had carefully documented all of Bishop's dealings and operations down to the smallest detail, explaining that he was only waiting for his own CID case to come to his commander before he turned his information over to him.

Ransom confirmed that some eight months ago when he was just a "Turtle" at his unit, he was approached by his platoon Sergeant Bishop, who offered him a chance to have sex with an American girl. Ransom explained that he was totally inexperienced in anything having to do with sex: women, girls, or females in general. The closest thing to a female type relationship he ever had was when Malory Benson used to sit next to him during the Chess Club meetings. She would lean against him and had, on more than one occasion, placed her head onto his shoulders and her hand onto his leg. Although he found it terribly exciting, it was also distracting and each time she had done so he had lost a major chess piece off the board.

Bishop, however, was willing for a price to set him up with an American girl whom he promised would be willing to not just talk with him, but would be willing to have sex with him. Ransom explained that finally being able to have sex, to him, was worth his whole paycheck, and for nearly a month he had spent nearly his entire paycheck on sex. Ransom explained that because he was willing to let the girls use his barracks room to conduct their business, he was allowed to go first and received a reduced rate. The whole idea of prostitution was somewhat foreign to him but he became acquainted with the operation first hand.

O'Toole and O'Brien were somewhat taken aback as Ransom began to describe how things developed as if he were telling a story in the third person, something that had happened to someone else but that he had observed first hand. He started going into detail about the actual sexual aspects, detailing the difference in price between a hand job, a blow job, or regular sex and the difference in price between the different girls. He made a comment about anal sex being extra but he wasn't positive about that because it had never interested him. He continued to rattle on when O'Brien finally had to stop with what they would later refer to as the "Penthouse Forum version" of events and got back to the how things actually operated.

Ransom admitted he was actually very grateful for experiencing his first sexual encounter. True he had to pay and that cut down on the romance aspect, but that didn't matter. He was able to prove to himself that his equipment at least worked and he was properly programmed. Ransom discovered that he liked females even more than he thought he liked them. So he found himself having sex with the girls when they first started, as part of the arrangement in order to use his room, and then would go to the end of the line and would pay the normal fare when it was his turn again. Then as everyone else went happily away satisfied, he went to the end of the line and paid again, and then to the end of the line and paid again, sometimes four or five times on a payday.

"You mean to tell me you took four or five shots a night?" O'Brien asked scratching his head in disbelief.

"Well sometimes less, sometimes more; it was more like four times on average," Ransom answered as a matter of fact and pushed his glasses further back onto his nose. "I was apparently trying to make up for any previous lost opportunities." He looked over at O'Brien and O'Toole as if to ask if he should continue.

"Jesus Christ." O'Brien looked as if he were lost in his own thoughts. "I'm sorry, continue, I'm still trying to wrap my head around four times a night."

"Well," Ransom thought O'Brien was really asking for a better explanation, "I'm twenty four years old. I realize as I grow older and mature that I'm a pretty nerdy guy and not very attractive to most women. Not that I wasn't always interested in women but it never seemed to work out even in college. So up until six or seven months ago I had never been with a woman or a girl. I just, never knew what to do or how to do it. So I figured I was just making up for some lost time, and like every other good thing this was eventually going to go away so I had better get all that I could while I could. I really had it all worked out in my head." Ransom explained his actions and rationale as if he were explaining the benefits of one insurance plan over another to two customers.

"OK, well if everything is going so well, then what happened?" O'Toole was dying to ask.

"Well, there comes a time when the desire overwhelms the ability to pay." Ransom looked over at them both and shrugged his shoulders in resignation. Ransom sighed as he continued to explain,

"So, I wasn't able to go as much as I wanted. I was still having the first go around, but that really didn't seem to do it for me anymore. Then because I was spending so much of my money on the girls, my car note in the states and my college loans were going unpaid so I started getting collection notices. I sort of realized how stupid I was. I had spent nearly the first four months never even leaving the camp except to over to CRC or Camp Stanley for something." Ransom shook his head.

"I feel like I'm in the middle of some encounter session," O'Brien commented.

Ransom paused and smiled, pushing his glasses back onto his nose. He looked at both O'Brien and O'Toole as if waiting to continue. O'Toole raised his hand palm side up as if to say continue on.

"I realize now my big mistake was listening to Sergeant Bishop. I should have been a little more careful and thought through his offer to float me a loan, then another and then another. Of course, I was borrowing money from Bishop and then giving it right back when I went with the girls. It didn't take too long before I finally realized that I was so far in debt I was never going to get out of it. So that's when I decided to write my car and college loan checks a couple of days before payday, then I wouldn't have the money to spend but the notes would be taken care of at least. I told Sergeant Bishop I needed some help because I couldn't pay all of the interest. I thought he would work with me, you know, but I found out he's not a bank. He held off doing anything to me by making me move out of my room on paydays. He stopped my special rate with the girls and put me on what he called a special repayment program, which meant right after payday he took me over to the PX and made me cash a check to pay him. I tried to tell him that I didn't have that much money because of the loans I had already written the checks for and so I didn't have that much money in the account. But he didn't seem to care and said that was my problem. He wanted his money or he was going to have someone kick the shit out of me and make my life miserable. Well of course, I rather not go through the shit kicking part, so the checks started to bounce and when I couldn't cash anymore at Camp Sears, he had one of his guys take me over to CRC and then Camp Stanley, to cash them."

"So that's why you were spreading bad paper all over?" O'Brien asked.

"Yeah, sounds dumb, doesn't it?" Ransom sighed.

"How much do you owe Bishop?"

"Well, right now, just over two thousand dollars. That's principal and interest, of course."

"How much?"

"Well, right now, two thousand one hundred and fifty dollars."

"Holy shit! Why didn't you say anything?"

"Who am I going to say something to? Sergeant Bishop is my platoon Sergeant, he's a senior NCO, and I'm just a PFC. It was going to be my word against his unless I had some evidence to back me up. No one else in their right minds would back me up or believe me."

The room grew quiet for a moment, "So you have a college degree?" O'Toole asked.

"Yes, I have a Master's degree in Electrical and Mechanical Engineering from California Polytechnic Institute.

"What? How old are you?"

"Well I'm 23, but I was able to start college when I was 16 and finished at 20."

"You're kidding me? At 16 you went to Cal Poly? What the fuck are you doing in the rmy? What's your MOS?

"I'm a wheel vehicle mechanic and truck driver sometimes," Ransom straightened up in his chair and looked at the shocked faces of both O'Brien and O'Toole. There was a pregnant pause as if the information was sinking in. Ransom thought they wanted more of an explanation and provided, "I had a lot of theory and book learning in my head, but I wanted to get out in the real world and really work on some vehicles so I could put things I learned in college to work in real life. It's been quite rewarding actually, Except for the part where I'm about to become a convicted felon. That was sort of a slight miscalculation, which really wasn't a part of my plan."

XX

O'Brien and O'Toole allowed Ransom to continue; they were amazed at how much information he had about the entire operation: who all was involved, who else owed money to Bishop, the other soldiers who in similar circumstances were forced to give up their rooms for Bishop and his crew to use on paydays. Most interesting were the women, Ransom was able to identify only one of the four women as being an American Soldier, assigned to the 51st Signal Battalion right on CRC. The others were actually civilian prostitutes Bishop had brought over to Korea from Detroit. They were staying somewhere in Seoul with another friend and were brought up on the bus on paydays. They stayed the night may be two and then went back to Seoul somewhere. Ransom proved to be an encyclopedia on everything about Bishop and his organization. They were especially interested in First Lieutenant Prichard who Ransom identified as the 'Motor Officer' in charge of the maintenance facility where Ransom and Bishop and most of the other soldiers on his floor worked. Prichard was undoubtedly involved, by providing cover for Bishop and his activities. It was clear to everyone in the platoon that they could not go to Prichard about Bishop without Bishop finding out about it and coming straight back to them and make them pay. Several soldiers made that mistake and were visited by someone working for Bishop and were threatened or beaten up.

Ransom explained that he himself was never present when Prichard and Bishop ever talked about the operation or about any complaints, but said he knew they had taken place.

"How do you know they took place if you weren't there?" O'Brien asked to clarify.

"Well, I knew I would need some evidence because it was going to be my word against theirs, so I had to find some evidence."

"OK, so what did you find?"

"Well none of course. So I did the next best thing. I recorded their conversations," Ransom straightened himself in his chair.

"You did what?" O'Brien stood up.

"I recorded their conversations in their office and in Bishop's room. Like Nixon in the White House, you know? That's where I got the idea. I have quite a collection actually."

"How did you do that?"

"Well I'm also an electrical engineer, remember? It's just a matter of placing a microphone then stringing wire back to a recorder. I had a simple switch that I was able to activate when I knew they were together or when I saw Bishop and his crew go to his room," Ransom answered as if it were obvious to everyone else but them.

"You know, of course, that it's illegal to record someone's conversations without their permission."

"Actually, I think it's illegal for the government to tape conversations, not private citizens," Ransom offered in a matter of fact response.

"Hey, let's worry about that later," O'Brien said trying to change the subject back to the important stuff."

"So, you say you have tapes of these guys discussing their operations?"

"Of course, they're in my room,"

"Jesus Christ, why didn't you say that before?"

"Well, you never asked and I was saving this for when I got my punishment," Ransom shrugged his shoulders. O'Brien looked over at O'Toole who was starting to turn red.

"Jesus Christ," O'Toole stood up quickly.

"Sir?" Ransom looked up not understanding the comment.

"OK, we're stopping right now and going to go get those fucking tapes. This is giving me a headache."

Later that afternoon they both sat down with O'Brien's reel to reel tape player and two sets of headphones and began to digest what was on the tapes, and then record them over to a cassette tape. It only took 30 minutes into the first multi-hour tapes to realize they had hit pay dirt. The recordings picked up Bishop, Prichard and several others all discussing in some manner or form their parts in the operations. Both O'Toole and O'Brien agreed that this was far larger and far more advanced than anything they had ever heard of in the Army. Included were conversations with two of the prostitutes who confronted Bishop about wanting to return to the U.S. Bishop was clearly heard growing irritated over the girls' clamoring to go home. He finally raised his voice in one instance shouting, "Shut the fuck up. You're going to stay here for as long as I say you're going to stay here." He then went on to warn them that if they went to any police he would make sure they never made it out of the country. He would make sure their asses were plowed under some rice patty somewhere or thrown to the hogs to eat.

O'Brien and O'Toole looked at each other and each recognized that they were no longer just dealing with pandering or pimping these females. They both realized they were dealing with a situation of forced prostitution, white slavery. This upped the seriousness and importance of stopping Bishop and his band of thugs.

The next day they were at the office early waiting for Stack to arrive. When he did, they both walked into his office carrying half a dozen reel to reel tapes and their case file.

"Close the door and give me the bottom line," Mr. Stack leaned back and put his hands behind his head and then placed his feet on his desk on top of a few manila folders. O'Toole closed the door behind them and stood in front of his desk with a tablet full of handwritten notes and O'Brien put the reel to reel tapes on the edge of the desk and sat down.

"Well Chief," O Toole started to count off the various offenses on his fingers, "we got multiple counts of Extortion, Distribution of Drugs, Cruelty and Maltreatment of Subordinates, Conspiracy, black marketing, conduct unbecoming an officer, pandering, and maybe even have a real good case of kidnapping and white slavery."

"Worst of all is that we've only listened to a couple of hours of tape and there are like days and days' worth of stuff to go through. There's no telling what else is there." O'Brien piped in and offered, "Nixon would be proud,"

O'Toole came over and sat down in the chair next to Stack's desk. "Chief, this is a lot bigger than even we thought."

"How solid is your information?"

"Chief, we haven't checked everything yet, but whatever we have checked has been right on time." O'Toole answered and placed his hands on his hips. "And these tapes, they're openly discussing their business, names, money, everything you can think of. I tell you I've never heard of anything like this before."

Mr. Stack took his feet off the desk, scooted the chair closer and began to rub his chin with his right hand as he thought for a moment and finally asked, "How many people are we talking about being directly involved?"

O'Toole answered straight away, "I'd say off hand, ten or twelve are deep into the shit, maybe more on the outer edge so to speak, spread out across our whole AOR; Camp Sears, Camp Stanley, Camp Essyons, even here at CRC."

"Don't forget there's someone in Seoul who's keeping the girls until they're brought up here on payday," O'Brien added.

"Oh yeah, right," O'Toole agreed. "I bet they're hooking down in Seoul too, you know, probably on off days."

"Do prostitutes get off days?" O'Brien asked and chuckled.

"Shit, I don't know, but I can't believe they're just sitting around on their asses waiting to come up this a way."

Stack broke into the banter and began issuing instructions, "Get everyone identified, that's the first big step. Make sure we know exactly who we are looking for." Stack looked over at O'Toole and tilted his head as if to give the assignment to him. "Get over to JAG and get Captain King briefed up about the whole case, especially the tapes. I want to make sure there isn't going to be a big issue with us using them. I don't think so but let's make sure."

"All right, Chief," O'Toole scribbled in his notes. "We have a pretty good idea on most of them; there were a couple of new names we hadn't heard before. From the tapes, I know Bishop is pretty pissed off at some dude named Dee Dee or Bee Bee," O'Toole shrugged his shoulders, "They talked about him a lot on the tapes. It was kind of hard to understand what they were saying, but it was pretty clear he was pissed at 'em whoever they are."

"Competition?" Stack asked. don't know Chief, maybe. Maybe a former partner, I don't know. But I can tell you Bishop was definitely pissed off. I mean he was talking about having him whacked or fucked up or something," O'Toole explained.

Stack nodded his head in understanding, "What about the female soldier doing all the hooking. Was that verified?"

"Yep," O'Toole looked down at his notes, "her name is PV2 Susan or Suzanna Allard, assigned to A Company 51st Signal Battalion. Nothing else on her so far."

"Company "A", you said?" Stack asked and looked up.

"Yeah," O'Toole reconfirmed the information from his notes.

Stack nodded, "I know the commander from Company A; we were in Nam together as enlisted during my first tour. Give me her information, I'll check her out."

There was a knock on Stack's office door and the three of them stopped talking.

"Chief, it's Bob." They all recognized Bateman's voice behind the door.

"Come on in." Stack called out and Bateman came into the office, surprised that O'Brien and O'Toole were inside. He was initially surprised and then was somewhat chest fallen that he was not included in what seemed to be a high level discussion of some case.

"What's up Bob?" Stack asked.

"Well, I went to the Field office up in Casey yesterday afternoon and I was doing some checking on my crime prevention survey at the Post Exchange. Did you know that this area had more shortages or unexplained losses at Camp Red Cloud than any other place in Korea?" Bateman sounded so proud to have discovered that factoid.

"Really?" Stack tried to sound encouraging.

"Yeah, even more than Yongsan or Pusan and they are like 3 times larger.."

"I'm sure we're going to find out why that is, aren't we?" Stack asked.

"Oh yeah, I'm on it." Bateman then looked around at the other three aware that this obviously was not a part of their conversation. "What's going on? Did I interrupt something?"

"No, not really, just sitting here bullshitting for a while first thing in the morning, even before I had my morning coffee," O'Toole volunteered.

Stack looked over in irritation towards O'Toole and then back at Bateman, "We have a big case brewing and we're going to need your help. I want you to put your PX case and other cases aside for the next few days. We have other priority stuff we need to do," Stack continued with his instructions for all three for another 30 minutes before sending them out to get started. He cautioned them all to watch what they say to anyone else until they get a handle on who all is possibly involved.

Sean returned to the detachment after work, dropped off his uniform and equipment, and packed a few things to bring back to Pok's house. As he was walking out to the road, he saw a civilian vehicle roll slowly by the detachment and then stop next to him. The windows were slightly tinted and Sean couldn't see inside until the window rolled down. It was O'Toole driving and O'Brien in the front passenger seat.

"Sean me boy!" O'Toole called out in a very bad imitated Irish accent as the window rolled down.

Sean walked over and then squatted down to be eye level with them. "Hey, what's up," he asked.

"Wanted to come by and talk with you for a second," O'Toole said and made a motion with his hand to get in the back seat, "Come on we'll give you a ride."

Sean got inside the rear seat behind O'Toole, with his small bag of clothes and other personal items. "Thanks. What's up?" he asked again.

O'Toole drove off and O'Brien turned to the left from the front seat as if to look at him. "Need to talk to you about your source."

"Sean, we'd really like to talk to him ourselves," O'Toole called out over his shoulder as he drove down the street.

"Well, OK, I know he's in the field right now. But I would have to ask him to come and talk to you. I mean he made me promise," Sean replied.

"Look Sean, we understand about maintaining confidentiality of your source, we understand completely. But now things have changed, this has really become some big shit," O'Brien said.

"Sean, this isn't for sharing with anyone outside this car understand?" asked O'Toole, looking into the mirror to see Sean's reaction.

"Sure," Sean agreed and shrugged his shoulders.

O'Brien started, "Look, everything your source came up with has checked out, including names, events, locations everything. This thing you came up with is big." O'Brien paused to look at Sean.

"Wow, that's great. I wasn't sure, you know. This was my first time doing anything like that." Sean felt very relieved and excited that he had apparently helped out.

"You did great," O'Toole turned briefly towards him and then back around to look out of the windshield, "But, something has come up and we're going to have to talk to your source ourselves. This is like life and death, understand?"

"Well," Sean tried to formulate his response, "I understand but I gave my word not to get him involved."

"Look, this is beyond a promise to some snitch." O'Brien countered.

Sean thought to himself, *a promise is a promise regardless who it was given to. This wasn't like promising his mom to write while he was away or take his vitamins every day. This was a serious promise and he looked into another man's eyes and had given his word not to divulge his name. Sean had to think what his word was worth, even to a 'snitch'. Although at the time he didn't consider Broadbench a snitch. He was just someone that gave him information.*

"Guys look, I gave him my word," Sean tried to explain but was cut off.

"Your word?" O'Brien raised his voice as if trying to get his attention, "Hey, fuck your word. We need to talk to him."

"I told you he's in the field. I'll contact him as soon as I can and see if he'll come in." Sean tried to remain calm although he was getting a little distressed from being challenged.

"That might not be good enough, Specialist," O'Brien elevated the conversation suddenly changing from informal first names to a more formal use of Sean's rank. O'Brien tried to assume a superior position over him and continued, "You gave your word to some snitch it was good intentioned, but that doesn't mean anything. I'd give him up, O'Toole here would give him up, and so would anyone under these conditions."

"Look Sirs," Sean stressed the word "sirs" as if to emphasize his response back to O'Brien. "I gave my word and that's good enough for me. If you'd go against your word, well that's your problem and your honor. Not mine." Sean could feel his anger rising. "So, you got to do what you got to do. So will I. Now, I'll track him down as soon as I can and try to convince him to come and talk to you. That's all I can do." Sean turned to look out the window and started to breathe deeply to remain calm.

O'Brien turned around in the passenger seat and faced forward. They rode the remainder of the way to Pok's house in relative silence, with Sean passing along the directions to O'Toole. As they pulled up to the street, Pok was coming out of the metal gate onto the sidewalk.

"Hey, doesn't she work at the PMO?" O'Brien pointed at Pok who had stopped on the sidewalk waiting for the vehicle to stop or pass by.

"Yeah, that's Miss Park. You can let me off right here, please." Sean gathered up his things.

"Sean, no hard feelings right? You got to understand this thing is much larger than we thought and your source has got to have some more information that could help us." O'Toole tried to maintain a relationship.

"It might be a matter of life or death, OK? So we could get him out of the field tomorrow if we had to," O'Brien tried one more time.

"Sirs, I understand. I'm sorry. This whole thing was all new to me. Next time I'll know not to make such a promise, but my word is my bond even for things like this." Sean opened the door to get out but turned back, "What good is a man's word if he's not bound by it? It's something my dad taught me."

O'Toole rolled down his window as Sean closed the rear door. "Sean, we understand. Get ahold of him as soon as you can, OK?"

"Yes, Sir, I will." Sean walked to catch up with Pok who had walked across the street while the car was parked.

The CID vehicle drove away at a rather fast pace. "Motherfucker!" O'Brien punched the dashboard. "We should have grabbed him up and taken him to the office right now. This is horse shit obstruction of justice. Who the fuck does he think he is?" O'Brien folded his arms and looked out the window in frustration.

"Nah, partner, not obstruction. That's honor," O'Toole leaned over as he drove. "Misplaced maybe for us right this minute. But, I got to tell you, I respect that little shit a lot more than I did before. Did you hear what he said? He told you to kiss his ass for sure. I swear that little fucker has a set of balls man." O'Toole looked out the window repeated to himself, "A man's word is his bond? Jesus Christ, O.B. who says that anymore?"

Sean walked across the street and caught up with Pok as she stood outside the small little store where she was buying a couple of packets of Raman Noodle soup. She was finishing the transaction as he walked up and greeted her.

Parked fifty yards up the road was a blue Toyota panel van with the engine running. "That's him right there," Jamie Broadbench spoke out identifying Sean to the Korean male driver and American soldier sitting in the passenger seat.

"Got him, is that his woman?" The American soldier asked.

"Yep, they live across the street on the left." Broadbench confirmed.

"All right, got it."

"Tomorrow, get here early and catch them somewhere and do it." Broadbench ordered and then asked the Korean, "you can drive tomorrow? Early yes?"

"Tomorrow early," the Korean said and nodded. "OK, and you all know what I want?" Broadbench asked.

"Yeah, Jamie we got it."

Sean and Pok started to walk across the street arm in arm laughing at some personal joke between them, while all three sets of eyes in the panel van were watching them as they opened the metal gate and went inside the small yard towards the house.

"Listen to me, don't fuck around with this guy; he's an old country boy and he'll kick your ass if you're not careful. Don't take no chances." Broadbench sternly warned.

"All right, Jamie we got it." The American soldier answered somewhat irritated at the constant warnings by Broadbench.

"All right, let's go then." Broadbench ordered and sat back against the seat.

The Korean driver put the van in gear and started down the road slowly passing by the gate as it shut behind Sean and Pok with all three occupants looking at them as the gate closed.

XXI

Over the next few days little by little, Sean moved into Pok's house. First it was his small overnight kit, with toothbrush, razor, shaving cream and the like, then a few clothing articles. Then he started bringing in civilian clothes and underwear. Pok gave up one drawer in the five-drawer chest of drawers and he was happy. He kept his uniforms at the detachment area to save space. Reggie's girlfriend Myong finally was able to come up and find a job in the local area. They found a small apartment just outside Camp Red Cloud above one of the shops. They each agreed to pick up the other up at 0400 when it was the other's scheduled day shift so they could each get a ride to work. Sean surprised Pok with a small 15" black and white television set from the Post Exchange and a couple of packets of Jiffy Pop. They spent several nights popping corn and watching a movie on Armed Forces Radio Television Service or AFRTS or "A Farts" as it was more commonly known. Pok had never tasted popcorn before and it was an instant hit. They sat in bed with a big bowl of popcorn between them and watched a movie and teased each other.

"Yobo," Pok called out from the kitchen, "Time to get up, lazy man. Breakfast almost ready." Sean was scheduled off for three days and he enjoyed a little extra time in bed. They decided the night before to go into town and pick up their suit and dress that were ready. In typical fashion, Pok rose earlier again, slipped out of bed slowly so as to not wake up Sean and made coffee and a few hard-boiled eggs for breakfast. It gave her a great deal of pleasure to prepare something for them to eat. She had pretty much gone against most everything traditional in the Korean Culture as she grew up. She had gone to school, gotten a job, and moved out of her family's house to go out on her own. But now with Sean, she had a man in her life for the first time and suddenly she understood why her mother had always seemed so dedicated and loyal to her father. Scurrying around the small kitchen to prepare breakfast, knowing Sean would appreciate her efforts put her in a good mood. She at last knew she could be a good wife too, someday.

Only after everything was ready did she call out for Sean to get up. "Yobo, time get up." She walked into the bedroom; her house slippers lightly scraping the floor as she shuffled across the floor and offered him a fresh cup of coffee. Sean had gotten up and put his feet over the side of the bed, when she first called out. He looked over at the clock on the night stand and realized he had slept until almost eight o'clock. Such luxury. He could hear Pok approaching and looked up to accept the cup of coffee. He took a sip of what visually could pass for strong tea. She was getting better at making coffee, but still a little on the weak side. But at least you couldn't see the bottom of the cup anymore like her first attempts.

"Yobo," Sean looked up at Pok who was standing before him. He sat the cup on the night stand and reached out and put his arm around her and put the side of his face into the middle of her abdomen and felt the warmth of the soft house coat. "Have I told you I loved you this morning?"

"No, you don't tell me ever." Pok answered back and made a face as if she were pouting," I think you a bad GI," and ran her fingers through his short hair.

"I'm very sorry to neglect you," Sean replied and hugged her.

"Neglect? What is neglect? What does it mean?" Pok asked and reached for her Korean-English dictionary on the nightstand and started flipping through the pages.

"Well, in this case, it's like I didn't pay enough attention to you, so I neglected you," Sean explained.

"Ah so, yes. I understand. You neglect me this morning." Pok put on the sad pouty face again and looked down as if she were dejected, "It break my heart." Her hand went to her heart as if in pain.

Sean looked up at her and they both giggled the lover's giggle, a small bit of nothing that made them both smile and feel appreciated. They enjoyed a nice relaxing breakfast, much less than her first attempt. A few hard-boiled eggs some toast and jam and they were satisfied. Pok sat on one side of the small table reading a Korean newspaper and Sean sat on the other reading the Stars and Stripes newspaper from the previous day. He couldn't help himself from looking over the table several times at Pok and smiled to himself. He had seen something similar at his own house as he was growing up. During the winter, both his mom and dad would sit at the table for a long time while each reading their paper drinking their coffee and making comments to each other. It was a strange feeling to find himself doing the same thing with Pok.

Eventually the coffee ran out, and the papers were read and they decided to get dressed. Sean had made arrangements the day before to meet Reggie and his girlfriend Myong downtown for lunch and perhaps some beers. Reggie had the day off too and it was going to be their first chance for the girls to meet each other. Once they got dressed, Pok called for a taxi to come and pick them up. When it arrived a few minutes later, it parked on the street and honked its horn; Sean and Pok were already walking down towards the gate. They opened the heavy metal gate and walked onto the street. Sean opened the back door to the taxi. As Pok got inside, he looked up the street and noted a blue Ford panel van parked across the street with two persons sitting inside. As he started to get into the back seat he noted the van starting up as well. Sean really did not pay that much attention to the vehicle, excepting it was unusual to have any vehicles parked along the narrow street in front of the house.

Pok and Sean exited the taxi when it reached the downtown shopping areas. Sean paid the 300 won fare and they both got outside. It was the start of a nice warm early summer day, with just a little humidity; it reminded Sean of similar days in June in the Mississippi delta when he was growing up. Looking around, he was already starting to feel comfortable walking around the market area, recognizing the different shops now from visiting them with Pok. It was going to be a great day casually walking hand in hand along the small street looking into the various shops and even better because of the surprise he had in store for Pok. It was so good, Sean had counted the days down in great anticipation until they could return to get their clothing and he could spring a surprise on her. They walked hand in hand, Pok no longer concerned with any public perception of holding hands with an American. She was keenly aware that any Korean woman seen in the company of an American soldier would almost automatically be thought of as a "business woman." It wasn't as if she didn't care what others may think or assume about her and Sean, she simply decided that it was worth whatever silent contempt she may have to face. She had her man who happened to be American, but he treated her well, loved her, and she was in love with him.

They weaved their way through the small shopping area until they eventually arrived at the tailor shop. Entering again, they were greeted by the same old man who seemed genuinely pleased to see them again. They had gone back a week before for a fitting and were very satisfied with the product. As they were walking towards the store the old man had seen them approach and had gotten the suit and dress ready to go; they were already on a stand when they walked in the door, wrapped in heavy dry-cleaning plastic. After their greeting, Pok looked over at the stand and put her hand over her mouth and gasped. She was floored at the final product. She first took the suit from the stand and put it up against Sean and smiled a broad smile of approval. She then turned around and took the dress from the stand and put it up against her and waited for Sean's reaction. Sean then smiled back in approval and the old man sat back with his hands behind his back obviously pleased at the reaction. Sean then nodded to the old man who quickly reached into his pocket and pulled out a small velvet covered box and handed it over to Sean very conspiratorially.

"I think this will make it look better," Sean said as Pok caught the movement between them.

Sean held the dress up against her neck and told her to hold it in position. Her eyes widened as Sean opened the box to show a small strand of pearls. He pulled them out of the box and reached over and placed it against Pok's neck. The pearls accented the black dress splendidly.

"Look good, numba one," the old man said while nodding approvingly.

"Sean," Pok could only say as tears formed in her eyes. She took the pearls into her hand and held them up to see and then quickly clutched them to her chest as if they were a great treasure and closed her eyes momentarily as if she were afraid to open them and discover it had been a dream. As her eyes closed, the tears ran down both her cheeks. Sean looked over at the old man who was smiling approvingly. He exchanged quick glances with Sean and nodded his approval. Pok finally opened her eyes again and held the pearls out in front of her to take a good at them. She smiled broadly and opened her arms wide to give him a hug, wrapping both arms around his neck and holding on tightly. She finally released him and then took the pearls and held them out in front of her to finally take a good look at them. She wanted so much to say something, but she was speechless.

"Anything for you sweetheart," Sean said happy that he was able to surprise her. He had dipped into his savings and bought them at the Post Exchange a few days before and brought them to the tailor shop before he got off work the day before. When he saw the look in Pok's face, he knew it was a worthy investment.

Pok turned to the older man and spoke in polite Korean. She turned around and looked back at Sean the tears now flowing out of her eyes. The old man appeared with a small box of Kleenex and held it out for her. Taking out a few sheets, she spoke to the man again and they both laughed.

" I…I don't know what to say." Pok finally managed to get out as she wiped the tears from her eyes and dried those that had run down her cheeks.

"Say I love you," Sean offered.

Pok smiled and nodded agreement. She reached out to give him another double arm hug and held on tightly. "I love you," she whispered in his ear and smiled.

"That's what I wanted to hear." Sean hugged back and then broke her hug and stepped back to look into her eyes.

"Not because this," Pok said as she held up the small velvet box.

"I know," Sean smiled back.

"This cost too much money," Pok said as she opened the box again and looked over the necklace. "You don't have to do this," she said, but was thrilled that he had done so.

"Nah, you numba one Yobo, its GI custom," Sean looked back and smiled. He was also on cloud nine and was very happy his surprise was so well accepted. Pok took a few more sheets of Kleenex and dried her eyes and then looked quickly into her compact mirror to see if her makeup had run at all.

Sean settled up with the bill, and Pok put the velvet box into her purse and was beaming as they walked out of the tailor shop. Sean was also smiling and carrying the suit and dress by their hangers over his right shoulder and the other two small packages they had bought earlier from another shop in his left hand. As they walked out of the store, a slender white male wearing a black leather jacket, blue jeans, cowboy boots and red baseball cap walked quickly up and suddenly stopped in front of Pok. Unable to stop, Pok bumped into him and was pushed back, running into Sean who was also just coming out of the store.

"Oh, I'm so sorry," Pok said embarrassed and slightly bowed in apology and stepped back.

"Well yobo-seyo," the man answered back and took a tooth pick out of his mouth. "That's OK, it was good for me too."

Sean was bumped back slightly as Pok was forced back and he then looked up to see what was going on. As the tall man spoke, another shorter white man came from behind the taller man to him, and got up in Sean face. Sean tried to step back and recover, but he was up against the tailor shop door. With Pok up against him from the front, the door behind him, and his hands both carrying something, there was nowhere for him to go.

"Hey, can't you control your little kimchi pussy?" The shorter man raised his voice and leaned forward getting right into Sean's face.

Sean tried to move his head back so he could even see the shorter man's face and make out who he was or what was going on. The sudden confrontation had taken Sean by surprise he could tell they were both Americans and by the short hair and general dress they were obviously soldiers.

"What's your problem man?" Sean finally recovered enough to speak as he looked at both the tall and short man.

"Hey, you're our problem dickweed. Can't you control your little Kimchi bitch?" the tall man said and grabbed Pok by the arm. He jerked her out of the way and immediately moved directly up to Sean. Reaching up, he grabbed Sean's left hand with both hands and held it down against the wall, at the same time the smaller man reached out and grabbed Sean's right wrist with both hands. Sean reacted by trying to step forward, he managed to come out of the doorway, but the combined weight and strength of the other two men pushed him against the exterior wall of the tailor shop.

"Nice try dickweed but you ain't going anywhere yet," the taller man said through gritted teeth into Sean's ear.

"You know why he can't control his little bitch? Because he can't mind his own fuckin' business." came a third voice, this one from a slender white male, wearing a blue nylon jacket, blue jeans, and mirrored sunglasses who was now standing a few feet in back of the other two who were trying to hold Sean against the wall. "Now you just stand there a minute," Mirrored Glasses said and smiled.

Sean could feel his blood boil as he sized up the three men and his own situation. He was backed up against the wall of the tailor shop with both hands still clutching the packages now held down by the two other men. The first soldier was up against him to his left side and the second male was up against him on his right, his arms held against the wall. The third man, who by his actions and comments appeared to be in charge of the other two suddenly reached out and took Pok, who was standing in the small gathering crowd, somewhat in shock with what was happening around her. He reached out and grabbed her by the arm and spun her around to face Sean, the man holding her in front of him with his arms wrapped around her.

"Maybe this little kimchi bitch needs some training so she won't bump into people innocently walking down the road." Mirrored Glasses spoke and leaned his head forward and stuck out his tongue to lick at her ear. "What do you think? You need some extra training?"

"Look, we're sorry. No harm intended now just let her go," Sean said as he looked from side to side sizing up each man up as he looked at them. As he looked around, he suddenly was gripped with a feeling of absolute calm. He was over the immediate shock of the unprovoked attack, and now having looked at each man in turn, he knew he could kick their asses, without a doubt. But first he wanted to get Pok out of the way. Sean didn't even try to struggle against the two men holding him; instead he became somewhat passive and limp, forcing them to use more energy to hold his arms up and tightly against the wall. He simply let go of his packages and let go of the hanger holding his suit, freeing both hands.

"Sorry? You're sorry? You bumped into my friend and you're sorry," said the taller man. "You are sorry, you mother fucker, you know why?" the taller man leaned forward and whispered into his ear.

"No, why?" Sean answered and looked from each man to another his eyes squinting as he concentrated on the man holding Pok. He knew there was a fight coming on and he was trying to figure out how to avoid getting Pok hurt.

"Because you're meddling and getting involved where you don't belong." The tall soldier came forward and put his chest up against Sean and leaned forward. He could feel the warmth of his breath.

"Meddling in what?" Sean asked and turned his head to face the tall man.

"Bishop," the tall man whispered.

"Bishop?" Sean asked as if he didn't understand, but he knew right away who he was talking about.

"Yeah, Bishop. You shot your mouth off to CID about Bishop, didn't you? Did you think we wouldn't find out?" The tall man pushed him hard against the wall.

"Boy, you need to keep your mouth shut if you know what's good for you," Mirrored Glasses said. "Otherwise we're going to have to teach your Korean slut here to suck some dick." The man lowered his head and licked her neck. "I bet we could make some money off of this one. She's awful sweet, and sure smells pretty."

Pok started to shake and he could see the fear in her eyes as she looked up at the man holding her and then over to Sean, who had properly sized each man up by this point. He knew he could take both men that were up against him, but he was uncertain about the man that was holding Pok.

"Nah, he ain't gonna say anything else are you? He's not so big and bad without his little stick and pistol is he?" The tall man leaned close to whisper in his ear.

"You know you can't spell wimp without an MP?" the shorter man emphasized by shoving against him.

"You talk to CID again and we'll come back," the tall man whispered to Sean. "It won't be so nice next time. Not a lot of talking, just some ass whooping, you understand?"

"Yeah?" Sean answered and let the packages go to the ground. He looked over at Pok and Mirrored Glasses who was still holding her and grinning a toothy grin.

"Yeah shit head," the smaller man said and then pushed his right arm against the wall.

Sean looked back at the smaller man to his right, looking directly into his eyes. He could feel the calm being replaced by a determination and resolve that Sean had felt before on the football field when they had desperately needed short yardage and the team was counting on him to plow through the line and save the game. He was going to have to do it. But this was way different, and he knew it.

"Look, let her go, if you have a beef with me let's settle it, but let her go," Sean said defiantly as he felt his blood starting to boil and his heart start to race.

"Nah, I like this little Korean pussy, why should I let her go?" Mirrored Glasses asked and kissed Pok on the ear and then pressed his face against Pok's face smiling back at Sean.

It's strange the things you think about when you're under stress, when you feel threatened, genuinely threatened for your safety or the safety of the one you love. Sean was amazed of his thoughts as his heart pounded through his chest, he became quite focused. In the middle the small street in Uijonbu Korea, with a man on either side of him holding him against the wall and another one holding the women he loved, he remembered something his father once told him. "Son," he said, "No one ever gets anything out of fighting except hurt. So, you should avoid it whenever possible. No one ever respects the man who fights for no reason or fights to prove they are tougher than another man, or even worse uses their size against a smaller man. It's a foolish waste of time and your God given talent and ability and I'll not have it in my house. But," he remembered his dad looking at him directly in the eye, "there is always the time when you cannot talk your way out or when you are forced to fight, because some other man is going to injure you or your own family. When that time comes, let the other guy talk, brag, beat his chest, and bolster his nerves, because when you get to the point where there is no way out, the time for talking is over. Then rise up and beat the living crap out of him. Don't give him a chance to recover and don't think you have to offer him a chance once things get started. That time has passed."

Sean looked over at the taller man, he now was focused like a laser beam on him, he began to smile a slight Mona Lisa smile that betrayed the actual intensity behind it and said, "Let her go, because I'm going to kick your ass in just a minute if you don't." It was the basic rattle warning from one man to another to beware and tread lightly.

"Yeah, well I might just kick your ass right here and now right in front of your little Kimchi cunt," the tall man said as he moved his face just inches from Sean's face, obviously not picking up on the sign.

"Whew," Sean moved his head back he knew it was time. "Man," Sean spoke, "did you eat shit for breakfast? Cause your breath smells like you've been eating shit." Sean looked directly at the tall man as if he were issuing a personal challenge to the man.

"Smart ass motherfucker," the tall man said through clenched teeth and quickly reared back to throw a punch. But Sean could see it coming and at the last millisecond he lowered his head and the tall man's fist struck the top of Sean's head rather than his face, basically hitting Sean in one of the hardest places on the human body. Sean could hear the taller man's knuckles pop and saw the tall man grab his hand then turn his face towards Sean. He was in obvious pain and was grimacing, but his movement had left Sean's arm free. Not wasting a second, Sean reached out and pulled the man to him and plowed his forehead full force against the bridge of the tall man's nose. The shorter man, distracted from the sudden violence, was taken by surprise when Sean jerked his right arm free from the wall and his grip and then pushed the shorter man away. holding his nose and face with both hands to pinch the flow of blood from his nose and get the tears out of his eyes caused by the blow to his face. Sean then turned to the taller man who had staggered back a few steps, Sean raised his right fist up and struck him solidly behind his right ear which sent him down onto both knees. The smaller man recovered and finally reacted by striking Sean in the face with a good right fist of his own, striking Sean's right cheek and sending his head back hard against the brick wall. Hitting the wall momentarily dazed him, but he shook his head rapidly a few times and his sense retuned.

The smaller man then let loose with a flurry of fists on Sean who was still dazed. Sean's legs started to buckle when the short man reached out and grabbed him by the front of his shirt with both hands and spun him 180 degrees around. He let go, sending Sean across the small street and into the shelves of merchandise displayed outside of another small shop. The shelves were loaded with brass tea kettles, figurines, vases, and trays. Sean hit the wooden shelves hard and fell to the ground, with some of the merchandise falling onto the street on and around Sean. The sound of the brass objects hitting the ground rang out over the normal hustle of the shopping area and attracted serious onlookers who were now aware of the fight and were speaking in loud Korean both calling for someone to call the police as well as offering encouragement to one side or the other. Sean managed to quickly get onto all fours trying to regain his footing, but the tall man had also recovered and although he was now bleeding profusely from his nose, he managed to land a direct hit to Sean's face with his right foot that sent Sean sprawling backwards onto the ground again. Sean rolled quickly over onto his stomach and up to all fours again as he had done in football drills a thousand times and was immediately trying to regain his footing and get off the ground. As his hands moved to balance him, he came into contact with a heavy object; he glanced over and saw it was an eighteen-inch solid brass figure of the Statue of Liberty. Sean could see the blur of movement coming from in front of him as he grabbed the figure tightly into his hand and in a single motion, swung the heavy object around and struck the smaller man in the right shin with corner of the heavy base. It cut through the blue jeans and struck the shin bone, ripping into the muscle and flesh as it glanced off the bone. A blood curdling painful cry emitted from the shorter man who fell to the ground grabbing for his lower leg that now was gushing blood.

Almost immediately the taller man again stepped up to Sean and threw another kick at his face. Sean saw this blow coming and turned slightly, deflecting the blow onto his left shoulder. It knocked him off balance, but he quickly recovered. In one swift motion Sean grabbed the heavy brass figurine gain but now with both hands and like he was swinging a sledgehammer, brought the base of the Statue of Liberty down on the tall man's left foot that was nearest to him, striking it with all of the force he could muster. The tall man now let out his own scream and fell to the ground and began to roll from side to side, crying out and withering in pain.

Sean, pulled himself up to a standing position. He looked around at the taller man still rolling on the ground and detected movement towards him from the right. The shorter man, now limping badly, was still coming at him as if to sucker punch him. Sean glanced over to the still standing shelf of merchandise and picked up a large brass tray. Just as the punch was thrown, Sean pulled the tray up like Captain American holding his shield and the shorter man struck the shield with his right hand. He again screamed in pain, backed away holding his right hand and fell to the ground landing hard on his knees. Sean was stunned by the shock of the punch thrown by the smaller man but managed to regain his balance. Breathing heavy he looked and saw that both the taller and shorter man had no fight left in them. He then turned to Mirrored Glasses and wiped the snot and blood from his face. He started to walk forward, but before he could attack, he noted that Mirrored Glasses was now holding a knife to Pok's throat.

Sean hesitated and stood still to evaluate the situation. He was breathing hard, but he was not tired only pumped up. The knife to Pok's throat was a game changer. He was still dazed from a couple of good shots to the head and was now bleeding from his nose, a cut on his cheek, and a laceration over his right ear. But he didn't care. He stood back and clenched and unclenched his fists sizing up the last man and thinking about how to get Pok away from him. Knife or no knife, if Pok was not in danger, he would have charged at sunglasses without hesitation or concern for his own safety but Pok's potential danger changed everything.

"All right, motherfucker," Mirrored Glasses shouted out, his voice betrayed his fear over what he had just seen. "That's enough. Anymore and I'll cut her fucking gook throat."

Sean looked deep into Mirrored Glasses and breathing heavy he turned to look at the location of the other two men. They were still both down and clearly out of any further fight. Sean looked up at the man and wiped his nose with the back of his hand.

"Let her go, or I'm going to kick your ass." Sean spat out, in no mood to negotiation with anyone and took a step towards sunglasses. He could see the look of fear in Pok's eyes as the knife was pressed hard against her throat.

"I'm telling you motherfucker, I'll cut her throat if you take another step." Sunglasses had pulled Pok closer to him and pressed the knife hard against her through. It was clear he was concerned for his own safety. "Now step back and I'll let her go."

Sean stood still and contemplated his options. From behind he could hear the other two men, he turned around and saw them holding onto each other, their arms around each other shoulders as they walked and limped passed Sean. Both were bleeding profusely and although they wanted to say something, both had decided they had enough and only wanted to get away. The men walked passed and continued on, the crowd that had gathered opened up like the Red Sea and they stumbled through. As the men passed sunglasses looked at them and then back at Sean.

"You got off easy this time," Mirrored Glasses spat out, "Next time we just go after this Kimchi bitch. Keep your mouth shut about

Bishop or you're going to be a guest at a Korean funeral." He pushed Pok forward hard into his arms. He then turned and disappeared himself into the crowd.

XXII

Once Sean realized they were no longer a threat, he took a couple of steps, leaned back against the wall, slid down to the ground and tried to catch his breath. He was still dazed. Pok kneeled down in front of him in tears, trying in vain to apply Kleenex to the wounds to stop the bleeding. Sean looked up at her and smiled. He knew he was not seriously hurt, and he was more concerned with Pok. Minutes later four Korean police officers came running up to them. At first they came and seemed to be ready to arrest Sean, pushing him down onto the ground and starting to apply handcuffs. They had seen the brass items all over the street and Sean leaned up against the wall bleeding and assumed he was at fault. After Pok and a dozen other witnesses all shouting out at once in unintelligible Korean finally managed to tell them what happened and pointed down the street as the direction of travel of the suspects, their attitude suddenly changed. Two of the officers ran further down the road to try and catch the other unknown men who were involved.

Once Sean had regained his breath and shook the cobwebs from his head, he managed to stand up. Placing his arm around Pok, he accompanied the Korean Police officers back to the police box located at the end of the street. Sean was actually okay, with just a bloody nose and two small cuts that bled far worse than the injuries would indicate. Both had stopped bleeding in a matter of minutes after he sat down at the police box.

As they were waiting at the police box, Sean looked through the window and noticed Reggie and Myong arriving outside in a taxi.

"Yobo," Sean called out to Pok, "there's Reggie and Myong."

Without a word, Pok walked outside and called out to Reggie. Sean could see her talking and explaining in English to Reggie who then bolted into the police box. Then he saw Pok and Myong speaking in rapid Korean outside.

"Who did this?" Reggie asked as he came inside the police box and sat down next to Sean.

"Shit Reg I wish I knew. We were just walking around and suddenly these three dudes came out of nowhere and started a fight."

"Three of them, huh? Did you know any of them?"

"No, never saw them before," Sean wiped his nose again of a small amount of blood still draining out. "Hey Reg, ask the Korean police to call CID ok? I got to talk to them."

"Was this about what Broadbench told you about?" Reggie asked.

"I think so, better tell CID they got a leak or something," Sean looked up at Reggie and shrugged his shoulders.

Reggie conveyed Sean's request to Pok who translated to the Korean police and a call was placed for the duty agent to respond to the police box. Reggie also managed to get some wet paper towels and Sean took them and wiped off the dried blood from his hands and face.

Sean looked over at Pok and Myong and noted they were engaged in animated conversation with each other and with the Korean police.

Twenty minutes later, PFC Eddie Wickham from the MP Detachment and Mr. Choi the Korean Interpreter showed up to take a MP report on what happened. Wickham came over to Sean and Reggie with his notebook and started making some notes as to what happened, while Mr. Choi walked over to Pok who he recognized from the PMO and sat down next to her. Pok was relieved to finally have someone she recognized. It took another 30 minutes to get things settled as to what had happened, the old man from the tailor shop arrived with their purchases and he also provided his information to the police that verified that Sean and Pok were assaulted and were only engaged in self-defense. The brass shop owner was in tow carrying the Statue of Liberty with him, thinking it might be used as evidence. He also agreed that it was the other three men who were to blame, and he did not wish to press any charges against Sean for any damage.

Sean looked up as the Koreans were talking to each other and saw Agent O'Brien finally drive up to the police box in his civilian vehicle, his own Korean Investigators with him. Sean got up and walked outside to talk with him.

"I'll be right back Reg, stay here OK?" Sean stood up and walked outside.

O'Brien recognized Sean immediately and was shocked at his appearance. "Man, what the hell happened to you?" O'Brien asked as he walked up to Sean.

"Bishop is what happened to me," Sean said flatly and then spit blood onto the pavement.

"Bishop? Bishop did this? What are you talking about?" O'Brien asked, not quite understanding.

"Three guys, three American soldiers started some shit with me and my girl as we were out here shopping," Sean started to explain.

"Bishop was one of them?"

"No, three white guys," Sean wiped the corner of his mouth with the back of his hand, "but they basically told me to shut up about Bishop and then threatened my girl."

"They mentioned Bishop specifically?" O'Brien asked to make sure he understood correctly.

"Yeah, said I had gone to CID and I had better shut my mouth, or my girlfriend was going to get hurt. Even put a knife to her throat." Sean then turned and spit again onto the group.

"You got to be shitting me," O'Brien asked as he looked through the window of the police box at the activity inside.

"Look," Sean looked around and walked up closer to O'Brien. "I haven't told anyone anything about Bishop. You guys were the only ones that I talked to so how does Bishop know I was talking to you? Who have you guys told?" Sean looked directly in his eyes and the accusation was very obvious.

"Wait a minute," O'Brien put his hands up, "I swear to you; this hasn't been briefed outside of CID channels to anyone, not even any of these commanders."

"Well someone knows something. I mean, fuck man." Sean expressed frustration and touched the cut above his eye to see if it was still bleeding.

"OK, who knew you were coming here?" O'Brien asked and pulled out his notebook.

"No one that I know," Sean looked somewhat offended by the thought. "I mean we were going to meet Reggie Phillips another MP from CRC and his girl and go to lunch and have a few beers," Sean explained and turned his back in frustration.

"All right, are you OK? Do you need to go to the dispensary to get looked at?" O'Brien asked looking over Sean.

"Nah I'm all right, a little cut up and a knot on the back of the head is all. But, I can tell you two of those guys had better go somewhere because I know I broke one's foot and cut another's leg pretty bad. They were bleeding like stuck pigs when they ran away. Well, they limped away actually. At least one of them will be going to a hospital; I'm pretty sure about that."

"All right I'll put the word out. We'll find them." O'Brien took out a small notebook and made a few notes.

"Look, something is wrong. I'm not telling you your business because I don't know it, but there has to be some leak somewhere," Sean stated the obvious.

"We'll get it unfucked," O'Brien promised. "You sure you're going to be OK?"

"I'm OK, just do something," Sean turned to look in the police box and then back at O'Brien, "my girl shouldn't be involved in anything like this. Who is this Bishop guy anyway?"

"He's a bad one all right but didn't think he was this bad." O'Brien put his notebook back into his pocket and waved at his interpreter who was still inside the police box to join him outside. "Look, I'm going back to CRC to start tracking these guys down. I need you to come up to the CID Office on CRC and make a full written statement. Shouldn't take more than an hour or so."

"All right. Let me take care of my girl and I'll meet you there in a while." Sean turned to go back to the police box and met Pok, Reggie, and Myong who were all standing at the doorway.

"Reg, we got to go up to CRC and make a statement, you guys want to just slide off and we'll do it some other day?"

"Are you kidding me, I want to hear all the details, besides it's my night off, I want to drink a few beers."

"All right, well, let's do the statement and then come over to our house," Sean looked over to Pok, "Is that OK?"

"It's ok," Pok answered and nodded her head. She then turned to Myong and then spoke rapidly in Korean who nodded her head and answered her back. The exchange went back and forth two or three times.

Reggie and Sean looked at them as they talked back and forth and then over at each other and smiled.

"You know we're never going to get a word in edgewise right?" Reggie observed as the girls continued to talk.

"Ok, ok, let's talk later, we have to go to CRC and make statement," Sean finally tried to break in and move everyone along. "We'll meet you up at the CID, Reg?"

"Sounds good, we'll be there right behind you." Reggie waved at them both and then escorted Myong outside and over to the waiting line of taxis.

It actually took nearly two hours at the CID, going through an interview and then taking a written statement. Sean went with O'Brien back to his office while the CID Interpreter stayed up front with Pok and took her statement in Korean which would later be translated into English. About half way through the process, O'Toole appeared at the office and sat down in O'Brien's office and assisted with the interview. They talked at great length trying to figure out who may have been involved.

O'Toole spent the better part of an hour on the phone to every medical clinic in the area asking for any soldiers who may have come in for any treatment for leg or foot injuries. So far no one reported anything which could match the injuries described by Sean, but all agreed to be on the lookout and then notify CID if any such injuries were reported. Eventually there were no more questions to ask and Sean, feeling like someone had just worked him over fairly well, was ready to go home. O'Brien offered to take them all back to Pok's house and even better, agreed to stop at the Class VI store and buy some beer and wine and a sack of ice. They all squeezed into the car together and finally made it home. Sean had a pounding headache, and his face was starting to puff up a bit from some of the solid punches that he had received. He knew what he wanted as they finally were able to pile out of the car and collect their things, Sean reached in to the brown paper shopping bag and took out a can of beer from the plastic ring and handed it to Reggie who accepted it gladly. Sean then took out one for himself and opened it. Saluting Reggie by raising the beer into the air, as the girls opened the gate, he took a long deep drink. Reggie followed suit and then followed the girls into the metal gate and up the few steps to the house. Everyone stopped of course to remove their shoes; it was a Korean custom that street shoes were not allowed in the house. They were left on the front steps, and several pairs of loose fitting sandals or slippers were left for them and guests.

Sean excused himself and asked if he could please take a shower and get some of the blood off of him. He took two beers and a change of clothes with him and then walked into the bathroom. Sean took another pull of the beer and looked into the mirror above the sink. If the truth was known, he had actually felt worse and had been hurt worse from playing football a time or two, yet still his head was somewhat pounding. He reached back and felt a good-sized knot on the back of his head that hurt to touch. He finally ran his tongue through the inside of his mouth and didn't feel any cuts inside. His forehead was already swelling and bright red and was going to bruise up for certain, but he smiled thinking it was going to be far worse for those other two. One probably had broken a few bones in his hand and maybe even his nose thanks to that forehead, so it was probably worth it. The sides of his head were both red and swelling and a scrape over his right ear was somewhat painful. But other than a black eye very likely from the kick to the nose, he thought he made out all right. He opened the other beer as he waited for the shower to warm up. He was grateful to get out of his clothes that both looked and smelled as if he had wallowed around on the street. Once the water warmed he stepped inside and almost immediately learned that he had also scraped his knees, and that knot on the back of his head was also scraped because the water burned as it ran over each injury. But it felt good, especially when he was able to cup his hands together and then splash water over his face. His nose hurt a little but he didn't think he had broken it.

He took a good fifteen minutes and would have liked to have taken an hour or so, but he knew he had to entertain his guests. The shower was just what he needed, and he felt refreshed, but thirsty since he had drank both of the beers during his shower. While he was getting cleaned up, the girls had jumped in and quickly put together a good supper of spiced pork, rice, and fresh cucumber and onion kimchi that Sean liked so well. The peppers stung his upper lip but it was still good. The beer was cold and went down very easy and Sean helped himself to several more. After supper Pok and Myong chased them out outside to let them get the kitchen cleaned and Reggie and Sean walked around and took the small exterior stairway up to the roof. The cool night air felt good and they sat down in the small lawn chairs that Sean had bought at the Post Exchange.

"Sorry to mess up your day, Reg." Sean sighed and looked over at Reg and saluted with another raised beer.

"Ah, who cares? I mean, at least I didn't get the shit kicked out of me," Reggie looked over and started to laugh.

"Yeah I guess you're right, you should be having a good time anyway," Sean started to laugh but it made his head hurt.

"This is weird man, I've never heard of anything like this before," Reggie commented and took another drink from his beer.

"Yeah, I know that's what people keep saying," Sean looked back and shook his head.

Pok and Myong were already becoming fast friends as well and except for the circumstances, they ended up having a real good time. But both Pok and Sean were happy when Reggie and Myong decided it was time to go home. They had a grand exit with hugs and so longs and goodbyes, the girls exchanged numbers and agreed to get together in the coming days. Sean was overjoyed when he could finally close the door and shut off the light. He was tired and the dull ache of his head was dampened by the beer but had never gone completely away. After giving Pok a hug and then brushing his teeth, Sean finally made his way to the bed and collapsed. Before Pok could come in and turn off the light he was fast asleep.

It took some effort to finally crawl out of bed the next morning. It seemed like every part of his body was sore. As he swung his feet over the edge of the bed his head started to pound, as if he had a hangover to top off the rest of his body. Standing up was also an adventure in discovering additional spots that hurt. He managed to find his way into the bathroom and stood over the sink and looked into the mirror. His face was certainly puffier and a dark purple contusion was already forming on his forehead and over the right ear. It hurt to the touch and was going to be ugly for couple of days but otherwise he thought he was going to survive. After his morning wash up he looked around the house but Pok was nowhere to be found. There was a pot of coffee all made on the automatic coffee maker and Sean poured a cup, then slowly made his way to the front door and went outside. It was a cool morning, with just a hint of humidity and Sean took a deep breath and stretched, causing several pangs of pain to shoot out into his back and left shoulder and causing him to stop. He sat down on the top of the stairs and looked at the small garden that made up the interior of the house. Almost silently Pok came out of the house and without a word sat next to him and wrapped both arms around him placing her head on his right shoulder.

Pok had not talked very much about her own feelings and fears over the incident the previous day. She thought she had been very strong and supportive through the incident and while they were at the police box and then the CID office, she had managed to put up a brave unafraid front. But, it had been a complete façade. Actually she had slept very little the night before and when she did, she had nightmares of having the knife placed against her throat. Sleeping was so much out of the question in the early morning hours she gave up all attempts and simply got up. Even after taking a long hot shower and shampooing her hair twice, she could still smell the body odor and breath of Mirrored Glasses.

Pok had never been subjected to anything like that in her entire life. She had grown up sheltered in a family with privilege and wealth and had never experienced any type of personal confrontation. When Mirrored Glasses pulled her to him and wrapped his arms around her, she was almost too shocked to respond. She could still remember looking across at Sean pushed against the wall of the small shop and then the look on Sean's face; at first it was surprise as he looked from side to side and then over to her. She saw something she had never seen before, when Sean's expression turn from surprise to cold anger. It came over him like a wave, his eyes had narrowed and he became focused on the two men holding him, and then calm. As if he had resolved the situation in his own mind. She knew then he was about to do something and it had frightened her as much as excited her. When he struck, Pok had never seen such rage in anyone in her entire life. The sudden physical explosion from Sean when he struck out against both men had shocked even Mirrored Glasses who had stepped back a few feet, dragging her away further. Then out of his own fear, he had unconsciously squeezed her to the point she was having difficulty in breathing.

From her memory, most of the fight was just a blur of activity as Sean responded and struck out as either of the two men presented themselves. Even when Mirrored Glasses put the knife to her throat she was more concerned with Sean. He was obviously hurt, and bleeding, yet he took a couple of breaths and started advancing towards her. Mirrored Glasses had gasped and grabbed her even tighter; she was so close to him she could feel his heart beating out of his chest. She had a knife to her throat, yet she could see Sean advancing towards her and she strangely felt safe, or at least knew she soon would be.

Now that Pok was sitting down next to Sean and holding him in her arms, she felt safe again, yet at the same time was apprehensive. Was this to be her future life? She could not imagine going through anything similar again, but who could have predicted such things in the first place. Pok decided that regardless of the future, Sean would be there to protect her; she had seen it herself. He was the knight in shining armor that women dream of finding.

XXIII

Camp Red Cloud, Korea

Monday morning, Grubner came into work and as per his routine asked to take a look at the weekend blotters, the chronological list of cases reported to the MP Station. The Commander saw and approved each night's blotter before it was sent out to the numerous offices and officers on CRC that got a copy of the blotter. It was like the MP's had their own camp newspaper. Grubner always got caught up on what happened the preceding day first thing in the morning as he drank his first cup of coffee. Mostly the entries were fairly routine – reported thefts, some simple possessions of drugs, often reports of soldiers picked up by patrols doing something stupid. It had all been rather unimportant and uninteresting until he came to one particular entry for Saturday. This once made him put his coffee cup down and light up a cigarette as he read and reread the entry several times to make sure he understood what had happened.

Assault consummated by Battery, Article 128 UCMJ; Aggravated Assault, Article 128, UCMJ; and Communicating a threat, Article 134, UCMJ.

He read down the blotter entry, line by line, three unknown white males, time and place; Victim number one, York, Sean P. Specialist, 3rd MP detachment, APO SF 96358 ; Victim number two, Park, Pok Suk, Korean female, Time and date, Saturday, time 11:45.

DETAILS: Investigation by unit 21(Wickham) revealed that York and Park were shopping together in downtown Uijongbu City when they were accosted by subjects 1-3 who made verbal threats against York and Park. Subject (1) and (2) then shoved York up against a wall and physically held him while they made additional verbal threats against Park who was being physically restrained by Subject #3. The altercation then turned physical when subject #1 struck York in the head, with his closed fist, and York responded by defending himself and struck suspects number 1 and 2. During the course of the struggle, and in self-defense, York struck subjects 1 and 2 with a brass figurine and injured them on their leg and foot. Subject number 3 then produced a knife and placed it against Park's throat threatening to harm her if York did not stop fighting subjects 1 and 2. Once the fight stopped, the three subjects then fled the scene. All three subjects remain at large. CID O'Brien accepted investigative jurisdiction of this case. No charges are pending against York or Park by the Korean National Police (KNP). There was no alcohol involved in this incident. Investigation continues by CID O'Brien.

He looked down at the blotter again and noted that the MP detachment Commander was notified of the incident at 1500 on Saturday but apparently the commander didn't feel it important enough to call and tell him about it. Even worse, as far as he was concerned, CID had gotten involved.

"God damned officers," Grubner thought to himself. He was the detachment sergeant in this outfit and anything that happened to any soldier in it, concerned him. How was he supposed to maintain order and discipline if the commander was keeping things from him? He knew how that worked. Let something bad develop and he was going to be expected to fix it, instead of being on top of things and preventing it from happening in the first place. Grubner put his cigarette out and looked at his watch, there was a weekly squad leaders meeting in less than fifteen minutes, he was going to take care of this developing problem today and put another nail in that little shit's coffin. After the morning squad leaders meeting, he called Whitehouse aside and handed him the blotter, "You know about that?"

Whitehouse looked over the blotter and recognized the report.

"Yep, that was Saturday. York called me at the house on Saturday afternoon from the CID office. I know all about it." Whitehouse handed back the blotter report.

"Well this conduct is inappropriate for a MP and I want a counseling statement. Perhaps he needs to spend some time on post for a while."

"Top, look he was minding his own business when these three guys threatened him. One held a knife to Miss Park's throat. We should be lucky he didn't beat them to a pulp. I'm sorry I don't have a problem with it at all. This was just self-defense, plain and simple and CID says the same thing."

"Well good, now I have a lawyer in my unit." Grubner looked at Whitehouse with contempt.

"Nope, not even, but I am telling you, if you were to threaten my wife like that, I'd kick the crap out of you too. Nothing he did is out of order from what I or any other man would have done themselves."

"Well, that's not the way it works, there was no reason for him to strike back. He could have retreated or walked away. If someone hits him, that's an assault. He makes a report and we go and get them. Once he hits back, that's engaging in an affray. Fighting plain and simple and engaging in an affray is a criminal offense, too. I want a counseling statement on it on my desk tomorrow when I come in."

"Top this is bullshit and you know it," Whitehouse called back to Grubner who had already started walking away.

"Staff Sergeant Whitehouse, this is not a debate or a request. This is an order; do you not understand the difference between the two?"

"I understand the difference, Top."

"Good, then why do we constantly have to go over this point?" Grubner turned around and then turned back, "I expect my order to be obeyed, or to see your stripes on my desk because you refuse to carry out my order. I suggest you pull his pass too; keep him here for a week or so, maybe that will calm him down." Grubner put on his hat and walked out of the PMO and lit up a cigarette. It was going to be a better day then he had expected.

It was tough for Sean to leave and head back to camp Monday morning to get ready for work, he was still a bit sore from the fight, but he was even more concerned about Pok. If someone could have found him walking downtown in the shopping area, what would stop them from coming out here to the apartment? They had discussed the possibility, but Pok had discounted it completely and did not even want to think about that possibility. He admired her for that and was relieved to see her act so brave, although he could not say for certain how much was for real and how much was just putting on an act.

When he finally got dressed at the detachment and made his way to the MP Station for guard mount, Sean was met by SSG Whitehouse who jerked his neck to the side to indicate Sean should follow him. They walked into the back area to talk. Whitehouse pulled out another sheet of paper and Sean recognized what it was immediately.

"Looks like they worked you over pretty good," Whitehouse said as he looked up at Sean's face.

"Yeah, it hurt like hell on Sunday morning, but I'm OK now. Looks worse than it feels," Sean answered.

"I take it the other two look a lot worse," Whitehouse smiled back and looked down at a piece of paper he had in his hand.

"You can take that to the bank," Sean smiled. It seemed that Whitehouse was trying to tell him something but was hesitating.

"Look, I got something for you again," Whitehouse held out another counseling statement and gave it to Sean.

"Sarge you got to be kidding me." Sean looked down at the piece of paper.

"Look, this ain't my doing. This comes directly from the Detachment Sergeant." Whitehouse tried to answer back and shook his head. "I don't know what you've done but somehow you have pissed on this man's parade."

"I swear to God Sarge I don't know." Sean looked down on the paper and read the comments. "Engaging in an affray? Come on Sarge. Those guys were trying to kick my ass, what am I supposed to do?"

"Don't get caught apparently," Whitehouse shrugged his shoulders as if he didn't know either.

"I guess." Sean signed the form and dropped the pen unceremoniously onto the paper. "You know this is getting old Sarge."

"I know this is wearing me thin too." Whitehouse took another drag from his cigarette. "Look, he 'suggested' I take your pass and keep your ass on compound. I'm not going to take his suggestion but don't mess up and make me regret it OK?"

"Thanks Sarge," Sean said and turned away then turned back, "Hey, I got word this morning from Bea, she said the points finally dropped and I made my E-5. Orders should be coming in any day now."

"Oh yeah? Good, I'm looking forward to a good promotion party." Whitehouse then turned to the typewriter, put his eraser pencil in his mouth, and started typing.

"You bet Sarge." Sean gave him a thumbs up and walked back into the briefing room.

After the standard briefing by Whitehouse, he announced Sean's pending promotion to everyone. It was good for backslaps and shakes of the hand in congratulation. It's always a good event when promotions come about. Guard mount was routine and short and by ones and twos they all walked outside to check the lights, the engine oil, and radios on the jeeps to make sure they were set to go for the night's patrol. Sean walked over to his assigned jeep and put his small notebook between the seat and transmission hump.

"Hey, Sean," came a voice from in the small tree line adjacent to the small parking lot.

Sean looked over and tried to see who owned the voice.

"Sean, over here," the voice spoke again more plaintively than before.

Sean walked around to the rear of his jeep and over to the small wood line. Sean almost ran into Jamie Broadbench who was standing just inside the thicket of trees and bushes.

"Jamie, is that you?" Sean asked as he walked forward.

"Yeah, hey how are you? I thought you might be working tonight." Jamie walked over and stuck out his hand to shake Sean's hand.

"Just get out of the field?" Sean asked.

"No, got out early; we came home Friday morning."

"Cool, I've been waiting for you." Sean turned around and called out to his partner who had raised the hood of the jeep and was checking the oil. "Hey, I'll be right back." He received a wave as a response and Sean put his arm over Jamie and started walking further back away from the parking lot.

"So are you working on Bishop?" Jamie asked. "I thought he might have been arrested already."

"Nah, I told you it was out of my league. I had to go to CID. I went to them the next day and gave them everything you told me."

"So?" Jamie asked.

"So, I guess they're working on it, I mean how should I know? It's not like they're going to tell me anything."

"I thought you were really interested in doing something?" Jamie asked.

"Yeah, well I am but I told you I'm just a uniformed MP, I'm pretty far down on the totem pole on stuff like that." Sean stopped walking and turned to face him.

"Yeah but I thought what I gave you was all tied up pretty as can be."

"Yeah, I guess it was. I don't know." Sean shrugged uncertain.

"Aren't they doing anything?" Jamie seemed so insistent.

Sean turned his head from side to side to see if anyone else was around. "I guess they're doing something," Sean was starting to get irritated. "You know Jamie, CID does their own thing; they're not going to tell me anything. But I know they really want to talk to you. Maybe that's the best thing, that way you can ask them what they're doing. "

"Nah, not me. We been through this before, you know the deal," Jamie countered and immediately became defensive.

"I know and I haven't told anyone who you are, but that still doesn't mean they don't want to talk with you."

"Well I gave you everything I would give them, so I don't see the need." Jamie kicked a few small rocks with the toe of his sports shoe. "Besides I don't trust anyone over at the CID to keep their mouth shut, fastest way to get hurt is to talk to those guys. Don't you think?"

Sean reflected on the comment momentarily, "I don't know."

"Really? I heard Bishop's boys paid you a visit over the weekend."

Sean hesitated and then looked directly at Broadbench, "How did you hear about that?" Sean looked up at him.

"I ...eh I .... I was working as the Staff duty driver. Saturday night. It was in the MP Blotter." Jamie quickly answered.

Their conversation was interrupted by a shout from the MP Parking lot,

"Sean, we got a call. Let's go." It was his patrol partner calling out as the jeep started and roared to life.

"All right, be right there." Sean called out and then looked over at Jamie. "Look the CID is working on it, you need to trust me and go and see them."

"Nah, they don't need me, they have you." Jamie put up his hand as if to say good bye and walked away.

Sean turned and walked back to the MP parking lot and got into the front passenger seat of his patrol vehicle. His partner threw the transmission into 2nd gear and then peeled out of the parking lot and raced for the main gate.

"Where we going?" Sean called out as he grasped the hand hold on the small dashboard to keep from falling out.

"Fight downtown at the UN Club, you up for it?" The driver called out over the racing engine and looked over at him.

"Shit, I'm always up for it," Sean replied with enthusiasm that he didn't really feel.

XXIV

O'Brien and O'Toole were at their office early typing and pecking away on their Olivetti manual typewriters, trying to update their case file from all of the activity the previous day. Stack would certainly want to read it first thing in the morning, and they already knew it was better to have it waiting than to have Stack pissed off because it wasn't there and ready to go. Excuses were not readily accepted by Stack or any other CID Supervisor. Excuses were typically greeted by an abrupt "Bullshit" which tended to succinctly express their opinion. Such a comment first thing in the morning led to a very miserable rest of the day, so they typed on.

After updating their case file, they had a full day of planning and briefings scheduled. Such operations and investigations were wonderfully exciting, but they had a down side and paperwork was it. How wonderful life could be if being a CID Special Agent was like a TV detective. Arresting and interrogating people, finding that hidden magic piece of evidence, occasionally being able to shoot some bad guy that needed shooting, and yet magically never having to actually sit down and write a report. Ah, to live in such a fantasy world; wouldn't life be great. Sadly, their world consisted of documentation and the general CID philosophy of *"if it isn't written down, it didn't happen."* They had already come up with a general plan of action of how they were going to take down the entire operation in one day with simultaneous arrests throughout their area.

By the time Stack made it to the office they were finished and had the file sitting on his desk. They were starting their second pot of coffee. They were planning on a round robin tour to make personal notification to the various commanders of the results of their preliminary investigation and their general plan of action. Experience showed it was not wise to suddenly and unexpectedly ambush a division commander and other senior officers by apprehending some fifteen soldiers including a senior NCO, several mid-level NCO's, and a Commissioned Officer without letting them know it was about to happen. Such slights were not easily forgiven and never forgotten. Although general officers were prevented by army regulations to interfere or stop any CID investigation, it was always better to give them a heads up when a big case was coming. Mainly because CID cases tended to generate calls from the media or a higher ranked general officer who would also want to know what's going on.

Their first stop was at their own nominal higher headquarters at the Camp Casey CID Field Office. As a branch office, Camp Red Cloud, along with a few other smaller offices just south of the DMZ were all subordinate to the Camp Casey Field Office. CW4 Henry De Franco, the Operations Officer for Camp Casey Field Office, and Stack's boss, came into the office an hour early to get a full briefing. He was an old school CID agent and came up through the ranks, actually starting his CID Career in Korea immediately following the war in 1953, even before there was a CID. At the time there was a shortage of investigators and he managed to swing a transfer from the infantry over to the Provost Marshal's Office. After a short but intense four week training course someone put together in one of the small camps outside of Seoul, he was conducting felony investigations. At one time he thought he was going to spend a few years doing investigations and then would change back to the infantry, but after a few years of working in an office and sleeping in a barracks instead of a foxhole or a tent, he decided he was much happier inside than outside.

De Franco listened intently to the briefing and approved wholeheartedly of the concept as outlined by Stack. He agreed to commit additional Agents from the field office and other offices in the area to help out as needed.

"All right," De Franco nodded his head in satisfaction after hearing the briefing. "I like it. I'll send you everyone I can round up, and get some more from down south if we need it. You got a date yet?"

"This next payday, the 30th," Stack answered.

"All right, that's awful quick. Can you put it all together?" De Franco asked.

"Already working on it, Chief," O'Toole spoke up, but Stack also nodded in agreement.

"OK, I'll brief Region on what's going on," De Franco knew he had to notify his boss at the CID Region Headquarters down in Yongsan so they would not be surprised with what was going on. "Where are you going now?"

"We'll start with the Division Commander, then DIVARTY Commander, then the other major commanders. We're on their calendars already for this morning," Stack answered as he stood up and collected his papers from the table.

"All right good deal," De Franco also stood up and took a drink of his coffee.

"Can you brief the Major?" Stack asked and smiled, referring to the Field Office Commander.

"Yeah, let me do that," De Franco sighed. "You don't need Sherlock Holmes up your ass." De Franco looked away and shook his head in frustration. "I'll try and keep him out of your way."

"Thanks. That'll help out."

"Yeah, well you owe me," De Franco mumbled to himself not looking forward to briefing the Major. "Well, let me start making some calls. Give me a call this afternoon; let me know how everything is going."

"All right. Will do." Stack reached out and shook his hand and then started out the door.

O'Toole and O'Brien then offered their hands as well.

"O'Toole and O'Brien, The Irish Mafia huh? You two scare me," De Franco commented to them both as he shook both of their hands.

"Ah come on, Chief, you know you love us." O'Toole smiled and shot back.

"Yeah, I loved getting the clap too; I just didn't love it after I got it." De Franco sneered back and then started to smile.

"Ouch Chief, that hurt," O'Brien called out as they exited the office and closed the door.

"You two don't fuck this up," De Franco called out to them as they walked out his office door.

Most senior army officers had a love hate relationship with CID. When they were in trouble or had a problem, they loved CID who could come in and find out what was going on and help them root out the problems. But there were other times, when they hated them, like when CID came to them with a problem they were not aware of or were about to bring a spotlight on something that could make them look bad. In this case, CID was presenting a very grave problem indeed – drugs, extortion in the ranks involving senior NCO, prostitution, and it was spread throughout the Division Artillery. Even CID did not know how far this was going to go, or who else was going to be involved or what they might eventually find out.

The Commanding General for the 2nd Infantry Division had welcomed them into his office warmly, shaking each one of their hands as they came into the room and were introduced to him. The General was dressed in his khaki short sleeve uniform with his ribbons all in place and two large silver stars on each epaulet. Based on Stack's earlier call to arrange the briefing, the division command also had in his Chief of Staff, a full bird Colonel in heavily starched fatigues, wearing the crossed rifles of an Infantry officer on his collar, jump wings and a Combat Infantry badge with a wreath and two stars indicating his third award the 101st Airborne Patch on his right shoulder indicating the last unit he served in combat. The Sergeant Major was a short and heavyset fireplug of a man, dressed in heavily starched fatigues, airborne wings with a star, and the CIB with two stars, the 82nd Airborne combat patch on his right shoulder. The Sergeant Major had a wad of chewing tobacco stuffed in his mouth and carried a small Styrofoam cup around with him to collect his spit. The movement of his jaw up and down accented the battle scar to his right cheekbone from grenade fragments from Viet Nam. Also present was the Division SJA, or Staff Judge Advocate, who was the commander's legal advisor. The SJA was an older, slender Lieutenant Colonel, with military issued black framed glasses. His uniform was also heavily starched, but it was probably two sizes too big, and he wore his pants high above his waist. Also, there was no combat patch on his right shoulder meaning that somehow during the 10-12 years of his career he had managed to avoid serving overseas in a combat zone.

The General sat behind his desk and leaned back listening to Stack deliver his briefing. as Stack made a point or discussed a particular issue he looked over at the Chief of Staff who apparently understood the meaning and wrote a note down. As he listened intently, he was becoming somewhat visibly upset. He recognized this could end up being a very black mark against him as he went for his third star and promotion. He certainly did not want to be known as the division commander who had the next "Khaki Mafia" operating under his nose and he knew nothing about it. He had been a Battalion Commander when that incident unraveled in Viet Nam and he lost a good Master Sergeant from his headquarters company who played a minor role, but enough to get court marshaled after 23 years of service. His bad judgment had destroyed a good career with two wars under his belt. Instead of retiring, he was sent to Leavenworth as a private for eight years of hard labor and a dishonorable discharge.

The General knew the possible ramifications when criminals took hold. He also knew it was not going to get better by not cooperating or by standing in the way of CID. Instead he had looked over at Stack who was briefing him.

"Does the Corps Commander know about this yet?" The division commander finally asked as Stack paused during his briefing.

"No sir, we wanted to brief you first. We'll be talking to the Corp Commander this afternoon," Stack answered. He knew the Division Commander would want to get out in front of his problem, so when briefed, the Corp Commander would be told the Division Commander was already engaged and cooperating completely.

"All right," the General paused, "Mr. Stack I'll brief the Corp Commander on all this, now what else do I need to do?" the General asked.

"OK sir, "Stack nodded his head to the General's request," we want to go brief your DIVARTY Commander and several of the Battalion Commanders. I'm afraid it is spread all over and we'd like to coordinate picking up all of these guys. We could also use some of your Military Police units to help us take them into custody and transport to CRC."

"When are you set to go?" the General asked.

"This payday, Sir, in two days," Stack answered back.

"Payday?" The General asked to confirm the date and wrote a note to himself.

"Yes sir. That is when we expect the women to be back this way and we can catch them, too. Also the drug dealers should have received their dope so we have a chance to catch them before they get rid of it."

"All right, what does my lawyer say?" The General looked over at the SJA who was still reading some of the briefing packet supplied by Stack.

"Well," The SJA looked up from reading the statements and various reports prepared over the last few days, provided by Stack, "if these are accurate we certainly have a problem."

Stack looked over at O'Brien and O'Toole with his eyes rolling slightly upwards, as if to acknowledge the SJA's firm grasp on the obvious.

The General took a few seconds to evaluate the limited legal opinion. He looked over at the Chief of Staff, "Ron, get me DIVARTY on the phone." The Colonel stood up and walked over to the General's desk, picked up the receiver on the phone, and dialed a number.

"Sir, one thing we have to be very careful on this, if the word gets out, things aren't going to go like we want. We've got to catch them by surprise so OPSEC is going to be an imperative."

The General nodded in affirmation, slightly irritated at the suggestion they would somehow spill the beans.

"Eddie, this is Ron," the Chief of Staff spoke into the receiver, then paused to listen a few moments, "...Yeah, stand by on that, the Boss wants to talk with you right now." The Chief of Staff handed the receiver to the General.

"Eddie, real quick," the General leaned back in his chair, "you're supposed to be getting a briefing in..." he looked over at Stack for a time reference.

"Two hours sir," Stack said.

"In two hours from the CID right?" the General looked at this watch, "look, I've just received the same briefing. I think it would be beneficial to have your Battalion Commanders present for that briefing. Your decision, but I think it would be helpful."

"Yes sir, what's...." The DIVARTY Commander tried to ask a question but was cut off.

"Ed, I'll touch base with you later, just get your Commanders together; listen to the briefing; then if you have any questions call me or Ron back and we'll talk. Right now, this is very close hold, so bring your folks over so as not to create any loose talk. Got it?"

"Yes sir."

"Ed," the General turned more serious, "Mr. Stack from the Red Cloud CID has my full support on this situation he's about to brief you on. Are we clear on that?"

"Crystal clear, sir. Message received."

"Good, we'll talk later." The General hung up without waiting for a response and looked over at Mr. Stack. "OK, Mr. Stack, I think you will get all of the cooperation you need. If not, please call the Chief of Staff or the Sergeant Major here, I'm sure they know which button to push. Col. Rush here will get a hold of the Division PM and coordinate whatever MP assets you might need. Anything else we need to do?"

Stack and the others stood up and walked forward towards the General's desk, "No sir, thank you," Stack reached out his hand to the General.

The General stood up and shook Stack's hand. "Gentlemen, I want to be very clear on this. You get all of these sons of bitches in my division. I don't care if I'm left with a single battery or a single rifle company. I want those criminals identified and prosecuted. We're not sweeping anything under the carpet in this division, understand?" The General stood up with his hands on his hips. "This is like a cancer and you have to dig it out, but I want it all dug out at one time. I don't want to be screwing with this my whole tour, got it?"

"Sir, yes sir." Stack nodded briefly to the general and then turned and walked out of the office, nodding to the S-3 Operations Officer and the Sergeant Major as they departed.

"Ron, after this thing goes on payday I want a key leader and Sergeant Majors conference here in the morning and block out everything on my calendar for that day."

"Yes sir," the Operations Officer made a note on his pad.

"Sergeant Major, I want you to stick around for a while. We need to talk."

Stack, O'Brien, and O'Toole then drove over to Camp Stanley through the mid-morning traffic. The drive wasn't so bad and it was a pretty good road, having just been repaved prior to their arrival in country. But, Korean vehicle traffic was a mishmash of vehicles, from old men on bicycles, to oxcarts, to large trucks and military tactical vehicles, all the way to the smaller Kimchi taxis that darted in and out of traffic. Driving in Korea could be an adventure and could never be called a 'Sunday drive through the country.' Driving a US military vehicle of any size and shape was especially adventurous since they were often considered to be targets of opportunity for any Korean with daring do or sufficient monetary problems that made risk of life and limb worth striking the American vehicle in order to collect money for his effort. Hitting an American vehicle without becoming seriously injured or killed was a prized skill to have. The rewards could almost be worth the risk. Hit a chicken with a truck and the Americans would pay, not just for the chicken, but also for all the chickens it would have in the future. Hit an oxcart and you're paying not for the ox and cart, but for future oxen and future carts and loss of income. It could be very expensive for the Americans. Korean Safety law number one established without questions pedestrians always had the right of way. As the urban myth was passed down to every American driver, if a Korean falls out of a tree and hits your truck, you'll be at fault; so be careful and don't fool around. Given all this, it took all of two hours to make their way through the highway and then through Uijongbu city to Camp Stanley.

The briefing at the DIVARTY Headquarters briefing room went off without a hitch, especially after the phone call by the Division Commander and then two subsequent calls back to the Chief of Staff for clarification. Like the General, the DIVARTY Commander didn't exactly relish the idea that something criminal was happening within his unit but he knew he had to act and do something or things could quickly spin out of control. The three CID Agents walked into the room and noted the other senior officers and DIVARTY Commander were already sitting around a highly polished red mahogany table. Stack took up an empty chair to the right of the DIVARATY Commander while O'Toole and O'Brien took seats lined up against the wall. As they sat down, O'Brien nudged O'Toole to look at a cartoon that nearly took up the whole wall – a figure resembling Napoleon standing with hands on his hips surrounded by artillery pieces and cannon balls with the words underneath: *"Artillery, lends dignity to what otherwise would be an ugly brawl."*

Stack started off the briefing with the general details of the various allegations they were investigating. It was also not a complete shock that the soldiers identified during the briefing to the Battalion Commanders were not unknown. Most of them were already known to be or were suspected to be criminals or poor performers, or on the Commander's list of least favorite soldiers. Far from being defensive, as often happens, the Battalion Commanders were actually very supportive, giving them a chance to clean house once and for all. They recognized if this could be broken up right away and these criminals punished, the other soldiers would see that as a welcomed change. It was clear from the tone of the meeting and the general cooperation that the Division Commander's intent was being fully implemented. Stack presented his general plan of action to apprehend everyone they had identified as being involved in this organization at one time. The impact of taking in everyone at once, although they were spread across three or four smaller installations, would have a dramatic effect on their interviews and subsequent investigations. Additionally there were several rooms and other locations that would have to be hit with search warrants at the same time. His plan was to show up at the various installations and have the soldiers waiting for him at the Battalion HQ for them to pick up.

That idea didn't suit one of the Commanders who had another idea. "Sir, I think we're missing an opportunity here." He looked over at the DIVARTY Commander who nodded for him to continue. "We have a payday formation every payday anyway right?" He looked around the room to the other Battalion Commanders. "We hand out awards, do promotions, make any announcements, and then give the routine safety briefing to the whole battalion right?" The others nodded their heads. "Well," he looked over at Stack, "I'd like you to pick my shitheads right out of the battalion formation, so I can use them as an example of what happens when you're a shithead in my battalion."

The idea met with general approval and chuckles.

"Good idea Tom," one of the other Battalion Commanders answered nodding approvingly. "You know I am personally shocked. I don't think any of us had, at least I didn't have, any idea this was happening. It's not such a shock that a soldier may get involved in something illegal. But, I've never seen or even heard of anything to this extent or so well organized as you're claiming there, Chief. I think we've had a complete breakdown in our junior NCO ranks and we gotta fix it. But you know Sir, Tom is right; we can make this a positive thing. Show the good soldiers that we are paying attention, and we're not going to let this happen. Send a signal to the junior NCO's to wake their asses up."

"Sir, I have to agree," another Battalion Commander chimed in. "If this is as bad as you're saying Mr. Stack," he looked over at Stack, "then we've got some serious problems. We need to be making an example out of these soldiers."

"All right, Sergeant Major, what's your opinion of all this?" the DIVARTY commander asked.

"Fuck 'em sir. These ain't soldiers, these are shitheads. Soldiers wouldn't be involved in this shit," the Sergeant Major spat out in disgust causing everyone in the room to laugh out loud.

"Sergeant Major please don't feel you have to hold back. I mean, feel free to express yourself," the DIVARTY Commander commented somewhat tongue and cheek and caused the room to erupt in laughter again. After regaining order, the Commander looked over at Stack and began in a more serious note, "All right Mr. Stack I think we can make this happen. I'll let you get with each of the Battalion Commanders for details as to when and where. Gentlemen, I have to brief the CG after everyone has been picked up. Once CID has picked up your soldiers, I need you to contact the adjutant with the names of the soldiers, so I can send it up to Division. Everyone got that?" The Commander looked around the room and was satisfied that everyone got the message.

"OK Gentlemen, let's make this thing happen," the commander spoke and then stood up, causing the entire group to stand up at the position of attention and salute the commander as he left the room.

XXV

The remainder of the briefing was on arranging the most dramatic pick up of each soldier. Several of the Battalion Commanders had other suspects they thought were also involved or had been told were involved in dealing drugs but had never been caught. Could they get picked up as well to show the remainder of the unit they were not getting away with anything? Stack shrugged his shoulder. It was just a matter of logistics for him. He had additional agents coming in; it was just going to take a bit longer. He would have to arrange something for the soldiers to eat since they would likely be there over lunch and maybe longer.

The Sergeant Major spoke up in response to Stack's concern, "Chief, I'll take care of that, we have plenty of "C" rations lying around. I'd let those shitheads starve but don't want to be accused of not taking care of my soldiers."

At the conclusion of the meeting Stack and the two others finally made their way out of the conference room.

"Jesus Christ," O'Toole spoke as they left the headquarters building and walked to their parked car. "This reminds me of Branded, doesn't it?"

"Branded?" Stack asked uncertain of the connection.

"Yeah you know the TV show with Chuck Connors and he plays some Calvary Lieutenant who was like wrongly accused of being a coward in some friggin' battle with the Indians."

"Bitter Creek," O'Brien interjected.

"What?" O'Toole answered back not understanding.

"Bitter Creek. That was the battle with the Indians in the TV show," O'Brien said matter-of-factly.

"Yeah, Bitter Creek, that's it." O'Toole nodded as he remembered. "Anyway, Chuck Connors is literally drummed out of the army; some senior officer rips his rank off his shoulders, cuts off his buttons to his uniform, and then breaks his sword over his knee. Then they walk him out of the fort, the drums playing behind him and then close the gate behind him. "

"So then what happens?" Stack asked.

"I guess he gets butt fucked the rest of his life, you know." O'Toole shrugged his shoulders. "This is like Branded you know? These Artillery guys are friggin' serious." O'Toole shook his head as they piled into the vehicle.

The DIVARTY briefing was followed by a briefing to the 19th Support Brigade Commander, the next higher commander above the Battalion located at Camp Sears. This briefing was a little longer and more detailed because the main players were senior NCO and Officers, and much of the criminal activity was taking place inside their barracks. Because of the involvement of senior people, Stack could not be certain how far up the chain of command might be involved in the criminal activity.

The 51st Signal Battalion Commander was the final briefing, since one of his soldiers was allegedly identified as being one of the prostitutes. The Commander was as thin as a rail, and gray-haired, Lieutenant Colonel, conspicuously wearing a West Point ring on his right hand, ushered all three agents into his office. It was really no surprise to him that PVT Allard was in trouble. He became aware of the soldier almost from the day he took command several months before and she had received one of his first field grade Article 15's, or non-judicial punishment, for some disciplinary infraction. Her boyfriend was also previously assigned to the battalion but had been chaptered or kicked out of the army for drug abuse some three months prior to his arrival. Her chain of command reported that right after he left country, her general appearance and duty performance went down, to the point where she was removed from working at a radio relay station on one of the isolated outposts a few miles from Camp Red Cloud, to working down in the A Company orderly room pushing papers so she could be closely supervised. She had already been demoted twice just since her arrival, once for failing to show up for duty, and once for sleeping on duty. She was looking at a possible chapter discharge herself if she would not change her duty performance and attitude. But the Commander was surprised that she was involved in prostitution. He remarked that at one time according to her commander, she was actually fairly attractive and was very motivated in her duty performance. He had seen pictures of her taken prior to his arrival, and she appeared to be bright and cheerful. But it's clear that something had happened because she was pretty rough looking now, like she had a lot of miles put on her over the last few months. Besides, she had enough medical appointments scheduled in the next few weeks to keep two doctors busy full time. The Battalion Commander was briefed that she was going to be picked up the following day at her company headquarters. He agreed not to inform the Unit Commander until payday and would have her waiting at the orderly room for CID to pick her up.

Their last briefing for the day was at the Camp Red Cloud Provost Marshal's office. There was going to be a lot of activity coming and going early in the morning and a lot of "visitors" coming to the MP Station needing to be processed and released back to their unit. Stack, O'Toole, and O'Brien pulled up to the PMO tired from their whirlwind tour of the area. As they pulled into the parking lot and got out of the car, SFC Grubner was standing in the front doorway of the PMO smoking a cigarette. The sight of the CID agents parking and then walking in mass towards the PMO sent shock waves through him. He had seen that once before in his life when he was picked up by the CID in Germany. Grubner threw his half-smoked cigarette butt onto the parking lot, retreated back into the PMO to his office and closed the door like an ostrich trying to hide his head in the sand.

"I'm Mister Stack from CID, is the Detachment Commander in?" Stack announced somewhat matter of fact as they all walked in the small orderly room outside the Commander's office.

"Yes sir. I think he is on the phone; stand by please." Bea stood up and walked the few steps over to the Commander's office door and knocked on the door casing.

Stack looked around the small office and noted Miss Park was standing alongside the other clerk in the small office. Both of them had been looking at some type of spreadsheet on the desk before they were obviously interrupted by CID's unexpected appearance.

"Miss Park, how are you today?" Stack asked softly.

"Very fine thank you," Pok answered back and looked back down at the spreadsheet as if she were embarrassed by the comment to her.

"Come on in sirs, the Commander will see you." Bea called out as she walked back over to her desk and sat down. Trying to look busy she could not help looking up as they entered the Commander's office. Generally, when CID came to a unit meant they were coming after someone.

Stack, O'Toole and O'Brien walked into the office and shook the Commander's hand.

"Captain Cruz, how are you doing?" Stack greeted the Commander and extended his hand across the desk.

"Mr. Stack," the Commander stood up and shook his hand. "Good to see you. To what do I owe the pleasure of this visit?" The captain sat back down uneasily to listen. He realized as he leaned back in his chair that his heart beat was starting to increase. He had never considered Grubner's comments about CID being interested in either of them to be anything more than delusional on his part. But, here, less than a week after being told CID was looking at them, here they were. If Stack was coming by to make small talk why did he have to bring two other agents with him?

"Sorry to barge right in like this, but we need some assistance." Stack started off.

"OK, what can I do for you?" Cruz answered uneasily.

"Well we have a fairly large operation going to kick off early payday morning, and we would very much like to use a few of your people to help out."

"OK, we'll help out as much as we can, what's going on?"

"Well, we have a lot of people we are picking up and apprehending tomorrow for a wide variety of offenses. They're spread all over the area, so we are getting some additional CID agents, and some MP's from the 2nd Division are going to be helping us too. I'd like to use your MPI folks, partnered up with my CID and we can spread my CID a little further that way."

"OK, that's no problem. I'll get a hold of Sergeant Pete; I'm sure he can make his folks available."

"Great that was our biggest problem. We'll have MP's from Camp Stanley and their MPI, your MPI, and if we could ask for two of your uniforms, I think we will be set."

"Two uniforms, I think we can make that happen."

"Well there's actually a special request. I know this is unusual, but we would like to request Specialist York specifically and then one more you can spare."

The Captain leaned back and put the pen he was holding down onto the paper where he was making notes. "Why the special request?"

"Well, York is really the one who came up with the information we used to even start on this particular investigation." Stack leaned forward in his chair, "He developed his own source and then came to us and gave us the information. If it wasn't for him, we wouldn't have known anything about it."

"This is what York was doing up at your office last week?" Captain Cruz asked.

"Yes sir. He came up with the information and we debriefed him. It took a few hours to get all the details."

"Well, what did he come up with?"

"Right now, it's still close hold need to know, but we will be reporting everything and all of the details tomorrow." Stack leaned back. "We will be all assembling here payday morning around 0600 at the CID Office."

"You have enough room at the CID Office?"

"Well it'll be tight for sure," Stack admitted.

"Well, why don't you use my dayroom at the MP Detachment?"

"Thank you sir, that'll be great. We're giving a final briefing to the other CID Agents and MP's. If you want to come up, please do so and you can sit in the briefing and have an idea of what is going on. You just need to sit on it until 0900 payday morning. Once we have made our key apprehensions you can brief whomever you think necessary. We have already briefed the 2nd Division Commanding General and other Commanders involved. I have an appointment with the Corp Commander tomorrow morning and I'll brief him then."

"All right, I'll detail York and another MP to you and they'll be there 0600 all set to go. I'll be there in the morning as well, and make sure we have some coffee all ready."

"All right, thanks sir. We'll get out of your hair. We still have some last minute things to get set up."

The CID agents at Camp Red Cloud were fortunate enough to occupy a building large enough to sleep ten but with only four assigned to the office at one time there was actually plenty of space for a small lounge, which of course they built into a small bar. It was established Army regulations that Officers were not billeted with enlisted, but CID was a strange animal of a unit and Stack chose to live at the barracks with the other three enlisted agents. It was not unusual for any senior officer to stop by on a Friday night to have a beer with the CID and talk about problems, or just looking to get away from everyone else. In the early evening the day before the operation, Stack, O'Brien, and O'Toole sat sipping a few beers trying to relax. They were finally as ready as they could be and were exhausted. After briefing, coordinating, and planning, their heads were filled with possible outcomes, potential problems, possible successes, and the realization of the common military axiom, *"No plan survives first contact."* The key was going to be flexibility, because once started, this type of operation tended to develop rapidly, taking on a life of its own. Soldiers who are involved in such organized criminal activity tended to stay together and were extremely loyal to their criminal leaders as they were engaged in their criminal acts. They remained loyal all the way up until they were apprehended, then they suddenly discovered the importance of taking care of themselves. What starts out with 6 or 7 may turn into 12 or 15 as each suspect starts talking, seeking a way to get himself out of the spotlight, by dropping dimes on his so-called brothers in crime.

They were getting an additional six agents who were rounded up from all over the area to use for the operation, available for one day and one day only. It would be good and a lot of fun to bring everyone together on what promised to be a major operation, but at the same time, Stack realized right away of the amount of work that was going to be generated. If they only had help for one day they were going to have to hustle with no playing around. Stack knew most of the agents coming up to help, he was happy with the choices. They were experienced and he knew he could count on them. They were still talking about the case, taking notes on things that still needed to be done, and drinking beer until around eleven o'clock when they all decided they had done enough and needed to get to sleep. Each shuffled off to his room and tried to get a few hours' sleep. Four thirty came early at the CID billets as the alarms from the four separate rooms went off in close proximity to each other. For this particular morning, there was no possibility of "five more minutes"; when the alarms went off, they all got up and started moving. Slowly to be certain, but one at a time they emerged out of their individual rooms and made their way down to the latrine at the end of the small hallway to shower, brush their teeth and otherwise wake up.

XXVI

In a Quonset hut a few blocks away, Sean's alarm also went off. Because he had to get up so early and Reggie was unavailable to pick him up, he decided to spend the night on camp. Sean put on his house shoes and robe and walked out of the side door and over to the latrine in the middle of their small detachment area. When he walked inside, Reggie was standing at one of six sinks shaving. He had also decided to spend the night at the detachment area. He was selected to help out for the operation and it was one of the few times that he was able to work with Sean since their arrival.

"Hey, GI you ready to kick some ass today?" Reggie asked as he rinsed off his razor.

"Absofuckinglutely," Sean answered with a yawn and walked over to the sink and stared into the mirror mounted above the sink. He turned on the water and splashed it onto his face, his eyes burned as he closed them. They were red from lack of sleep since he had slept fitfully, anticipating the operations. Although in his mind he had done little, still he was interested in seeing what would happen. He was also interested in identifying Bishop's little punks that ambushed him downtown. There was going to be a reckoning today and he wanted to see it happen. The MP Detachment day room started filling up shortly after five thirty as vehicles and personnel from all over the area started to arrive for their briefing. The Detachment Commander was already inside, along with Bea who was busy setting up the large coffee pot. Slowly but steadily the various participants kept coming. They came in ones, and twos, and threes until the large room was nearly filled. As each person entered the room he found his way over to his own peer group. Uniformed MP's from the 2nd MP Company stood or sat together and the MPI and CID agents went to another part of the room and stood in their group. In addition to the CID Agents and the six uniformed MP from Camp Stanley, several other MP Officers in uniform had also arrived to attend the briefing, including the 2nd Infantry Division Provost Marshal, a Lieutenant Colonel, the Platoon leader from the 2ⁿᵈ MP Company, a 1ˢᵗ Lieutenant from Camp Stanley, and Captain Cruz.

"Oh, just what I need, a bunch of friggin' MP Officers." Stack thought to himself as he came into the day room and looked around.

Stack walked over to the small group of senior officers, greeted everyone, and then shook their hands – first to CW4 De Franco, who looked like he would rather be somewhere else, then his own field office commander, Major Dyke, then the other three officers by rank in turn.

"You all set Mr. Stack?" Major Dyke, his field office commander, asked in a command voice as if he was somehow involved in the operation.

"Yes sir, running a little late; we had a little last minute tweaking to do this morning, but we're all set."

"Looks like a very well-planned operation," Major Dyke began to expound.

"Thank you sir, I think it'll be OK," Stack answered rather noncommittal.

"Come on let's get some coffee," De Franco interrupted and began to push Stack away from the group.

"What are they doing here?" Stack asked in a whisper as they walked towards the coffee urn set up on a small table.

"Oh Geez, you wouldn't believe it," De Franco leaned over and whispered as they were walking. "Dyke finds out the Division Provost Marshal was coming and he gets so excited I thought he was gonna blow a load onto his friggin' desk. This guy is so far up the PM's ass, I'm not sure he's getting enough oxygen to his brain."

"RLOs," Stack responded in secret CID code; an RLO meant a *Real Live Officer*, referring to any actual commissioned officer, especially Military Police Officers who were assigned to a CID unit. This helped distinguish the difference between Commissioned officers and a warrant officer who was a CID Special Agent. Depending how it was used, the term "RLO" could connote a teasing acceptance into the CID world by a good deserving officer who may have made a slight faux pas in CID etiquette or procedures but was generally a good officer; or it could reflect general condemnation and disrespect to one or more senior officers who were always trying to get themselves involved in CID agents business, where they had no place to be. CID

Agents could decipher the general meaning with the tone in their voice or how it was used.

"RLOs," Stack repeated and shook his head as he walked a few steps and stopped in front of the coffee urn on the small table.

"Look," De Franco started and then looked around if anyone else was listening, "don't give Dyke a chance to address the troops. He's got like the Gettysburg Address all written down in his pocket. I swear to God." De Franco looked back at the group of officers standing around talking quietly.

"You're kidding me?" Stack asked pouring a cup of coffee.

"Nah," De Franco shook his head. "I'm telling you I could hear him practicing in his office last night when he decided he was coming over too." De Franco mimicked, "Once more into the breach dear friends…. I tell you it was so awe inspiring I wanted to throw up."

"Jesus Christ this is going to be a long day." Stack took a sip of his coffee and smiled.

"Worse yet, you know these friggin' MP officers, if Dyke addresses the troops then the PM has got to address the troops, then the friggin' Captain will feel obligated, I'm sure the Lieutenant will feel it necessary to tell us about his own experience. You know what that could mean. It'll be a nightmare." De Franco took a sip and they walked to the center of the room.

"Like a trip to the dentist and proctologist at the same time." Stack shook his head. "Is Dyke going to stay here all day?"

"Nah. I'll get him out of your hair as soon as you guys hit the road."

"Good man," Stack smiled.

"You owe me," De Franco said in response.

"Chief," O'Toole spoke in greeting as he walked over and interrupted Stack and De Franco. "We're just waiting on the guys from Camp Howze, they had a longer way, probably just a few more minutes."

"All right, have you already made up the teams and passed out the folders?" Stack looked at his watch; they still had a few minutes so they went back to sipping their coffee.

"Here you go," O'Toole handed him a list with names, arrestees and where they were supposed to go.

"All right, take a break and have a coffee. We'll give them a few more minutes," Stack answered and turned back to De Franco.

It was another ten minutes of casual conversation and last minute details before the final two CID agents arrived from Camp Howze. They were greeted by cat calls and teasing from everyone else in the room for being the last to arrive.

Stack took their arrival for his signal to get started on his briefing. He refilled his coffee cup and then made his way to the front of the room where a wooden podium had been placed.

"All right, all right, let's take a seat." Stack started to get the room in order and a general calm returned to the room.

"Gentlemen, thank you all for getting here so early in the morning," Stack looked over at the two agents from Camp Howze and teased, "or, in the case of Camp Howze, getting here eventually."

A ripple of laughter and cat calls went through the room. Stack held up his hand to regain control.

"I want to first off thank Captain Cruz from the Camp Red Cloud MP's for the use of the dayroom and use of his MPI and uniformed troops." Stack nodded at the Captain. "Also thanks to the 2nd Division PM and 2nd MP Company for their assistance today with their MPI and Uniformed troops," he waved his hand over to the six uniformed MP's standing together in the back of the room.

Stack looked around, he had mentioned everyone present. Time to get started. "All right, today we are going to be making simultaneous apprehensions of eleven soldiers and hopefully at least three civilians and conducting searches of at least four billet's rooms. All of these apprehensions will take place on four different compounds. We want to try as best as we can to pick them all up at the same time. All suspects will be transported back here to CRC where they will be advised of their rights, interviewed, processed and released back to their units. Now we've already briefed all of the Battalion Commanders and they know we are coming."

"Hopefully they haven't blabbed it all over," came a voice from a CID agent in the crowd followed up by an exchange of undistinguishable comments and opinions between the group.

"Well the Division Commander seemed to put a lot of interest into this operation, so I think for once we may have a chance to actually catch these guys by surprise," Stack answered back. "Otherwise, I think someone might have some explaining to do."

Stack looked down on his notes and continued with the briefing, "CID Agents, you should have received your folders, right?"

Stack looked around the room and saw nods of agreement. "Inside are the names and information of the soldiers you are apprehending, along with any special instructions. Some of you also have a search warrant inside your folders. We got those yesterday from the Military judge to execute today. So after you pick your suspect up, get them transported here to CRC and then go execute your search warrant. Have your assigned uniform MP's bring the soldier back. Uniform MP's, I need to make sure I have at least two of you back at CID building at all times to keep order. We don't have enough space inside, so we have a bench set up outside. I need one of you inside and one outside. There's no talking, no farting around. They just sit until we are done with them. After we are finished with the interviews, then they will be taken to the MP stationed at CRC and then released back to their units on DD 629. A few of these suspects are going to the MPI Office here on CRC- Agents take a look at your folders, these are the females. I want them interviewed up there. We're hoping to snag at least three civilians. Depends on how things go what happens to them afterwards. A couple of general things that's important. First, we know a lot of the players, but we want anyone else that's involved. If we can identify them, then we pick them up today too. You all have the list of names of all suspects we are picking up, so if someone spills another name of the group, then let me know. I'll be at my office acting as the conductor for Grand Central Station. Second, we are looking generally for where these girls are coming from and who is keeping them down in Seoul. The Yongsan office has some agents ready to respond down there if we can give them a name and place. Third, there is at least one other suspect out there we can't identify. We only know him as Bee Bee or Dee Dee and we think he may be a white male but that's about all for right now. So we want to make sure we ask everyone who has waived their rights about who that is so we can go and scarf him up as well. Last, we're still looking for two shitheads that were involved in assaulting Specialist York over here last weekend." Stack pointed over to York who was standing alongside Reggie in the back.

"For those of you who are not aware, it was Specialist York standing back there who developed all of this information and brought it to us. He did an outstanding job as far as we are concerned." There was general applause from the group as they turned around to see York. Sean sheepishly raised his hand and was nudged by Reggie who was smiling.

"Now like I said," Stack raised his hand to get order and then continued, "Over last weekend some soldiers, we think are members of this group, tried to physically intimidate and threaten York because he had reported this incident to us. Unfortunately for them, York didn't feel intimidated and in the course of a minor physical scuffle, York injured two suspects, one on his lower leg the other on his foot. We think they were serious enough injuries to have gone to a dispensary or hospital for treatment but so far we haven't gotten any reports of any such treatment. So, bottom line, be looking for anyone limping." There was general laughter from the group.

There were a few last minute questions and Stack answered them. He looked at his watch and then back to the rear of the room where he could see Major Dyke trying to signal him as if he wanted to say something. He could see that he was holding a piece of paper in his hands.

"*Holy shit,*" Stack thought and immediately blurted out, "OK, folks we're running late, please get with your respective partners, you have about five minutes to review your packets and then let's get out of here. Look here, for division soldiers, your suspects will all be in formation at 0715; as soon as the Battalion Commander takes charge of the formation, we are to walk up. They will call the battalion to attention and then call for the soldiers to come out to him. We are to take them into custody, cuff them, and walk them off the parade ground or wherever they are assembled. The Battalion Commanders will then continue, you just move off and get back here or over to the room to search. Someone will be standing by to let you in. Who has the three black female civilians?"

O'Brien and three others raised their hands.

"OK, they are supposed to be coming up from Yongsan on the bus arriving at CRC main gate 0730. They are supposed to be picked up by someone and brought over to Camp Sears. Pay attention, because we want both the women and whoever is coming to get them. Got it?"

"Got it, Chief."

"Mister Stack," Major Dyke started walking forward towards Stack raising his arm as if trying to catch his attention.

Stack ignored Major Dyke and closed his folder and started to walk away from the podium. "OK, let's get going- good luck." With those final instructions the group stood up and immediately started to gather around their partners or their groups.

"Mister Stack," Major Dyke walked up next to Stack. "I wanted to say a few words to the troops."

Stack looked around at the group who were already pairing up and milling around. "Oh, sorry sir, but we're running sort of late right now, so maybe later." Stack said in response and then turned away to another CID Agent who was trying to ask him a question. He left Major Dyke alone holding his speaking noted in his hands.

"Sean," O'Toole walked up to Sean and Reggie. "You two are on my team."

Sean and Reggie looked at each other and nodded in approval.

"We got the big prize." O'Toole announced proudly.

"Bishop?" Sean asked.

"Yep, none other. Thought you'd like a chance to say hello to him in person," O'Toole smiled.

"Yes sir, I would." Sean smiled and nudged Reggie.

"OK, let's get your shit together and get going," Stack looked at his watch and shouted to the entire group. It was going to be cutting it a little tight for the farthest teams but if traffic cooperated they would have a few minutes to spare.

Everyone started to file out of the room and find their respective vehicles. MP's combined with CID vehicles started lining up on the small side road as if in caravan. As each team was formed, Stack gave them a wave to get going and they started heading across the small camp towards the main gate. It took almost ten minutes to 'launch' all of the teams, then Stack looked around at the empty room with just the senior officers and De Franco left behind. Feeling much like Eisenhower at D-Day after all of the planning, once you give the execute order, there is nothing else to do but sit down and start second guessing about your plan and what you may have over looked. Time would tell.

XXVII

"Battalion," the Sergeant Major screamed out the preparatory command standing in the middle of a U-shaped formation of soldiers in the middle of the parade ground.

"Battery," echoed the four battery commanders over their right shoulders, nearly in unison.

"Attend-shun." The Sergeant Major finally spat out the command of execution and the entire three-hundred-man battalion moved together as one to the position of attention. The sound of boot heels clicking as they came together echoed across the small parade field. The Sergeant Major looked from left to right across the battalion formation in front of him. Once satisfied, he did a parade ground perfect about face movement and came to the position of attention himself and waited for the Battalion Commander to walk up and stand before him.

"Sir," the Sergeant Major snapped a perfect salute and held it while he reported, "the battalion is formed." The Sergeant Major stood ramrod straight and looked into the commander's eyes.

"Thank you, Sergeant Major. You may post," The Battalion Commander dropped his salute and the Sergeant Major dropped his sharply executed a right face, moved off to the rear of the Commander and assumed the position of attention glaring back at the assembled troops.

"Stand at," the Battalion Commander shouted out the preparatory command to the assembled formation.

"Stand at," echoed the four commanders over their shoulders to the assembled troops.

"Ease," the Battalion Commander shouted the command of execution and watched the formation move their left foot approximately shoulder width apart and place their hands behind them at the small of their backs. The Commander hesitated momentarily to look over the assembled troops.

"Gentlemen," the Battalion Commander started speaking in a voice loud enough to carry across the formation. He began walking, slowing in front of the troops and continued, "I look forward to these payday formations, because it is a time for me to recognize good soldiers and acknowledge their hard work and dedication to duty. In fact, one of my favorite things to do as a commander is to re-enlist a good soldier and present various awards they have earned during their tour."

The Commander let his words sink in and then began again, "If you remember when I took command, some six months ago, I said there were many things that were incompatible with military service and completely incompatible for any solider in this battalion." The Battalion Commander paused walking and turned to look from side to side as he addressed the formation. "Those incompatible things included racism, insubordination, malingering, stealing from another soldier, and drug abuse of any sort." He looked around and moved a little to the left as he continued talking. "If you remember, I said I would aggressively prosecute and punish any soldier involved in any of these activities to the farthest extent possible. Today, I am sad to report that we have soldiers assigned to this battalion who apparently did not believe me. They didn't listen to their chain of command when they repeated and enforced my standards. I guess they didn't think they would be found out; they thought they were so smart that they could get away with dealing drugs, running a criminal enterprise right in the middle of this battalion, victimizing their brother soldiers, making them unfit for duty with drugs, or taking away their hard-earned pay. Well for those of you engaged in this activity, today is the start of judgment day."

The Battalion Commander turned around, faced to his rear and made a motion with his hand. In response and on cue, a 2nd Division MP Jeep and an unmarked CID vehicle drove onto the parade ground, moving at a slow pace towards the battalion commander and his command group. The Commander turned around and watched the vehicle approach as did every other member in the battalion. There were mumblings and rumblings as the vehicles approached, the battery commanders each turned their heads and called out, "At ease back there, at ease in the ranks." The noise lowered slightly but did not stop.

The two vehicles drove within ten feet of the Battalion Commander, stopped and turned off their engines. Two uniformed MPs got out of their vehicle, walked around to the front of the jeep and came to a position of parade rest facing the assembled battalion. The two CID agents exited their vehicle, dressed in suits and ties and walked over to the Battalion Commander, who came to the position of attention and saluted. The lead CID agent saluted back. It is military protocol and tradition for the lower ranking to execute the salute first to the senior ranking. The Battalion Commander raised a lot of eyebrows when he executed his salute first. The first CID agent handed the Battalion Commander a small piece of paper which the commander took and then turned to face the battalion again.

"Like I said, gentlemen, this is the start of judgment day and a come to Jesus time for several of our soldiers who are going to have to make a big decision that will affect the rest of their career and life." The Commander looked around to make sure his words were being heard, "Listen up; if I call your name, you are to double time up here to these CID agents. They need to talk to you about your activity. When they are done, the Sergeant Major will come and get you and bring you back to me."

The Battalion Commander let his words sink in and then read four names from the paper. The soldiers each left the formation and doubled timed up to the CID agents. All had a deer in the headlight look as they walked tentatively up to the waiting CID agents. Immediately, two of them were taken into custody and placed in hand irons by the uniformed MP and put into the back of the MP Jeep. The other two suspects walked up to the CID agents who were also waiting with hand irons. They then searched them and placed them into the rear of the CID vehicle. After the suspects were all loaded up, the CID agent turned to the Battalion Commander and the two exchanged salutes again. The agents and MPs all entered their vehicles and drove away. The Battalion Commander then looked down and called out another series of names, with instructions to report to the Battalion Headquarters. They were the second round of soldiers the commander believed might know something about the drug activity who would be picked up later and interviewed as well.

After the other six soldiers left the formation the Battalion Commander then called the Battalion formation to attention and released them back to their own commanders. This scene was more or less repeated four other times that morning as soldiers throughout the division artillery were apprehended, searched, placed in hand irons and then started their way back to the CID office at Camp Red Cloud.

Sean and Reggie, followed by O'Toole in the CID vehicle, were waved onto Camp Sears by the Korean Security Guard. They drove directly over to the Battalion Motor Pool and parked outside. They exited their vehicles and as a group led by O'Toole they walked inside the maintenance building, across the open work bays where soldiers were busy sweeping and mopping down the floor. As they walked up to the small office door, Sean looked around and saw the activity within the bay had all stopped as soldiers were now paying complete attention to their arrival and apparent destination. Without hesitating, O'Toole opened the office door and walked into the small office and approached Bishop who was sitting behind his desk.

"Sergeant Bishop?" O'Toole asked as all three came into the office and stared at the man sitting behind the desk who was filling out some document with a no. 2 yellow pencil.

"Yeah, I'm Sergeant Bishop," Bishop answered, put down his pencil and leaned back in his chair. "Whatcha need?"

"Sergeant Bishop, I'm Special Agent O'Toole from CID and you're under apprehension for extortion, pandering and half a dozen other offenses we'll advise you of later."

"What are you talking about?" Bishop attempted to protest and stood up slowly.

"Sergeant Bishop, we'll talk about this at the CID office. Right now, just turn around and place your hands against the wall," O'Toole directed.

Bishop hesitated momentarily and looked back and forth to the four persons crowding together in the small office.

"Sergeant Bishop, I'm not in any mood to be messing around," O'Toole became more intense. "One more time, turn around, put your hands against the wall." He then turned to Sean and Reggie, "Specialist York, please go around and take charge of Sergeant Bishop."

Sean started moving as Bishop started to turn towards the wall hesitatingly. Sean came up to him and put his left hand on the middle of his back and began to slowly guide his hands to the wall and then tapped his boots signaling him to move back and widen his stance. Once in position, Sean started to do a pat down search. There were no weapons, but Sean could feel what he thought was one of those small green notebooks in Bishop's upper left blouse pocket. Sean started to unbutton the pocket flap to remove the book, but as he moved to unbutton the pocket flap, Bishop reacted by taking one hand off the wall and moved it quickly to try and secure the pocket and prevent removal of the notebook.

"Now, wait a minute that's mine," Bishop protested.

Sean reacted by moving his hands around to Bishop's back, and then leaned against him, whispering into his ear through clutched teeth. "Sergeant Bishop, put your hands back on the wall. If they come off the wall again I'll drop you to the ground Sarge."

"Sergeant Bishop, put your hands back on the wall," O'Toole called out.

"That's my property; you have no reason to take my property," Bishop protested loudly but replaced his hand on the wall.

O'Toole was clearly not in the mood, "Sarge, you're under apprehension now. We have the right to search you and everything on your person. Now relax. York, do your thing."

Bishop lowered his head. As Sean started searching again, he could feel Bishop trembling. He reached around and was able to unbutton the shirt pocket and then remove the small notebook inside. The notebook was handed over to O'Toole who briefly took his eyes off of Bishop to look through the various entries in the notebook.

"Thank you, Sergeant Bishop, this is one of the things I'm looking for."

Sean continued the search and removed a small key ring from Bishop's front pocket and handed it over to O'Toole.

"Sergeant Bishop, are these your room keys?" O'Toole held up a small key ring.

Bishop looked over and then answered, "Yeah."

"OK, I'm taking these too." O'Toole put the keys into his pocket for safe keeping and continued, "Sergeant Bishop, I want to advise you that we also have a search warrant for your room. Another agent will be meeting us soon to do it. I'll give you a copy of the warrant at the CID office."

"Put your head against the wall Sarge," Sean asked in a calm voice and Bishop leaned forward and complied. Sean reached up and took Bishop by the left wrist and brought it down to Bishop's left hip and put his hand into the cuff. He then did the same with the right hand. Double locking the cuffs Sean grabbed Bishop by his right upper arm and started to guide him from behind the desk toward the office door. He turned him around and only managed to take one step when the office door opened again. The others started to move for the door as well but ran almost headlong into 1LT Prichard, who opened the door and entered the office, which was quickly becoming very crowded now with five persons inside.

"What's going on in here?" Prichard was visibly surprised and upset. "I'm the motor officer, Sergeant Bishop what's going on?"

"They're jacking me up sir," Bishop called out and shook his shoulders as if trying to get free. "This is all bullshit."

"Sarge, knock it off," Sean spoke through gritted teeth. This seemed to settle him down as he looked to his left and saw Sean and to his right and saw Reggie.

"Lieutenant Prichard?" O'Toole stated rather please to find him so easily.

"Yeah, I'm Lieutenant Prichard and this is my shop and this is my senior NCO. What is going on and who are you?"

"I'm special agent O'Toole from CID and I've just apprehended Sergeant Bishop here and am taking him to the CID office for questioning."

"Apprehended?" 1LT Prichard asked.

"It means the same as arrested. Make sense now?" O'Toole answered.

"Under whose authority? I didn't authorize this. Who's your commander?" Prichard began spitting out questions not waiting for an answer.

"Hey, calm down, you're going to have a chance to talk with him, because I'm here to pick you up too."

"Me?" Prichard said rather loudly as if to intimidate. "You're here to pick me up?" Prichard put his hands on his hips and pushed his chest out as if he were trying to intimidate the CID Agent by seizing control.

"First of all, back the fuck down Lieutenant." O'Toole looked Prichard directly into the eyes not intimidated in the least and then continued, "Second of all, yes, I'm here to pick you up, because you're under apprehension too. Now don't be stupid," O'Toole added and glared back.

Prichard's attitude seemed to soften slightly from the rebuke. He seemed to step back but he was not ready to give up completely and countered, "That's bullshit! I'm an officer you, can't talk to me in this manner and you can't just drive up here and take me in. I'm going to go see my Battalion Commander right now." Prichard turned towards the door but was stopped when O'Toole reached out and grabbed his arm.

"Lieutenant, don't worry about your Battalion Commander, your Brigade Commander already knows we're here for you." O'Toole responded calmly but very matter of factly, "Now, because you're an officer, I'll walk you out to my car without handcuffs. But, if you don't calm down or if you start acting stupid I'll put you down and make you do the chicken and then take you out in cuffs like the sarge here."

"Is that a threat?"

"No, it's not meant as a threat at all. It's a statement of how it's gonna be," O'Toole answered back and looked intently back at Prichard. "Now step back, turn around, and let's move out of here."

Prichard hesitated only a few moments as his mind raced. He finally decided there was nothing else to do so he stepped back. O'Toole opened the office door and then escorted Prichard out of the office followed by and Sean and Reggie who were positioned on either side of Bishop with one hand each on Bishop's arms. Exiting the office, they walked quickly towards the now opened vehicle bay door, followed by every eye in the maintenance bay. It was only a few seconds before they were at their vehicles and they started placing their prisoners inside. LT Prichard was quickly patted down for weapons by O'Toole at the CID vehicle and then placed into the front seat. Bishop was escorted back to the MP Jeep and placed carefully into the back seat. Sean and Reggie walked back to the front of their jeep to observe a second CID vehicle pull up and O'Toole talk briefly to the driver and hand over Bishop's room keys.

"Must be going to search the room," Reggie commented.

"Probably," Sean agreed.

Reggie nudged Sean and jerked his head towards two soldiers who had followed them from a distance from the maintenance bay out into the parking lot. They were now standing and staring at them, each holding a push broom, but neither were sweeping. They slowly walked over towards the side of the MP Jeep and leaned forward towards Bishop. "You OK Sarge?" one of them spoke and walked slightly forward towards the jeep as if he were trying to talk to Bishop.

"Hey, you two get out of here," Reggie called out and moved over to the side of the jeep. "You don't need to be talking to him."

The soldier looked over at Reggie and then back to Bishop, "Everything OK sarge? You need us to do anything?" The soldier asked.

"Hey, I said get out of here," Reggie moved over and put himself between the soldier and the jeep, placing his left hand over his nightstick.

"Yeah, well who the fuck are you?" The soldier straightened up and stared back at Reggie, gripping the broom handle tightly.

"I'm the fuck who's gonna drag your ass to the MP Station in handcuffs again if you don't get out of here right now. Remember the last time?" Reggie said as he focused on the soldier and began ever so slowly to raise his night stick out of his carrying ring so it could be quickly removed and brought into play if needed.

Sean turned and walked towards Reggie to give support if needed, keeping his eye on the other soldier who was starting to look around the area as if to see if anyone else was around.

"Now," Reggie withdrew his night stick and slammed it against the jeep making a loud noise and startling the soldier standing in front of him. "I said hit the bricks GI." The sudden noise surprised both the soldier and Sean who was also startled at the sound.

The first soldier recovered slightly, stepped back and looked back at Reggie who was now gripping the night stick in his right hand, his left hand holding the other end. It was in the ready position and looked like he was obviously willing to use it. He leaned forward on the push broom and spit onto the ground. He then looked up and faced Reggie, with a sneer on his face. He looked back down at Bishop sitting in the backseat and then turned around slowly and walked away towards the second soldier who also was glaring back.

"Too bad we have other things going on, that one needs an attitude check." Reggie tapped the night stick in the palm of his hand several times as if he were imagining the type of adjustment he actually needed.

"What was that all about? You know him from before?" Sean asked as he came over to Reggie.

"That's two of the guys who tried to beat up your boy Broadbench the other day at the Hamilton Club," Reggie explained as he kept his eyes on the two who had walked a short distance away and then turned around again.

Sean looked over at the two now leaning against their brooms again, "Oh yeah?"

"The one that was up close to the jeep trying to talk to Bishop is the one that got speared in the head at the dispensary," Reggie explained.

"Really?" Sean looked back at the two who were walking slowly away looking back over their shoulders.

"Yeah, he's a piece of work all right." Reggie walked around and got into the driver's seat and started up the jeep. "More talk than anything else, typical bad ass; really tough when it's four or five to one, not so tough by himself."

They were interrupted by O'Toole who whistled to get their attention and made a circling motion with his finger, signaling to mount up. O'Toole then got into his car and started up, Reggie jumped into the driver's seat and started up and got behind the CID car. Seconds later they were driving away.

"Sergeant Bishop," Reggie who was driving asked over his shoulder and then looked into the rearview mirror. "Do you know who this is?" Reggie nodded his head towards Sean.

"Who gives a fuck man?" Bishop asked as he looked out the plastic window in the rear seat.

"No really, do you know who this is?" Reggie asked again.

"I don't know and I don't care." Bishop looked out the side of the jeep trying to be left alone.

"This is Sean York, from the Red Cloud MP's. Doesn't that sound familiar?" Reggie called back over his shoulder.

Sean turned around to stare at Bishop who was looking back at him but it was clear that he was not making a connection nor interested in any other conversation.

"Sorry Sean, he must have short term memory loss or something," Reggie volunteered and smiled as they exited camp Sears and went onto the main road back to Uijombu and Camp Red Cloud.

"Yeah, maybe." Sean turned back around and stared out the front windshield. He felt somewhat strange; he had expected at least some acknowledgement or recognition from Bishop, but he was certainly playing it cool. But, actually he was getting the feeling he didn't have any idea who Sean was.

XXVIII

The large fifty passenger blue colored shuttle bus from Yongsan drove through the main gate of CRC within minutes of its scheduled arrival. After entering the main gate, it stopped to allow a Korean security guard to get on board, it then made an immediate left-hand turn, drove up the street and then turned around and stopped at the bus stop just a few yards from the main gate. The Korean security guard stepped off and checked the identification of any passenger who was disembarking. O'Brien and another agent were standing inside the main gate shack drinking coffee from Styrofoam cups as the bus arrived. Two other agents were parked in a CID vehicle just up the street also sipping their coffee.

"Showtime," O'Brien stated to no one in particular as the bus pulled up and then the Korean security guard stepped off the bus. O'Brien and the other CID Agent dropped the remainder of their coffee into the trash can, stepped outside and began walking slowly towards the bus as it was offloading passengers. As they walked forward, a black female stepped off the bus and presented some type of identification to the security guard, then walked a few steps and stopped as if she were waiting for someone else to get off the bus. She was followed by two other soldiers in uniform, then two other black females, each providing some type of identity card for the security guard to validate their authorization to offload onto the installation. One of the last passengers off the bus was a rather large black male, standing at least 6'4" 250 lbs, dressed in a bright yellow matching set of sweatpants and sweatshirt, white tennis shoes, short Afro style hair cut, and a pair of gold framed sunglasses, and although they were still some distance away they could make out the large gold chain linked necklace placed around his neck.

"Jesus Christ," O'Brien looked at the other two standing next to him, "that's a big motherfucker."

The three black females started slowly walking towards the main gate with the black male walking a few steps behind them as if he were herding them towards the personnel gate and towards the Kimchi cabs parked outside. The bus pulled away and drove past O'Brien and the other CID agent who were now nearly upon the small group. O'Brien looked beyond them and could see the CID vehicle start up from behind the small group. The agents inside the car turned their lights on and off and started to drive slowly up the road.

"Good morning ladies," O'Brien called cheerfully out to the small group and held his hands up as if to signal stop, displaying his CID credentials and gold badge as identification. "I'm Special Agent O'Brien from the Army CID. I'd like to see everyone's identification please."

The females hesitated in their tracks and all turned to the man walking behind them, but instead of addressing O'Brien, the large black man opened his arms wide and began to literally push the three women forward. The girls responded by walking slowly, but unwillingly, forward towards O'Brien and the other CID Agent. The large black male looked straight ahead as if he was not even acknowledging the request. O'Brien planted himself firmly in front of the women and spread his own arms out wide in an effort to physically stop them.

"Stop right here and show me some identification," O'Brien demanded. The girls all tried to stop and were actually leaning backwards to avoid running over O'Brien, but they were all pushed forward as if the black man intended to use them to steamroll right over O'Brien. O'Brien held his ground and brought the march to the gate to a brief halt, causing the black man to finally call out in a rage.

"Get the fuck out of our way cracker or I'll fuck you up!" The black male looked intimidating towards O'Brien and put his hand menacingly into his sweatshirt pocket, as if he had a weapon inside the pocket.

"Cracker really? Do we got to go there?" O'Brien sighed and shook his head back and forth.

The girls looked back and forth from O'Brien towards the black male and they separated to the left and right like a stream of water hitting a boulder. O'Brien was now face to face with the black male with no one in between. Unfortunately, there was a considerable size difference and O'Brien was forced to literally stare up at the man who towered over him by a good five inches.

As they stared at each other, O'Brien could see the CID vehicle pull up quietly just a few feet from the group and the two CID occupants exited the vehicle but left the doors open so not to make any noise. O'Brien smiled back at the large man, seeing his reinforcements arrive he felt much more at ease. "One last time, give me some identification or you're going to have some trouble."

"Motherfucker, you and your cracker friend are about to get some trouble, I'm a black man minding my own business and you're hassling me for no reason. This ain't no Birmingham Alabama, and I'm walking anywhere I want to walk and you're not stopping me. Now, get the fuck out of my way and let a free man mind his own business."

The black male moved menacingly forward towards O'Brien who took a step back and reached and placed his hand on his .38 caliber revolver that was on his hip in a leather holster and at the same time placed his left hand as if signaling the large male to stop. Seeing him reach for this pistol made the man hesitate and stop.

O'Brian raised both hand as if he were going to personally stop them. "Now, everyone stop right now," O'Brien commanded, this time his voice being sterner to get their attention.

"Girls you go on and walk out the gate, let me take care of these cracker mother fuckers," The black man instructed the women. The three women moved off to the side, not so much wanting to get to the main gate as much as wanting to get away from being in between the two.

"This is a big mistake," O'Brien called out as the women shuttled quickly by him but were intercepted by the uniformed MP that had started to advance on them from the gate. The large man now had two CID Agents directly in front of him, and two more coming slowly from behind but as of yet still unobserved. O'Brien could see the two agents advancing from behind, stood up from his alert position and took his hands off of his pistol.

"All right, since you won't listen to me, I'm now placing you under apprehension for failure to obey a lawful order and communicating a threat. That's like saying you're under arrest." O'Brien tried to make the man understand the situation and continued, "Now, I want you to put your hands on the back of your head and go down to your knees." O'Brien stood with his hands on his hips and motioned with his own arms to put his hands behind his head and then motioned him to get on his knees.

The large black male smiled and hesitated almost in disbelief over his challenge. Several moments later the man decided to press the point and took one more step towards O'Brien.

"Hey, hey, hey," O'Brien raised both hands again as if he were making a stop signal and then made one last attempt to avoid any physical confrontation. "For the last time, do what I tell you to do or I'm gonna have to take you down and you're going to know pain. Now I personally don't care if you come horizontally or you come vertically, makes no difference to me. But, one thing is for certain, you're coming with me. So, make it easier on yourself." O'Brien widened his stance and got prepared for any sudden moves.

"Yeah? You talk some big shit for such a little punk. You think you gonna give me some pain? I'm gonna rip your head off and shit down your neck."

The man moved forward another step when he was suddenly and viciously struck on the right knee by a full roundhouse blow from a MP night stick wielded by one of the CID Agents who had walked up behind him. The man called out in pain. His knee gave out and he fell to his right knee, with his left foot still on the ground but leg bent. He howled in a rage and started to stand up as he was struck a second time on the small sweet spot of muscle between his neck and right shoulder, again delivered in a round house fashion with all of the force the agent could muster. The blow temporarily stunned his right arm. This second blow was followed up quickly by a diving tackle from behind delivered by the second CID agent. As he was hit, the agent wrapped his arms around the big man's arms and plowed the man forward hard. Because his arms were pinned against his torso, his couldn't bring his hands up to brace his fall and he hit the asphalt face first, scraping his forehead and jamming his sunglasses down onto the bridge of his nose. The blow was not enough to render him unconscious but it was enough to stun him enough to resist any further. As if they were in a cattle roping contest, the big man's hands were pulled around to the small of his back to have cuffs applied. Unfortunately, the man was so large the wrists could not be brought together to apply the cuffs, so the agents placed one set on the left hand and a second set of cuffs on the other and then put the two sets together.

"Wow," O'Brien bent over and looked down onto the ground at the stunned black man and then over to the other agent standing by him, "I bet that hurt."

It was several seconds before the man recovered enough to realize what happened and realize he was hurting. He started yelling out blood curdling cries of pain from his knee, shoulder, head, and a multitude of threats and general profanity.

O'Brien looked down at him with his hands on his knees, "Yep, that really must have hurt."

It took a minute for him to calm down enough for the agents to help him back to his feet. His knee hurt so bad he was forced to lean on one of the CID agents and hop on one leg over to the CID vehicle where he was then placed across the hood and searched. Inside his right sweatshirt pocket was a roll of quarters that were rolled in paper and then wrapped in tape designed to fit into a clenched fist. If he would have managed to punch someone with that fist it could have done a lot of damage.

"You know, you'd think I'd feel bad for you being hit from behind like that," O'Brien watched the other agents get into position to help him to his feet, with the man still bellowing in pain and threats. O'Brien tiled his head as he considered the thought, "But you know, I really don't feel bad at all."

Once the man was under control, O'Brien walked back towards the main gate and addressed the three females who were being held in check by the uniform MP.

"Sorry about that interruption ladies," O'Brien approached them with a smile, "but I still need to see some identification please."

This time, without any hesitation at all, the three women reached into their respective purses and handed O'Brien the brown identification cards normally issued to the wives of soldiers and other military family members. O'Brien collected each one in turn and looked at them quickly. The pictures all appeared to match the holder and as he casually looked, all had been issued on the same date and their individual card serial numbers were in sequential order. Interesting, he thought, wonder what the chances are of that happening by accident.

"All right, listen we'd like to talk to you this morning down at the CID office, OK?" O'Brien looked over at the women who all nodded but still had not said a single word since they had gotten off the bus. O'Brien looked at each one of them and was greeted with a nod of agreement from each. He put their identification into his shirt pocket and minutes later a female MP arrived at the gate and patted them down for weapons and searched their purses. Eventually all three were put into one of the CID vehicles and the still unidentified black man was put into the front passenger seat of the MP jeep and all were taken to the CID office. Since all of the other agents were already out picking up suspects or conducting searches, Stack took it upon himself along with one of the local MPI agents to drive the short distance across CRC to pick up PV2 Suzanna Allard at her unit and return her to the CID office. It only took a few minutes to arrive at A Co 51st Signal unit headquarters, Stack along with the MPI Agent entered the office expecting to find Allard waiting for them.

"Can I help you, Sir?" One of the clerks asked looking up from her typewriter.

"Mister Stack from the CID office. Is your first sergeant or commander here?" Stack asked, rather irritated at the delay or miscommunication.

The first sergeant overheard the conversation and walked into the orderly room and looked around.

"Where's Allard?" the first sergeant called out to no one in particular and walked over and stood next to Stack.

Stack looked around the orderly room, everyone had stopped working and you could have heard a pin drop onto the floor.

"I said, where's Allard?" The first sergeant barked out in a loud voice, obviously wanting some answers, "She go on sick call again?"

"I don't know, top, she hasn't been in here yet," Answered one of the buck sergeants sitting at a desk.

The door to the orderly opened and a senior NCO walked inside, taking his hat off as he entered the room.

"Robinson," the first sergeant addressed the NCO, "I told you to have Allard up here at 0800. Where is she?"

"I told her this morning at breakfast, top. I was just coming in to make sure she was here."

"God damn it," the first sergeant spat out through clenched teeth. Without another word he grabbed his hat from the small coat rack and put it on his head, "I'm heading over to the female barracks. Robinson, let's go." They headed for the door and walked rapidly across the small open area to the barracks.

Stack and the MPI agent followed close behind. All four men walked into the barracks and up to the third floor. At the top of the stairs, the first sergeant stopped and knocked loudly to announce his presence, "Male on the floor." The first sergeant called out loud enough to wake the dead so as not to surprise any female soldiers who might be walking out of the shower or latrine. They then preceded a few rooms into the billets and Robinson pointed to Allard's door marked with a small 3 X 5 card with the name PV 2 Susan Allard typed across the card.

The first sergeant knocked heavily on the door and called out, "Allard!" Knock, knock, knock, he pounded on the door with even more enthusiasm, "Allard," he called out again, "This is the first sergeant, are you in there?" No response. "Allard, get your butt to the door."

The first sergeant looked up and shrugged his shoulders to Stack who nodded in agreement. The first sergeant reached into his pocket and took out the master key that opened every door in the billets. He put it into the lock and pounded on the door one last time. When he received no answer, he opened the dead bolt and slowly opened the door, calling out again as he turned the door handle.

"Allard, this is the first sergeant."

There was still no answer so he opened the door further and turned on the lights. It took a few second for the overhead fluorescent lights to come fully on. Standing at the doorway, they could look across the room at a bunk that seemed to have a body fast asleep on the top of the blanket.

"Allard," The first sergeant shouted into the room and knocked on the door but there was no response.

He walked inside the room followed a few feet back by Stack. He stood over the bunk and looked down at the slender blond female, dressed in a long john shirt and a pair of sweat pants with white socks. He reached out and shook her but received no visible response; it was as if she were passed out. Stack looked over at the small night stand and saw four medicine containers, the plastic containers were opened and the caps off, but there were no medications inside. There was an opened can of beer sitting next to them. The first sergeant again shook

Allard but received no reaction. Stack pushed the first sergeant out of the way and opened Allard's eyes. He could see a slight reaction of the pupils to the light but they were slow reacting, and he noted her breathing was very shallow and somewhat labored as if she were having difficulty breathing.

"Shit, she's OD'd on something." Stack looked around the room then quickly, without thinking, reached down and picked her up in his arms. He called out to the MPI, "Go get the vehicle over here fast. First sergeant, call the dispensary tell them we have an overdose coming in. Grab up those empty vials and take them up there too. We're not waiting for any ambulance."

XXIX

Stack carried Allard all the way outside and placed her carefully into the back seat of the vehicle, and then jumped in next to her with his arm around her., They sped away. Minutes later, they arrived at the small medical dispensary and were met at the parking lot by two medics with a gurney who helped get her out of the backseat onto the gurney and then rushed her into the small ER room. The first sergeant arrived within minutes carrying the four pill containers so they knew what they were dealing with.

It was touch and go for a few minutes, but eventually the doctor came out into the small waiting room and announced they had managed to pump her stomach and he thought she was going to make it. He was, however, sending her down ASAP to the 121St Army Hospital in Yongsan to be further treated and for some inpatient mental examination. In just a few minutes, a MEDIVAC helicopter was touching down at the small pad on CRC and Allard was wheeled outside, an IV in place, and loaded into the side of the aircraft. In less than a minute, she was strapped in and the helicopter was lifting off and on its way.

"Damn that was a close one, Sir. Good job," the first sergeant reached out and shook Stack's hand.

"Thanks, first sergeant. I'm gonna have one of my guys come up and interview you guys about what happened, OK?" Stack then jerked his head to the MPI agent and they both walked outside and back to the CID vehicle.

"Sheeeeeeit," The MPI agent commented with gusto as he got into the car and slammed the door.

"Yeah, hell of a way to start the day," Stack responded and started up the car. He had some phone calls to make himself and was trying to remember exactly what happened.

By the time Stack made it back to the office, O'Brien was already back at the CID office with the large black male, who had been finally identified as Sergeant Trumain Washington also from the Headquarters Company, 19th Support Battalion, Camp Sears. He was sitting in the small waiting room of the CID office still with his hands cuffed behind his back and a pained look on his face, slowly limping to his seat where he could finally sit down. He grimaced from the pain in his right shoulder and right knee but the fight was clearly out of him. Stack was briefed as to the need for physical force to take Sergeant Washington into custody and the successful apprehension of the other three females who were currently up at the MPI Office being interviewed. Based on an initial phone call, the females were already talking their asses off.

Stack went back to his office to make a few important phone calls. The first was to Yongsan to have Allard interviewed at the hospital by CID agents from the Yongsan office and the second call was to brief his own headquarters on the overdose of Allard. He was still talking when he could hear the loud footsteps of several persons walking in combat boots down the small hallway towards O'Toole's office. Stack stood up and walked to the door and peered down the hallway. He saw Sergeant Bishop in cuffs being turned to face the wall and leaning forward until his forehead was touching the wall.

"Sergeant Bishop, I'm going to take these handcuffs off of you. If you act like a senior NCO, I will treat you like one. If you act like an asshole, I'll put them back on, understand?" O'Toole spoke into Bishop's ear.

"I got it. I don't want no problems," Bishop said in a very low, almost resigned, voice.

O'Toole nodded at Reggie who started to unlock the cuffs. One at a time, he placed the free hand onto the wall. He instructed Bishop to stand up and O'Toole then escorted him into his own office and shut the door. Reggie and Sean then walked out into the small waiting room and noted the arrival of several other suspects from Camp Essyons and Camp Stanley. They came into the CID office where they were checked in, and then escorted outside to sit on a bench that had been placed against the wall for their use.

"York," Stack walked out of his office carrying a piece of paper, "here's the next one for you. Go and pick up these two from Camp Sears, they're at the Battalion HQ."

Sean took the paper with the names and put it into his pocket. At the same time, Stack motioned for two uniform MP from the 2nd MP Company to come to him and he handed them a piece of paper listing two names for them to pick up at Camp Stanley. They in turn walked out to get their next two suspects.

Picking up Bishop had given Sean a lot of satisfaction; it seemed as if that helped complete the circle. But at the same time, he was troubled because he didn't get the feeling that Bishop actually know who he was. He didn't react to his name or presence one way or the other, as if he could not put together Sean's name to any specific reason for him to care.

"Hey are you in there?" Reggie asked Sean as they drove through traffic.

"Sorry man, I was just thinking to myself, that thing with Bishop, you know, that really seemed flat. It just didn't seem to fit. Like we knew something he didn't. I mean, I didn't see any reaction, did you?"

"Nah, not really. You know I thought that was sort of weird, too."

"Yeah, weird," Sean said and then stared out the window. Almost thinking out loud he turned to Reggie, "You'd think if he sent someone to threaten me or kick my ass he would have at least shown some reaction for me being the one to pick him up, you know?"

Reggie nodded in agreement and continued to drive while Sean looked out the window. They rode most of the way to Camp Sears in silence. They went through and made their way to the Battalion headquarters. Once inside, they saw several soldiers sitting in a group of chairs just inside the door. Sean walked in and up to the small service counter that separated a small waiting area with the various desks of S-1 or the personnel section.

"We're here to pick up a couple of soldiers for CID," Sean explained to a female sergeant who walked up to the desk loudly chewing her gum. She didn't answer at all but just pointed a pencil to the group of soldiers seated in front of her.

"Logan, Willis," Sean read from the small piece of paper. Two soldiers raised their hands and Sean pointed to the door. They stood up and walked outside without saying anything, leaving the other two soldier sitting on the chairs. They walked out to the MP Jeep where each was searched and placed in hand cuffs and then placed into the back seat. Sean and Reggie got into the front seat and drove back like an armed taxi cab. They made a little small talk and joked around somewhat, but Sean was relieved to be finally back at CRC to get out of the jeep and stretch his legs a little.

They walked into the CID office and saw SFC Bishop sitting in the small reception area by himself. He was leaned back with his legs stretched out in front of him, his head resting against the wall. They dropped their newest prisoners at the CID office and they were in turn placed outside to wait with the growing number of soldiers from various units in the area. The bench outside was getting full as the interviews started to back up.

"York," Stack stuck his head out of his office and called him back.

Sean and Reggie walked to his office and saw O'Toole standing near a book case. Stack had already sat down behind the desk.

"Yes sir," Sean addressed Stack as they came inside.

"Sean, we've interviewed Bishop. He didn't say that much about what he was doing, and claims he has no idea about anyone attacking you."

"Chief, we were thinking sort of the same. He didn't show any reaction at all when we picked him up."

"So, what do you make of it?"

"No idea Chief," York shrugged his shoulders and looked over at Reggie then back to Stack. "Is anyone else talking?"

"Yeah, most are spilling their guts, they are pissing all over Bishop, Belk, Washington, and a few others we didn't even know about." Stack began, "We picked up over a pound of marihuana all bagged up in Belk's room, some scales, and about a quarter pound all bagged up over on Camp Essyons, along with a few note books in Bishop's room, that we're gonna have to go over in more detail. But so far it looks like we are making a good sweep."

O'Toole broke in, "The girls are also talking, Chief. They've been staying at someone's house in Yongsan and been tricking over there too, coming up here every two weeks. Guess whose house they were staying at?"

"No idea," Stack took a sip from his coffee and waited to hear.

"Bishop's cousin," O'Toole blurted out.

"No shit?" Sean said surprised.

"No shit." O'Toole started to chuckle. "We've got guys in Yongsan on their way over to pick him up right now. He works at the ID card section at Yongsan and he managed to sneak them in and give each of them a dependent identification card.

"And ration plate," Bateman piped in.

"And a ration plate that got them into the PX," Stack completed his statement and looked over to Bateman. "We got Bishop's notebook and larger notebook in his room and nearly five thousand dollars in cash he had in a small safe under his bed."

"The girls have all said they were brought over for 30 days by Bishop and were all ready to go back home but were being held here and threatened, like a white slavery deal," O'Toole provided.

"Wow, pretty good so far. Anything on Bee Bee or Dee Dee?" Reggie asked.

"Not so far," O'Toole shook his head and looked down. "No one wants to go down that path for some reason. Everyone seems to just change the subject or clams up completely."

The conversation was interrupted by Stack's phone ringing. Sean turned to O'Toole, "So everything seems to be playing out like you thought."

"Yeah about 75% anyway, which is pretty good in these operations. I don't know if you heard, Allard overdosed."

"Who?" Sean asked.

"Oh yeah, she was the soldier hooker; you didn't know her name, did you? Anyway, Chief goes over to pick her up and she's not there, finds her in the barracks OD'd on some prescription drugs. Had to take her to the 121 Hospital to have her checked out."

Sean nodded taking it all in; Reggie lightly punched him in the arm as a way to show his approval.

Stack hung the phone up and was taking a note.

"You guys run over to the Dispensary at Red Cloud. Those pill vials from Allard were left there by mistake by the unit first sergeant. My guys are all covered right now but we got to get them. Take a few minutes and go pick them up and bring them back, OK? We need them on an evidence custody document, so pick them up as if they were evidence, OK?"

"Sure, Chief, we got it."

"Go in the very back of the clinic to the records section. They're supposed to be sitting there on a desk waiting for ya."

"Chief, sorry to interrupt," Bateman finally had a chance to put his two cents into the conversation. "I think you better come in here, I got Prichard in my office and I think he's ready to see the light. He's about to roll over on Bishop and wants to talk about Bee Bee." Bateman looked around the office as if to receive accolades from the others.

"Bee Bee? Who is it?" O'Toole broke in.

"Well he hasn't come off of that yet, but he's scared shitless of him I can tell you that much. I think he's about ready to come off the name, but I could use some help to push him over the top."

"Be right there," Stack answered and stood up and adjusted his pants. "Well boys, looks like this is starting to come together. Stay here and watched the phone," he ordered O'Toole who nodded in return.

Sean started out the door with a little bounce to his step. Things were coming together and he felt somewhat relieved that whatever information he had was not just bullshit. He was in much better spirits as they made the short ride up to the dispensary and parked in the front parking spaces.

They started into the front door but Reggie waved Sean over to walk around the building, "There's a back door we can go right into records and avoid the crowd in the front," Reggie suggested and Sean shrugged his shoulders.

Walking in front of the large windows in front of the dispensary they made nearly everyone on sick call and inside waiting on their turn to see the medics turn and watch them walk around. Uniformed MPs always seemed to make everyone pay attention. They walked around the building still cracking a joke or two on their activities that morning. Coming to the back door, Reggie walked up the two wooden steps to a small landing in order to reach the rear door. As he reached for the back door to turn the knob it flew opened and a tall soldier dressed in medic whites ran right into him, forcing him backwards, knocking his helmet liner off, and causing the soldier to fall forward, landing nearly on top of him. Sean reacted quickly to untangle the two, reaching out to stand the tall soldier back up and then reaching down to help Reggie back to his feet.

As Reggie came to his feet and tried to recover, Sean reached down for his helmet liner. As he stood back up he noted that the soldier was trying to adjust a wooden crutch under his right arm and was wearing a large brace on his right lower leg. Sean looked up and into the eyes of the soldier.

"Motherfucker," Sean called out and immediately grabbed the soldier by his uniform blouse. He shoved him hard back onto the closed back door to the dispensary, brought him back and slammed him hard again, causing the crutch to fall to the ground.

"What are you doing? Are you crazy? It was an accident! I'm sorry!" the tall soldier yelled out.

"You think I would forget you, asshole?" Sean spat out just inches away from the man's face.

"Sean, what are you doing?" Reggie came up and helped restrain the soldier.

"This is one of those assholes that tried to threaten me last weekend."

"You're shitting me. Are you sure?" Reggie spat out.

"I've never seen you before man; what are you talking about? Now let me go," the tall man called out. "Help, police brutality," he screamed trying to get someone from inside the clinic to come outside.

"Never seen me before," Sean looked into his eyes and then raised his left leg and kicked him in the right leg over the brace.

The tall man screamed and grimaced in pain.

"That bring back any memories?" Sean said through clenched teeth as he grabbed him and pulled him forward and then shoved him back against the wall again.

"OK Sean, I got him," Reggie maneuvered himself to get between Sean and the soldier. "You're under apprehension for assault and battery." Reggie grabbed the soldier and then spun him around and shoved his face against the wall causing him to call out again. Quickly, Reggie reached back to get his hand cuffs and placed them on the soldier.

The back door opened and another soldier leaned forward to see what was going on

"Military Police," Sean called out. "Move back inside and close the door."

The door closed immediately with a slam. Reggie moved the soldier off the wall and spun him around and carefully started him down the two steps. Hopping unsteadily, the soldier made it down with Reggie's help.

"Sean get the crutches and those vials, I'll take care of him," Reggie called out over his shoulder.

Sean had managed to calm down from the surprise, "All right, give me a minute. Meet you up front."

Sean walked inside the rear of the dispensary and was met by a staff sergeant dressed in medic whites who was about to go outside to see what was going on.

"I'm Sergeant Briggs and that's my soldier. What is going on?"

"Sarge, he's under apprehension for assault," York responded. "What's his name?"

"Apprehended for assault? But we saw him run into you guys. That was an accident. This is bullshit."

"Not for running into us, for something that happened last weekend," York tried to explain. "That's when his leg was injured."

"He was in a car accident," Briggs responded.

"Is that what he reported?"

"Yeah last Saturday afternoon. I was working the duty. Cut it up pretty bad," Briggs explained.

Sean felt better knowing he had caused him some pain. "All right, someone will be back to talk with you. Now what's his name?"

"Specialist Anderson."

"Did he come in with someone else on Saturday?"

"No, he came in by himself."

"Did anyone else come in on Saturday with a foot injury?"

"Yeah, we had another soldier come in with a broken foot, had something pretty heavy fall on him in the motor pool. He was really messed up."

"What unit was he assigned to?"

"Hmmmmm, I don't remember. He was only here for a few minutes because we were already getting ready to do a MEDIVAC down to 121 Hospital for another patient. This guy's foot was crushed really bad, nothing we could do here but stabilize him. I heard they sent him to Tripler in Hawaii on the air ambulance flight for orthopedic surgery. Guess he's going to be there for a while. "

"All right, hey get me that information on the guy too, OK?"

Sean put off any more questions concerning the soldiers and their injuries and took control of the four prescription vials, placing them into a small zip lock baggie he kept in his shirt packet for evidence. He reached into his clip board and withdrew a property receipt and started writing it out. Later, SSG Briggs returned with the second soldier's name, Specialist Floyd, Co A 51st Signal Battalion. SSG Briggs then signed the property receipt and Sean took control of the vials and walked out of the dispensary and back to the MP Jeep. Anderson was in the back seat, vocalizing how much pain he was in and how uncomfortable he was sitting. Listening to him drown on was making Sean's blood boil all over again.

"Shut up asshole. You ought to consider yourself lucky you're not in Tripler with your friend Floyd," Sean commented as he got into the front passenger seat. "Let's go Reg, I've been thinking on something."

"Right on," Reggie called out and started the jeep. He sped to the CID office.

They returned to the CID office, Sean raised up the front passenger seat and leaned forward to grab Anderson by the uniform. He was about to jerk him completely out of the back seat, when Reggie came over and pushed Sean away.

"You go inside, I'll take care if this guy."

Breathing hard, he nodded his head, turned his back and walked into the CID office with the medication vials. Reggie escorted Anderson into the CID office and sat him down on one of the empty chairs. Sean sat down on a chair in the middle of the CID office lobby and tried to take a few deep breaths to calm himself down, forcing himself to start thinking rationally and not go over and beat the crap out of him as he wanted to do. He looked over at the Korean secretary sitting at her desk trying to work through all of the day's activity.

Sean settled down and his mind started functioning again from the latest excitement. He asked the secretary to see the copies of the MP blotters for the last two weeks, and then he walked over to an adjacent empty desk and leafed through the blotters. He went back almost ten days of MP blotters and found the entry describing the assault against Broadbench at the Hamilton Club. He leafed through the blotter until he found the right entry and then read what happened. It had been written as a basic bar room fight with everyone being charged with engaging in an affray.

"Hey, Reggie come here a minute," Sean called over to Reggie who had taken Anderson out of his cuffs and sat him down on a chair. Anderson stretched out his leg and was in obvious pain.

"Yeah," Reggie walked over.

"Hey, those guys today you saw today at Camp Sears you said were involved in the bar fight at the Hamilton with Broadbench? Remember, you told me that morning when I took Broadbench back to his unit that the other subjects were from the engineers?" Sean asked looking from the blotter.

"Yeah, well, they were all wearing those red broken heart engineer battalion shirts, so I thought they were from the 44th. But I didn't write the report so I just assumed they were with the engineers."

"Look," Sean pointed to the MP blotter that identified the two soldiers involved in the fight as being assigned to Headquarters and Headquarters Company 19th Support Battalion, the same unit as Bishop. Then he moved his finger over to the left into the column that was used to record administrative data, including who came to sign for the suspects when they were released back to their units.

"SFC Bishop," Reggie read the name out loud in the left column and looked up and deeply sighed.

"Yep, Bishop signed for those guys. Do you remember what Mr. Stack was saying this morning about some guy they were still looking for, someone they called Bee Bee or Dee Dee?" Sean asked.

"Yeah."

"Well what if they were talking about someone with two B's in their name like Broadbench?" Sean asked.

"Holy shit never occurred to me. You think this was Broadbench and this fight was really an attempt to kick his ass?" Reggie asked as he tried to put it altogether.

"I don't know, but it makes sense to me. He gets the shit kicked out of him, maybe even tried to whack him, who knows. The first thing he wants to do is drop a dime on Bishop to get some revenge or something. You know I saw Broadbench just the other day. He showed up outside the MP station and said something about reading about what happened to me in the MP blotter and saying something like it was Bishop's work. But, I just remembered something," Sean looked back through the MP blotter and found the case involving his attack. The case number was there, the offenses were there but there was no synopsis or description of the event and no mention of his name or unit. It read only in capital letters, "RESTRICTED ENTRY". Just underneath the page with the basic information, was a second sheet that did have the full entry. Sean explained his point, "I forgot, anything having to do with senior officers, lawyers, or MP's are always made as restricted entries. So, regular units don't get any blotters on anyone like that. This second sheet with all of the details is added to only certain select units like MPI, CID, and the commanding general, but other blotter reports would only have the first sheet. Look, here," Sean pointed to the Restricted Entry, "No names on the regular sheet. So how would he know anything about me being involved? He couldn't have accidentally learned about what happened. He had to know somehow. So how does he know?"

"Dude, this is getting fucked up," Reggie answered and looked at Sean.

"Now, this is the shit head that tried to threaten us that day," Sean pointed at Anderson still sitting on the chair. Sean continued, "There was a second guy, remember? Well I just found out there's a guy MEDIVAC to Hawaii, guess he needed some orthopedic surgery," Sean said with a slight grin very satisfied with himself.

"Good job man," Reggie patted him on the back.

"Yeah, but guess what unit the other guy was in?"

Reggie shrugged his shoulders and shook his head.

"Company A 51st Signal. Guess where Broadbench is assigned?"

"51st Signal?" Reggie guessed the obvious.

"Better. Company A, 51st Signal." Sean sat the clipboard on the table and looked up at Reggie.

"Gee, you think it's a coincidence or something?"

"Yeah or something."

XXX

"We got to tell Mr. Stack." Sean looked up at Reggie who nodded in approval. "I'll bring this right back OK?" Sean held up the clipboard containing the MP blotters and spoke to the Korean secretary who nodded in understanding and answered the ringing telephone on her desk. They walked back towards the individual offices and knocked on Stack's office door.

"Come in," Sean recognized O'Toole's muffled voice on the other side.

O'Toole was on the phone when they entered the office. Sean looked back at the blotter reports and waited patiently while O'Toole finished up his conversation and signed off.

"What's up?" O'Toole asked as he hung up the receiver and continued writing some notes on a small pad.

"Well we got the vials from the dispensary like Mr. Stack told us," Sean looked over at Reggie.

"Alright, I'll sign for them and I think there is a list up front for the next customers to go pick up," O'Toole spoke without looking up.

"Mr. O'Toole," Sean hesitated.

"Yeah?" O'Toole looked up, pen still in his hand.

"How are you coming with identifying Bee Bee?"

"Nothing so far. Mr. Stack is inside with the Lieutenant, but nothing so far."

"We think we know who he is," Sean announced looking over at Reggie who nodded in agreement.

"What?" O'Toole raised up and laid his pen on the desk.

"We think we know who Bee Bee is," Sean repeated and then gave him their thoughts and suspicions on the identity of Bee Bee.

"Stand by right here." O'Toole seemed satisfied after hearing a few basic facts and knew he needed to get Stack involved. He got up quickly and walked down the small hallway to Bateman's office. He knocked twice and then opened the door and stuck his head inside. Stack was leaning towards Prichard who was leaning back with his hands folded across his chest.

"What?" Stack snapped irritated at being interrupted.

"Chief you need to take a break and come here," O'Toole interrupted.

"In a minute," Stack looked back at Prichard. "The Lieutenant and I are talking." Stack spat out in a disgusted tone.

"Chief, you really need to take a break and come here," O'Toole repeated. When Stack turned to look at him, O'Toole nodded and smiled and motioned with his hand to come out.

"You think about it for a minute, I'll be right back." Irritated, Stack stood up and walked out of the office. He closed the door behind him and then turned to face O'Toole.

"Chief, we think we know who Bee Bee is." O'Toole beamed with a "I know something you don't know" Cheshire cat smile.

"Really?" Stack said and started up the small hallway to his office. Entering, he saw Sean and Reggie standing in front of his desk.

"So, talk to me," Stack walked passed them and sat down at his desk. "I'm all ears."

O'Toole looked over at Sean and nodded for him to start.

"Sir, we think Bee Bee is a guy named Broadbench, from A Company 51st Signal."

"Broadbench, Bee Bee, all right maybe. What else you got?"

"Well sir, sort of a long story, but that's the guy who gave me the original information on Bishop."

"Yeah?" Stack leaned back in his chair.

"Well, I met him after he's picked up after a fight downtown; he says a couple of soldiers jumped him. We find out today that the guys that jumped him were from Bishop's unit and Bishop was the one that actually signed for them at the MP Station that night."

"OK," Stack started putting things together.

"Well I met Broadbench that morning and we talked and I tried to, you know, get him to be my source. You know, who knows what he might know about any small stuff, you know the deal." Stack nodded his head understanding the tactic and Sean continued, "Well, he came back that night and told me this stuff about Bishop."

"OK," Stack said and nodded his head that he was following.

"Well the next day I come up here and talked to you guys and tell you everything he told me. Then the next weekend is when I get accosted downtown by the three assholes, and we, or at least I, thought they were from Bishop to scare me or something."

"Yeah, go on?"

"Well today when we pick up Bishop, he shows no reaction to me, like he didn't even know me."

"Yeah Chief, and I asked him during the interview, but he acted like he had no idea what we were talking about," O'Toole volunteered.

"But, we go to the dispensary like you asked and there is one of the guys who assaulted me working right there. He's outside right now injured leg and all."

"So what does this have to do with Broadbench?"

"Well, the other guy is Specialist Floyd. He's in Broadbench's unit and he's been MEDIVAC to Tripler in Hawaii for orthopedic surgery on his foot."

"Still not seeing it."

"A couple of days after the incident downtown, Broadbench comes by the MP Station as I was going on duty. He mentioned the assault downtown and again blames Bishop, right? He says he learned about the assault from reading the MP Blotter at staff duty, but Chief, it went into the blotter as a restricted entry. Meaning only you guys at CID, and a few others, ever had the whole report. There is no way he could have known about it from the MP Blotter."

"Well, that is interesting. The Lieutenant here wants to make a deal. He wants immunity from prosecution for giving up this Bee Bee and completing the circle with Bishop, saying he has a lot of information but wants a deal. I have SJA coming in right now." Stack turned his chair to stare out the small window in the wall behind him.

Several quiet moments past while Stack contemplated their next move.

"Alright, makes sense to me and we don't have anything else." Stack started talking to no one in particular, "Let's get this guy that York says was involved in his assault and get him interviewed. Get O'Brien on that. You," he pointed at O'Toole, "take York and Phillips here over and pick up this guy Broadbench and bring his happy ass over here. I'm gonna go ram something up this Lieutenant's ass and have a come to Jesus moment right now. Are we done?" Stack stood up and looked around the room but no one made any comments. "Alright, do it and let's see how this all works out."

With that, Stack walked out of the room and back to the office down the hallway. He opened the door and saw the Lieutenant leaning back in the chair, his legs stretched out in front of him and his arms folded. His head was lowered and chin resting on his chest.

"Hey, sit your happy ass up in here; you think you're on a holiday?" Stack came in and tapped Prichard's foot with his.

Prichard raised up in his chair but looked over at Stack with mild contempt.

"I'm sorry to piss in your corn flakes this morning Lieutenant, but things have slightly changed." Stack paused a moment and watched to see Prichard suddenly start paying more attention. "So, tell me, you ever been to Kansas, Lieutenant?" Stack asked him and leaned against the wall.

"Kansas?" Prichard looked up not understanding the question that seemed to come out of left field.

"Yeah Kansas, have you ever been to Kansas? It's that flat spot in the middle of the country, with lots of farms, windmills. Dorothy. Toto?" Stack deadpanned the statement.

"No, never been there." Prichard looked down again as if he were irritated with the question.

"Yeah, well you're about to earn an all-expenses paid vacation to Kansas," Stack gave a slight smile and looked over at Prichard who was suddenly wide awake and listening to every word. Looking directly into his eyes Stack began, "Let me be clear on something you're not getting immunity today. You're not getting immunity tomorrow, and you're not getting immunity next week. What you are going to get is a paid trip to Kansas. Leavenworth Kansas. I figure for about ten years." Stack paused to let his comment sink in, "You see, senior officers don't like junior officers that conspire with criminals to sell dope, extort money from junior enlisted soldiers, and force female soldiers into prostitution, along with other crimes. You see, they don't think that is conducive to good order and discipline. It tends to make the army nonfunctional." Stack let the words sink in then continued, "Senior officers don't like a nonfunctional army. It makes them uneasy."

Prichard rose up in his chair and began to look over at Stack again folding his arms across his chest. "You ain't got shit, man," Prichard blurted out.

"Really? A few minutes ago I was interested in Bee Bee, remember?" Stack asked and looked down to face Prichard at eye level.

"Yeah, I told you, give me immunity and you'll get everything. I told you that already." Prichard sat back in his chair smugly.

"Yeah, you did. Only, in the last few minutes we already found out who Bee Bee is, so why do I need to offer you anything?"

"Bullshit!" Prichard spat back defiantly.

"Right, you're so clever, aren't you? And Bishop and his crew are so big and bad, aren't they?" So tell me, if they're so big and bad and they are so smart, then why are they all sitting outside my office now? If they were so clever and such bad asses, then why are we picking them up all over our area and searching their rooms and taking their dope from them?" Stack let his comments sink in. "Right now you need be thinking about something very hard. What's going to happen when every enlisted guy goes to court and starts saying I was obeying orders from the Lieutenant? I was just a lower enlisted soldier, what choice did I have? Right now, I tend to believe you were just stupid and really had a minor involvement. As soon as I walk out this door without any information, as far as I am concerned you are the senior person involved, you obviously were the big boss. Makes no difference to me which report I write. Might suck for you later on, but makes no difference to me."

Prichard uncrossed his arms and bent down, placing his arms on his legs. Stack recognized the signs that he was on the ropes and moved in for the kill.

"Lieutenant, I'm offering you a life line. But I'm only throwing it once. I'm going to ask you one time, if you come up with the right answer we're going to talk some more. If you act stupid or try to lie to me I'm walking out and there won't be an option that doesn't include prison. Of that you can be certain." Stack paused. "Now, you say you know who Bee Bee is, tell me."

There was silence in the room. Stack looked down at Prichard and saw his chest start to heave as he began to breathe heavy, contemplating his fate. It was followed rapidly with a muffled sniffle, and he could tell that Prichard's eyes were starting to water. Looking down, he could see his hands trembling.

Prichard rose up in his chair again and tried to straighten up. He wiped his eyes with the back of his right hand. "It's not like that at all. I wasn't involved in any of those things. I never sold any dope or was involved with any prostitutes."

"Lieutenant, you're not listening to me. I don't give a fuck about any of that shit. I asked you a question, the only question I care about right now is Bee Bee. I want to know who Bee Bee is, or I walk and you're out of here and the next time I see you will be in court. I can make you look like Al Capone, or Little Orphan Annie, depends on how I write it up."

"You said you already know who he is," Prichard looked up and sniffed again.

"Lieutenant, I do know. I'm trying to help you out here by showing you're going to be telling me what I already know, but I want you to tell me. You're the one who started out telling me all the information you know on Bishop and this Bee Bee. I want to know if you're going to be telling me the truth or going to continue to bullshit me."

"I'm going to tell you the truth, I swear."

"Good. Then who is Bee Bee?"

Prichard lowered his head and sniffed again using the back of his hand to wipe his nose. Stack looked over at Bateman who was grinning.

"Lieutenant you're starting to bore me."

"I want a deal." Prichard raised his head again. "I need immunity before I do anything."

"Deal? You want a deal?" Stack raised his voice slightly, "Sure, I'll give you a deal. The only deal you're going to get is this: tell the truth and I'll make it known to your commanders you cooperated. That's it. Or remain silent and I'll tell your commanders you remained silent. Your choice, that's your deal. You're either going to be a young inexperienced Lieutenant who used bad judgment or Al Capone with a gold bar. So that's your deal take it or leave it. Now you're starting to bore me with all of this conversation. If you're not interested, I have to go ask someone else and they can tell me. One last time before I get up and leave, who is Bee Bee?" Stack leaned back against the wall and waited for his comments to sink in. After a few seconds of silence, Stack stood straight up and started for the door.

"Dumb ass," Stack shook his head and opened the door to leave.

"Wait," Prichard rose up in his chair and wiped his nose again.

"Nah, you had your chance. I don't give a shit anymore. I can get it from someone else."

"No wait," Prichard called out as if calling for a life line, snot beginning to run down his nose. "Please."

Stack turned and looked back, "Alright, then give me a name."

Prichard grimaced and the tears started to flow down his cheek.

Stack was unimpressed by the display, "Name, give me the name."

"Broadbench," Prichard finally said and then lowered his head.

"Jamie Broadbench. From A Company 51st Signal, right?" Stack asked matter-of-factly.

Prichard looked up and wiped his eyes with the back of his hand, "Yeah,"

"I tried to tell you we knew already. I only wanted to make sure you were going to tell the truth. Now, you're going to tell the truth from now on, right?"

"Yes sir," Prichard answered.

"OK, then you're going to sit down with Mr. Bateman here and tell him everything you know about everything, right?" Stack asked and looked over at Bateman who nodded.

"Yes sir," Prichard nodded.

"If you leave anything out," Stack started but was interrupted by Prichard.

"I won't. I won't leave anything out, I swear," Prichard spat out and wiped his eyes again.

Stack opened the office door and walked outside into the hallway and walked back to his office where he sat in his chair and turned around to stare out the window. This operation was taking an unexpected twist. He was still trying to figure out a reason for the hesitation to identify this Broadbench when he was interrupted by the ringing of his phone.

As they departed the CID office, O'Toole suggested they go get a quick cup of coffee at the snack bar and discuss their plan of action. The coffee was most welcomed, it was already getting to be a long day and it was just approaching eleven o'clock. O'Toole grabbed a packaged "Honey Bun" as they passed through the food line to get their coffee and they all sat down and talked.

"We call this is a CID brunch," O'Toole pointed to his honey bun and coffee. "Alright, so tell me about this Broadbench."

Reggie started out, "Well we took him in after a fight at the Hamilton Club, I guess about ten days ago. He said he was jumped by a couple of guys. The other guys all invoked their rights so they never said anything about what started it. I tell you one thing, that's a tough SOB. He took on four guys and was whipping their ass when he got cold cocked by someone from behind."

"Country boy," Sean nodded and sipped his coffee.

"So how did you hook up with him?" O'Toole asked.

Sean went through his contact with Broadbench that morning and then him coming back that night to tell him everything about Bishop.

"Think he was diming out Bishop for revenge?" Reggie volunteered.

"Maybe. Maybe he was using us to get rid of his competition?" O'Toole took another bite of his honey bun. "Guess we'll have to find out. Where does he work?"

"51st Signal Battalion Motor Pool."

O'Toole looked at his watch, "We need to get going before they break for chow and before word gets back to him. Is he going to go easy?"

"Makes no difference to me," Sean said matter-of-factly. "You know what we say, horizontal or vertical, he's coming with us. Might have to stop by the dispensary first, but he's coming with us."

They drove over to the 51st Signal Battalion Motor pool and drove through the gate of the small fenced in compound. They parked in front of the maintenance bay and walked inside. Towards the back was a group of soldiers who were sitting around laughing, smoking cigarettes and drinking coffee or sodas. One of them looked up and saw them come inside and nudged the others who in ones and twos stopped talking and looked up to observe them. Sean looked around and just off to the side, sitting at a small desk along the wall, was Jamie Broadbench talking on a telephone. Sean pointed him out to O'Toole and they shifted their walk over towards him. Broadbench looked up and saw the three coming towards him and looked around the desk. He pocketed a small notebook and put it into his right shirt pocket and then hung up the phone.

"Hey, dude what's going on?" Broadbench stood up smiling in surprise by the visit.

"Specialist Broadbench, I'm Mister O'Toole from CID," O'Toole displayed his credentials and gold badge as identification. "You need to come with us right now. "

"Well Ok, I need to tell my platoon Sergeant first."

It wasn't lost on O'Toole that he didn't ask why he had to go to the CID office, but O'Toole decided not to go into it right then and there and directed, "Don't worry, we'll tell your sergeant, just come with us right now."

"Sure," Broadbench walked around the desk and walked up to Sean and asked in a hushed voice, "So, what's this about?"

"You don't know, Jamie?"

"No of course not. Did you say something?"

"No. I ran into Anderson today at the dispensary. You know Anderson, right?"

"No, I don't know any Anderson. What is this about?" Broadbench only halfheartedly protested.

"Shut up Jamie. Let's go." Sean jerked his head to the left motioning Broadbench to walk to their jeep.

They arrived at the jeep. Broadbench was patted down for weapons and then got into the back seat. Reggie walked around and got into the driver seat. While Sean took his night stick out of its ring and placed it between his seat and the transmission hump, his attention was drawn to movement to his right. He turned and saw a soldier wearing mirrored sunglasses; The same type of mirrored sunglasses worn by the man who held the knife to Pok's throat. The soldier was holding a clipboard out in front of him and reading whatever was clipped to it, oblivious to anything else. The soldier stopped walking and started to write something on the clipboard. Sean started to walk slowly towards him becoming convinced with each step this was the same man. When he was about 30 feet away, the soldier happened to look up and saw Sean walking towards him. He immediately recognized Sean and dropped the clipboard to the ground and without a moment's hesitation immediately turned on his heels and tried to sprint away. A second later Sean started after him.

"Halt, Military Police," Sean yelled out at the top of his lungs, but thought to himself he hoped he would keep running. Although he had a few steps on Sean, it was no contest. Sean turned on his open field running and even in combat boots was on top of him in a matter of seconds. He brought him down with a textbook perfect open field tackle, hitting him hard on the back, both arms wrapped around his waist and drove him forward onto the pavement. The soldier hit the blacktop hard and with Sean slamming into his back and knocking the wind out of him. He was still gasping for air as Sean recovered. Within seconds, Sean had the soldier's hands behind his back and was applying cuffs to him.

Sean then stood up and although he was breathing heavy, reached down and picked the soldier up by the back of his uniform blouse and brought him back to a semi standing position. "Get up you piece of shit," Sean said through clenched teeth as he shoved him back towards the MP jeep. "Not such a badass without a knife and two friends, are you?"

The soldier was gasping still trying to catch his breath and was having trouble stumbling back towards the MP jeep. O'Toole ran up to assist with Reggie just behind him.

"What the hell was that all about?" O'Toole asked.

"This piece of shit was the one that held the knife against my girl's throat."

"That's a lie. I've never even seen you before," the soldier blurted out in a pained voice.

"You're gonna wish you never saw me before," Sean yelled into his ear and pulled up on the handcuffs causing a pain in the man's shoulders.

"Woah, Sean, Sean," Reggie squeezed in between Sean and the soldier. "We got it, man. Take it easy."

"Reg, this is the asshole that had the knife to Pok's throat," Sean called out.

"We got it man. Go back to the jeep. We got this guy. Go back to the jeep and settle down."

"York," O'Toole called out to take control of the situation, "go on, we've got it now."

Sean looked around and breathing heavy, started walking back to the jeep. His dander was worked up now and it was all he could do to calm himself down and not go back to beat the living crap out of the soldier he had just apprehended.

"Holy Christ, did you see that?" Reggie said to O'Toole as he held the soldier up by the blouse and looked at Sean walking away.

"Haven't seen an open field tackle like that in a while," O'Toole said back and then looked at the soldier who was still trying to stand on his own. He reached out and tried to straighten the man's mirrored sunglasses that were now missing one of the lenses. "Gonna have to talk to him about knocking the shit out of people he tries to arrest, though." O'Toole looked at the skin abrasion on the man's forehead, nose and chin from hitting the pavement so hard. "Gonna be a few minutes before we get anything out of this one. Come on, help me get him to my car. I'll take him back."

Broadbench started speaking as soon as Sean came back to the jeep, "Sean, I hope you don't think…"

"Save it," Sean spat out. "Right now, you don't want me to start thinking about anything."

Reggie came back to the jeep and got inside the driver's seat, while Sean mounted into the passenger side and they drove away. Sean looked down at his hands, both were skinned, but his right hand was bleeding from scraping the pavement. He then looked down and saw that the toes of both boots were now scuffed and deeply scratched and the left knee of his pants and left elbow of his blouse were ripped open.

"God damn it," Sean looked down at his scraped and bleeding hands and uniform which now had several blood stains from his hands bleeding onto his pants. "I scratched up my boots. Now that pisses me off."

Sean looked over at Reggie and they both started to laugh hard at the concern expressed over his uniform and boots instead of his own injuries. They continued to laugh all the way back to the CID Office. Broadbench sat handcuffed in the back seat of the jeep not certain what to expect when they arrived. He had tried to talk to Sean several times but was greeted by a "shut up" for his efforts.

Once they parked, Sean raised the front seat up and carefully helped Broadbench out of the back and escorted him into the CID Office. As they walked into the CID office, Stack was up front talking to the Korean Secretary and looked up as the door opened.

"Chief, this is Specialist Broadbench," Sean announced. as he looked to the left at the chairs in the waiting room, he noted that SFC Bishop suddenly was alert, raised up in his chair and staring intently at the new arrival. Broadbench stared back in contempt. They were both looks of death and no doubt if they had the opportunity one of them would have killed the other.

"What the hell happened to you?" Stack asked looking at Sean's bloody hands.

"I found the other guy involved in threatening me at the motor pool," Sean offered as an explanation.

"Jesus, what does the other guy look like?" Stack asked in amazement.

"A lot worse than that Chief, I promise you that much," Reggie volunteered.

Stack nodded his head in approval, "Well, Specialist Broadbench, I've been looking forward to talking with you for a while now. Come this way."

XXXI

Broadbench walked ahead of them in a criminally experienced swagger and followed Stack into the small hallway into one of the smaller offices. Thirty minutes later, O'Toole came inside with the other soldier. Sean looked at him and for the first time saw the name tape across his right chest as "Smiley" and his collar showed that he was wearing Sergeant Stripes.

"Phillips, take him back to my office and take his cuffs off," O'Toole looked over to Reggie who nodded. "York you stay here and watch these people," O'Toole waved towards the several soldiers sitting in chairs waiting for interviews . He then walked to the back of the CID office.

Sean started to protest when Reggie piped up, "Sean, go and wash your hands man. You're bleeding all over the place. It looks gross."

Sean looked down and could see that he had stopped bleeding but his hands were covered in dried blood from the scrapes on his knuckles. He walked to the small latrine just inside the CID office and went inside. There was a sink and a mirror. He put both hands on the sink and then looked into the mirror. He took his helmet liner off and noted that his face was a little flushed and his hair was a mess from sweating and then drying. He turned on the cold water and washed his hands and then washed his face. The cool water helped finally calm him down. He looked back at the mirror and could not believe he had acted the way he did. It was totally out of character and lacked the discipline he prided himself on. But when he recognized the man who held the knife to Pok's throat, something happened to him that he could not explain. It was as if someone turned on a switch and he went into sudden attack mode. It was not like him and the emotion and intensity surprised him and made himself feel uneasy. He looked into the mirror and wondered if he could have really seriously hurt the man if he had been alone with him with no witnesses. He splashed more water on his face and finally became aware of the stinging of his hands. He looked into the sink and saw a reddish tint to the water as it went down the drain.

Sean took a few paper towels and dried off his face and felt surprisingly better. He had his control back. He brushed his hair back with his fingers, put his helmet liner back on and did the best he could to straighten up his uniform. He then walked back outside and was much calmer. Reggie was outside in the small office waiting for him.

"You OK?" Reggie inquired.

"Yeah, thanks man. That helped." Sean sighed in relief.

"Ol' Sergeant Smiley is gonna sing like a bird, man. You know you scared the shit out of him."

"Yeah. You think?"

"No, I mean you literally scared the shit out of him. O'Toole said they had to stop on the way to the CID Office because the guy had literally shit himself. He begged O'Toole to let him change his drawers before they went to the CID office. O'Toole said he let him wipe himself off and throw the drawers away in the motor pool latrine. And that is a no shit story," Reggie announced and they both started to laugh.

"York," came a voice from down the hallway.

Sean and Reggie walked down and found O'Brien standing there with a file folder.

"Chief Stack told me to tell you guys you're done for the day."

"I thought we had other guys to get picked up."

"Yeah, but every time we send you out for one guy you come back with another two. No seriously, Chief says you both did a good job and he will contact you both tomorrow., For right now, get out of here and go get yourselves cleaned up. Go have a beer or something. All right?"

"Sure, OK," both Sean and Reggie replied, although they were somewhat disappointed at missing out on the rest of the day. They both walked outside and felt the warm sun coming through the trees.

"You know what we need?" Reggie asked.

"What?"

"We need beer. I suggest we go downtown and have a few beers. We'll get the girls to come by and get us later on and we'll just act stupid for the rest of the day."

"You know, that's a good idea."

Reggie and Sean drove back to the PMO and turned in their weapons and vehicle. Sean walked down the small hallway to Pok's office. She was inside talking to one of their interpreters, Mr. Pak.

"Yobosayo," Sean said grinning a big grin and walking into the office catching them by surprise and in mid laughter.

"Ah Hello," Mr. Pak responded and bowed slightly towards Sean.

"Sean," Pok called out, "what are you doing back here?"

"Hey Mr. Pak," Sean first waved at the older Korean man sitting at the desk and then turned his attention to Pok. "Hey we're all done for today," Sean briefly explained and motioned for her to come out into the hallway.

Pok quietly apologized to Mr. Pak for the interruption and then followed him into the hallway.

"Yobo," Pok said in concern as she looked at the blood on Sean's uniform and scrapes on his hand. "What happened?"

"I found those three men who threatened us. We arrested all of them this morning."

"You found them?" Pok asked incredulously.

"Yes, it's a long story, but they won't be bothering us anymore," Sean beamed in his report to her.

"But what happened to you?" Pok reached for his hand to look at the scrape and then down at his uniform.

"Well I had to catch one of them, he tried to run away."

"Yeah, he tried to get away, but he sure didn't go far," Reggie interjected as he walked up to them in the hallway.

"Oh," Pok looked up and smiled at Reggie. "Hello Reggie."

"Did you tell her?"

"No, not yet."

"I'm taking your Yobo downtown to the Paradise Club and we're going to have a few beers. You need to come down after work and pick him up. Myong is coming to get me later too."

"Paradise club, ah you have new girlfriend there?" Pok looked playfully at Sean.

"No, unless my Yobo leaves me all alone," Sean teased back.

"You tell new girlfriend, she big trouble if I come there," Pok wagged her finger at Sean and tried to look serious.

"OK, I'll tell her but don't be late," Sean looked back and then leaned down and kissed Pok lightly on the forehead. "We're going to go change and then see you after work OK?"

Pok nodded agreement and then walked back into her office as Reggie and Sean walked outside almost arm in arm laughing at the day's events. For a MP, days don't get much better

The interview of Broadbench was somewhat anticlimactic. He walked boldly, almost swaggering, into the smaller office reserved to conduct interrogations and sat down in the chair next to the desk. Stack came in and moved around him to sit down in the chair. Broadbench looked somewhat bored with the process as Stack began to talk with him. Stack looked over and saw that he certainly appeared to be a cool character. Broadbench provided all of his background information, his name, rank, social security number, and unit. He continued answering additional administrative questions over his home of record as if he were filling out a job application or applying for a loan. Stack was taken aback slightly by the overall lack of concern displayed by Broadbench. He leaned back in his chair, put his pen back down onto the desk top and looked back over at Broadbench who was collecting and removing invisible lint from his uniform.

"You seem very comfortable for someone that is in pretty deep shit," Stack finally said to him to see his reaction.

"Look," Broadbench looked back at and smiled, "do what you have to do; I've got nothing to say. Just contact Mr. Jack LaFontain in Jackson, Tennessee. He's my attorney and he will take care of everything." Broadbench reached into his uniform blouse pocket and withdrew a small business card and passed it over to Stack.

Stack pointed to the desk for Broadbench to place the card. "So, you have an attorney already?"

"Just call Mr. Jack LaFontain," Broadbench responded as he started cleaning his fingernails., "Otherwise, I have nothing to say."

"Well, I'm about to read you your rights anyway and you will see that you do have a right to an attorney, and it can be anyone you want it to be, as long as you pay for it. But, I don't call lawyers for anyone."

"No problem, I'll contact him when I get back to the states," Broadbench announced and then placed his hands together on his lap.

"Back to the states?" Stack leaned back again.

"Yeah, I assume you're going to charge me with something and that's why I'm here, right?" Broacdbench straightened up in his chair as well. "Well I'll contact him when you send me back for trial."

Stack started to laugh out loud almost uncontrollably. Broadbench looked over and was somewhat unsettled, not expecting the outburst for a response to his statement.

"I hate to burst your bubble young man, but you're in the army. We can take you to court right here in Korea. We don't have to send you back." Stack then started laughing out loud but caught himself after a few seconds. "Sorry, but that was a good one. I've never heard of that before."

Broadbench looked over at Stack as if he were trying to see if he were being truthful.

"Look, let me get through the rights advisement and you can do whatever you want to do. You can talk, you can remain silent, you can request a lawyer, and you can do whatever you want to do." Stack came forward and picked up a form sitting before him. "I just wanted to get your side of the story since your friends aren't as experienced with these things like you seemed to be and they, of course, are pissing all over you."

"They ain't saying anything," Broadbench smiled knowingly.

"Yeah? You're sure of that, are you?" Stack looked over at him and gave him another smile. "Anderson isn't having any trouble at all. And Smiley," Stack emphasized loudly, "Smiley, literally shit himself when he was picked up, did you know that? He's shitting all over you now, two rooms down. So if you don't want to talk, who cares? I got their side of the story. That's good enough for me. Might be bad for you of course, but it's OK with me. Do you really think those guys are going to take a fall for you?"

Broadbench turned slightly to the left and stared straight ahead, his face flushing.

"Gee, you don't seem too confident now," Stack said and then paused momentarily. "Wow," he began again, "it's getting stuffy in here. I think I just heard a big sucking sound as your asshole is sucking up all the oxygen in here," Stack said in a very matter of fact tone. Broadbench did not take the bait and continued to concentrate on the wall across from him. Stack paused but was fairly certain that he was not going to waive his rights. Stack then went through the rights warning procedure and Broadbench true to his initial statement indicated that he didn't want to answer any questions and wanted to speak to an attorney. He signed the form formalizing the rights advisement and Stack stood up.

"OK, wait here for the time being. Someone will be right back for you." Stack took the form and placed it into a small manila folder and then walked out of the room. Hopefully the others were in fact talking. That, however, was not a problem he would soon learn; both Anderson and Smiley were talking their asses off. He made a motion for one of the uniform MP in the outer office to come back and stand outside the interview room.

"Watch him, will ya?" Stack instructed the 2nd Division MP as he came up to the door.

"Got it Chief," The MP responded and cracked the door open slightly to be able to observe Broadbench sitting on his chair.

Stacked turned and walked few feet away to his own office and dropped exhaustedly onto his chair behind the desk. Only moments later he was interrupted.

"Chief, want some coffee?" O'Toole leaned into the office holding a full carafe of coffee.

"Hell yeah, bring it in here." Stack looked around his desk that was now littered by reports and other documents generated by the various apprehension and interview teams thus far in his operation and eventually found his coffee cup. O'Toole walked inside and filled the cup that Stack was holding out. Stack looked up and saw that it was already almost four o'clock and things were still happening. "How many more do we have to interview?"

"Last count, about three or four of the soldiers the Battalion commanders wanted interviewed. MPI are doing those. O'Toole has Smiley and I'm finishing up Anderson. O'Toole said that Smiley is still talking. Shit, I think he might confess to Kennedy's assassination before this is all done."

"I thought I smelled fresh coffee," Bateman suddenly appeared at the door carrying his coffee cup and interrupting the conversation.

O'Toole walked forward to Bateman. "Please be generous to your server," he joked as he poured the coffee.

"Chief, I think you better read this." Bateman took a sip and then handed Stack a couple of typewritten pages.

"Is our Lieutenant cooperating now?" Stack took the pages and set them down in front of him and started to read.

"Yeah, through his tears." Bateman chuckled, "You should have seen, Chief. He broke this guy down like a shotgun, it was a classic."

XXXII

"Well, this fills in some spaces," Stack commented as he began reading the statement rocking back and forth in his chair. Prichard was apparently coming clean with everything and had laid it all out, how he had been compromised and blackmailed early on. Bishop had set him up with one of the prostitutes, 'as a date', who then photographed their sexual encounter. Bishop simply threatened to send the pictures to Prichard's wife. Then to keep him on the leash and on the reservation he also loaned him some money to help pay for some expensive car repairs back home, and then he had him. Prichard found himself on the hook like everyone else. Only Bishop never put pressure on him to repay, only reminded him of the debt and was expected to provide cover for Bishop and his activities.

"You know, I think Prichard was actually relieved that this was finally over," Bateman observed as he took another sip of his coffee.

Stack leaned forward and sat the statement down on his desk in front of him and then rose up, took his glasses off and rubbed his eyes and bridge of his nose. Taking his coffee cup he took another sip as he read the statement and commented, "Well this explains a lot."

"Prichard is screwed," Bateman volunteered.

"That might be an understatement," Stack responded and then leaned back again. "OK, let's regroup on this for a second. We've got all the women interviewed, right?"

"All interviewed and all made written statements," O Toole acknowledged. "All were brought over by Bishop who paid their air fare. They knew him from the neighborhood in Detroit."

"How did he get in contact with them?" Bateman asked.

O'Toole looked over the report prepared by the agents who interviewed the girls, "Some relative of Bishop's approached them back on the block and offered them a chance to make a lot of money and travel. He said it was only going to be for a couple of weeks then they would come back home. They went down, got their passport and wham, bam, thank you ma'am here they were. Bishop picked them up from Kimpo when they arrived and took them over to his cousin's house on Yongsan. He takes their passports and they ain't going anywhere."

"What did his wife say about that?" Stack asked. "I'd like to be a bug on the wall when this was brought up," Stack's eyes widened and he smiled, causing a chuckle from the other two.

"Well, not much since it doesn't appear that she ever made it over." O'Toole went through the multi-page report until he found the right spot and continued "He had an accompanied tour to Yongsan, so his wife was authorized to come over with him. His household goods were packed up and sent over but his wife apparently never did make it over. So there he is living in housing on post with no wife or kids. So he has a three bedroom apartment going to waste. He brings them over and they stay. He pimps them on the side for special customers, but on paydays, he puts them on the bus for Camp Red Cloud. Then the next day, they come back."

"Nice scam," Bateman said and nodded in appreciation of the criminal mind.

"Oh gets better, the cousin works at pass and ID section, so guess who he brings into the office to get a dependent ID card and ration plate so they can go to the commissary and Post Exchange?"

"The girls?"

"Yep, one day he just brings them in one at a time and they each posed as his wife. They get a new dependent card and new ration plate. Then later he destroys the authorization paper work the following day and there is no record of it."

"Jesus this thing goes on and on," Bateman shook his head.

"How much money are they making?" Stack interrupted. "I just barely skimmed over his books this afternoon. Unreal the records this guy was keeping, he could almost be an accountant." Stack reached out and picked up the small ledger book in front of him on another stack of documents.

"Chief, these girls were each doing ten to twenty customers every payday at 20-50 bucks a shot, sometimes more."

Stack did a quick calculation, "Wow, roughly two thousand dollars a payday."

"Holy shit." Bateman commented, "That's around four thousand a month, maybe more if they were tricking in Yongsan."

"Plus whatever he was making loan sharking, and whatever he was making dealing dope," O'Brien added.

"How much were the girls getting?" Stack asked.

"So far not much," O'Brien shook his head and read from the report. "Bishop was taking almost all of the money for himself. Looks like the girls wanted to go back home but after getting their ass whooped they decided it was better to shut up about it."

"You know, I'm not catching the link with these guys," Stack finally announced and rubbed the sides of his head. "I mean it's almost like we got two separate groups here. I can't see any connection with Bishop and Broadbench. In fact other than Broadbench getting his ass kicked by Bishop and then diming out Bishop, I'm lost."

"Chief, I think I can help," O'Toole announced as he strutted into the office with a mile-wide grin on his face, "because I've been interviewing the friggin Rosetta stone."

"Smiley?" Stack asked.

"Yeah, Chief," O'Toole began looking around to the others in the room. "I swear to God that guy hasn't stop talking since I closed the office door. I thought I was going to have to gag the little fucker to get him through the rights advisement before he started pissing on himself." There were chuckles from everyone.

"So, what's the link between these guys?" Stack asked.

"Chief, this Broadbench is a scary mother." O'Toole started out, "You ever heard of anything called the Dixie Mafia?"

"The what?" Stacked asked as if he did not understand.

"The Dixie Mafia," O'Toole posed the question again and then looked around the room.

"All right, I'll bite, what is the Dixie Mafia?"

"Chief, according to Smiley, this Dixie Mafia is like a loosely associated group of redneck thieves and criminals down south. You know, deep south as in Mississippi, Alabama, Louisiana, and Tennessee and they are certified bad asses."

"OK, so what does that mean?"

"Smiley says that this Broadbench is part of that group," O'Toole started to explain and clarify, "Well actually his daddy is like a leader of part of that group but Broadbench is right up there too."

"So what does that mean," Bateman asked and looked over at Stack to judge his reaction.

"Look, we were looking at Bishop as this big bad ass right?" O'Toole looked around the room and saw everyone nodding in general agreement. "Well, actually it's this Broadbench that's the real bad ass." O'Toole started to explain the entire background as if he had been holding back an ocean and could not hold it any longer.

"Chief, according to Smiley, Broadbench was an active member of this Dixie Mafia. These guys are involved in home burglaries, thefts, armed robberies, dealing drugs, and contract murder. I guess in the criminal world down south they're some real bad asses."

"You know I think I did hear something about these guys when I was down in Fort Rucker," O'Brien offered up., "Aren't they around Biloxi or something?"

"Could be," O'Toole shrugged his shoulders. "I've never heard about 'em." O'Toole then continued, "Anyway, Broadbench here is a part of that group, but he gets pinched after some job they did in Tennessee. He was just like seventeen or eighteen and the judge decided to use the old line of, either go to prison or join the army. "

"I thought they stopped that," Bateman interjected but O'Toole chose not to answer him.

"So, he joins the army and after his initial training, he is sent to Korea. Once he gets here he looks around at all of the criminal opportunities and he starts right in."

"Like what?" Stacked asked.

"Well he's a truck driver, right? Within the first couple of weeks he starts making the POL run from Inchon to Camp Sears. He drives down picks up a load of army Mogas, drives it back and drops it off at the POL point. Well, he makes some contact with some Koreans and starts diverting fuel he gets from Inchon over to Korean fuel trucks that he meets on the way back. Smiley says he's diverting 250 to 500 gallons at a time. Then he comes to the POL point and drops his load. He then alters the delivery amount to reflect a full load was dropped off. He was making at least one, sometimes two trips a week, getting like fifty cents a gallon, which is cheap for Koreans. It was a cool scam, no telling how much gas we lost."

"Jesus is there no end to this?" Stack asked.

"Well it gets better, during these thefts, he makes contact with some other Korean bad guys who want to deal marihuana and other dope. Broadbench starts buying dope by 10 pound-lots and starts selling it to other Americans who in turn deal it down to baggies and sell it to the soldiers. Want to take a guess who's one of his biggest customers?"

"Bishop?" Stacked asked tentatively.

"Bishop," O'Toole nodded in agreement. "Turns out Bishop and Broadbench were actually partners in crime in a lot of ways."

"Well isn't that interesting?" Stack leaned back in his chair and started thinking.

"Nah Chief it even gets better," O'Toole commented and started again. "Look, you know about Private Allard hooking right? Well come to find out, it was Broadbench that brought her to Bishop."

"What?"

"Yep," O'Toole started again, "Allard's had this boyfriend, another soldier who was running up all kinds of debt with Broadbench with drugs. He apparently was an absolute junkie. The guy eventually is chaptered out of the army but he owes Broadbench beaucoup money, but by now he's back in the states and out of his reach. So Broadbench goes to Allard and basically says to her, "you now owe his debt to me. If you say no, then I'll kill your boyfriend and you'll still owe me money." She says no and threatens to go to his commander. Broadbench then beats the shit out of her and then Broadbench, Anderson, and some other guy named," O'Toole looked through his notes, "Nix, raped her one after another. Really messed her up, you know."

O'Toole looked around the room but everyone was staring back at him in disbelief. He then continued, "Afterwards, he brings her over to Bishop who by this time had brought the other girls over. Bishop buys Allard for her debt and now Allard is forced to prostitute herself to pay down her debt that she now supposedly owes to Bishop."

"What? That's white slavery," Bateman offered.

"No shit." O'Toole continued with his narrative, "So, everything is going OK, right? But there is trouble in Muddville, because Bishop wants to branch out into other areas. So he starts making contact with Broadbench's Korean source for dope and tries to make a separate deal and cut Broadbench out of the loop so he can make even more money. But, the Korean source tells Broadbench so there is this big confrontation like Al Capone and the O'Bannon gang in Chicago or something. Then things seemed to get worked out and they play nice for a while but Bishop again tries to cut Broadbench out of the loop with another source of dope. Again the Korean tells Broadbench what's going on." O'Toole then looked around the room and saw that everyone was staring intently at him. "Now are you ready for this?" O'Toole paused.

"Yeah, keep talking. I'm listening."

"OK, Chief, you remember like last month we went up to Camp Colburn to help them out with a murder they had up there?" O'Toole looked over to see if Stack was following him, "You know, the black private who was found all beat up with throat cut in the gutter in the ville? We all thought it was a robbery or maybe drug related, because we found out he was dealing some dope on the side. But, we never got anywhere, and other than identify some customers there were just no leads?"

"Yeah," Stack asked and tilted his head to hear better.

"That guy, was supposedly Bishop's man. He was supposed to be meeting with a Korean to talk about getting their own dope and was met instead by Broadbench, Anderson, and Nix."

"Nix?" Stack questioned and made a note.

"Yeah, that's the guy who was with Broadbench when they raped Allard. He's already back in the states." O'Toole explained.

"Shit, I'm going to need a program to keep track of this stuff." Stack was writing down notes trying to keep up.

"Anyway, they beat the shit out of this guy and then to make a point they cut his throat. They threw him out into the street gutter and then they came back down here. No one knew who they were up there so we were like chasing a ghost or something."

"This guy Smiley says Anderson was there when they killed him?"

"Yeah, was real emphatic on that point."

"O.B.," Stack looked over at O'Brien, "did Anderson say anything about this shit?"

"Not yet, but I think we're going to talk again," O'Brien put his coffee cup down and walked out of the room and back to his office where Anderson was still sitting in his chair with his arms folded in front of him.

"Well, it takes a while but Bishop eventually decides to take Broadbench out himself. He set him up to whack him, that's when he was attacked at the Hamilton Club. They were beating the shit out of him when the MP's showed up. It was the next day when he approached York with the information about Bishop, basically planning to let us take out Bishop and he would just stand around and pick up the pieces. So he tells York about Bishop thinking that York would go out and arrest him and problem gone."

"So he tells York, but then he attacks York? That doesn't make any sense," Stack questioned.

"Broadbench was upset that nothing was happening, he wasn't patient enough to let the plan go forward. He decided he needed to push York by threatening him and his Korean girl, while blaming it on Bishop."

"Geez, this is almost too complicated," Stack put his head into his hands. "You have all of this in a statement?" Stack finally asked.

"Almost done, Chief. I'm finishing it off right now. But I wanted to come down and brief you. He knows more for sure, but I needed a break."

"OK, we're going to have to sit down and figure this out. Shit I need a drink." Stack raised up in his chair again and looked over to Bateman, "Find out who has that homicide case from Camp Colburn. We're going to need some additional facts on that one. Then find out about this Nix, we're going to need to pay him a visit back in the world."

"Right, Chief," Bateman walked out of the office like a man on a mission.

Stack looked around the small office and then at his desk at the papers and reports lying around him and then at the small piece of notebook paper he had used to make some notes. He looked over at the clock on the wall, it was almost the end of the duty day and he had some phone calls to make. He knew it was going to be several more hours before he could even think of calling it quits. Stack thought to himself for a second, *How exactly did this thing start?* Then he remembered, the MP coming to the office out of the blue with some wild story. He was brought back to reality by the loud ringing of his desk phone. It took several rings for him to find it underneath the various papers and reports.

"Red Cloud CID, Mister Stack," Stack answered on the fourth ring.

"Elliot Ness, this is De Franco," De Franco came back on the other end. "Just calling for a SITREP. What's your Irish Mafia doing? I got people I have to brief and I've been waiting all afternoon."

"Well I was just about to call you. Are you sittin' down? Cause you ain't gonna believe this bucket of shit we got going on up here."

XXXIII

"I've been talking to Mr. Stack from the CID Office this morning," Captain Cruz said looking up at Sean who was standing at parade rest in front of his desk. "He says the operation yesterday went beyond his wildest dreams and they're still picking up other suspects and evidence."

"Yes sir," Sean answered back and looked straight ahead, not sure where the conversation was going. He had been instructed earlier that day to come to the orderly early before guard mount to talk to the Detachment Commander.

"I don't know if you know it or not, but not only did they smash two criminal groups that were preying upon soldiers, they also gathered up a large amount of drugs and drug money, solved an organized fuel diversion operation, and even solved a homicide." Captain Cruz leaned forward and looked over his note he had on his desk, "Not bad for a few days work, is it?"

"No, sir. Not bad at all, I guess," Sean answered and smiled to himself feeling very proud of what he was able to help do. He had no idea how the case had gone after they had left. "Thank you for telling me sir."

"Frankly York, I've been shaking my head in amazement. I don't think anyone was expecting anything like this." Cruz leaned back against his chair, a broad smile on his face.

"Me either sir," Sean flushed not quite knowing how to answer. Such praise made him feel uncomfortable, never knowing exactly how he was supposed to respond.

"Well how did you manage all of this?" Then Cruz put his hands behind his head, "I'm serious, I really want to know how does a regular uniformed MP come up with something like this? CID hasn't told me how this all went down."

"Sir I, well, I, well I don't know how to explain sir. I really just picked up some information and passed it on sir. CID did the rest." Sean tried to explain not really understanding the question.

"What about the three soldiers that attacked you?"

"Well I just happened to run into them when picking up others and I recognized them."

"I see," Captain Cruz straightened up and shook his head smiling. "Alright, well, no big deal, I was just curious." Captain Cruz leaned forward and replaced his forearms on his desk, "Well we've got Anderson and Broadbench in the D/Cell. They've been here all night waiting for some paperwork to get them down to pretrial confinement at Camp Humphreys. The others are over at Camp Stanley and headed down there, too."

"Yes sir," Sean smiled at the thought of all of them behind bars where they belong.

"Right, well just wanted to let you know how things turned out." Captain Cruz looked up, "York, I want you to know I'm very proud to have you in this unit."

"Thank you, sir," Sean had recognized the final comment as a dismissal; he immediately came to attention and saluted. "Thank you very much, sir."

The Commander returned the salute and Sean dropped his arm, executed an about face and walked outside to the small orderly room where Pok was waiting for him.

"Everything OK?" Pok questioned as he came out of the office.

"Everything OK. He said I did a good job." Sean continued on to explain exactly what the commander had told him as Pok smiled a broad grin at the accolades for Sean.

"Hey GI," Pok whispered to him, "I take you to lunch today?"

"I don't know. What if my Yobo finds out?" Sean answered back with a grin and looked into her eyes.

"It's OK, I talk with her," Pok smiled.

Sean walked through the door into the small area to the side of the MP desk and looked into the D/Cell where Broadbench was sitting on the edge of the metal bench, his legs dangling over the side, hands on the bench gripping the edge. Sean saw that his boots were on, but the laces had been removed as was his uniform belt.

"Hey," Sean called out to him as he stood in front of the cell, looking through the bars. He had calmed down a lot since the previous day, and although he was still upset, he was over the anger.

"Well, look at you," Broadbench looked up and smiled. Sluggishly he leaned back to put his back against the cinderblock wall and brought his legs up, wrapping his arms around his shins.

"Jamie, how you doing?" Sean asked.

"Well, it was a tough night, this bench is hard," Broadbench answered and looked back at Sean smiling.

"Yeah, not meant for long term occupancy," Sean looked at the second D/Cell and could see Anderson curled up on his left side, his back to the D/Cell door, still dressed in his medic white uniform.

"Yep, that's for sure. Well, they're going to take us to jail this morning I hear. I guess they didn't want me to hang around the company area." Broadbench smiled and started shaking his head a few times and then pushed himself forward until his feet hit the floor and he stood up. "I guess they think I might infect someone or something."

"Probably think you might try and run on 'em," Sean smiled.

"I'm in Korea; you think we could blend in with the people or go hide in the hills or something?" Broadbench smiled at the thought.

"I don't know, you sure fooled me for a while," Sean smiled back.

"Yeah," he reached up and rubbed his chin as he was contemplating what all had happened the previous day. "I probably should have thought that whole deal out a little better." Broadbench smiled, stepped forward and put his left hand on the cell wall and leaned over.

"Yeah, maybe so." Sean nodded in agreement and smiled back.

"You wouldn't want to take me over to the snack bar again, would ya?" Broadbench smiled innocently. "A biscuit and coffee would be good right about now."

"Nah, can't see it Jamie," Sean smiled and shook his head as he looked back through the bars.

"Yeah, well I'm not hungry anyway I guess." Broadbench stood up, walked forward and put both hands on the bars. "Look, I was hoping to see you before I go Jamie paused for a second. "I wanted to say no hard feelings, you know?" Broadbench reached his hand out through the bars. "I never told those guys to beat you up, just to nudge you a little bit."

Sean looked down at his hand sticking through the bar and reached out and shook it with his right hand. "Well they nudged alright," Sean pumped his hand twice and then let go.

"I told 'em they better take you seriously or you'd kick their ass, but they didn't listen." Broadbench looked down and shook his head in frustration.

"Yeah, I guess good help is hard to find."

"Ain't that the truth?" Broadbench seemed to drift off a moment as if trying to think of something to say, "Boy you sure fucked up ole Floyd." Broadbench smiled to himself and then looked up at Sean.

"Who?"

"Floyd. The guy you hit on the foot with that metal thing."

"Oh yeah?"

"Yeah, you crushed his foot man." Broadbench shook his head as if he were remembering, "It was bad. Anderson too, he took like fifty stitches."

Sean glanced over at Anderson who was still sleeping on the bench and shrugged his shoulders not knowing exactly what to say.

"Ah, fuck 'em," Broadbench smiled. "They're big boys and shoulda listened to me."

"York," Whitehouse called out from the MP Desk breaking up the conversation, "got a duty call."

"Alright," Sean called back and looked over at Broadbench who was still looking down. "Well, I got to go, so you take care of yourself, you hear? Just do your time and get on back home."

"Oh, I'll be alright. Don't worry about me; I ain't ever going to prison." Broadbench chuckled, as if he were laughing at some personal joke only he understood.

"You don't think so?" Sean looked back incredulously.

"Oh, I'm sure of it. In fact, I'll be stateside and home way before you are." Broadbench smiled back broadly as he pressed his face partway through the space between the bars.

"York, God damn it, you got a duty call," Whitehouse called out again, this time with more enthusiasm.

"Alright Sarge comin'," Sean smiled back and nodded to Broadbench, not sure how he could respond to such a positive statement.

Later that afternoon the paperwork was finally completed and charges sworn out by their respective commanders and Bishop, Broadbench, and Anderson were all ordered into Pretrial confinement. Their units responded with a vehicle, a driver and an armed NCO escort who then took off for Camp Humphreys to the army's confinement facility. Belk joined them two days later after he threatened a soldier he believed had given a statement against him. CID had picked him back up for the new threat and in a matter of hours, Belk found himself sitting in Camp Stanley MP Station waiting for his own trip to Humphrey. SGT Smiley had immediately agreed to testify against everyone in exchange for a lighter sentence in his own court martial.

Sean and Reggie returned to their normal duties and were treated as near rock stars by their other squad mates because of their participation in the investigation. Other than a few times they had seen each other coming in and out of the gate or when they came down to the MP station, Sean had no further contact with CID about the case. He had no idea what was happening with the case. Instead he quickly fell back into the same routine of coming to work, working, heading home and then going back to   work.

During the next three day breaks however, Reggie and Sean tried to get together and socialize at least once. The girls also managed to get away for a girls' day out on occasion and were becoming very close friends as well. The summer was finally full upon them. The three or four weeks of monsoon, where nearly every day the clouds came over and gave forth a heavy shower for an hour and then cleared up, filled the rice patties up and generally washed down the streets. At the end of June, they were fixated on the events over the hijacking of the French airliner to Uganda and holding of Israeli hostages. Through the Stars and Stripes and the news from the American Forces radio and TV, it was the full topic of conversations. There was almost universal agreement; they were convinced the Israelis were going to kick someone's ass over this.

"You know we were in basic training during the Yom Kippur War. Man we were certain we were headed for Egypt to kick some Arab ass," Sean volunteered during one of the broadcasts thinking about the threats of the drill sergeants that they were all heading to *Bum Fuck Egypt* and had better pay attention. That seemed like such a long time ago, although it was just coming up on three years.

The hostage drama finally played out over the 4th of July holiday, with Israeli forces flying a Commando unit in and conducting a rescue at Entebbe airport. The rescue seemed to add to the general feeling revolving around the Bicentennial 4th of July celebration. The girls both thought it interesting how enthusiastic both Reggie and Sean were for their nation's 200th birthday, toasting each other repeatedly as they sat on the lawn of the parade field and drank beer. They had all come onto Camp for the traditional fireworks display, with the army band playing American patriotic songs. Pok had to admit she had even felt a certain thrill when the Star Spangled Banner was played at the end of the concert. It had been the high point of the summer up to that point.

Both Sean and Pok had settled down into something more or less resembling married life and both were very happy with the arrangement. Sean had brought up the subject of meeting her parents to Pok several times, but each time she had artfully deflected the idea, in the traditional Asian way of never saying no, but never saying yes, and never making any arrangements to do so. Pok was certainly falling in deep love with Sean and their talks of a future together were becoming more and more frequent. Although Sean had wanted to officially propose marriage, every time she thought he was getting close, she managed to change the subject. Pok was scared to death of such a proposal and how it would change their relationship. She truly loved Sean with all of her heart, but she was not so certain how it would be received by her father and older brothers. He father had already tried one time before to arrange a marriage for her with another older Korean businessman that she had managed to avoid. But her father was a very traditional man and she was uncertain if he would ever accept Sean, a foreigner into the family. Pok realized at some time soon she would have to make a decision about their life together and approach or confront her father, but she hoped to put it off as long as possible. Sean had at least another six months go to before he was even scheduled to return to the states so she believed she still had time to work something out. She wanted with all of her heart to marry Sean and be his wife, but at the same time she was also scared about leaving Korea and coming to live in America, and she knew Sean could never stay and live in Korea with her. She was also concerned at Sean's family's reaction to her and her family's reaction to him. For the time being, she decided she would rather continue to live in her dream world where such problems did not exist than face the reality of their situation.

Sean's immediate concern was his promotion to Sergeant which he had expected several weeks before. Almost on a daily basis he found himself at the detachment orderly room talking with Bea and trying to track down his promotion orders supposedly coming from personnel, but so far nothing. It wasn't until he received his end of month check for July and he opened it up and saw that he had received a significant pay increase. There was only one reason to get a pay increase; the army did not make such mistakes. Sean went back to the unit orderly room and picked up his leave and earning statement. There it was. He read the very top line containing his hand and rank and pay grade. It read E5, the army was saying his orders had come through and they had promoted him. If the army was paying him to be a Sergeant then he wanted to wear the stripes. Sean was in the orderly room waiting to talk to Bea who was on the phone. He was contemplating his next step when he was interrupted by Grubner who walked into the orderly room.

"York, what are you doing in here? These people have things to do." Grubner snapped, "So take your happy little ass out of here."

"I just picked up my LES Sarge." Sean held up his monthly leave and earning statement to Grubner, "Look, the army is paying me for being a Sergeant, but I haven't got my orders yet."

Grubner ignored the document Sean tried to show him.

"Look, when your orders come in, if they come in, then you'll get them now get out of here."

"But Sarge," York started to protest.

"I said take your happy ass out of here," Grubner was not interested in hearing Sean's point.

"What's going on out here?" The Commander asked casually walking out of his office into the orderly room.

"All taken care of sir," Grubner stated as if it would end the conversation.

Sean's face flushed and he could feel his anger begin to rise and he blurted out, "No sir, it's not taken care of," Sean glared over at Grubner. "Sir, I've been waiting for my promotion orders now for almost four weeks. I come in here every day expecting they will be here. Sir, look," Sean handed his LES to the commander, "I've already gotten my promotion raise sir, my LES shows I'm an E-5, that means the Army says I'm an E-5 already. I just want my orders."

Grubner flashed an angry look towards Sean and tried to reassert himself, "Sir, I can take care of this."

"No, this is bullshit." Captain Cruz intently looked over the LES and then turned to Grubner, "Sergeant, I want you to unscrew this thing by tomorrow. If the Army says he is an E-5 then I want some orders saying that and I want them by tomorrow. Understood?"

Grubner's face flushed in anger, "Yes sir I'll take care of it." Grubner turned around and opened a file drawer and shuffled through the files as if he were looking for something.

"Alright," Cruz turned to Sean, "I'm not sure what's going on right now, but the detachment Sergeant will track it down and we'll get an answer tomorrow. Good enough?"

"Thanks sir. That's all I'm asking." Sean responded and gave the universal thumbs up sign as approval.

"Alright then, congratulations," Cruz said and nodded approval towards Sean.

The next day a frustrated Grubner retrieved the promotion orders out of his top desk drawer where he had placed them some three weeks before and simply put them into the daily distribution. He never said another word about them. Once Sean finally managed to pick them up, it was clear from the date on the orders they should have been given to him weeks before. But Sean didn't care anymore he just wanted to be able to wear his stripes. There was a short and personal promotion ceremony with the rest of his squad and the specialist rank was removed from his collar and the three stripes of a sergeant were put in their place. SSG Whitehead put on the new stripes and then took his fists and gave him a good shot with both fists on each collar. Tradition required they be struck in order for them to stay on.

Sean beamed in a broad smile as he walked into Pok's office. She looked up from her typewriter and smiled and then her eyes widened when she recognized his new stripes. Standing up, she ran around the desk and gave him a big hug. Coming from a military family herself, she knew how important this was for him and she was very proud.

"How do they look?" Sean beamed and stood up straight.

"Look good, you numba one Sergeant now," Pok smiled approvingly and traced her finger over the rank insignia on his collar.

"More money too," Sean proudly announced.

"Oh yeah, more money too," Pok smiled an approving toothy smile. "More money is good."

SSG Whitehouse took him to lunch and went over his philosophy of being a NCO and how important it was to set a good example and take care of his troops. Sean enjoyed the lunch and talk very much. He had suffered under bad leadership before and always vowed he would not treat his soldiers like he had been treated from time to time. That evening the other five junior NCOs from the detachment all got together and brought him to the Papasan Club, the NCO club on Camp Red Cloud, to celebrate. Sean had seen the club many times from the outside driving by but because he was not yet an NCO, he was not allowed to go inside. He accompanied SSG Whitehouse and the other NCO into the club and they sat at a table. Sean willingly bought round after round of beer and drinks, taking great pleasure in joining the club and getting the club card to show he was now a member. It was nearly curfew when they broke up and Sean walked back to the MP Station to get a ride home. Pok was actually still up and opened the door for him as he staggered, more than walked, up the steps to the house. She was smiling, shaking her head as he came up to her. She was wearing her white terrycloth robe, but underneath she was dressed only in one of Sean's white tee shirts that covered her slender body down to mid-thigh with her hair in a ponytail tied with a blue ribbon.

"Hello Yobo," Sean said and smiled as he took off his shoes at the door.

"Come inside GI, my boyfriend come home soon," she returned his smile and they both laughed. He ran up the remaining steps and reached out and picked her up and took her in his arms, then carried her to the bedroom and laid her gently onto the bed.

XXXIV

Sean was sleeping soundly with Pok's head laying on his chest and his arms around her when the phone next to his side of the bed rang. Sean managed to reach out and answer on the second ring.

"Hello," Sean tried to clear his throat.

"York?" a female voice on the other end called out.

"Yeah, this is Sergeant York," Sean corrected.

"I'm sorry Sean, that's going to take some getting used to," the voiced giggled. "This is Bea from the detachment. The Captain asked me to call you and tell you he wants you to come into the detachment today at 1330 in uniform."

"Today? I'm supposed to be off," Sean semi protested.

"I know, but the Commander just said for you to come in uniform and get here by 1330."

"Alright, I'll be there," Sean put the phone back onto the cradle and then sighed. He looked up at the lock and realized he had already slept past ten thirty and decided he had better get up. Pok must have gotten up quietly and gone to work at her regular time. Although generally a light sleeper, he hadn't heard a thing.

At a little before 1330, Sean walked through the front door of the provost marshal's office and into the detachment orderly room. He was very proudly displaying his new stripes on his collar.

"The Commander's on the phone. He'll be with you in a minute," Bea advised as he came into the office. She then went back to writing on some form.

Sean walked around and made small talk with everyone, then started reading some of the posters on the wall to pass the time. He walked down to Pok's office but the door was closed. When he opened the door to look inside, the space was empty. He figured she was out running an errand or something. As he stood around bouncing back from heel to toe to pass the time he could hear the commander's phone ringing inside his office and seconds later the commander walked briskly out of his office, his hat already on his head.

"Glad you are here early. Come on. Bea get the jeep," Captain Cruz said as he passed by Sean and he walked out of the office. Sean fell in behind and followed him out of the front door and into the small parking lot. Bea, with hat in hand following close behind, walked past them and got into the commander's jeep parked in front.

"What's up sir?" Sean asked as they all made it to the Commander's jeep packed in a reserved parking spot in front.

"We've got places to go and people to see," Captain Cruz said with a smile then pulled the passenger seat forward and signaled for Sean to get into the back. Once Sean was loaded in, the Commander sat down in the front passenger seat and Bea got into the driver seat and fired up the jeep. They drove straight up to the I Corps Headquarters and Bea parked outside in a visitor parking spot and they all got out. Sean had recognized the building immediately of course from the many times he had parked nearby to conduct the flag call ceremonies, raising the flag in the morning and taking it down at the end of the duty day. Sean followed Captain Cruz into the headquarters, still uncertain what was going on. Once inside, Sean removed his hat and then looked around. There was Mr. Stack, O'Toole, O'Brien and Bateman all dressed in suits and ties milling around a small alcove just inside the main door. It was Sean's first time seeing the agents since the big round up. Other than waving to them as they came in or out of the main gate in their vehicle over the last few weeks, he had not really talked to anyone or found out how the case was going. He was greeted by each of the agents very warmly.

"Hey there he is, Sherlock York," O'Toole said and thrust his hand out to shake Sean's hand. The remaining agents walked over one at a time and shook his hand. Sean then looked around not quite understanding what was going on, but noted that all of the CID agents were dressed in suits and ties.

"What's going on?" Sean asked and looked around at the group.

"You don't know?" O'Toole asked and then looked at the others.

"Know what?" Sean asked.

At that time a young Lieutenant from Headquarters I Corps staff walked into the small foyer and made a motion for the group to follow him. They all slowly filed into a large very comfortable office suite and then single file they went into another office off to the side. Sean followed behind the CID agents and as they came inside, he immediately recognized the I Corps commander dressed in heavy starched fatigues, with three black stars on each collar. Sean started to come to attention, never having been in the company of a general officer before, but noticed the remainder of the group stood straight but held their hands folded in front of them. Sean looked at the Corps Commander then to a full bird Colonel standing next to him; he could make out the crossed pistol insignia of a military police officer but didn't recognize him. From his peripheral vision he could make out two other officers, he didn't recognize them either, but saw they wore the gold leaves of majors. But then he looked again and to the left of one of the officers he saw Pok, standing there dressed in his favorite yellow dress, wearing her string of pearls and her hair in a pony tail tied with a yellow ribbon. She was smiling broadly. Sean looked back at the room again trying to figure out exactly what was going on.

"Come in gentlemen come in, there's plenty of room," the Corps Commander said and waved his hand to indicate they should form a semi-circle in the office. Sean shuffled along until the general was satisfied.

"Gentlemen, I have been briefed as to your activity here in the I Corps area over the past month or so and I want to tell you personally how pleased and proud I am of each and every one of you." The general started speaking without notes, "Nothing breaks a commander's heart more than to see the events that have played out over these last few weeks. Anytime we have senior NCO's and Officers maltreat their subordinates, it's unacceptable. Especially when it's every officer's and NCO's moral and legal responsibility to watch over these young soldiers placed into their care. I'm looking at this situation as a cancer that over time wove itself into our community and tried to kill it. But, you members of the CID and Military Police, you were like my surgeon in this situation; you identified the problem and helped me get rid of it. For that the US Army, I Corp, and your nation are very grateful."

Sean felt his face flush and looked around the small room as the CID Agents stood straight up and listened politely. The general then continued for several more moments of general praise for the group. Sean was distracted as he looked over and saw Pok standing in the room off to the side with Captain Cruz, smiling at him and touching her strand of pearls lightly with her fingers and a big toothy smile.

Sean came back to reality when he looked over and saw the four CID Agents walking slowly forward from where they were standing and forming a line in front of the general.

"Attention to orders," a major standing to the side of the general began to read from a piece of paper held out in front of him. It took a second for Sean to realize that the four CID agents were apparently being presented with an award for their work on the recent case. Sean looked up and after reading the citation, the general stood in front of each agent, pinned a metal to his suit lapel and shook his hand. A cameraman from the Public Affairs Office came forward and took photos as the medal was presented. A second photo was taken when a small green case with the award citation certificate inside was presented. The certificate would be placed into a picture frame and later mounted on the wall of their office for all to see.

The simple ceremony of awarding the medal and presenting the certificate was repeated four times and then the general stepped aside, and the small group applauded them all. Sean looked on very pleased and was smiling at their success. Mr. Stack was then called up to say a few words. When he finished, he stepped back, and the small group applauded again.

The four agents returned to where they had been standing, the medals still pinned to their suit coats. Sean looked around and was still a little confused as to why he was standing there when suddenly out of nowhere, the general called his name.

"Specialist York," the general looked over at him and made a motion to come up to where he was standing. "Gentlemen, I am very proud of all of your efforts in this matter. But what's more important in my book, is that this was brought about by one of the most junior members of my law enforcement team. Specialist York come on over here." The general turned to the side to look over at Sean. "Oh, excuse me Sergeant," The general hesitated a moment when he caught Sean's three stripes on his collar, "I mean Sergeant York. So when did that happen?" The general smiled as he recovered from his error.

"Just yesterday Sir," Sean started hesitatingly as the group politely chuckled. Sean smiled in return not certain how to respond or what was happening.

"Well by all I've heard, it apparently is well deserved." The general patted Sean on the back and looked at the others surrounding him. "Congratulations on that, too Sergeant York." The general started again, "my CID Commander here seems to think you were responsible for initiating this whole investigation. Colonel Goodfellow, the Commander of the 7th Region CID," the general motioned to the full Colonel to his side, "in conjunction with Mr. Stack here," the general made a motion to Mr. Stack, "asked me to personally make this presentation to you and I whole heartedly agreed. I wish that other young soldiers were as dedicated and professional as you have demonstrated." The general looked around at the assembled group waiting patiently and continued, "I know I can get a little long winded so I'm going to take a pause and ask Major Faulkner to please publish the order."

"Attention to orders," Major Faulkner was apparently one of the two unidentified majors he observed as he walked into the office. "This is to certify that the Secretary of the Army has awarded the Army Accommodation Medal to Specialist Sean P. York, 3rd Military Police Detachment, APO SF 96358, for his outstanding dedication to duty during the period of 9 May through 1 June 1976. Specialist York provided the key information leading to the apprehension of nineteen military offenders and four Korean civilians who were engaged in a wide variety of criminal acts affecting the good order and discipline of several units within the I Corps area of responsibility. Specialist York's actions were in keeping with the highest traditions of the I Corp and the US Army. Signed, Erick C. Goodfellow. Colonel. MP, Commanding." Faulkner closed the small folder and walked forward to the general holding a small blue felt case.

The Corps Commander stepped in front of York, and Major Faulkner handed him the ARCOM medal, Sean looked down as the general attached the green ribbon and medal onto his left blouse pocket. He then turned to Faulkner and accepted the green plastic case which had the citation inside and handed it to York, shaking his hand.

"I'm very proud of you Sergeant; you've done your unit and your country proud," the general whispered as he attached the medal and then shook his hand.

"Thank you sir," Sean said back. The general turned to smile at the PAO cameraman. The general held onto his hand until the photographer took three or four pictures.

"Alright gentleman let's give the awardees our personal congratulations," the general started by shaking Sean's hand and patted him on the shoulders. Sean, uncertain what to do, stood still while the group filed passed him and each in turn shook his hand and made a few comments. It was very overpowering to Sean who had no idea anything like this was going to happen. Pok joined in the line of well-wishers and gave him a two armed hug and squeezed him tight. She had been invited by Captain Cruz to attend and was beaming in pride over the award.

After a few minutes, Major Faulkner, the general's aide, began to herd the group outside the office as the general had to get back to work. Sean and Pok made their way out of the commander's office behind the others and stopped briefly into the small foyer just inside the front door to the headquarters. The PAO cameraman was waiting outside for everyone with a hometown news release for all awardees to sign. Afterwards he would send the photo and a short description of the event to everyone's local newspaper so they could print the photo and award citation. It was part of the army's public relations to show hometown folks what the army was doing and hopefully encourage others to enlist.

"Sergeant York," Captain Cruz said as they finally got outside. "Just a minute."

Sean stopped and turned around to face Cruz. "Sir," he automatically called out.

"This is Major Faulkner, the general's aide," Captain Cruz made the introduction, causing Sean to come automatically to the position of attention to greet the senior officer.

"At ease Sergeant," Major Faulkner patted Sean on the left shoulder and looked briefly over at Pok who was standing next to him. "Per the general's direction, and with the concurrence of your commander, you've also earned a four-day pass. You just need to work it out with your commander as to when exactly." He reached out to shake York's hand. "This was a very good thing you did Sergeant; I can tell you the general was very pleased."

"Thank you sir," Sean answered back and shook his hand.

"Sergeant York," the commander interjected, "I've already authorized Miss Park to take two days of vacation and since today is Friday, I want you to take the next four days off and enjoy yourselves. After all you've been through, you deserve some time off, got it?"

"Yes sir," Sean looked down at Pok. "Sounds great. Thank you, sir."

"Thank you so much," Pok bowed slightly and then looked up at Sean grinning, almost beaming with pride.

"Alright so I'll see you back for work on Tuesday." The commander stood by his jeep and held the seat forward, "You guys want a ride back?"

They looked at each other "No sir, we're going to walk and enjoy the day," Sean called back.

Captain Cruz nodded and smiled as if he understood, then turned and jumped into the front passenger seat. Bea started the jeep and then drove off with a start, catching the Commander by surprise. Sean watched the jeep drive away and then looked down at his shirt and looked at the medal.

"Wow, I never expected this," Sean said as he removed and then looked at the green ribbon, three white stripes down the middle, and attached medal.

He had received many awards in high school for football and baseball and even the honor roll once, but this was different. He had done something no one expected and he was being rewarded. He seemed to grow in pride as they started to walk. He momentarily reached out and gave her a hug, but it was not proper to walk holding hands or with his arm around her in uniform, so they walked along the sidewalk slightly bumping into each other as they walked as a substitute for holding hands.

They walked back to the main gate and then caught a taxi to their house. Once inside the gate Sean turned and took Pok into his arms and gave her a deep kiss. She returned the kiss enthusiastically. The kiss lead to a double armed hug and Sean lifted her up off the ground and began to spin her around, causing Pok to start giggling with joy.

Sean finally lowered her to the ground and stepped back.

"Come on Yobo, I have something for you," Sean spoke softly and then took her by the hand and led her up the steps to the house. Once inside he walked her back to the bedroom and sat her on the bed. He then turned to the small dresser, opened a top drawer which contained his underwear and retrieved a small box that contained a ring. A ring he had bought two months before but had hesitated to bring up the subject until now. He turned around to face her as his mind was spinning he asked himself if this was the best time; he quickly answered, if not now, then when? He could not put it off any longer. Sean smiled at Pok and dropped to one knee before her.

"Yobo," Sean began, "you know I love you."

"I love you too," Pok said back and looked into his eyes. She was confused, but then looked down as Sean brought out the small box and opened it. Her eyes grew wide and she saw the small silver ring inside.

"Pok, I…" Sean began nervously. He had planned for this moment many times in the recent past and he was now committed. "Pok would you marry me? Make me the happiest man in the world?" Sean raised his hand and opened the lid to expose the ring inside.

Pok looked back at the ring and then into Sean's face. Her eyes teared up as the time she had anticipated, and yet carefully avoided, had arrived. She was torn: she truly loved Sean, but he did not understand the difficulties this would bring for both of them. He lived in an American world where anything was possible, she came from a world of traditions. But she was suddenly overcome by a wave of emotion and love. She reached out and put her arms around his neck and then slid down to the floor on her knees and grabbed his head and brought it to her and she kissed him deeply.

She broke the kiss then leaned back. "I marry you Yobo," she finally managed to say. Then the tears began to flow.

"Oh Pok," Sean embraced her again. "You make me so happy." Sean embraced her. He released her and leaned back and took the ring from the box and reached for her left hand and placed the ring onto her ring finger.

"Sweetheart," Sean began as he held her hands in his, "I know this is not easy for you, but we can make it. I love you more than anything in the world. We can make it."

"I know," Pok look at him and smiled. But she knew Sean had no idea how difficult it was going to be with her family.

The rest of the day they spent making love, talking about their future, and making plans. Sean's mind was racing now, all the things he had to do. He would have to tell his parents now, certainly before they were married. He would have to get permission from his unit, and then fill out a ton of paperwork to marry a Korean National. Suddenly the long running fantasy was a reality and seemed almost overwhelming. But he was satisfied he had met his life partner and believed he was ready for whatever the future brought.

ABOUT THE AUTHOR

Arthur S. Chancellor

Steve was raised in California and enlisted in the US Army as a Military Policeman right after high school graduation in 1973. He served as a MP in Arizona, California, Korea, Kansas and Panama. In 1981 he was accepted into the US Army CID where he worked felony crimes at various military posts across the US and overseas. He later commanded three different CID units and in 2001 retired as a Chief Warrant Officer Four as the Operations Officer for a CID Battalion responsible for five different CID units. Once retired Steve was employed by the Mississippi State Crime Lab as a senior crime scene analyst and conducted the examination of violent crime scenes across the state. In 2004 Steve was transferred from the crime lab to the Mississippi Bureau of Investigation (MBI) as the first Director of the MBI Cold Case unit. In 2008 Steve returned to Army CID as a civilian where he is employed as a Supervisory Special Agent at Ft Bragg, NC. Steve has a master's degree and undergrad degrees in Criminal Justice, is a Graduate of the FBI National Academy and has been a college adjunct instructor for Austin Peay State University, Clarksville TN, University of Mississippi, Oxford, MS and Clayton State University, Morrow, Georgia. Steve is a fellow with the American Academy of Forensic Science (AAFS), and a member of the International; Association for Identification (IAI), and the International Homicide Investigator's Association. Steve has also authored a text on *Investigating Sexual Assault Cases*, and co-authored the texts *Staged Crime Scenes: Investigating Suspect Misdirection of the Crime Scene*, and *Death Investigations: The Second Edition*.

Made in the USA
San Bernardino, CA
18 August 2018